TRAITOR

BRIAN NICHOLSON

Order this book online at www.trafford.com
or email orders@trafford.com

Most Trafford titles are also available at major online book retailers.

Printed in the United States of America.

ISBN: 978-1-4269-4604-2 (sc)
ISBN: 978-1-4269-4605-9 (e)

*Our mission is to efficiently provide the world's finest, most comprehensive book publishing
service, enabling every author to experience success. To find out how to publish your
book, your way, and have it available worldwide, visit us online at www.trafford.com*

Trafford rev. 11/11/2010

Trafford
PUBLISHING® www.trafford.com

North America & international
toll-free: 1 888 232 4444 (USA & Canada)
phone: 250 383 6864 ♦ fax: 812 355 4082

Also by Brian Nicholson featuring

John Gunn

GWEILO

AL SAMAK

ASHANTI GOLD

FIRE DRAGON

CALYPSO

SHARK

To D, Charlie and Sasha

ACKNOWLEDGEMENTS

I am very grateful for the help of many people who gave me advice about various aspects of TRAITOR, but there are those who require a special mention: Nick and his colleagues in the Army Air Corps and RAF for their advice on matters aeronautical; George for his gunnery advice; John for his Japanese advice and David Stockman for his cover design.

FOREWORD

In 1988, after a series of leaks and defections in MI5 and MI6, the Prime Minister tasked a relatively young Major General, who had retired at the age of 48, with the reorganisation of the United Kingdom's Intelligence Services. After retirement he had redirected his talents into management consultancy and turned two failing companies from near bankruptcy to healthy, profit-making concerns.

Within a year of being given the remit to set up an effective, efficient and secure intelligence service, he had created the British Intelligence Directorate. Both the espionage and counter-espionage departments were brought under the same roof where their efforts were constructive rather than conflicting. Very few MI5 and MI6 personnel survived the stringent security vetting initiated by the new director. The two buildings at Millbank and Vauxhall Cross were retained, but only for a limited period during the changeover, as an overt intelligence front. In reality they had little more than a clerical role for storage and retrieval of historical classified material.

Kingsroad House was purpose-built for BID in Cale Street to the north of the King's Road. Outwardly it claimed to be the head office of Express Delivery Services (EDS). Access to EDS was by the main entrance on Cale Street while access to BID was either via the main entrance or via the 10th floor of the adjacent multi-storey NCP car park. There were two other headquarter buildings; one in Kingston-on-Thames and another in Southampton. Both had a similar layout to Kingsroad House, but possessed subtle variations in case security was compromised.

Kingsroad House had fourteen above-ground floors, with a helipad on the fifteenth floor. There were three basement levels, which contained BID's emergency medical centre – the main medical facility was at Maidenhead – an extensive transport department, stores, a small armoury and a shooting range. The lowest basement level also provided access to four passages that could be used by BID staff to leave the building avoiding any form of surveillance.

BID became operational in April 1990.

PROLOGUE

JAPANESE INVASION OF
HONG KONG, 1941

In the regimental command post at Stanley Fort on the southern tip of Hong Kong Island, the fire orders from Captain Ronnie Lequesne, one of three Observation Post (OP) officers of 12 Battery, 5th Medium Regiment, blurted indistinctly over the radio through heavy static.

'Regimental Target........Target Mike 55.........fire by order....... all...five rounds gunfire......fire!...over!'

Target Mike 55 was the number of a pre-planned and recorded defensive fire target on the forward slope in front of the Shing Mun Redoubt on the Gin Drinkers Line, the inner defensive line prepared by the defending British and Commonwealth forces against a Japanese invasion. It stretched from Kwei Chung Bay in the west to Port Shelter in the east, passing through Beacon Hill, Lion Rock and Tate's Cairn – the line of hills separating Kowloon from the New Territories to the north. The key defensive point of the line was the Shing Mun Redoubt – a series of concrete bunkers connected by underground passages - and Ronnie Lequesne, with his small OP party was in a slit trench on the forward slope of the line with a platoon of B Company, 2nd/14th Punjab Regiment.

'I say again.......fire by order.....all....five rounds gunfire.....fire!' he repeated, accompanied by even worse static.

Each of the Regiment's eighteen 5.5"guns fired five rounds, totalling 90 rounds of high explosive shrapnel covering an area of 100 by 300 yards, arriving with no warning amongst the advancing Japanese. However, Major General Maltby, the Commander of Hong Kong's Defence Forces, had been expecting a naval assault on Hong Kong, so the majority of the ammunition was armour-piercing shells to penetrate the steel hulls and decks of ships; the result was a very limited supply of high-explosive, point-detonation and airburst ammunition to defeat an infantry assault by land.

The Japanese had been fighting in China since 1937, gradually moving south towards the border with Hong Kong, but Maltby had ignored the threat, convinced that he had adequate forces to defend the island of Hong Kong, if not Kowloon and the New Territories. But the Japanese infantry, under the command of Colonel Toi Teishichi, proved the inaccuracy of Maltby's assessment by reaching Needle Hill - directly opposite and overlooking the Shing Mun Redoubt - on the afternoon of 9th December – only two days after the attack on Pearl Harbour and 24 hours after crossing the Sino/Hong Kong Border. They had beaten a path with frightening speed via Smuggler's Ridge Hill, which most had thought to be an impossible approach to the Gin Drinkers Line strongpoint, doggedly pushing through - despite heavy casualties - under the concentrated fire of every artillery unit in range.

Ronnie and his OP party with two sections of sepoys from 'B' Company under the command of a Havildar and Naik, were forced to retreat to the New Territories' Devil's Peak on the Lei Yue Mun Peninsular. A planned counter attack on the Shing Mun Redoubt for 10th December never materialised because there were woefully inadequate resources to redeploy for such a manoeuvre. On 11th December, the British withdrawal from the mainland to Hong Kong Island started, covered by the 7th Rajputs and Winnipeg Grenadiers who were the last to cross to the island. During the evacuation, a young Canadian Grenadier was captured by the Japanese and beheaded. This was but a hint of the brutality that would follow.

Ronnie's Battery Commander ordered him to redeploy to the east of Hong Kong Island to support a brigade covering North Point and Lei Yue Mun. He occupied a position near the 500 foot peak of Mount Parker, which provided a commanding view of the Lye Yue Mun narrows between the mainland and the island. It also afforded clear communications back to his battery and regiment in Stanley. His Indian soldiers had lost contact with their company, so were now a welcome addition in man and firepower.

On 15th December, the Japanese began the systematic artillery and aerial bombardment of Hong Kong Island. After two demands for surrender were rejected, they crossed the harbour on the evening of 18th December with three regiments, suffering only light casualties from the artillery deployed on the west of the island because of crest clearance problems caused by the steep slopes of the island's geology. Below Ronnie's position, the Sai Wan coast battery was quickly over-run by the Japanese infantry and, despite surrendering, every man was executed. Once again, Ronnie and his small band of Gunners and Indian soldiers had to withdraw as intense fighting engulfed the centre of Hong Kong Island at the Wong Nai Chung Gap. Amidst the bloodshed, a courageous Canadian of the Winnipeg Grenadiers, John Osborn, earned a Victoria Cross when he threw himself onto a grenade to save the lives of his comrades. The Japanese quickly defeated the brigade defending the west of the island and secured the route through to the south. There they embarked on a brutal massacre of prisoners, including all the medical staff at the Salesian Mission on Chai Wan Road and all the men, women and children at the Repulse Bay Hotel, who were executed on the beach like cattle. On Christmas morning, the Japanese entered the British Field Hospital at St Stephen's College and proceeded to torture and kill all 60 injured soldiers; they raped the female medical staff and then bayoneted them.

The Island was now split in two; Ronnie had lost touch with both his battery and the regiment in Stanley. The Japanese had captured the island's reservoirs so they had no access to fresh water. On the afternoon of Christmas Day, Sir Mark Young, the Governor of Hong Kong, surrendered to the Japanese Commander, Lt General Sakai Takashi, at his Headquarters in the Peninsular Hotel in Kowloon. Ronnie, with his OP party and Indian soldiers, surrendered that afternoon and were taken with all the other POWs over to Kowloon. There, Ronnie was separated from his soldiers, who were taken to a POW camp at North Point. The Canadians and Royal Navy were interned in a camp at Sham Shui Po. He was taken with all the other British Army officers to a camp near Argyle Street. Ronnie's wife, Helen, and their two children, Rory and Katie, aged six and four, together with nearly 3,000 other civilians, were taken to the Stanley Internment Camp on the peninsular on the south side of Hong Kong Island. There they remained until the Japanese surrendered in August 1945.

Ronnie's prison camp, located between Argyle Street and Prince Edward Street in Kowloon on the mainland, like all the camps - consisted of single floor wooden barrack blocks surrounded by barbed wire and sentry posts. The Japanese did their best to persuade all the POWs in the camp to sign a 'non-escape' agreement, assuring them that conditions and the food would improve if they agreed. Ronnie, together with other officers from the Royal Artillery, Royal Scots and Middlesex Regiment, steadfastly refused to sign any agreement with the Japanese, but some did and to Ronnie's shame, one of them was a recently arrived subaltern from his own Regiment.

Lt Peter Drummond had been furious at being removed from his oriental studies degree at Cambridge and conscripted into the Army; he had stopped just short of claiming to be a conscientious objector, realising that that could well land him in prison for the duration of the war. He spoke both Chinese and Japanese – a logical choice for the posting to a unit in Hong Kong – and until the Japanese invasion had been usefully employed as an assistant to the Regiment's Intelligence Officer.

Drummond's blatant efforts to curry favour with the Japanese guards in order to secure better conditions for himself had earned him pariah status; he was avoided by all the other POWs. This didn't go unnoticed by the Japanese who compounded the situation by removing him from the 30-man barrack room with the rest of his regiment and placing him with other 'trustees' who had signed the agreement.

In the nine months from January to September 1942, there were more than a dozen escape attempts from the camp, all made by the 620 officers who'd refused to sign the agreement. All but one failed; the Japanese guards were somehow always forewarned. The name of the officer who coordinated the escape plans was a closely guarded secret and he was only referred to by his nickname, 'Horse'. After the one successful escape, 'Horse' was tortured by the Japanese guards for five days to force him to reveal the names of the other officers involved in the escape plans. The Japs failed to break him and he was eventually dragged, beaten and bleeding from the tin box in which he was incarcerated into the middle of the POW's parade ground. Once all the POWs had been assembled, 'Horse' was blindfolded and then beheaded with a Samurai *katana* sword. The Jap guards then used his severed head as a football and kicked it around the parade ground causing a riot amongst the POWs which resulted in several of them being shot.

When caught, the escapees were beaten and tortured with renewed vigour, the majority dying from their injuries, malnutrition and disease. One of the men who'd signed the agreement and subsequently rescinded it, warned the officers that it was Drummond who was alerting the Japanese guards to their planned escapes. He also told them that Drummond frequently dined with the Commandant of the Camp. The British POWs developed a plan to remove the traitor permanently, but it was thwarted by the Japanese, who decided to ship the POWs to Japan as slave labour in the coal mines and munitions factories, thus releasing thousands of Japanese workers to be conscripted for the war in Burma.

On 29th September 1942, Ronnie Lequesne and 600 other officers from the camp, together with another 1,200 POWs from the other camps, were herded aboard a decrepit ship named *Lisbon Maru*. In cramped filth and squalor on the ship's orlop deck down in the bilges, they departed for Japan. Before the ship weighed anchor in Victoria Harbour, while the last of the POWs were being transferred from a stinking refuse lighter to the ship, Peter Drummond was escorted aboard by the Camp Commandant and taken to a cabin on the boat deck.

Two days later, when the *Lisbon Maru* was off Shanghai, the submarine *USS Grouper* fired five torpedoes at her. Four missed, but the fifth hit the stern of the ship and it started to sink. The submarine came under fire from patrol boats and aircraft and left the area, taking note that Japanese soldiers were being rescued from the sinking ship. Its crew could not have known about the 1,800 POWs still on board. Neither did they know that the Japanese had locked the hatches on the holds containing the POWs, leaving them to drown.

Of the 1,800 POWs, only 748 made it back to Britain. The *Lisbon Maru's* decrepit state meant that in some of the holds the POWs were able to break down the hatches and escape, but others were so ill and weak from malnutrition and disease that they drowned before they could be freed. Ronnie was among those who managed to break out of their hold and were rescued by Chinese fishermen who ferried them ashore and then passed them from one guerrilla group to another. With three other Hong Kong expatriates, Ronnie remained in China for nearly three years, moving from village to village every few weeks to avoid the Japanese soldiers. After their surrender in the wake of the Hiroshima and Nagasaki bombs and the execution of Isogai Rensuke, the Japanese Governor of the occupied territory, Ronnie returned to Hong Kong and was reunited with his wife and children.

But he would never be able to forget the incredible bravery of 'Horse' whose refusal to break under the most appalling torture had saved so many lives. Nor the horrific spectacle of 'Horse's' execution and his own revulsion at seeing Peter Drummond helping the Japanese to lock the hatches on the *Lisbon Maru*, pushing back his desperate comrades as they weakly begged for their lives. That day, Drummond murdered more than 1,200 of his fellow British officers.

CHAPTER 1

'Gunn,' he answered, holding his cellphone tucked under his chin with a bite-size piece of hot croissant and apricot jam in his left hand and a scalding cup of coffee in his right.

'John, it's Miles; just had a call from Peter Stancombe – you've met him, he's the Head of SO15 at the Met.'

'Yes sir,' Gunn replied having swallowed his mouthful of croissant.

'He's asked if you could call in at New Scotland Yard in, say....... twenty minutes?'

'Any idea what it's about sir?' Gunn asked, glancing at his watch as he left the small kitchen in his mews house at Elm Park Lane in Chelsea and went up the stairs to his bedroom.

'It's an odd one; there was a hit-and-run fatality outside Victoria Station last week. The man was killed instantly.'

'Witnesses?' Gunn asked, pulling on his trousers.

'None; not even a vague description of the type of vehicle which killed the man. A group of soccer supporters, who had missed their train, found him and were just sober enough to call the police.'

'Why me, sir?'

'The man's name is Lequesne.....Rory Lequesne.' Miles Thompson, the Deputy Director of the British Intelligence Directorate and Head of its Espionage Department, had incorrectly pronounced the 's' in the surname. 'Does that mean anything to you, John?

'Yes sir – if it's the same Lequesnes that my parents know; the Lequesnes are an expatriate Hong Kong family whose ancestry dates back to the foundation of the Colony in 1897.' Gunn was

1

now dressed in lightweight slacks, shirt and black slip-on loafers. He grabbed a tie from the wardrobe and the matching lightweight jacket of the suit and, still cradling the mobile between chin and left shoulder, left the bedroom pausing momentarily at the door to glance back at the tousled head of blonde hair peeping out from the duvet.

Gunn's family had an equally long connection with Hong Kong; his father and grandfather had worked for Euro-Pacific Construction and after leaving the Army, he had planned to join the Hong Kong- based company until he was recruited by BID. He had just successfully completed his SAS induction course when the Commanding Officer of 22 SAS Regiment had told him that he had failed to reach the required standard. BID had manipulated the result of the SAS course because its in-country agent in Hong Kong had been murdered. After failing to find a suitable replacement at very short notice from either its own resources or from the Diplomatic Service, BID had trawled the records of the Armed Forces which had revealed that Gunn spoke fluent Mandarin.

After the assignment in Hong Kong he had accepted the offer of permanent employment with the British Intelligence Directorate. His specialist area was South-East Asia because of his fluency in Chinese and colloquial ability in Bahasa Indonesia – the language of the largest Muslim nation in the world. With a height of 6'3"and and a weight of nearly 200 lbs, Gunn was the antithesis of the ideal agent for that part of the world where the average height of the male was 5'7". Gunn had acquired the ability to adapt, when it was needed, by walking with a stoop or by the simple practice of remaining seated whenever that was possible.

'Oh, is that how it's pronounced?.......well, Peter Stancombe has a Chief Inspector Nesbit with him – he's the investigating officer in this case – who's anxious to speak to someone with an in-depth knowledge of Hong Kong. I know that you've taken some leave after that last assignment, but I'm hoping that an hour or so helping out the Met won't cramp your style.'

'Not a problem, sir; I'm on my way,' Gunn replied going back down the stairs, grabbing his keys off the hall table, slotting the

Glock 26 into his ankle holster and then letting himself out of the front door into the mews.

'Give me a quick heads-up after your visit John. Remember we now have a new Director who's very keen at being kept in the loop..... particularly on any liaison between us and the Met.'

'Will do, sir,' and Gunn ended the call and turned right into Brompton Road, flagged down a taxi and asked for New Scotland Yard.

*

Sir Jeremy Hammond had been the Director of BID since 1990 when it had replaced MI5 and MI6. After some twenty years as the Director, he had decided to retire having recommended to the Prime Minister that his Deputy, Miles Thompson, should succeed him. However, the Prime Minister had rejected the recommendation and had appointed a career diplomat and lifelong supporter of the PM's political party. Sir Ian Davidson had recently completed his appointment as British Ambassador in Tokyo and had moved to the appointment of Director of BID two weeks previously.

Whilst Sir Ian was more than familiar with the remit of the MI6 officers who had been in the embassies and high commissions prior to the creation of BID, the appointment of an 'amateur' intelligence director was highly unpopular with both the BID hierarchy, the Parliamentary Opposition and the broadsheet Press. During the 1988 reorganisation of the UK's Intelligence Services, Sir Jeremy Hammond had removed the MI6 officers from embassies and high commissions in favour of in-country BID agents whose identity was only known by the Ambassador, his Head of Chancery and the Defence Attaché. That removal of 'the friends' – the term used when referring to the Secret Intelligence Services - from every embassy and high commission had succeeded in reducing the leaks, but had upset the hierarchy of the Diplomatic Service who viewed it as a condemnation of the Service's integrity.

No one had been more outspoken about this diminution of role for the Diplomatic Service than Sir Ian Davidson and he had made it quite clear when questioned by the media after the announcement of his appointment that he had every intention of making some changes.

*

Gunn was met in the main lobby of New Scotland Yard by Commander Peter Stancombe who introduced him to Chief Inspector Peter Nesbit.

'So how's the new boss settling in at the 'house'?' Commander Stancombe asked when they reached the Chief Inspector's office. The 'house' was a nick-name for Kingsroad House, the head office building of BID.

'Really no idea, Commander,' Gunn replied taking a seat in the chair indicated to him by the Chief Inspector. 'I've been on leave for the last two weeks so have yet to catch up with any gossip about the new Director. So how can I be of help with Rory Lequesne's death?' Gunn continued, diverting the conversation away from the controversial appointment of BID's new Director.

'I'll leave the two of you to discuss Lequesne's death. I've got to make another statement to the IPCC about the death of Jean Carlos de Menezes at Stockwell tube station,' and Commander Stancombe picked up his briefcase and left the office closing the door behind him. Peter Nesbit sat down at his desk and turned to Gunn.

'Sorry you've been dragged off leave, Mr Gunn.....'

'John.'

'Thanks....John. I believe you knew Mr Lequesne?'

'Yes I did. How well do you know Hong Kong?'

'Not at all....never been further east than our annual holiday in Cyprus.'

'OK....even after Hong Kong was handed back to the Chinese in 1997, many of the long established ex-pat community remained there. Rory Lequesne was my father's age....late sixties or seventy....'

'Seventy-two.'

'Right.....and yes I did meet him, but my father would know much more about him than me. I thought this was just another road death......tragic as that always is for the family and anyone else connected with it.'

'So did my guys until SOCO and the forensic boys arrived. Lequesne was murdered. After 'itting 'im the vehicle reversed over 'is body and then drove forward over 'im again crushing 'is skull. 'e'd been staying at the Travel Inn in Belgrave Road....only a couple of 'undred yards from where 'e was killed.'

'How did you know where he'd been staying,' Gunn asked.

'The plastic key card for 'is room was still in 'is wallet....as was about forty pounds.'

'So wha....'

''ang on a sec, John.'

'Sorry.'

'Don't apologise; I'm not explaining this well. As soon as they found the key, two of my constables – one was a WPC – went to the hotel. When they got there the receptionist told them that a plain clothes officer 'ad already gone up to the room.' The CI paused, ran his hands through his thinning hair and then continued. 'They didn't 'ave a fucking cat's chance in 'ell poor sods.......never paused to think 'ow another officer could 'ave got there before them or to call for back-up, just went straight up in the lift to the second floor.....the room was 203....opened the door with the room key and saw this man pulling out drawers from the fitted wardrobe. 'e shot both of them. Dan Mason was shot in the 'ead and died instantly. WPC Richards was saved by 'er stab-vest. The man barged out of the room knocking WPC Richards onto the floor. 'Zoe....that's WPC Richards.... is back on duty and it's from 'er that we learned what happened.'

Gunn remained silent as the CI paused. He felt that any comment expressing sorrow or concern would not only sound inadequate, but trite and meaningless.

'Anyway,' the CI continued, 'apart from confirming that Lequesne's death was murder, that wasn't the reason I went to see Peter Stancombe; we've been good friends ever since 'e was an instructor at the Police College at 'endon when I was a cadet. I knew he had close connections with BID and I wanted to speak to someone who knew a lot about Hong Kong. There's another reason I'll get to in a bit.'

'Why?.......apart from the obvious fact that Rory Lequesne lived there,' Gunn asked, still unclear as to why it had been necessary for the Police to approach BID for help with a murder.

'Because we found what that man was looking for in Lequesne's 'otel bedroom,' and the CI got up from his desk and went over to a steel cabinet, opened the door and removed a small, well-worn, leather attaché case.

*

'Thompson.'

'Miles, Director here. Pop into my office please as soon as possible.'

'Very well, Sir Ian, on my way,' and Miles Thompson put down the phone and walked the twenty or so yards along the corridor of the twelfth floor to the Director's office. As he left his outer office he cast a raised-eyebrow glance at his PA who shrugged her shoulders.

'Ah, Miles, come in,' the Director invited as his Deputy was shown in by Melanie, the Director's PA. Miles was left standing while the Director finished signing off a file. Whether this crass behaviour was purposely designed to humiliate the person who had been recommended for the Director's appointment or just bad manners would have to remain a matter for conjecture. As no gesture had been made, Miles walked over and sat in one of the armchairs. Conjecture was solved as the Director looked up from the file, his expression revealing his irritation that his deliberate 'put-down' of his Deputy had been ignored.

'I can come back, Sir Ian, if you're busy, but my PA intimated that that there was a degree of urgency in your request for me to pop into your office as soon as possible.' Miles had purposely used the exact words used by the Director.

'No, no, that's alright,' and the file was closed. Even from where he was seated, Miles could see that the file was the routine float file which circulated around the Assistant Directors with low-grade classified material confirming the attempted humiliation by the man behind the desk. 'How long has Melanie been the Director's PA?'

The question took Miles completely by surprise. Was that why he'd been summoned 'as soon as possible' to the Director's office?

'About five or six years, but Martin King, our Head of Human Resources, would have the exact details, Sir Ian. Is that what you wanted me to discuss with you?' Miles was unable to exclude the ridicule in his tone.

'No, no, no Miles but you've been with BID since its formation so I thought I would just check.' Possibly imagined by Miles, but there was the insinuation of 'and that's quite long enough'. 'I can't say I'm impressed with her performance during my first fortnight here. I may wish to replace her.'

'That's your prerogative Sir Ian. Martin King's the man who'll arrange that for you.' Silently Miles wonderd what Melanie had done to upset her new boss.

'Right, thank you Miles. Now, the reason I wanted to speak to you.'

'At last,' Miles thought silently and then aloud, 'yes, what can I do to help?'

'At my weekly 'prayers' for all Heads of Departments this morning you mentioned that you had sent one of our agents to help the Metropolitan Police. What's that all about?'

'A man was killed by a hit and run driver last week a few hundred yards from Victoria Station. The police identified him as a Rory Lequesne..........' Miles stopped in mid-sentence at the startled expression on the Director's face. 'I'm sorry Sir Ian; is there a problem?'

'No, no......go on Miles,' but every vestige of colour had vanished from the Director's face.

'Very well,' Miles restarted his account, 'and discovered that he was an expatriate resident of Hong Kong. The investigating officer knew nothing about Hong Kong and Peter Stancombe – the Head of SO15 – asked me for help. John Gunn comes from one of the oldest expatriate families in Hong Kong, speaks fluent Mandarin and was free. He's at New Scotland Yard now helping them.'

'And you did this without reference to me?'

'Yes of course Sir Ian. I wouldn't dream of bothering you with such a routine request from the Met.'

'Please let me have a full report on the matter,' and the Director stood up indicating that the 'summons' was over. Miles Thompson stood up, unable to hide the look of mild incredulity on his face.

'Very well Sir Ian,' Miles replied calmly and walked out of the office closing the door behind him. As he passed Melanie he very quietly asked her to come and see him during her lunch break.

*

'How did this man miss that?' Gunn asked as the Chief Inspector placed the small case on the table beside him and pulled up another chair.

'Because it wasn't in the room. We found a key to a left-luggage locker at Victoria Station in Lequesne's 'ip pocket. The case was in that locker.'

Gunn held up his hand, 'hang on.......so let me get this right, Peter. The car ran over Lequesne, but the killer, or killers, didn't have time to search the body because the soccer supporters appeared on the scene. Right so far?'

'That's 'ow we see it.'

'So, as the killer didn't have his room key, he - or they - must have been following Lequesne for some time.......presumably waiting for the opportunity to kill him. Why for God's sake? What's in that case Peter?' Gunn asked pulling his chair closer to the table. The CI opened the case revealing a jumbled collection of diaries, papers and notebooks. 'So what's so valuable with that lot that it cost Lequesne his life?' Gunn asked leaning forward to get a better look at the contents of the case.

'I've 'ad the case at my 'ome for the last four days. All of these papers, diaries and notes belong to Ronnie Lequesne, Rory's father. Did you know 'im?'

'My father and Rory, as children, were both in the Stanley Internment Centre at the southern end of Hong Kong Island. That's where the Japanese held all non-Chinese nationals after their victory in the Battle for Hong Kong. Rory's father, Ronnie, was in the

Royal Artillery serving with 5th Medium Regiment. He was taken prisoner by the Japs, as was my grandfather, and sent to a POW camp in Argyle Street. That's in Kowloon, Peter, on the north side of the Harbour.....damn!' Gunn paused, 'I should have thought to bring a map of the territory with me.'

'No problem, go on.'

'Many of the officers and soldiers in that POW camp - and other camps - died from beatings, torture, mal-nutrition and executions for attempted escapes....... sorry, I'm banging on a bit....'

'On the contrary, what you're telling me is 'ighly relevant as you'll discover shortly. Go on.'

'Ronnie tried to escape, but was caught, beaten, tortured and then with most of the other officers in that camp was shipped to Japan in an old rust bucket called the '*Lisbon Maru*'. Their destination was a slave labour camp in Japan, but the ship was torpedoed by a US submarine off Shanghai. The POWs had been locked in the ship's holds and hundreds of them were left to drown as the Japs abandoned the sinking ship. Ronnie escaped with the other prisoners in his hold by breaking down the rotten hatch, was rescued by Chinese fishermen and taken to China where he was looked after by the guerrillas. My father told me many years later that as a young boy, on a number of occasions, he could remember seeing Ronnie and other surviving officers in deep conversation about their exploits.....phew!......that's about it. Any help?'

'And some!.......and now I understand the reason for the letter that was on the top of the papers in the case which is addressed to you,' and the CI handed the envelope to Gunn.

> '*Should anything happen to me and this case is found I would be most grateful if the case and its contents could be given to John Gunn who works for the British Intelligence Directorate.*'

'*Dear John,*

I have no wish to be melodramatic, but if you are reading this it means that I am dead.

Your father and I have always been the greatest of friends and many were the evenings that we talked about our fathers' exploits during the Battle for Hong Kong. I know that Ronnie, my father, would not have survived his time in the POW camp in Argyle Street had it not been for the courage, unselfishness and strength of your grandfather.'

Gunn paused from reading the letter as he recalled his father's reticence to discuss anything about his grandfather's death in the battle for Hong Kong. He then continued reading the letter.

'My old father became somewhat obsessed in his later years with chronicling every detail of his time in the POW camp and the last voyage of the Lisburn Maru. Most of his research was focused on the treachery of that traitor Peter Drummond who has to be guilty of the murder of hundreds of British and Canadian officers who were locked in the holds of the sinking ship after it was torpedoed by the US submarine. Drummond remained in Japan helping the Japs with their war effort, but unfortunately was not killed by either of the two atomic bombs in 1945. As part of his research into what he rightly believed were war crimes, my father went to Japan, but never found Drummond or anything about him. It was as though he had never existed.

I took up the task after my father's death fifteen years ago. During the probate of his estate I found all the papers which are in the case which is now in your possession. I discovered that Drummond did survive the war, changed his name, married a secretary from the British Embassy in Tokyo and remained in Japan for the rest of his life.

At that stage two events occurred: the first was my realisation that every effort had been made by the Japanese to protect Drummond's identity. The second was that my research had made me a target for the Japanese Mafia – the Yakuza.

There have been three attempts to kill me and so I have decided to come to London to warn you that Drummond's treachery continues – even though he must be in his eighties now. My sister was killed by a hit-and-run driver in Australia; they never found the culprit, but I'm certain that it was a part of this conspiracy. I'm the only one left who can warn you of this threat. There seems to be a connection to both the Yakuza and 'Aum Shinrikyo', the organisation that attacked the Tokyo Subway with Sarin gas in 1995 and now calls itself 'Aleph'.

I leave it to you to decide if this is just the ramblings of an old man or something worth investigating.

With kindest regards
Rory'

CHAPTER 2

'You asked me to call in during my lunch break, sir.'

'Yes, come in and take a seat Melanie,' and Miles Thompson pushed the file he was working on to one side and got up from his chair behind the desk and joined her in another armchair. 'I understand that things might not be going too smoothly with the new Director?'

'Is that what he said?'

'In so many words; so what's the problem?'

'Ever since his first few days here he's spent a lot of time each day down on the tenth floor in the Top Secret restricted section of the secure records vault.'

'Nothing wrong with that, is there Melanie?'

'No sir, of course not; but he's confined his interest to just one section of the records.......the one that's excluded from the Freedom of Information Act and the 30 year rule on disclosure. The files he's been looking at are those stamped with the 100 year restriction relating to the Second World War, Japan's role in that war and the agents from the Special Operations Executive operating in Japan.'

'OK, I hear what you're saying, but as he has just completed a four year tour as Ambassador in Tokyo, is it not reasonable for him to be particularly interested in the records relating to Japan's role in that war,' Miles suggested, guessing that the real cause of the clash of personalities had yet to be revealed.

'Sorry sir......I'm not explaining this very well....'

'That's OK, take your time.'

'No one's allowed to remove those files or any of the contents of those files from the vault.'

'Of course.'

'Two of the most sensitive files.....the ones relating to the work of the SOE agents, their betrayal, how they were captured by the Japanese Secret Service.....the *Kem*.... something or other....'

'*Kempei tai*?' Miles offered.

'That's the word, and the torture they suffered are in the Director's office.'

'Are they still there?'

'Yes sir....or they were. As soon as you left the office, the Director said he was going out and would not be back until after lunch. He didn't take the files with him.'

'So has this happened before?'

'Yes sir. That's what's annoyed him because I mentioned to him that the files shouldn't have been removed from the vault. He went ballistic....I thought he was going to hit me at one point.'

'But how did he get the files past Martin King when he signed out of the Secure Records area?' The comment was rhetorical, not expecting an answer from Melanie.

'No idea sir.'

'Where are the current files when he left the office?'

'They were pushed into his desk drawer.'

'Not locked?'

'Not locked.'

'Where are they now?'

'I locked them in my safe.'

'Right,' and Miles picked up his phone and dialled Martin King's number. He was at his desk and Miles told him that he would be with him in a few minutes. 'Come on Melanie, let's get those files and then you go out to lunch.'

The two of them went back along the corridor to the Director's office where Melanie opened her safe and handed the two files to Miles Thompson who scribbled a receipt for her and dated it. Melanie then headed for the lift while Miles returned to his office with the two files. Before he went to see the Head of Administration and Finance, he wanted to have a quick scan of the files' contents. Flicking through the contents from the back folios of each, it took less than a minute to discover that at least two or three folios were missing from each file. If the folios had been removed, for whatever reason, then Martin King would have a record of the date of removal and the reason for that removal.

In both the files, the missing folios had been removed from papers relating to the betrayal and arrest of the SOE agents. Miles closed the files, placed them in his brief case and headed for the stairs down to the tenth floor.

*

'My Chief Superintendent has agreed to let me sign out the papers to you although they've been logged in as evidence in Lequesne's murder and the shooting of my two constables. Is that OK with you, bearing in mind that at least two people are dead because someone wants to get their 'ands on the contents of that case?' Chief Inspector Nesbit asked, pushing a police form across the table for Gunn to sign.

'Yes, that's OK,' Gunn agreed and signed the form. He closed the attaché case and got up from his chair.

'Very grateful for any information you can give me that 'elps us get that bastard who shot PC Mason.......and, of course, whoever killed Lequesne,' the CI added, handing over the duplicate copy of the form which Gunn had just signed. He was then escorted by the CI down to the lobby of New Scotland Yard where the two men parted. Gunn glanced at his watch – nearly 12.30; rather longer than the twenty minutes forecast by Miles Thompson.

Gunn walked out into Broadway where he picked up a taxi which dropped him off in Beaufort Street at the junction with Elm Park Lane. He paid the taxi driver, accepted the receipt and walked the short distance to his house, removing the house keys from his pocket. There was a right-angle bend in the mews after some twenty yards and then Gunn's house was a further twenty yards on the left. To the right of the front door was the dining room window and to the right of that the up-and-over garage door. The door wasn't shut properly. Had he failed to close it properly the previous evening when he'd put the Jaguar away? Highly unlikely, Gunn reasoned, as he'd only just acquired the five year old, midnight-blue, XKR convertible to replace his previous classic sports car. In fact he could clearly remember shooting the bolts on the door the previous evening.

Gunn returned the keys to his pocket, transferred the small attaché case into his left hand and walked past his front door to the right hand end of the house where a small alleyway led into Elm Park Gardens. A short distance along the alleyway on the left was a gate into the back garden of his mews house. He unlocked the gate and went into the garden, hiding the attaché case under a rhododendron bush and closing the gate behind him. Gunn removed the Glock 26 from its ankle holster and walked silently along the moss-covered brick path to the back door. He'd left Claudine either asleep, or feigning sleep, when he'd left the house earlier. Had she gone out of the garage door? Highly unlikely, Gunn reasoned, as he inserted the key into the Chubb lock on the back door.

The door was wrenched open, pulling Gunn off balance into the kitchen and a numbing chop to his right wrist sent the Glock spinning out of his hand under the kitchen table. He rolled forward onto the floor, swinging his legs in a scything movement which caught his attacker's legs, bringing him down onto the floor and saving Gunn from a vicious knife thrust which ripped through his jacket from the breast pocket down to the side pocket. His attacker was large with a shaved head and tattoos covering almost every inch of exposed flesh. He recovered quickly and threw himself at Gunn driving the knife in front of him aiming it at Gunn's stomach. Gunn caught the hand holding the knife, twisted it, rolled over, pulling the man with him as the wrist snapped with an audible crack, quickly drowned by the screams of pain from the man as Gunn broke all the fingers in his right hand, releasing the knife. Gunn grabbed the knife and drove it up to the hilt in the man's neck, releasing a gusher of blood from his mouth as he collapsed, choking out his life blood onto the kitchen floor.

15

There was a shout from somewhere upstairs and heavy steps on the stairs before the kitchen door burst open and another man appeared, covered in blood, gripping an automatic in his right hand. His left arm had been almost severed just above the elbow. Gunn's Glock still lay under the kitchen table; the latter was made of solid Indonesian teak, a trophy of a previous assignment in that country, and had survived the onslaught of the first attack on Gunn. He dived under the table, scooping up the Glock and pulling the table over between himself and his second attacker. The man fired; his shot hit one of the table legs and went no further. The 9mm, steel-jacketed bullet from Gunn's Glock 26 went through the man's right eye and lifted off the back of his head, splattering it over the kitchen door.

Gunn scrambled to his feet, desperate to know what had happened upstairs. He pulled the dead man away from the door and raced up the stairs to the bedroom where he'd left Claudine some three hours earlier. The room where he had left Claudine asleep looked as though a bomb had exploded there. Blood was everywhere – mostly on the bed, but also splattered on the walls, carpet and smashed furniture. The immediate evidence showed that there had been a furious fight as Claudine fought for her life. She lay on the carpet beside the bed, her right hand still grasping the butt of her Colt .45 automatic. It would have been a bullet from that which had partially severed her attacker's left arm. Gunn knelt beside her, feeling for a pulse in her neck as he pressed the speed dial number for BID's emergency medical support at Kingsroad House. His call was answered immediately and battling to keep his emotions and despair in check, he asked for immediate life-saving paramedic support.

There was no pulse and the bullet wounds in Claudine's chest and stomach provided the mind-numbing evidence for Gunn that she had failed in the battle to save her life. For Gunn it was as though there was a time vortex and it was only the furious ringing of the front door bell that sent him rushing down the stairs to admit the BID paramedics whom he led back up the stairs to the bedroom. Gunn stood back as the highly competent team got to work, but after just a few minutes the team leader of the paramedics turned to Gunn from where he knelt beside Claudine and shook his head. Claudine was dead.

The team leader led Gunn out of the bedroom back downstairs while his team removed Claudine's body from the bedroom into the ambulance. Gunn dialled Miles Thompson's mobile number.

'Thompson.'

'John Gunn, sir. I'm at my house. Claudine's dead. The men who killed her are also both dead. Please send the 'clean-up' squad. The paramedics are bringing Claudine,' Gunn paused, unable to say "Claudine's body", 'back to Kingsroad House.'

'Dear God..........' Miles began, but Gunn had ended the call.

*

In the miserable days that followed Claudine's death, Gunn cancelled his leave and returned to work – anything to avoid wallowing in his own self-pity and to keep in check the rage which twisted his gut like some rampant ulcer. One of his first duties was to fly to Guernsey to visit Claudine's father, Jean de Carteret. It had been on an assignment shortly after Gunn joined BID that he had rescued Jean from Hassan Hussein's mock medieval castle on Sardrière Island to the east of Guernsey's St Peter Port. That rescue had led to the start of the relationship between Gunn and Claudine and her subsequent recruitment by BID. Jean, her father, still took his small fishing trawler out every day and was surrounded by a close band of fellow fishermen who would help him through the worst of the grieving.

WPC Zoe Richards identified one of Claudine's killers as the man who had shot PC Mason at the Travel Inn in Belgrave Road. Both men had a string of convictions for armed robbery, GBH, enforcing protection rackets, drug dealing and intimidation. Their criminal services were available to anyone who paid them and as both had been killed by Gunn, the opportunity of identifying the person who had employed them had gone. CI Nesbit had told Gunn that even if they had been alive it would have been impossible to identify the 'Mr Big' – Nesbit's expression – as the hiring and payment would have been concealed by a maze of cut-outs. Claudine's funeral was a private family affair in the parish church of St Peter Port, but attended by so many people that the service had to be relayed by loudspeakers to those who could not get a seat inside the Church.

Only a week after Claudine's death, while Gunn was in Guernsey for the funeral, his house was broken into and suffered the chaos of a very thorough search. Nothing was taken from the house which probably meant that the Lequesne papers, once again, were the target of the break-in. CI Nesbit had offered to take back the attaché case, but Gunn told him that he had had no time to study the papers and as it appeared that the information contained in the papers might have contributed to Claudine's death, he intended to pick up the trail where Rory Lequesne's death had temporarily halted it.

In the days following the funeral, Gunn spent his evenings reading every scrap of information from the attaché case. His first task was to catalogue the papers into some semblance of a sequence of events. Once that was done he was able to follow Ronnie Lequesne's search for information about Peter Drummond, followed by his son's which picked up the trail when his father died. He went down to his parents' home in Sussex and spent a day talking to his father about his grandfather who had died in a POW camp. David Gunn was able to tell his son a great deal about the character of Ronnie Lequesne, but very little about his quest to trace the whereabouts of Peter Drummond. He told Gunn he knew that Ronnie had been obsessed with his duty to those who had died in the POW camp and in the *Lisburn Maru*, but apparently, he'd never discussed the detail of his research. The only way that Gunn could make any progress was to pick up the trail where it had been terminated by the killing of Rory Lequesne and Claudine. That meant a detailed examination of every bit of information in the attaché case.

After the Sunday spent at his parent's home in Sussex, Gunn phoned BID's Deputy Director at his home in Durham Place, barely half a mile from Gunn's mews house. Miles Thompson told him that he and his wife Libby were on their own and invited him to come round for a drink. After two attempts to ransack his house to find the Lequesne papers, Gunn was taking no chances with losing them, so they were returned to the left-luggage locker at Victoria

Station before he walked the short distance to the Deputy Director's house.

Miles answered the door and led the way into the sitting room where Libby greeted Gunn with a kiss and then announced that she intended to have an early night after watching the TV in the first floor lounge. Gunn sipped the single malt scotch which Miles had poured for both of them.

'Was your father able to fill in any of the background to your research into Rory Lequesne's papers,' Miles asked as he sat down in an armchair opposite Gunn.

'Not really....he was able to tell me a lot about Rory himself as they had known each other since childhood when both were in the Stanley Internment Camp as kids. But he really had no knowledge about what happened to Peter Drummond or what Ronnie Lequesne's search had discovered about him.'

'Have you been through all the papers?' Miles asked.

'Yes........they're in the form of diaries; meticulous in their detail of every step taken both by Ronnie and then his son, Rory, to trace Drummond. There are some horrifying details of what the POWs suffered at the hands of the Jap guards in the Argyle Street Camp; details that leave me no option but to pick up the trail that was halted by Rory's and Claudine's murder. The papers revealed that Drummond changed his name and received considerable help from the wartime Japanese secret service to conceal both his identity and whereabouts. The Japs used him just like the Germans used Rudolf Hess to spread propaganda.'

'This was the *Kempei tai*........?'

'It was, and as I've recently learnt had a very similar role... and reputation.....as the Nazi Gestapo and Totenkopf, or Death's Head SS Units. This consisted of POW and forced labour camps, interrogation and torture, difficult POWs used for human medical experiments, the provision of brothels for the Japanese troops and dissemination of propaganda. After the Japs surrendered in August 1945, the *Kampei tai* was disbanded and was replaced by the post-war internal police called *Keimu tai*.'

Miles Thompson did not interrupt Gunn, realising that his research was probably Gunn's way of preventing himself from dwelling on Claudine's murder.

'Pleasant bunch; can I top up your scotch, John?'

'Thanks.....just a small one.'

'So, where to next?' Miles asked as he poured another scotch for both of them and returned to his armchair.

'I still have ten days of leave so I'm going to pick up where Rory left off. I'm pretty certain that my research into Rory's papers will lead me to Tokyo. It'll be difficult as I don't speak a word of Japanese, but perhaps BID's in-country agent might be able to help?'

'Come into the office tomorrow, John. I know the police have asked you to pass on anything you discover if it helps in identifying who is behind Claudine's and PC Mason's deaths so your investigation must be done as a formal assignment. I will set that up tomorrow. Come to my office at about 11.30 and I'll brief you.'

'Many thanks for that, Miles.....and the scotch,' and Gunn left the Espionage Director's house.

*

The sadness of Claudine's death hung like a dark cloud over everyone in BID and had put Miles' investigation into the disappearance of folios from a Top Secret file onto a back-burner. He had returned the files to the Head of Finance and Administration warning him that he wanted a 100% check of all the documents in the restricted area of the vault. His first question to Martin King was to ask him how the Director had managed to leave the vault while in the possession of files on more than one occasion.

'Sloppiness on my part, sir,' Martin admitted. 'I had recently given him the full brief on accessing those sensitive files and assumed that he would stick to the rules. I'm still not sure, though, how he avoided the checks we have in place to prevent anyone leaving here with an unauthorised file.'

'That is you first task then, Martin; I want a complete overhaul of the security in your department. Now what happened to those missing folios from those files dealing with the capture of our SOE agents in Japan?'

'They're not missing, sir.'

'They damn well are, Martin....here I've made a note of the folio numbers,' and Miles slapped a sheet from a memo pad in front of Martin King.

'Would you come with me, sir,' and Martin picked up the memo and led the Deputy Director into the secure records vault. They went to the far right hand end of the vault where access was further restricted by another door with a combination lock. Martin tapped out the combination, opened the door and led the way into the air-conditioned room, glancing again at the file reference on the memo handed to him by Miles.

'Here we are,' and Martin had stopped in front of a shelf of files, each section clearly labelled with an alpha/numeric reference. He removed the two files which Miles had returned some ten days earlier. 'These are the files, sir, which you brought down to me and we both checked the folios and confirmed the ones that were missing.' Miles took the files.

'Yes, these are the files,' Miles confirmed as he opened the first one at the back folio and flicked to the first missing folio – 23A – which he remembered without checking his memo which Martin was holding. Folio 23A was a flimsy and faded signal from an SOE agent in Tokyo to SOE Headquarters at Hans Place in London's Knightsbridge. Miles remembered that the signal had listed the names of the agents who had been arrested by the *Kempei tai*. Folio 23A was on the file – in the right place and exactly as Miles remembered it. 'What was the next folio?'

'Folio 42, sir.'

'Right,' Miles muttered, 'let's see if that has also miraculously reappeared.........ah!......here we are, and here is folio 42,' Miles announced, holding the file open. And the third folio in the second file had also reappeared. They've all been removed and then re-inserted, but over the years many of the folios have been removed for photocopying so that proves nothing.'

'Exactly, sir,' Martin returned the files, 'except that you and I know that those folios were removed.'

'Presumably the Director came in here after I had returned those files?'

'Yes sir....at least twice. I would have to check the records.'

'Which in future will be rigorously controlled......yes?'

'Yes sir.'

'Very well, Martin, I'd better go and have a word with our Director,' and Miles left the Finance and Administration Department.

CHAPTER 3

'I suppose it was that PA of mine who went to you about those files,' was the Director's response to Miles when he questioned him about the removal of files from the restricted area of the records vault.

'As your Deputy, Sir Ian, I have the overall responsibility for all aspects of security whether that be physical, electronic or written and all the staff in BID know that,' Miles replied.

'I consider her first duty is to be an efficient and loyal PA to me.......not....not ....to run elsewhere telling tales......'

'Sir Ian, I believe I'm right in saying that Melanie had already advised you that the files you had in your possession should not have been removed from the secure records vault.......'

'Possibly......I don't remember,' the Director interrupted. Miles ignored the interruption.

'.........can you tell me, Sir Ian, why you needed to remove a number of folios from those files and then return them without clearing the procedure with Martin King?'

'I'm writing a definitive book about my time in Japan for the FCO and needed to verify some data,' was said abruptly indicating that that was the end of discussion on the matter.

'Thank you for letting me know that. You'll find that I have had to reprimand Martin King for allowing such a breach of security. You will also find that access to those files has been considerably tightened. I would be most grateful, Sir Ian, if you could help us by seeing that the enhanced security is effective.'

'Very well; now what's happening about de Carteret's murder and the death of the police constable. This agent of ours........Gunn....

seems to be something of a loose cannon.......' the Director stopped in mid sentence as he saw the look of amazement on Miles' face. 'Well, isn't he? I mean how are we to know what happened in Gunn's house.......it sounds like a rather sordid affair that should be handed over to the police....'

'No, Sir Ian,' Miles interrupted, 'definitely not. In fact I'm briefing John Gunn, who, incidentally, is probably the most effective agent in the Espionage Directorate, for an assignment to follow up the deaths of Lequesne, PC Mason and Claudine de Carteret.'

'On whose authority?' the Director snapped.

'Mine, Sir Ian.'

'And when was I to be informed of this?'

'At our weekly meeting.'

'I have no intention of sanctioning this assignment. I see this as a police matter and I'm now directing you to cancel this assignment for...er....for.......Gunn.' Miles could hardly believe what he was hearing, but realised that a confrontation would gain little, so bit his lip furiously.

'Very well, Sir Ian,' and Miles left the Director's office; shell-shocked would be an inadequate description of his reaction to the behaviour of BID's new Director.

Miles returned to his office where he found Gunn waiting in his PA's office. He glanced at his watch; 11.30.

'Come in, John.' Miles walked over to the windows with the view over the rooftops to the Thames. Gunn waited and then commented quietly.

'The boss hasn't approved the assignment, has he?'

Miles turned; 'no he hasn't.' Both men were silent and then Miles went over to his desk, opened a drawer and removed a card index of addresses, flicked through the cards, extracted one and copied the details onto a memo pad and handed it to Gunn. 'During your leave you might like to look up an old friend of mine. His name's Shiro Akagawa; he's a senior Professor at the School of Oriental and African Studies in Russell Square. He'll be expecting you.'

'Thanks Miles,' and Gunn turned to leave the office.

'Wait.......and that's how to contact Yukiko Yoshiwa....BID's in-country agent in Tokyo,' and Gunn took the proffered slip of paper.

'How long's he been with BID?'

'Only six months.........and it's 'she' not 'he'.

*

Gunn crossed the paved courtyard between the two college buildings of SOAS at the north-west corner of Russell Square. The School was a part of the University of London and in term time its courtyard would usually be filled with undergraduates, but in mid September the University was still 'down' and it was deserted. Gunn went up the short flight of wide steps into the modern, airy and mainly white-painted reception and registration area which was deserted except for one person at the reception desk. The young man at the semi-circular reception desk, who could have come from any Asian country directed him in perfect English to Professor Akagawa's office on the first floor of the building. Gunn knocked on the office door and entered in response to the loud and cheery 'come in!'

Professor Akagawa was slightly taller than Gunn had expected – 'probably five foot ten', he guessed, as he shook hands with a good-looking man in his late fifties or early sixties with a full head of iron-grey hair. Both men had bowed before shaking hands. Having spent the first thirteen years of his life with his family in Hong Kong, Gunn had met many Japanese businessmen who had visited the family apartment on the Peak and was aware of the importance of the greeting etiquette. He knew that the bowing routine could vary from a nod of the head to kneeling on the floor with head touching the ground and palms flat on the floor.

The office was decorated in Western style rather than Japanese with just one or two delicate flower arrangements and Japanese paintings and ornaments.

'Welcome Mr Gunn, do please sit down,' and the Professor indicated a comfortable upholstered chair.

'Thank you, sir; I'm really grateful that you've been able to spare the time to see me.'

'I have plenty of time Mr Gunn until the university year starts once more in October.' The English was accent-less and grammatically perfect. 'Now Miles tells me that you will be going to Japan – Tokyo most probably – and although you are very familiar with South-East Asia and speak Mandarin fluently, I gather you know very little about Japan.'

'Very, very little, sir,' Gunn emphasised, 'other than what I learnt from meeting the Japanese who visited my parents' apartment in Hong Kong.'

'Right, well I now know where to start, but first of all two things; my first name is 'Shiro' which means that I'm the fourth – and youngest – of my brothers. I would like you to call me by that name please. My surname, 'Akagawa' – literally translated means 'red river', but I won't bore you with my family's ancestry to explain the origin of that name. Secondly I'm going to introduce you to the tea ceremony – why? – because we Japanese, even in the twenty-first century, are obsessed with ritual, status, courtesy and what others think of us. Now to do this as your host I should be wearing a kimono, but we will dispense with that ritual of the *Way* – the proper way to drink tea - which was brought to Japan from China in the twelfth century.'

The 'makings' of this ritual had been laid out on the low round table between Gunn and the Professor. Shiro picked up a small bamboo scoop and ladled powdered green tea into a bowl followed by boiling water which he whisked until it frothed. Bowing, Shiro handed the bowl to Gunn.

'John, first bow and then take the bowl from me.'

Gunn did as directed, accepted the bowl and bowed.

'Now turn the bowl clockwise twice so that the front of the bowl is away from you. Sip the tea, wipe the bowl with your fingers from where you drank and turn the bowl anti-clockwise twice.' Gunn completed the ritual and returned the bowl to Shiro.

'Good; there are three rituals which form the classical arts of Japanese refinement. The first is *'chado'* – the tea ceremony which you have just mastered expertly!' was said with a smile, 'the second is '*ikebana*' or flower arrangement and the third is '*kodo*' – the incense ceremony. Enough of that, but I hope that has illustrated for you just how important it will be for you to have this knowledge of Japanese rituals.'

'I realise I've a great deal of reading to do before I leave for Tokyo in 48 hours,' Gunn acknowledged with a wry smile.

'I will give you a small book to read which covers the history and customs of Japan and an excellent guide book to Tokyo, but that is not the real reason that Miles wanted me to speak with you. Does the word *Yakuza* mean anything to you?'

'I think I've heard it used in connection with organised crime, but........' Gunn paused and Shiro continued.

'Correct; *Yakuza* is the Japanese Mafia. It is formed by different groups. Each group or family is headed up by an *Oyabun* who gives orders to his subordinates.....known as *Kobun*.'

YAKUZA

ヤクザ

YAMAGUCHI-GUMI

SUMIYOSHI-RENGO

INAGAWA-KAI

AIZUKOTETSU-KAI

TOA-KAI

SEPPUKU-KAI

'The largest of these groups is *Yamaguchi-gumi* which has its headquarters in Kobe from where it directs criminal activity throughout Japan. There are four other 'families' worthy of note and they are *Sumiyoshi-rengo, Inagawa-kai, Aizukotetsu-kai* and *Toakai*. All of these groups have a crest, monogram or tattoo – usually tattooed on the right wrist or engraved on a medallion hung round the neck. Here,' and Shiro passed a sheet of A4 to Gunn on which he'd photocopied the monograms. 'Sorry for the quality, but I did this in a hurry as soon as I got the call from Miles. At the top is the *kanji* script for *Yakuza*.'

'These *Yakuza* groups have a finger in every form of criminal activity, but particularly in sex-related industries fed by the importation of young girls from China and the Philippines. More tea?'

'No thanks,' Gunn declined the offer.

'After the war when these *Yakuza* groups re-emerged after the tight military control of the whole country, a new group surfaced calling itself *Seppuku-kai*......you will know that better as *Harakiri*, the ritual self-evisceration with the ceremonial *wakizashi* sword.'

'Unpleasant,' Gunn grimaced.

'Yes, very, but to a Samurai warrior an honourable death rather than to be captured by the enemy. You remember the Sarin gas attack on the Tokyo subway in 1995?'

'Yeees....' Gunn said uncertainly......'I was in the army at that time on an emergency tour in Northern Ireland.'

'That attack resulted in over 5,000 patients being admitted to hospital of whom 12 died. The organisation responsible for the attack was *Aum Shinrikyo* and its leader, Asahara, and seven other members were sentenced to death. They were hanged two years ago after their appeal against the death sentence was rejected. The organisation had about 2,000 members and after this atrocity changed its name to *Aleph* which continues to this day as a religious organisation permitted by the Japanese Diet although proscribed by the US State Department as a "terrorist organisation".'

Shiro picked up the tea bowl, turned it and sipped before continuing.

'The ardent fundamentalists of *Aum Shinrikyo*, whose goal was to bring down the Government and Monarchy, are known to have been recruited into *Seppuku-kai*. Everything I've told you so far is fact; now I'm going to move into a shadowy area of rumour and conjecture. The Japanese equivalent of your BID is the *Keimu tai*, which replaced the disgraced wartime *Kempei tai*. What I'm about to tell you is intelligence gathered from its surveillance of the dismissed members of *Aum Shinrikyo* who joined *Seppuku-kai*. *Seppuku-kai* was so well organised and its security so tight that the *Keimu tai* had an almost impossible task gathering any intelligence on it. Under-cover agents attempted to infiltrate it, but after all of them were found floating in Tokyo's Sumida River with the three bottom fingers of their right hands severed........'

'Why the three.....?'

'I'm sorry John, yet another *Yakuza* ritual known as *Yubitsume*. It comes from the traditional way of holding a Japanese sword. The bottom three fingers of the hand are used to grip the sword tightly with the thumb and forefinger slightly looser. The removal of those fingers indicates that the victim is no longer of any use because he cannot hold a sword.'

'Bloody gruesome, Shiro.'

'Yes of course, but still done today either as an act of repentance or punishment.....it is even possible to buy prosthetic fingers to cover up this form of punishment. However I digress and time is not on our side. You must at all times be alert to any of those monograms I've shown you.....they may be tattoos, the crest on a ring, a neck medallion....almost anything... anywhere. The success of this new group, *Seppuku-kai*, was put down to its leader who has been identified as Ken..........'

But Shiro was interrupted by a subdued cough behind Gunn; a hole appeared in the centre of Shiro's forehead a split second before he and his chair flipped over backwards staining the pale blue carpet with the contents of the professor's skull. Even before the obscene noise of the shot from a silenced automatic had cut off the Professor's words, Gunn had hurled himself off his chair to the right, somersaulting over his right shoulder as he pulled the Glock 17 from his shoulder holster. He fired his first shot while still rolling, head facing the doorway offering the smallest target possible to the Professor's assassin.

Another cough and a bullet slammed into the leg of the low table on which the tea ceremony had been performed, splintering it and emptying the table contents onto the carpet. All Gunn could see at the edge of the barely-opened door was the extended barrel of the silenced automatic and the hand holding it. His second shot was aimed at where the arm and body holding that automatic should be. The 9mm, steel-jacketed bullet from the Glock went through the door, losing little of its very high muzzle velocity, and the muffled cry from the other side of the door confirmed a hit.

Gunn ran forward in a low crouch holding the Glock in front of him, covering the gap between the edge of the door and the door frame. With his back to the wall beside the door, he kicked it open. Another bullet slammed into the wall beside Gunn's head as the gunman walked backwards unsteadily to the stairs leaving a trail of blood in front of him. Gunn dropped to the floor behind the office wall and holding the Glock in both hands fired round the door jam at the same moment as another bullet from the gunman went through the door and smashed the window overlooking the courtyard below. Gunn's shot went through the gunman's neck, hurling him backwards over the top step of the stairs down to the reception area on the ground floor.

Still holding the Glock, Gunn ran from the professor's office and taking the stairs two at a time reached the gunman only seconds after he rolled to a halt at the foot of the stairs. Gunn's first bullet had missed the gunman, but had been close enough to disrupt his aim. The second bullet had gone through the man's chest and the third through his neck smashing his spinal cord and killing him instantly. Gunn felt for a pulse; there was nothing.

The reception area was empty; not even the receptionist was at the desk. Gunn re-holstered the Glock, buttoned his jacket and walked out of the building.

*

The BID Operations Centre on the 14th floor of Kingsroad House was very similar to a scaled down version of NASA's Mission Control Centre at Houston – an interior with which nearly the entire world was familiar after the NASA moon landings at the end of the 20th century. In the middle of the Centre, the Director of Communications and Ciphers and Controller of the Operations Centre sat at a console on a raised dais from where he could see every part of his electronic world – and the humans who operated it.

The Controller of this electronic world was Terry Holt, a retired RAF Wing Commander. The Centre was divided into two – one third of the room supported the Espionage Directorate and the other two thirds, the Counter-Espionage Directorate. Apart from the rows and rows of flat-screen VDUs of all shapes and sizes, there were two huge electronic display screens in each part of the Centre; one showed a display map of the United Kingdom and the other, the World.

The Centre operated 24/7 for 365 days of the year with three, eight hour shifts. The image on the UK screen could be changed instantly to the whole, or a segment, of any village, town or city in the UK and the same scale of detail could be achieved on the World screen. The Centre was linked directly to GCHQ, BID's Cheltenham-based Signals-Intelligence Centre and to the CIA Operations Centre in Fairfax County, Langley, Virginia. It also had close links with the HQ of the French DGSE at Boulevard Mortier in Paris, the Canadian CSIS at Ogalvie Road in Ottawa, the German BND at Pullach near Munich and the Israeli Mossad in Tel Aviv.

Three of the VDUs in front of Terry Holt were switched to various news channels. The Centre had a full complement of 28 staff, but in spite of this there was only a low murmur of chatter and the steady whir of the air-conditioning cooling both humans and computer chips and circuits. Sky News was reporting on the worsening world-wide bank crisis when the presenter paused in his summary as he listened to a message in his earphone.

"We're interrupting this financial report to bring you some breaking news from the streets of London. Only 23 minutes ago a man walked into the School of Oriental and African Studies in Russell Square and shot Professor Shiro Akagawa, a senior professor at the School, which is a part of the University of London. Our reporter, Kate Balmer, is at the scene now." The scene on the VDU changed to the paved courtyard outside the entrance to SOAS and Sky's diminutive and pretty TV journalist, surrounded by a web of police blue and white scene-of-crime tape. "Kate, can you update us on what the police have discovered so far."

"Yes Simon; behind me you can see the main entrance to the School which has been screened off by the police. I have been told by Superintendent Mathews who's in charge of this crime scene that at 12.25 a man entered the building – you can see that on this CCTV clip."

The jerky-framed clip showed a tall man in a suit entering the building, speaking to the receptionist and then heading for the stairs at which point that CCTV camera lost him.

"The camera on the first floor then picks up the man as he entered the Professor's office. Superintendent Mathews has told me that the Professor was shot once through the head before the gunman left the office. On this clip you can now see the gunman leaving the office in a hurry before he goes down the stairs to the ground floor.............." but Terry was no longer listening to Kate Balmer's crime scene report. He'd frozen the screen as the gunman came running out of the Professor's office.

It was John Gunn.

CHAPTER 4

The taxi dropped Gunn in the King's Road at the junction with Jubilee Place - a route he sometimes used to cut through to Cale Street and Kingsroad House. As far as he knew the only person who knew of his visit to SOAS was Miles Thompson. So how come the reception for him with a silenced automatic? Or had the murder of the Professor been a terrorist act and his presence and his attempted murder just collateral damage? These and a string of other questions had raced through Gunn's thoughts as he made his way back to Kingsroad House to report to Miles Thompson on the murder of the Professor, the attempted murder of himself and how he had dealt with the assassin. He was passing Curry's Digital which had a shop window full of flat screen plasma and LCD TVs; all of them tuned to the Sky News Channel. He had passed the shop before he stopped and returned to the Curry's window. The journalist standing outside the now familiar background of SOAS was doing a talk-over of the CCTV clip which at that moment showed him running out of the Professor's office. But the clip showed nothing of the gunman nor did it show anything down in the reception area – which had a fair quantity of the gunman's blood smeared over the floor – when Gunn had walked out of the building. So who had cleaned up the scene of crime and turned him into the gunman who had killed Shiro Akagawa? If this information was out on the news channels then BID would certainly know. Even as that thought came to mind, Gunn's cellphone rang.

'What the hell's going on, John?' It was Miles.

'I'm standing in front of Currys watching this pantomime right now. The Professor was shot while I was with him. He was just about to tell me the name of the head of the Japanese Mafia group which emerged after the Sarin attack on the Tokyo subway when he was shot. The gunman also shot three times at me before I killed him.'

'But what's this story that's going out on the Sky News Channel?'

'For some reason, Miles, I've walked into an ambush. Someone knew of my visit to SOAS and had a clean-up squad in position to make it look as though I was the gunman. I'll have a bet with you that the gunman was using a Glock 17. Who else for crissakes, Miles, knew of my visit?'

'No one.'

'Right, that means that someone has bugged your office as that was the only place where it was mentioned between you and me.' While he was talking, Gunn waved down a taxi and climbed in. Holding his thumb over the mobile's minute microphone, he gave the driver directions to Beaufort Street.

'You'd better come in, John and we'll sort this out.'

'OK, on my way; be with you shortly,' and Gunn ended the call.

'Whereabouts in Beaufort Street, mate?' Gunn was asked by this driver.

'Thanks, right here'll do fine.'

'That's £3.60.' Gunn handed the driver four one pound coins and then walked briskly to his house less than 200 yards from where he'd been dropped by the taxi. He judged that he had no more than seven or eight minutes at the outside before they came to pick him up.

Offshore yachts have an emergency survival pack which is kept near the companionway for quick access if the boat has to be abandoned in favour of the life-raft. As an experienced yachtsman, Gunn had decided only a short time after being recruited by BID that a similar emergency pack was required at his house should he need to 'disappear' rapidly either within the UK or abroad. That emergency pack was a small stainless-steel case buried under the rhododendron bush at the garden entrance to his mews house at 1

Elm Park Lane. In the case was a selection of passports, Sterling and US currency, a handful of credit cards and driving licences which matched the passports, a roll of duck tape and small tool kit, four boxes of 9mm ammunition and his old Browning Hi-power 9mm para-bellum 13 round automatic.

He unlocked the padlock on the garden gate and opened it just enough to allow him to squeeze through. The speed and clinical efficiency with which those responsible for framing him for the murder of Shiro Akagawa gave Gunn ample warning to expect 'visitors' to his house. He wasn't disappointed. A fleeting movement behind the venetian blinds at the kitchen window which overlooked the garden provided Gunn with a glimpse of his uninvited visitors.

It was just over a week since his previous visitation which was a harsh reminder of Claudine's death. He paused at the solid wooden kitchen door. From the other side of the door he could hear muffled voices – not English, so certainly not a social call from BID or the police - and then the scrape of a chair leg on the tiled floor. Gunn removed his jacket which he dropped on the path. Holding the Glock 17 in his left hand he gently inserted the key into the lock. The next step required very fast simultaneous action. The door opened inwards from left to right. He sank down to a low crouch to the left side of the door, placed the Glock on the path then grasped hold of the door knob with his right hand and the key with his left.

✳

'Yes Angela,' Miles Thompson answered his PA's call.

'Terry Holt from Ops wants to speak urgently - I'll put him through.'

'Yes Terry,' and then Miles pre-empted whatever Terry was about to say, 'and yes, I've seen the breaking news on Sky and was just on my way up to you, but I spoke to Gunn first. He's coming in to give us his version of events. Is Mike Carrington with you?' Miles added before leaving his office. Carrington was the recently appointed Head of BID's Counter Espionage Directorate.

'Yes sir....and the Director,' Terry added.

'Oh shit!' Miles muttered under his breath as he left his office and took the stairs two-at-a-time up to the 14th floor. The Operations Centre had a reputation for remaining calm with only a subdued level of noise even during the most hectic events. As Miles entered the Centre he was horrified to see the Director airing his views on the current situation at a volume which reached all the operations staff. The Director spotted Miles immediately he entered the Centre.

'Ah!' the Director exclaimed, pointedly looking at his watch, 'our Espionage Director joins us. So this is the performance of your most effective agent is it? This is the biggest balls-up I've ever seen from the 'E' Directorate. And what the hell was Gunn doing visiting this Japanese Professor? I made it quite clear that I would not sanction any assignment from your Directorate that was connected with de Carteret's death.'

Apart from the very undiplomatic language used by the Director in the presence of a number of female operations staff, his remarks to his Deputy in front of the operations staff might well have provided Miles Thompson with more than adequate grounds to take the matter to an industrial tribunal. Once again, Miles ignored the Director's rudeness.

'Sir Ian, the agent in question is on his way here now. Could we perhaps let him tell me his version of this incident and then I will immediately ensure that you have the full facts to deal with any questions asked by the Media or the Cabinet Office Intelligence Committee.' The Director was about to demand that Gunn reported to him, but even he realised that was unacceptable. He looked around him seeing that all the staff were carrying on with their jobs and paying no attention to the group clustered around the Controller's console or to him in particular. Realising that his outburst had achieved very little except perhaps self-ridicule, the Director made what he hoped was a dignified exit from the Operations Centre.

'Mike,' Miles turned to the CE Director, 'could you come down to my office? John Gunn will be there shortly and I believe it's most important that both of us hear what he has to say.'

'Of course; thank you Miles. That entire episode on Sky News was ludicrously bizarre and even a child could see that those CCTV clips had been very amateurishly edited.......perhaps 'doctored' would be a more accurate word.' The E and CE Directors left the Centre together.

Mike Carrington had replaced Paul Manton as the CE Director. After a particularly unpleasant divorce with undertones of paedophilia, the latter had become involved in a pension conspiracy masterminded by the security supremo at Number 10 Downing Street. Manton had been silenced by other co-conspirators to prevent him talking whilst under sedation in the BID clinic at Maidenhead after a nervous breakdown. The Prime Minister was saved the embarrassment of the Media finding out about the criminal activity of his security supremo when he disappeared during the PM's visit to China.

Mike Carrington had proved to be a highly successful Head of SO15 – the Counter-Terrorist Command at New Scotland Yard - until a difference of opinion with the Commissioner of the Metropolitan Police had ended a promising police career. He had applied for the vacant appointment in BID as Head of Counter-Espionage and had been selected by the retiring Director, Sir Jeremy Hammond – the man who had been responsible for converting MI5 and MI6 into the British Intelligence Directorate.

'You say that John Gunn is on his way here to give us his version of his visit to SOAS?' Mike Carrington asked as the two men reached Miles' office.

'Should be here any minute now; he said he'd be here shortly. There's no point in speculating on what really happened. It is so utterly unbelievable that Gunn could have shot perhaps the key man to help him with his investigation into the deaths of Rory Lequesne..........'

'Who is?' Mike interjected.

'Sorry, I was forgetting,' Miles said rubbing his eyes, showing signs of the stress of the last two weeks and coping with a new Director who appeared to have little empathy with the intelligence organisation he'd inherited from Sir Jeremy Hammond. 'He was the man who was murdered in a hit-and-run killing in Victoria which started this whole bloody mess. He left behind a case of papers which recorded his and his father's search for a war criminal responsible for the deaths of hundreds of British POWs in Hong Kong. Gunn's family were close friends of the Lequesnes in Hong Kong. Lequesne's father was taken prisoner by the Japs and sent to a POW camp where escape plans of the British POWs were betrayed by a fellow British officer.'

'But it's now 65 years since the end of the war and even if this Lequesne character was only in his early twenties at the time the Japs overran Hong Kong, he would now be in his eighties..........if he's still alive,' Mike Carrington commented as he accepted a coffee from Miles' PA and walked across to the windows overlooking Cale Street and the river beyond.

'That's right, of course; no, Ronnie Lequesne died some years ago. Rory, his son, took up the search and believed that his investigation had made him a target for some secret organisation – probably Japanese. He had come to England to follow up a line of inquiry and this case of his contained a letter addressed to Gunn. When he was killed the police found the key to a left luggage box at Victoria Station in his back pocket. The case was in that box. The police then contacted me and asked if Gunn could go to New Scotland Yard to help them with their investigation into the hit-and-run killing. Although he was on leave, Gunn readily agreed to go and while he was there his house was broken into and Claudine was murdered. They also killed a policeman when he interrupted their search of Lequesne's hotel room where they looking for this case of papers. The rest I think you know, Mike, except that as Gunn still had ten days leave due him, had read the papers in the attaché case and was determined to honour Lequesne's request for him to continue the search, I suggested that he visit Professor Akagawa.'

'But who else knew that you had suggested he go to see the Professor?'

'No one; I did mention Akagawa's name while Gunn was in this office.....but only briefly. I wrote his name and the SOAS address on a memo note and handed it to Gunn.' Miles was certainly not going to add that he had also given Gunn the name and address of the BID agent in Tokyo.

'So either this office is bugged or Gunn has been under surveillance by someone ever since he became involved in this business.........or both.'

'Just so, which is why we must hear from Gunn exactly what happened at SOAS,' Miles added glancing out of the window as the muffled sound of police two-tone sirens reached the double-glazed windows on the 12th floor of Kingsroad House. Three police cars had pulled up in front of the building and six police officers hurried up the steps to the main entrance, out of Miles view at the foot of the building. 'Has this got anything to do with you?' Miles asked turning to Mike Carrington.

'What's that?'

'Six police officers have just come into this building looking as though they're hell bent on arresting someone.'

'News to me,' Mike Carrington muttered as he joined Miles at the window. 'But I have a nasty suspicion that we're about to find out soon enough.'

Hardly were the words out Carrington's mouth than they both heard Angela's loud protestations from the outer office quickly followed by the office door being thrown open by the Director, closely followed by a Chief Superintendent, an Inspector, a Sergeant and three police constables.

'Good heavens, Sir Ian, this is all a bit dramatic,' Miles Thompson said calmly. 'Can we be of any help to you and your police escort?'

'Where is he?' was demanded by the Director.

'I presume you mean John Gunn.'

'Of course I mean J.J.J........Gunn.'

'John Gunn is on his way to this building. When he gets here I hope that you will allow me to question one of my own agents first before he's arrested and questioned by the police.' The Director's mouth opened to say something which he might have regretted, but he was interrupted by the Chief Superintendent.

'That would be the best way to handle this, sir, if I might suggest. Once Mr Gunn has had a chance to debrief Mr Thompson, perhaps he could then come to New Scotland Yard where he can make a statement.' What the Director had not seen because he was facing Miles was the silent signal sent to the Chief Superintendent by Mike Carrington's head shake.

'Very well........you'll see that that happens, Miles.'

'Yes, of course, Sir Ian,' and Miles courteously escorted the Director and the police out of his office and then shut the door.

'Thanks for that, Mike.'

'My pleasure..........what a ludicrous charade. I'll be interested to know what really happened at SOAS.'

'So will I,' Miles said with conviction.

*

Gunn turned the key and door knob together, pushing the back door to his house fully open. What confronted him seemed like some gruesome tableau. Two men dressed in black overalls were seated at the kitchen table; both were wearing full head masks which covered their faces entirely except for the eyes. The masks explained the muffled voices – this was a quirky thought which registered for a nano second in Gunn's mind. On the table between the two men were two Uzi machine pistols and two unsheathed ceremonial Samurai swords.

The man with his back to Gunn had turned as the door opened and with a lightening reaction grabbed the hilt of a sword and hurled it back-handed at Gunn while the other man reached for the Uzi's trigger to fire it as it lay on the table. Gunn ignored the razor- sharp sword which slammed into the kitchen door and fired two shots from the Glock 17 at the man reaching for the Uzi. He had no idea if the men were wearing bullet-proof vests under the overalls which might have prevented a kill shot from the steel-jacketed 9mm bullets. Both bullets went through the man's forehead – one milliseconds after the other hurling him back out of the chair onto the electric hob. The other man gave vent to what Gunn assumed was some shrieking Samurai war cry, raised the second sword above his head and rushed at Gunn as he remained crouched in the doorway. Gunn fired four times; the first two into the man's chest where the powerful 500 joules muzzle energy of the Glock stopped him in his tracks and the second two into his head. The man was dead before his body collapsed onto the kitchen floor.

Gunn stood up and went into the kitchen, ripping off the mask of the man he'd just shot.........ethnic Asian as was the other man. As he dragged the second man over to the other one by the hob, his sleeve rose up revealing a tattoo which Gunn had seen only twenty minutes earlier in Professor Akagawa's office at SOAS. The folded sheet of A4 paper with the Japanese Mafia's monograms was in his jacket pocket outside the back door. He had been told that the most powerful and vicious of the mafia groups was *Seppuku-kai* – its monogram of a *wakizashi* sword in between the Japanese *kanji* script for *harakiri* was tattooed on the man's right wrist. Even Gunn, as a schoolboy, had known that Samurai warriors used these short swords to commit ritual suicide or *harakiri*, by plunging the sword into the left side of the stomach and drawing it across diagonally upwards from left to right thus achieving self evisceration. This was then followed by instant decapitation by an assistant skilled in that gruesome task.

He placed both bodies together, took the mobile out of his pocket and photographed the two men and then took a close-up photo of the tattoo on the man's wrist. The tattoo confirmed the nationality of Gunn's uninvited visitors as Japanese. 'This time we'll have proof,' he muttered as he went back out to the garden picking up his jacket and a small trowel by the back door as he went to the rhododendron bush. It took only seconds to remove the shallow layer of soil and retrieve the steel case with his 'emergency' kit. Back into the house where he checked the road outside the front door – there were no parked cars and despite the sound of the shots from his Glock there appeared to be no reaction.........'just as well I hadn't hoped for someone to come to my assistance at midday on a Monday in London,' he thought with a grimace as he closed and locked the front door.

He opened the connecting door from the kitchen into the garage where he was greeted with the sight of his dark blue supercharged Jaguar XKR. He checked the bolts on the garage door, patted the Jaguar's bonnet and then locked the connecting door. Gunn changed into jeans, light-weight hiking boots, shirt and anorak and placed the contents of the emergency case into his small back-pack with a sweater and change of clothing. Anything else he might need he would buy.

Gunn then went down to his study and dug out a padded envelope. Into this he placed the Glock 17 minus its bullets and then scribbled a note to Miles in which he suggested that the rifling striation marks on the bullets which killed Shiro Akagawa be compared with test rounds fired from his Glock. He addressed the envelope to Miles' home address. He then switched on his laptop and typed an email to Miles at his BID address:

From: jgunn@hotmail.com
To: mthompson@bid.gov.uk

'*Shiro Akagawa was murdered by a Japanese hit-man while he was talking to me. He was murdered to prevent him from telling me the name of the head of a secret mafia organisation which has connections with Aum Shinrikyo and which was responsible for the Sarin gas attack on the Tokyo subway. The man fired three shots at me which must have left behind forensic evidence for the police to examine. I shot the man twice. He fell to the foot of the stairs. There was blood all over the place. This killing had to be carefully planned and the instant clean up after I had gone and the editing of the CCTV indicate that I have been under surveillance ever since I agreed to help the police with their investigation into Lequesne's death. Rest assured, I will find who was responsible for Rory's, Claudine's and the PC's deaths.*

On return to my house a short while ago I was greeted by two more Japanese men who tried to kill me. They are both dead. They have tattoos on their right forearms which indicate that they are members of the Seppuku-kai Mafia. This will require a BID clean-up. I have attached a photo of the two men and the cult tattoo just in case another opposition clean-up occurs.

This is the tattoo which both men had on their right forearms.'

Having attached the photo of the two dead men and the tattoo to his email he sent it to Miles. Gunn checked the Browning Hi-Power and then placed it in his shoulder holster. He had one final check round his house, picked up the 'Jiffy' envelope addressed to Miles, slung the back-pack over his shoulder and let himself out of the back door, locking it and the garden gate as he went out into the narrow alleyway leading to Elm Park Gardens.

CHAPTER 5

'There's an email for you from John Gunn,' Angela told the Espionage Director as she placed a handful of letters to be signed in his in-tray. Miles Thompson immediately clicked on the ikon on his desktop computer and had only just finished reading the email when his phone rang.

'Miles.'

'Has Gunn shown up yet?' was the peremptory query from BID's Director.

'Not yet Sir Ian; I'm just on my way to your office.' Miles ended the call, picked up Gunn's email and photo from the printer tray and walked next door to Mike Carrington's office. Mike ended the phone call he was making as Miles came into his office.

'Problems?' Mike raised his eyebrows.

'Mike, Gunn's decided to go it alone to find Claudine's killers. I've little doubt he guessed....rightly....that he'd be arrested if he came here and wasn't prepared to waste time convincing both us and the police of his innocence. Can you please arrange for Jack Barclay's clean-up squad to go to Gunn's house immediately where there should be two dead Japanese gunmen..........'

'Killed by Gunn?'

'Yes.......I've got an email from him that I'll discuss with you later, but in the meantime he's a fugitive wanted by the police. I'm just on my way to see the Director. Could you please put out an all points bulletin to the police to arrest him and a stop on all ports, airports, airfields and yacht marinas.'

'Consider it done.'

'Thanks, I'll get back to you shortly,' and Miles walked back along the corridor to the Director's office where Melanie showed him immediately into the Director. There was no offer of a seat for Miles, just a curt inquiry.

'So what's this agent of yours done now?'

'Unfortunately he's decided to continue on his own with the investigation into Claudine's death and the war crime diaries he was given by Lequesne......'

'That means he's on the run from the police,' interrupted the Director reaching for his phone.

'Sir Ian, please wait while I brief you. The police have been alerted as have our own agents in CE and there's a stop on all ports and airports.' The Director removed his hand reluctantly from the phone. Miles took a seat in one of the chairs facing the Director's desk.

'So what further horrors has Gunn committed?'

'When he returned to his house........' Miles looked at his watch, 'about 25 minutes ago, he was attacked by two hooded and armed gunmen. He killed both of them.....'

'He.....he.....he's out of control. He'll ....'

'Sir Ian, please listen and then we'll decide on the appropriate course of action.'

'Oh....very well, but please be brief as there's a lot to be done.' Miles ignored this last statement.

'Both these men were Japanese..........' if Miles had said "the World will end in five minutes", it could not have had a more profound effect on the Director. The colour drained from his face and both hands grasped the edge of his desk. 'Are you alright, Sir Ian?' Miles asked.

'Yes....yes...I'm fine,' was gasped in a muted and hoarse whisper. 'How did Gunn know that they were Japanese?'

'They both had this tattoo on their right wrist,' and Miles showed the Director the photo and the diagram emailed by Gunn. 'You'll recognise the Japanese *Kanji* script. I'm not fluent in Japanese and had to check with Mike Dimmock – our South East Asia Director who does speak fluent Japanese – he told me that the tattoo is the monogram of the *Seppuku-kai* cult, part of *Yakuza*, the Japanese Mafia; one of the most vicious, ruthless and barbaric secret societies to emerge in Japan since the wartime *Kempei tai*. As you speak fluent Japanese, Sir Ian, you will know that *'seppuku'* is the spoken version of *'harakiri'*.

'The cult recruited the radical fundamentalists of *Aum Shinrikyo* who broke away from that organisation after the Sarin gas attack on the Tokyo subway and joined *Seppuku-kai*. The ultimate goal was the assassination of the Emperor, but that was abandoned by the more moderate members of *Aum Shinrikyo* which reverted to its religious roots under the name of *Aleph*. *Seppuk-kai* retains that original goal and intends to destroy the West's commercial monopoly over developing countries by assassinating key financial and business moguls of the G8 countries. It's also thought to have links with Al Qaeda, but that has yet to be confirmed.'

'The man who shot the Professor and fired three times at Gunn had the same ethnic Japanese appearance and was similarly dressed as the two men at Gunn's house. I now have Gunn's Glock' - Miles was not prepared to tell the Director that it was in the post - 'and we'll be able to do a test firing and compare the rifling striations with the bullet that killed the professor. If all of this checks out, which I'm certain it will, it means that Gunn is in the clear.'

The Director had said nothing during Miles' explanation, but his hands still grasped the desk. 'But the police are still looking for Gunn?'

'They are Sir Ian, but if Gunn can't evade the police and the surveillance at ports and airports then he isn't the agent that BID has trained him to be.'

'Where do you think he'll go?' the Director asked meekly.

'I should think Japan's a pretty safe bet, but I'll keep you informed,' and Miles stood up, retrieved the email and photo from the Director and walked out of the office.

As he left the Director's office he met Mike Carrington. 'Ah! Miles, I was coming to see you. I've just had a call from Jack and his clean-up team.'

'Don't tell me,' Miles said, expecting the worst, 'someone got there before him,' as they both walked into Miles' office.

'They did, but Jack, I understand, has had to clean up Gunn's house before and he took two vans. He went into Elm Park Mews from the Beaufort Street end in one van while the other van blocked off the exit from the mews onto Elm Park Road.'

'Take a seat, Mike,' Miles offered hardly daring to hope for a successful outcome.'

'Thanks........as they arrived, two men were dragging a black body-bag out of the front door. As soon as they saw Jack's van heading towards them, they dumped the bag and sprinted down the mews towards Elm Park Road where Jack's second van with three of his crew was parked across the mews exit. When the two men realised they were trapped, they drew handguns in an attempt to shoot their way out of the mews. Bad mistake........Jack's guys were expecting this and shot both of them.'

'At last we now have proof to support Gunn's version of events which our Director seems most reluctant to accept.'

'The clean-up team's on its way back now. There was no time for these Japanese guys to clean up Gunn's house. There was blood everywhere in the kitchen so Jack told me.'

'They were Japanese?' Miles queried.

'Both of them had tattoos on their right forearms.......sword with Japanese writing which Jack told me meant *harakiri*......you know it's.....'

'Like this?' Miles asked handing Gunn's email to Mike Carrington.

'Yes, that's how Jack described it.......he should be back here shortly.'

'Right, now I'll fill you in on the background to all this. Hopefully, we might be able to change our Director's refusal to let Gunn investigate this business as an official BID assignment.

*

Gunn turned left onto the Fulham Road as he walked out of Elm Park Gardens, crossed the road and went into his local barber's salon. He was still sporting the long hair and beard he'd cultivated for his last assignment amongst the Bedouin of the Iraqi Desert. All five seats were empty so he was attended to immediately by the salon owner, Maurice, and requested a shave and very short haircut.

He had completed his previous assignment only a week before the murder of Lequesne and Claudine and was still deeply tanned from the time he'd spent in the desert with Doyle Barnes - his career-long colleague in the CIA whom he'd known since they were both in their respective armies.

Doyle had been brutally beaten and tortured by nomadic Iraqi army deserters during that assignment and was still recuperating at a veterans' convalescence clinic in Flagstaff, Arizona. The removal of all facial hair and the short haircut completely changed Gunn's appearance. His next stop was at Superdrug where he bought a packet of black hair-dye before waving down a taxi to take him to Victoria Station. Before buying his ticket to Southampton Parkway, he removed his Browning and the spare box of 9mm bullets from his backpack and placed them in the left luggage locker. He then removed the key papers from the attaché case and put those in his backpack. That now left him with the Glock 26 in his ankle holster and a spare full magazine of twelve rounds, but without BID's authority to entrust his handgun to an aircraft flight crew.

That completed he went back to the concourse to buy his ticket. Right beside the self-serve ticket machines was a large plasma TV screen tuned to the BBC news channel which was showing a repeat of the syndicated Sky news item of the murder at SOAS. Now with a short haircut and minus his beard, no one paid him any attention as he fed his credit card in the name of Jaafor Ghasaan into the machine which then produced his ticket to the station for Southampton International Airport at Eastleigh.

Gunn glanced at his watch; his train was due to leave in just under ten minutes. At three in the afternoon, the train was almost empty. As soon as he was on the train he went to the toilet and started the process of dying his hair. This took some time and the train was well on its way before he emerged from the toilet. Apart from a dirty look from a plump female passenger with dark eyebrows and an obvious blonde wig who had possibly been forced to cross her legs while Gunn dyed his hair, not one of the other passengers paid him any attention.

Gunn took a seat in the near-empty compartment and for the next 45 minutes of the journey to Southampton Parkway analysed the events of the last five hours. Someone other than Miles knew that he'd gone to SOAS. Who? There were only two ways that someone could have obtained that information; either by bugging Miles office – that was unlikely as the whole building was swept and cleared every 24 hours, or he had been followed ever since he became involved in Rory Lequesne's death. Gunn discarded the bugging hypothesis and decided he had to assume that he would be followed wherever he went.

So why was the new Director so reluctant to authorise his assignment to pick up the search where Rory's death had left it? Even in the short time that Sir Ian Davidson had been in the appointment, the grapevine of gossip in the 'house' had been less than enthusiastic about the new Director. He had already been heard to express the view that the sooner the E and CE Directorates were separated in different buildings the better. This opinion flew in the face of the evidence of the last eighteen years which overwhelmingly supported the status quo. Was it a case of divide and conquer? Surely not.......
Gunn looked at his watch; quarter of an hour to go. The train had stopped twice since London. Had anyone got on who might be following him? If the tail was good, Gunn knew he would not spot him - or her - on the train. OK, so back to the current situation.

Seven people had been killed in the last ten days because someone wished to destroy papers relating to the identity of a man who had betrayed his fellow officers and soldiers nearly 70 years ago after the Japs had overrun Hong Kong. Again, why? What was so sensitive that it required a squad of killers from some freak Japanese secret cult – all tattooed like a juvenile urban gang – to be imported into the UK? Why did they need to stop anyone from discovering what became of the traitor who had defected to Japan in 1941? - apart from bringing him to justice if he was still alive, which was unlikely. Any further thoughts were interrupted as the train slowed and the voice recorded PA system announced its arrival at Southampton Parkway.

The train pulled into the station and stopped. It was only a short walk of some 100 yards from the station to the airport terminal. His seat was three rows away from the sliding exit door. No one from Gunn's carriage left the train and only one woman dragging a small, wheeled bag with flight baggage stickers wrapped round the handle got on via the door nearest to Gunn. His train had been the express service which only stopped at half-a-dozen stations on its way to Weymouth connecting with the ferry services to the Channel Islands. The next stop was Southampton Central followed by Bournemouth. The door started to close; unhurriedly, Gunn slipped out of the door as it closed behind him. No one else in the carriage made any movement to follow him. A young woman with nothing but a strapped handbag over her shoulder and a mobile phone in her right hand was the only person in the carriage who had paid no attention to Gunn. The other passengers glanced in his direction at the last minute exit. Platform 3 at Southampton Parkway was empty except for a porter pushing an empty trolley.

Gunn swiped his ticket at the automatic barrier just ahead of a woman with two young children and headed for the station exit. At the exit he paused, out of sight of anyone outside. Was there anyone with a cellphone clamped to their ear? The answer to that question was 'yes' – three people. One was the woman with two children, another was a middle-aged man with a weather-beaten face, sailing anorak and travel-bag – the station was the transit point for 'yachties' heading to and from the Hamble marinas – and the third was another young woman in jeans, trainers and fleece and just a handbag over her shoulder.

Gunn walked out of the station towards the taxi rank where there were four taxis. As he emerged from the station the young woman looked up and finished the call, possibly confirming that she and her accomplice on the train were on a joint surveillance task. Not very professional......unlikely to be connected to the Japanese cult; far more likely to be from BID's CE Directorate or Special Branch, Gunn guessed as he approached the leading taxi just ahead of the woman and her two children. Still talking on her mobile and trying to control her children, she changed direction and went to the second taxi as Gunn had hoped would happen. The driver of the first taxi was standing by the car. 'Hamble Point Marina,' Gunn requested loud enough for those in the immediate vicinity to hear as he got into the front seat of the taxi.

The woman with the children was doing her best to organise the children into the second taxi and load her two bags into the boot helped by the driver. The young woman was beside the third taxi which couldn't move until taxi number two moved. Gunn's taxi pulled out of the station onto the road. As the taxi came to a roundabout, Gunn turned to the driver: 'change of plan, could we go to Southampton Central Station please.'

'No problem sir,' was the immediate response from the young Asian taxi driver who did as bidden and took the exit from the roundabout to Southampton. There was no sign of any taxi following them. When they arrived at Southampton Central six minutes later, Gunn paid off the taxi and walked towards the station entrance. Now approaching Southampton's rush hour, the concourse was fairly full of commuters, but not so full as to conceal the young woman at the ticket window. Her surveillance partner had no doubt drawn a blank at the Hamble Point Marina and had asked her to return to the Parkway station, Gunn assumed, while he waited for her to leave the concourse and head for the track underpass to the London-bound platform.

As soon as she had left the concourse, he bought a ticket to Weymouth. The train was not an express and was due to arrive in seven minutes. In answer to his inquiry of the South-West Trains employee at the ticket window, his 'tail's' train was not due for eleven minutes. Gunn walked over to the WH Smiths news-stall and killed time flicking through a copy of 'Yachting Monthly' until his train pulled in, blocking his 'tail's' view of anyone boarding the train from Gunn's platform.

Just as he found a seat his cellphone buzzed with a text message. It was from Miles Thompson.

'Clean-up authenticates your account of events but you remain on police and BID wanted list for a statement about what occurred at SOAS. CE has no choice but to follow you. You are being targeted by the Japanese 'Seppuku-kai' cult because of your possession of the Lequesne papers. It's a very dangerous terrorist organisation linked to the Japanese Mafia and Al Qaeda with the goal of destroying the West's Banking and Commercial sectors by assassination of key personnel.'

Gunn switched off the cellphone, removed the 'sim' card which he put in his wallet and exchanged the cellphone for another one in his backpack which was an essential part of his 'emergency escape pack'.

After frequent stops, the train pulled into Weymouth just before 7pm. Gunn left the station and walked the short distance to the ferry terminal where he discovered that the next ferry to Guernsey left at 6am the next morning. Gunn bought his ticket at the Condor Ferries counter and asked if there was a local B&B which could be recommended.

'Plenty at this time of year now that the school holidays are over, sir.'

'Somewhere fairly close?' Gunn asked.

'You might try the Avondale, sir. That's in easy walking distance.'

'Sounds good, where's that?'

'You go back along the coast road for two or three hundred yards past the turning to the station and it's on the left facing the sea.'

'Many thanks,' and Gunn left the terminal and set off in search of the Avondale Guest House.

CHAPTER 6

'They've lost him,' confessed Fiona Ransby, the Assistant Director of CE4, the Counter Espionage team which dealt with political and diplomatic matters.

'Where was that?' Mike Carrington asked.

'At Southampton Parkway station.....it's the station for the airport. They thought he might leave the train there and Susan got off while Bryony stayed on the train.'

'Remind me Fiona....I'll get my head round all these names soon,' Mike Carrington admitted with a smile, 'Susan?'

'Nixon....... and Bryony Whistler.'

'Right........and they're both still in training?'

'Yes, they've been down at Maidenhead for the last four weeks with the rest of Induction Course 8/6.'

'Where did they pick up Gunn?'

'At his house..... we briefed them to cover both the front and the alley exit from his house. Susan picked him up as he walked through to Elm Park Gardens and warned Bryony who went into the Fulham Road and front-tailed him until he went into the barber. They nearly lost him when he came out of the barber. He's had that beard shaved off and a really short haircut which makes him completely unrecognisable from the person being shown on the TV news. From the barber he went to Victoria Station via the Superdrug store. If he bought anything he must have put it in his backpack,' Fiona paused and checked her notes. 'Yeah, they slipped up here; he went to the luggage locker area, but they didn't get the number of the locker he used.'

'No matter, go on,' Carrington encouraged.

'Gunn bought a ticket and boarded the train. He made no move when the train stopped, but then slipped out through the closing doors leaving Bryony no option but to stay on the train. She warned Susan who decided to wait outside the station. Gunn came out of the station, went to the first taxi in the rank and Susan heard him ask the taxi driver to take him to the Hamble Point Marina........ Miles Thompson briefed us that he might either leave the Country in a boat or plane as he's able to handle both.'

'She took the next available taxi, but he'd obviously made Susan....and probably Bryony as well....and had vanished. Bryony left the train at Southampton Central and took the train back to Southampton Parkway where they both met up. They decided to check out the airport in case he'd doubled back, but no one had any record of Gunn or had seen anyone looking like him. They did discover that a number of people had bought last minute flight tickets on Flybe's Flight BE633 to Guernsey which had already departed. The girls only had a long shot taken with Bryony's cellphone of the short-haired, clean-shaven Gunn and no one at the airport recognised it. That flight landed in Guernsey,' Fiona checked her watch, 'an hour and a quarter ago.'

'Many thanks; please tell the girls that's exactly what we wanted to know. They've done a good job as their first real test.'

'Really?' Fiona looked up from her notes in surprise.

'Yes, really.' Carrington walked out of his office with Fiona who took the lift while he went into Miles' office.

'Guernsey – we think...either by air or sea.'

'Good, I thought that might be the route he'd take. He'll meet up with Claudine's father, who'll probably take him to France in his fishing boat. Thanks for your help, Mike, particularly as we're both out on a limb as the boss hasn't approved this. I'll now take over and make sure we get an agent out to France asap to cover Gunn's back.'

'Pleasure, Miles,' and Mike Carrington returned to his office.

*

54

The Avondale was a Georgian-fronted guest house, one road back from the seafront with other guest houses on both sides. It was more than used to its clients staying over-night before catching the 6am ferry to Guernsey's St Peter Port in the morning. It was now only a fortnight until the clocks went back an hour to achieve daylight saving and which, to Gunn, clearly heralded the end of summer and the onset of long, dark evenings for the next six months.

As Gunn made his reservation, the receptionist looked with interest at the black cover and cedar tree motif on his Lebanese passport in the name of Jafoor Ghasaan.

'Not seen one of those before, sir. You been on holiday here?' was asked as he handed over his credit card.

'No, only on business, but I hope to come back for a holiday some time........when it is warmer,' Gunn added with a smile.

'Oh, it gets quite hot here in the summer........but not this summer. It's been really miserable. Did you want any supper, sir?'

'Yes that would be nice, but I thought you only did bed and breakfast. There will not be enough time tomorrow for breakfast if I am to catch the boat to Guernsey,' Gunn told her in careful, accented English.

'Right sir, here's your key and supper goes on until 9pm. Would you like an early call tomorrow?'

'No, that is alright; I shall pay my bill tonight after supper.'

'Very well sir.'

Gunn went up to room 11 on the first floor, dropped off his back-pack after removing his emergency kit and placing it in a separate carrier bag with the spare magazine for his Glock 26 which he took with him down to supper. After supper, he walked down to the sea front; it was now dark and still pleasantly warm despite a steady on-shore breeze. He dialled Miles Thompson's home number.

'Hello John.......I've been expecting your call.'

'OK, I'm now on my other cellphone. You have the number. Am I still wanted by the police and any change in the Director's embargo on my investigation?'

'Yes and no, in that order,' Miles replied. We lost you at Southampton when you switched off your cellphone. I'm assuming you're on your way to Guernsey to meet up with Jean de Carteret.'

'Possibly; I was expecting a visible police presence at the ferry terminal, but it was either carefully concealed or non-existent.'

'You can thank Mike Carrington for that. He's convinced his former colleagues in the Met that firstly, you're not a wanted criminal and therefore unnecessary to allocate scant police resources to a country-wide stop on ports and airports and, secondly, if you do leave the country it'll be by an east coast port.'

'Thanks for that; now two questions: what's the Director's problem with me and how much can you tell me now about this *'Seppuku-kai'* terrorist organisation?'

'Ian Davidson - very similar to your childhood in Hong Kong - was brought up by his parents in Japan. His father, Paul Davidson – a minor British Diplomat - was involved in the rehabilitation of that country after its humiliating defeat in the Second World War. His son was educated in Japan and became bi-lingual in English and Japanese. He was then sent to Cambridge where he graduated with an Honours Degree in Japanese and joined the FCO. He did three tours in Tokyo; first as a third secretary in the consular section, then as a first secretary in the commercial section when he met and married Sarah Peasmarsh – a secretary in the Embassy - and finally as Ambassador. He probably knows more about Japan and its impressive post-war economic success than anyone else in the UK. Little, if anything is known about his father, but that is hardly surprising such was the chaos and misery in post-war Japan.'

'So why the reluctance to let BID become involved in bringing the Japanese killers of Claudine and Rory Lequesne to justice?'

'I don't know. All I can tell you is that when I told him that we had proof of the killers' nationality from the bodies in your house, I thought he was about to have a stroke.'

'Interesting....and *'Seppuku-kai'*?'

'*Seppuk-kai* first appeared on the West's radar shortly after the end of the Second World War. Japan wallows in its love of secret societies, bushido and samurai warrior rituals. After the humiliation of Japan's defeat, *Seppuku-kai* had no difficulty in recruiting thousands of eager volunteers who wished to cleanse themselves of their defeat. Its growth worldwide amongst its ethnic emigrant population resident in other countries is very similar to the power base achieved by the Chinese Triads and the radicalised Muslims of Al Qaeda. I've tasked Mike Dimmock to dig up everything he possibly can on the organisation, but what he's told me so far.....and what we've seen them do in this city in the last ten days.....is warning enough of the fanaticism of its terrorists. The stated target is to bring down the commercial supremacy of the G8 nations by murder and financial mayhem.....'

'The world-wide bank crash?'

'Not proven, but some very worrying indicators that there was something more than just the financial incompetence of governments and moronic greed of the banking and mortgage sector of the financial world that precipitated the crisis. The Governor of the Bank of England is convinced there was more to it than just the greed and stupidity of the bankers allowing themselves to become engulfed in billions of dollars worth of unsecured loans. That greed was aided and abetted by meaningless controls devised by the Financial Services Authority and by a massive withdrawal by some Asian financial consortium of support for the toxic debts of Western Banks.'

'That possibly accounts for the financial mayhem, but have there, as yet, been any obvious - or not so obvious - deaths of key G8 tycoons?'

'Had you asked that question of me this morning I would have said "not as yet", but that may well have changed in the last few hours. Nikolai Lazarenko........'

'......he owns that huge yacht *Rozalina* that's twice the size of the Queen's old *Britannia*...'

'....is possibly one of the richest men in the world and controls most of the gas and oil resources in Russia. He was killed in a car accident this morning. The Mercedes in which he was being chauffeured in St Petersburg was crushed to a lump of scrap by a forty ton articulated lorry. It was virtually impossible to separate the bodies from the compacted remains of the car. The lorry driver disappeared before the police reached the crash.

'Not an obvious assassination,' Gunn interrupted.

'Indeed, but barely an hour later Gunther Mayerling....'

'I've seen him on TV at Formula One race meetings.....'

'.......I'm sure you have. He has a controlling share-holding in the German automotive industry and if Nikolai is the wealthiest industrialist, Gunther isn't far behind.'

'What happened to him?'

'No one knows.....he's vanished. He was last seen by his fourth wife – she's nearly young enough to be his grand-daughter - when he left the house this morning. No one has seen him since.'

'So the murders have started. Thanks for all that,' and Gunn ended the call and walked back to the guest house. He let himself in with the house key, paid his bill at the small reception counter and went up to his room. The curtains had been drawn and the bed had been turned down by someone. Presumably the same person who had opened his backpack, checked its contents and then refastened it, but not as it had been purposely left by Gunn.

*

'I have Rear Admiral Parker, the Head of Defence Intelligence on the line,' Miles was told by his PA as he walked into his office. He glanced at his watch.....8.20....so what had prompted this early call from the MOD? Miles pondered as he reached his desk and picked up the phone.

'Yes Neville, Miles here.'

'Can we go secure?'

'Of course,' and Miles pressed the button on his phone which initiated a sequence of electronic wizardry which scrambled everything said at one end of the link until it was unscrambled at the other end. Once they were in secure mode, the person on the other end of the connection sounded as though they were speaking from a large empty, echoing hangar.

'Sorry to call you at this hour, but I know you're an early starter and as I've been here all night in the MOD's Joint Ops Centre I thought I'd catch you before I go to my club to get a couple of hours sleep.'

'That's fine, what can I do to help.'

'There's a JIC on Thursday'..........why did some military people love talking in acronyms? Miles smiled at the Admiral's reference to the Cabinet Office Joint Intelligence Committee........'and my first question was to ask you if you had any news about the Chairman?'

'Andrew Allen will chair the meeting and my Director will be there representing our E and CE Directorates as usual.'

'He's recovered then?'

'He must have, Neville.' Miles knew exactly what the Admiral was referring to, but had no wish to speculate on the health of a fellow senior civil servant. Andrew Allen had collapsed at home and been taken to hospital some two months previously.

'Right, pleased to hear that.........can you give me a heads up on the death of Nikolai Lazarenko and the disappearance of Gunther Mayerling.'

'I'm not sure that we know any more than you until I've received our agents' reports. You will know that *Seppuku-kai* has declared on its website blog that it intends to destroy the G8's financial supremacy.'

'Presumably Sir Ian will give us all an update on what BID is doing,' which was a very fair comment from the Admiral, but Miles knew that it was going to be difficult for the BID Director to tell the JIC that the one strong lead that BID had was being followed up by what he referred to as a 'rogue agent' with no authority to investigate.

'Early days, but yes I'm sure he will,' Miles stalled, knowing that the real purpose of this phone call would eventually emerge.

'That incident yesterday at the School of Oriental and African Studies....?' the question was left hanging, hollowly on the echoing secure line.

'Yes, the agent shown on Sky News was one of ours and no, he didn't murder the Professor,' Miles stated evenly.

'*Seppuku-kai*?'

'Possibly.'

'Why?'

'Because he was about to reveal the name of a key person to our agent.'

'Aaah.......that would be reason enough to incriminate him with the murder.'

'Yes.....it would.'

'Just one more question....if I may Miles.'

'Go ahead, Neville.'

'Earlier this year one of your agents appeared in local papers in the Caribbean.....St Vincent I believe. That was just before the dramatic escape of *HMS Edinburgh* from Havana Harbour. Could that have been the same agent?'

'Now Neville........'

'Sorry, silly of me to ask.........but I think you've answered my question. If you've got someone of that quality on this assignment I'm damn certain we can look forward to a result. Thanks for your time, Miles. You must come and have lunch at my club,' and the Rear Admiral ended the call. Miles Thompson replaced the phone, released the secure speech button and then pressed the stop button on the digital recorder. For a few moments he stood looking out over the rooftops to the Thames beyond glistening like molten bronze in the early morning autumn sunlight. He had always found he drew strength and resolve from the very timelessness of the view.

'This nonsense over Gunn has got to stop otherwise BID will become a laughing stock,' Miles declared determinedly to his empty office. He ejected the mini-disc which had just recorded his conversation with the Head of Defence Intelligence and walked out of his office. 'I'm going to the Director, Angela,' he said, sticking his head round the door to his PA's office.

'Morning Miles,' he was greeted cheerily as he entered the Director's office. 'What news of your errant agent?'

'None Sir Ian, but before you attend your first meeting of the Joint Intelligence Committee on Thursday where you are certain to be asked by the Chairman to evaluate the threat level which *Seppuku-kai* poses to the UK.......'

'Was that in your brief and speaking notes?' the Director interrupted.

'.........it was, under the heading of 'Current Threat Assessment' on page three. I would like you to listen to just a short excerpt of a conversation I had a few minutes ago with the Head of Defence Intelligence.'

'Why?'

'Because it expresses the Admiral's opinion of our agent John Gunn, whom you've never met, but have a very prejudicial opinion of his ability despite the fact that we are now in possession of overwhelming evidence exonerating him from the murder of Professor Akagawa.'

Without waiting for the Director's agreement, Miles inserted the disc into the slot under his phone and pressed the fast forward button, stopped it and pressed the 'play' button........."if you've got someone of that quality on this assignment I'm damn certain we can look forward to a result".

'The Admiral is referring to the assignment some six months ago..........I'm sure you'll recall it Sir Ian.....when John Gunn, with help from our in-country agent and the CIA, engineered the successful release of *HMS Edinburgh* from Havana. That was followed in August with him saving the Prime Minister considerable embarrassment and BID and the Cabinet Office a great deal of money by uncovering a conspiracy to embezzle some £80 million from government funds.' Miles removed the disc from the phone. There was a stunned silence from the Director.

'But he disobeyed your instructions to report back here after that Professor's murder.'

'No Sir Ian; he said he was returning here until he saw that Sky News clip which made him change his mind. I did not tell him to come back to this building. On Thursday at the JIC the Chairman will ask you for two things: your threat assessment of *Seppuku-kai* and what you're doing about it.'

'That's covered in your brief.....'

'It is......I've suggested that the threat level to the UK public is 'moderate', but to key heads of banking and commerce is 'severe'.

The Chairman is almost certain to ask you what you're doing about that 'severe' threat. As at this moment, despite my formal request to you to sanction Gunn's assignment, the true answer is 'nothing', even though you have an agent with a strong lead who is following up that lead at his own expense.'

'I'm not prepared to sanction Gunn's assignment as I'm still convinced that he's a loose cannon – in spite of his record with BID. Japan is a nation steeped in thousands of years of ritual, culture and respect....'

'As in its barbaric treatment of POWs, Sir Ian.......?'

'That was an aberration which is bitterly regretted. If he goes crashing around like a bull in a china shop he'll do far more harm than good. And he doesn't speak a word of Japanese. Do we not have a Japanese speaker who could be tasked with this assignment?'

'Yes we do.'

'I am prepared to sanction an assignment into what threat *Seppuku-kai* poses to the UK provided the agent tasked is a fluent Japanese speaker.'

'And Gunn?'

'As far as I'm concerned you can send Gunn his P45 – he no longer works for BID.'

*

It was now just before 10pm. Gunn had no problem with the surreptitious search of his backpack. Understandably, after the suicide bombs on the London Underground in July 2007, the public's suspicion of any Middle-East-looking man with only a backpack about to travel on plane, boat or train would cause suspicion. Only a couple of years previously, an entire plane-load of passengers had refused to fly until three highly suspicious, villainous and hirsute, but innocuous Middle-East-looking passengers had been removed from the aircraft. That was something that terrorism strived to achieve, Gunn rationalised - widespread panic, fear and irrational prejudice amongst the population. It was more than possible that a phone call had been made to the police and despite Miles Thompson's reassurance that his arrest was now a low priority it was time for him to lay the second false trail for his pursuers.

On the back of his bedroom door was a notice informing guests of the action needed in case of fire, which identified an emergency fire escape at the end of the first floor corridor. Gunn opened his backpack and dug down inside it for a leather-zipped case which contained a selection of tools and a small torch that would be needed shortly. The set of tools was a vital component of his emergency escape pack. He pulled the tool-case up to the top of his backpack and then closed it, slung it over his shoulder, left his room key on the chest of drawers and walked out into the corridor closing the door quietly behind him.

The fire-escape led down to a gravelled area and then a long strip of untidy garden which ended in a six foot high wall. Gunn made his way through the garden which was helpfully lit by the street lights in the road at the far end. He had little difficulty in climbing over the wall and dropped down into the deserted street. At the height of the season there might have been more activity on the streets, but as Gunn made his way to the marina crossing two roundabouts and passing the station he'd arrived at some hours earlier, he saw less than a handful of cars and not a soul on the roads.

The marina was well-lit and, like the majority of marinas around the UK coast, secured by a fence with access via a combination locked gate. Gunn identified an area of the security fence which was not covered by CCTV and climbed over it.

'So far so good,' Gunn muttered, 'but now comes the tricky bit; a RIB or something bigger that has enough fuel to get me to Guernsey.' There was an abundance of the popular rigid inflatable boats with their glass-fibre hulls and inflated rubber topsides. These varied in size from an 8 foot yacht tender with a 5hp Mariner outboard engine to a 30 foot monster with three 100hp Yamaha outboards, 'and probably capable of about 60 knots,' Gunn murmured as he examined the large Mako RIB. He'd only been to the marina once before when he'd delivered a motor-yacht from Guernsey to Weymouth as a favour for a yacht charter company on

Guernsey. That brought back painful memories of the times that he and Claudine had spent cruising in the Channel Isles.

Weymouth Harbour was formed in the shape of a right-angle dog-leg with the harbour entrance on an easterly transit into Portland Bill – the isthmus which jutted out south into the English Channel. The ferry terminal and the majority of fishing boats were in the easterly part of the dog-leg. Further east was the lifting Town Bridge and then came the right-angle turn to the north which opened into a sheltered marina for hundreds of yachts, RIBs and motor-yachts. Gunn was hoping to find a suitable boat in the marina rather than the marginally busier commercial part of the harbour which still, at nearly 10.30pm, had plenty of activity amongst the fishing boats and trawlers.

He was examining a smart blue 'Humber' RIB with a 90hp Mariner outboard to see if it was fitted with spare fuel tanks when a snatch of conversation reached him. The voices were carried by the evening breeze from the long central pontoon which hosted the majority of larger motor-yachts.

'.........that should do it Dave........start 'er up and I'll check to make sure the bearing ain't running 'ot.' Gunn didn't hear the response, but a powerful diesel rumbled into life on a sleek motor yacht one pontoon away from where Gunn was kneeling on the wooden decking of another pontoon examining the fuel tanks of the RIB with his small torch. Gunn got to his feet. The men working on the motor-yacht had rigged a bright extension light over the area at the stern of the boat where they were working on the engines.

'.......yeah.....that's good....she's running sweet as a nut now.....'is nibs should 'ave no more bovver wiv' the bearings on that starboard engine's water pump....'kay, Dave, let's clean up and I'll buy yer a pint of Badger's Best at the George.' The engine stopped and 'Dave' appeared from the saloon. Gunn had crossed over to the other pontoon and was now only two boats away from the motor-yacht.

'What'd 'e want done wiv' the keys, Pete?'

''e's off at six to Guernsey.....be a miracle if 'e ever gets there...... with that juicy bit of crumpet 'e 'ad followin' 'im aroun'.' 'e'll motor like a bat out o' 'ell round to Poole, drop a 'ook before she drops her knickers and.....' but a fresh gust of wind denied Gunn the detail of what would happen next.

'.......anyway.......'e said...... to leave the keys under the mat by the saloon door once we'd refuelled 'er and replaced the bearings on the starboard engine water pump.'

'What abaht the alarm?'

'No, 'e said not to bother as 'e can never remember the code.'

'That was thoughtful of him,' Gunn muttered quietly with a broad grin on his face. The two marine engineers from the boatyard tidied up, disconnected the extension light, picked up their tool bags and set off along the pontoon on their quest for two pints of Badger's Best at the George Inn.

As soon as they were out of sight, Gunn left the boat from which he'd watched the men on the motor-yacht and walked along the pontoon to check the mooring warps of the motor-yacht; it was a very smart Fairline Phantom 40.

'Bloody side more comfortable than freezing my arse off in a RIB,' Gunn chuckled as he jumped aboard the motor-yacht, retrieved the keys from under the mat and opened the saloon door.

CHAPTER 7

The interior layout of the motor-yacht was very similar to a number of boats which Gunn had driven in the past. At the for'ard end of the saloon was a door which led into a double cabin and two heads. In the saloon there was a well-appointed steering position on the starboard side and a small galley on the port side. The large fitted sofa on the starboard side converted into a double bed and opposite this was the navigation station. Access to the fly bridge was by steps on the port side of the saloon door where all the gadgets and dials in the saloon steering position were duplicated on the fly bridge.

In the bookshelf by the navigation station was a pristine copy of Reeds Nautical Almanac for the current year. Without a single thumbprint on the outside edge of the pages, Gunn doubted if it had ever been opened. As he checked over the navigation instruments, Gunn recalled an anecdote he'd heard from a lifeboat coxswain. A small boat he and his crew had rescued barely seconds before it was swamped in the Shambles overfalls off Portland Bill was being navigated by means of an Esso road map of South-West England. He opened the almanac at the index, found Weymouth and turned to the relevant page where he discovered that from September to April the last opening time for the bridge was 8pm and if he wanted to get it opened he had to give an hour's notice to the harbourmaster by contacting him on channel 12. He also learnt that at high tide the clearance under the centre of the bridge was 14 feet and at low tide this increased to 23 feet. He then turned to the tide tables where he discovered that low tide had been one hour earlier.

'Thank heavens for that,' Gunn murmured to the empty saloon as he replaced the almanac in its slot on the shelf.

Gunn switched off the small flexible-stemmed light he'd used to read the almanac, pulled the Imray chart C12 out of the chart drawer and then went to the steering console and switched on the ignition. The fuel gauges indicated full. He gave each engine five seconds of pre-heat and then started the two, 375hp Volvo-Penta diesels which, after a burst of throttle, rumbled steadily at tick-over. Back outside the saloon, Gunn stepped down onto the stern bathing platform to ensure that the engines' cooling water was flowing out of the exhausts – particularly the starboard engine which had just had its pump repaired - followed by a quick check to see if anyone was paying attention to the Phantom 40 – perhaps aptly named '*Bonus*' by its owner. The breeze had subsided as Gunn released the bow and stern lines before returning to the navigation station to switch on the motor-yacht's navigation lights. Hanging inside a locker outside the owner's cabin was a very expensive Peter Storm yachting anorak which Gunn grabbed before climbing up to the fly-bridge.

Not a sign of interest from anywhere; Gunn gently eased forward the combined throttle and gear levers for both engines and *Bonus* moved sedately away from her pontoon berth and headed down towards the Town Bridge and the commercial harbour beyond. Bonus negotiated the bridge with at least four feet to spare above the raked aerofoil-mounted radar, anemometer and satnav aerial. There were two small fishing boats leaving the harbour ahead of *Bonus* which conveniently guided Gunn out to the Weymouth breakwater. Over to starboard were the lights of the Portland Harbour breakwaters and beyond them the quick-flashing Cardinal buoy marking the eastern extremity of the rocks forming the Shambles ledge. Gunn brought *Bonus* onto a course of 100° heading for St Albans Head to the east, increased the motor-yacht's speed to 20 knots, engaged the autopilot and then went down to the saloon.

It was now time to lay yet another false trail. At the navigation station, Gunn switched on the boats' Garmin satnav and the Furuno radar on which he set the alarm to 5 nautical miles. He opened the dividers to measure 10 nautical miles and swung them across the chart to the small ferry harbour of Newhaven – 10 miles to the east of Brighton.

'100 miles at 20 knots – should be there,' and he glanced at his watch, 'between four and five in the morning. Right, let's see where we are and if it's time to set a course,' Gunn announced to the empty saloon. As he reached the fly bridge, the East Shambles light was now on his starboard quarter. He disengaged the autopilot, brought *Bonus* onto a course of 90°, re-engaged the autopilot, had a thorough look all round the seas surrounding the boat, but there was nothing except the lights of a few fishing boats and the strobe light of a helicopter heading eastwards. Gunn returned to the saloon.

'Now Trevor,' – Gunn had found the name of Trevor Eversley on the boat's registration papers in the chart drawer –'I think it's time for a drink.' Not only was the boat amply stocked with booze, but the fridge and adjacent lockers were also filled with ample supplies of food. Gunn made himself a ham sandwich and armed with that and a single finger of Bells Scotch in a cut-glass rummer, he returned to the fly bridge.

Not unusual for September just before the autumn equinox, Gunn had often experienced some really balmy sailing weather and that night promised to fit that category. The wind was from the south at barely Force 2 and at an estimated sea state of less than 1 and crystal clear visibility, Gunn was determined to make the most of this stage of his departure from England. The boat's course along the south coast past the Isle of Wight, Portsmouth and the popular resorts of Worthing and Brighton provided Gunn with a chain of onshore lights to port while to starboard were the navigation and deck lights of the huge container and cargo ships in a never ceasing procession along the separation lanes of the English Channel.

It was just after 3.30am when the satnav beeped at Gunn to let him know *Bonus* had reached the waypoint where Gunn would have to change course to head for the entrance to Newhaven. Gunn had failed to include in his calculations nearly five hours of east-going tide which had reduced the time by nearly an hour. There were no boats either entering or leaving the harbour as *Bonus* passed the breakwaters at a sedate 10 knots and then reduced to 5 at the harbour entrance. The marina was on the port hand side opposite the Transmanche ferry terminal on the other side of the harbour. Two long pontoons extended out from the boatyard with many vacant moorings. Gunn selected a vacant finger pontoon between two motor-yachts of very similar size to *Bonus* where his arrival would hopefully go unnoticed for as long as possible.

Bonus slipped into her mooring almost noiselessly; Gunn jumped down and secured her bow and stern warps and then decompressed the two engines. Had anyone noticed his arrival? Gunn climbed up to the fly bridge from where he looked and listened. Not a sound except the distant noise of a car and another helicopter heading from south to north. Both the boats on either side of *Bonus* had large FOR SALE signs; expensive pastimes like funding the annual upkeep of yachts would be the first casualties of a recession, Gunn guessed, as he checked the warps before returning to the saloon. It was now 4.45am. He opened his back-pack into which went the passport in the name of Jafoor Ghasaan to be replaced by a new passport and driving licence in the name of Robert Bradfield. He then stretched out on the saloon couch and in seconds was fast asleep.

He awoke at 7.15am, washed and shaved in the boat's heads, locked the saloon door and after leaving the keys under the mat, jumped off *Bonus* and headed for the exit from the marina. He had decided that he needed to find a 'greasy spoon' cafe where he could firstly, get a high cholesterol breakfast of bacon, eggs and all the trimmings and where secondly, he could get directions to a car hire company. Gunn reckoned that he'd find a cafe open at that hour in the area of the ferry terminal and rail station. This meant a walk of about a quarter of a mile to the swing bridge and then back along the other side of the harbour. One or two cars were already on the concourse waiting for the first ferry........'probably been there all night,' Gunn sympathised as one unshaven and weary-looking driver struggled out of his car wrapped in a blanket. He spotted 'Harry's Shack' where he joined a number of even wearier-looking car and lorry drivers. Gunn went up to the counter where – Harry presumably – was adeptly creating doorstep-sized bacon sandwiches.

'Yes mate,' Harry looked up from the sandwich task.

'Nearest car hire company?' Gunn asked.

'Sure, Solomons in Quarry Road......go over the bridge, turn left and continue past the marina. Quarry Road's on your right.'

'Thanks, any idea when he opens?' Harry looked up at the clock on the wall.

'Should be open now.'

'Thanks,' and then under his breath, 'sod's law,' as Gunn left the 'Shack' and at a jog trot retraced the way he'd only just come. The breakfast with the trimmings would have to wait if there was a chance of catching the first ferry. Good as Harry's word, Solomans was open and in less than ten minutes Gunn, as Robert Bradfield, drove away in a well-used Ford Fiesta with 56,000 miles on the odometer. Next stop was back at the Transmanche office on the quayside where he bought a return ticket to Dieppe and was told that he was just in time for the 9am crossing as the ferry was still loading. The fluorescent-jacketed loaders were waiting for him as he drove onto the concourse and directed him up the ramp into the yellow-hulled ferry. The steel doors closed behind him, the warps were cast off and with three blasts on her siren, the ferry *Dieppe* left Newhaven.

*

When Miles left the Director's office the door remained ajar. Melanie got up to close the door but paused with her hand on the door knob, as she heard his cellphone ring. The Director took the call and after answering in English he switched to Japanese. On the verge of closing the door, Melanie heard the name 'John Gunn' spoken by Sir Ian Davidson. She reached across to her desk, picked up the small hand-held recorder which she used for dictation, pointed the directional mike round the edge of the open door and pressed the 'record' button.

Melanie could no more understand Japanese than 'double-dutch', but her antipathy towards her new boss and her awareness of his unreasonable behaviour with both his Deputy Director, Miles Thompson, and John Gunn focused her attention on Davidson's side of the call. She heard the name 'Gunn' mentioned again and then, very clearly, 'Guernsey', 'Weymouth' and 'Southampton Airport'.

Melanie picked up the cup of coffee which she had just made for the Director and walked into the office with the small cassette recorder held under the tray with her left hand.

The Director looked up in irritation. 'Put it on the table and knock in future before you come into my office.'

'Very well, sir,' unruffled, Melanie placed the cup and saucer on the table together with the biscuits and left the office, closing the door behind her, but not letting the catch fully engage on the strike plate.

As soon as she was out of the room the conversation continued with Melanie holding the recorder close to the gap in the unclosed door. The conversation continued for a couple of minutes with further references to 'Gunn' and 'Guernsey' and then the Director ended the call.

Melanie pressed the 'stop' button on the recorder and rewound the cassette.

*

Rather than summon an Assistant Director to his office, Miles Thompson always made a point of visiting an AD in his or her office. James Rayner was the AD for Russia and Eastern European Countries and the BID agent, Tatanya Kazakova, had been seconded to his Directorate for an assignment in Tibilisi controlled by David Simpson. He was met by James's PA, Tricia who showed him into her AD's office. Six months previously, Miles had chaired the selection panel of two ADs and two Controllers who had conducted the interviews of the final 12 candidates – of whom Tatyana was one - from the original 40 applicants to seek employment with BID.

Tatanya Kazakova's great grandparents had emigrated from St Petersburg in 1907 after the first Russian Revolution of 1905. Her grandfather had fought in the First World War in the newly formed Tank Corps and had commanded a tank at the Battle of Cambrai in December 1917 – the first time that tanks had been used in warfare. The family had established a light engineering company near Basingstoke in Hampshire which produced a selection of parts for the rapidly growing automotive industry.

During the Second World War, the family company was pressed by the Government into the mass production of parts for military vehicles. In spite of being exempt from military service because of the vital importance of his company's product for the war effort, her grandfather had insisted on enlisting with the Royal Tank Regiment and fought with 1 RTR at the Battle of El Alamein. He was promoted on the battlefield to Lieutenant and awarded a Military Cross while in command of a troop of three Sherman tanks.

Her father was born after the war and moved the company to Leamington Spa where it was closer to the hub of British car production in Birmingham. As the British car industry declined in the second half of the century, Tatanya's father, Alex, diversified his company into the production of glass-fibre hulls and high quality phosphor-bronze deck fittings for the booming yacht market. By 1975, it made no more sense to retain the factory in the Midlands and Alex Kazakova moved the company back to Hampshire to a boatyard at the extremity of the navigable part of the Hamble River. His daughter, Tatanya, was born in 1986 and on completion of her degree at Durham University, not only spoke Russian, but was also fluent in Japanese.

'James, I have an assignment that needs both a Russian and Japanese speaker......'

'........and so you need to know if Tanya has completed her assignment in Georgia,' James Rayner pre-empted his Director.

'I do, but can make do with two agents as long as each speaks one of those languages. This is a particularly sensitive and dangerous assignment. Look, I have to meet my wife for a sandwich lunch at Peter Jones, but could you come to my office at two?'

'Yes of course Miles, I'll......' but the office door opened and Tricia stuck her head round the door.

'Sorry to interrupt, but the Director's PA is in your outer office sir and Angela seems to think it's quite urgent.'

'See you at two James. On my way Tricia,' and Miles left the AD's office and went back up to the 14th floor. 'Come in Melanie,' he greeted the Director's PA and when the door closed behind her, 'take a seat and tell me what this is about.'

'I've no idea if I should be speaking to you about this sir, but if I don't I shall never forgive myself.'

'Go ahead, Melanie, I'll soon tell you if what you're telling me is out of court.'

'Just after you left the Director's office this morning his cellphone rang. The door hadn't closed properly and I could hear the conversation.'

'And....?' Miles interjected.

'I got up to close the door, but am certain the conversation was in Japanese.'

'Well he does speak Japanese, Melanie, and knows many Japanese diplomats in London.'

'Yes I know sir, but he mentioned the word 'John Gunn' at least twice and also 'Southampton', 'Weymouth' and 'Guernsey'. I'm aware of course that he won't agree to Gunn following up Claudine's murder and although I don't understand a word of Japanese it sounded very like he was giving instructions to someone to go to Guernsey.'

'I see....'

'....and when I went in with his cup of coffee, he was furious........ and highly agitated at the interruption. There, that's it sir. I know he wants to find another PA, but I felt I had to mention this to you before I go.'

'Thank you, Melanie. I do need to know this.'

'Oh, nearly forgot sir, this is a recording of the whole conversation,' and Melanie placed a micro cassette on Miles' desk and then left the office.

*

The crossing to Dieppe took five minutes over four hours, giving Gunn plenty of time to get the full English breakfast that he'd missed at Harry's Shack and buy a road map of Northern France – an item that had not been included by the car hire company. As France was one hour ahead of the UK, Gunn was on the A27 autoroute to Paris via Rouen by 16.30. He arrived in Pontoise, a suburb some 30kms to the north-west of Paris, at 19.20. He parked the Ford Fiesta amongst a number of similar sized Renaults, Citroens and Peugeots where there were no parking charges or restrictions in a housing estate between Pontoise and the small village of Ennery. Gunn locked the car and then with a strip of duck-tape from the emergency pack, he attached the ignition key to the inside of the right front wheel arch. It was full dark by now and no one took any notice of Gunn as he walked back into Pontoise, was directed to the station in Place Charles de Gaulle and caught the train to the Gare du Nord in Paris.

*

Tuesday early evening very rarely produced more than a handful of clientele at the Ship Inn in St Peter Port, which was why the two Asian men who had just entered the pub were so noticeable. Tom Le Page, the landlord of the pub, glanced at them as he pulled a couple of pints and when they made no move to order anything, wandered over to their table.

'Evening gents, can I get you anything?'

'Would you have tea?' the man nearer to Tom asked.

'Yes sir, I can do a pot of tea for you. Would that be two cups?'

'Yes, two cups please,' and as Tom turned away the man continued, 'and some information.'

'Do my best,' Tom smiled at the two men, 'and where are you both from?'

'We are tourists from Japan. Would you be able to tell us how to get to that lighthouse?' and the man produced a crumpled slip of paper from his pocket and showed it to Tom - Lighthouse on St Martin's Point, Guernsey.

'It's about two miles. Are you walking or taking a taxi?'

'We walk.'

'There's only one road that goes there, but as it's getting dark be careful because the road is very close to some dangerous cliffs,' and Tom told them how to get to the road from the pub. The 'dangerous cliffs' was a 200 foot sheer drop onto rocks below concealed by the convex slope of the cliff edge.

'Thank you, thank you,' was said by the same man and the only one who had spoken. Both got up to leave.

'Do you want your tea?'

'No thank you, in a hurry,' and both got up and left the pub.

The Ship was the regular haunt of Jean de Carteret and his was the only cottage beyond the lighthouse on St Martin's Point. Tom and all the regulars at the Ship had been devastated by the murder of Jean's daughter Claudine and when John Gunn had spent the week of the funeral with Jean, the companionship of Tom and the regulars at the Ship had done a lot to help with the grieving process for both men. During that week, Gunn had told Tom very briefly some of the background about the Lequesnes and the search for evidence to submit to a war crimes tribunal. What had stuck in Tom's memory of that conversation was the Japanese connection.

'So what the hell do two Nips want with that lighthouse at 6.30 in the evening? If those two are tourists then I'm King Farouk.'

'What you on about, Tom?' his wife asked as she served a customer.

'Nothing love, just going out the back for a couple of minutes.' Tom went out to his office at the back of the pub and dialled Jean's number on his cellphone. 'Please pick up, Jean,' Tom quietly begged.

'Hello.'

'Jean, it's Tom.'

'Yes Tom.'

'Two Japs have just left the pub. They asked for directions to St Martin's Point. They said they were tourists, but to me they looked like a couple of freaky Kung Fu types. John told us that he'd been investigating something to do with Japan when his house was ransacked and Claudy was murdered. Are you on your own, because if......'

'Thanks Tom.....for the warning. John hinted that something like this might happen. Nothing would give me greater pleasure than to meet up with these bastards.......and no, I'm not on my own. Four skippers from our small fleet - your regulars, Pierre,

Don, Michele and Tony - are here discussing tonight's fishing with me. How long have we got?'

'They're walking....so they said, so no more than twenty minutes....half an hour at most.'

'We'll be waiting for them.'

*

It was nearly 21.15 when Gunn's train pulled into the Gare du Nord. The train to Moscow departed from the Gare de l'Est which was only one stop away on the Metro. He had no idea of the train times to Moscow and rather than catch the Metro, he decided to walk the short distance to the Gare de l'Est and stretch his legs before spending two nights on the train to Moscow followed by the eight day marathon to Vladivostok on the Trans-Siberian train.

After asking for directions in his school standard French, Gunn took a left outside the station and then a right into the Rue d'Alsace which led to the Gare de l'Est. At the information kiosk in the ticketing area he was told that the train to Moscow left every evening from platform 6 at 20.20 and arrived at the Bielowruskaia Station in Moscow two days later at 08.35. Visas, of course, would be a problem – the sort of administrative detail which would have been handled by his controller at BID in the preparation and briefing stage before any assignment. Gunn decided that he would think about that later over a glass of wine.

He accepted the recommendation from the helpful woman at the information kiosk of the two star Hotel Londres on the Boulevard Barbes after her phone call confirmed a vacancy and made a room reservation. At the ticket office his plastic card in the name of Robert Bradfield secured a reservation in a sleeper compartment on the train the following evening. All of that sorted, Gunn set off to find his hotel. After he'd checked in, the hotel receptionist told him that the Consular Section of the Russian Embassy in the Boulevard Lannes would issue him with a visa immediately after he'd filled in the application forms in duplicate and handed over two photographs. However, she advised him to be at the Embassy by 08.30 in order to be at the front of the inevitable queue.

CHAPTER 8

Jean's fellow skippers had arrived at his house on their bicycles which were leaning on the wall at the front of the house. In preparation for the 'Japanese tourists', these were removed and placed in one of the three outhouses at the back of the cottage in which Jean kept his fishing gear. Amongst the spare nets, floats, lobster and crab pots, cordage and marker buoys were half-a-dozen, old fashioned rusty stevedore hooks, once used by dockers to handle cargo bundles and crates, but redundant now as all cargo was carried in containers and moved around by mechanical handling equipment.

The fishermen used them as gaffes when they hauled in large tuna and the occasional shark. The stem of the hook ended in a wooden 'T' bar wooden handle about a foot below the needle sharp hook. They all helped themselves to various bits and pieces and then returned to the open-plan hall-cum-lounge which for years had served as the cottage's focal point for the de Carteret family and their friends.

The land-line phone rang in the cottage, startling all of them. It was Richard Sauvrier who lived in the lighthouse keeper's cottage to tell Jean that he had just re-directed two 'Chinks', as he described them, who were looking for Jean's cottage.

'Right guys,' Jean addressed his piratical looking group of fishermen, 'I think this is how we'll play this. Tony, you and I'll sit at the table with a couple of beers. Pierre, Don and Michele I'd like you to go into the kitchen........here, burn these corks to blacken your faces,' and Jean opened a drawer in the kitchen dresser and handed over a couple of corks and a box of matches, 'but leave the door open ajar and here.....take this,' and Jean handed Don a small hand-held tape recorder. 'Never know it might be useful to have evidence of whatever is said. OK guys let's see what these Japs want with me.'

Perfectly on cue there was a knock on the front door. 'Come in!' Jean shouted from his seat at the table. The door opened carefully and first one and then the second man came into the room. Jean got up.

'Hello, what can I do for you?'

'You are Mister Carteret?'

'And who are you?' Jean asked without answering the inquiry.

'We come to speak to Mister Gunn.'

'No.....that was the wrong answer. I asked you who you were not what you wanted.'

'We have business with Mr Gunn,' was the stubborn response.

'No one of that name lives here and if you aren't polite enough to introduce yourselves you can both leave now or I'll call the police.' This caused momentary confusion; it was quite clear that the two Japanese thugs had expected to find an old man on his own and to be faced with a relatively easy task of intimidating him into revealing the whereabouts of Gunn. Instead of this they were faced with a strong, weather-beaten man in his early fifties and over six feet tall – with another man of roughly the same physique.

If there ever had been a plan of action, it was now falling apart and something had to be done quickly to try and reassert their authority over the situation. With some unintelligible Samurai oath, the only man who had spoken drew a short sword - almost as if by magic it seemed to Jean - from a long side pocket in his black combats. The action was the signal for the other man to do the same and the two of them advanced on Jean and Tony. They stopped in their tracks as the kitchen door burst open and three of the most terrifying 'ogres' appeared.

The three men had blackened their faces and each carried a net in one hand and a stevedore hook in the other. If it hadn't been so threatening, Jean would have cracked up with laughter. It was just like a scene from the film 'Gladiator' - the nimble *Retiarii* with their nets and tridents about to engage in gladiatorial combat with the clumsier *Secutors* with their swords and armour. Jean and Tony bent down and picked up metal angle irons with sharpened points which they had placed under the kitchen table. However, there was nothing clumsy about the two men confronting the fishermen with their razor sharp ceremonial *wakizashi* swords.

The three 'ogres' roared their defiance and advanced on the two diminutive Japanese swirling their nets and lunging at them with the needle sharp hooks while the other two men made scything sweeps and thrusts with their metal angle irons. Had it ended in a fight there would have been serious injuries, but the odds were heavily stacked against the Japanese men and in humiliation and sheer terror they dropped their swords and bolted out of the door chased by the three 'ogre' fishermen.

There, the ludicrous confrontation should have ended, with perhaps a call to the police, but the two Japanese had become disorientated and, in the dark, fled in the wrong direction. Thinking they were running towards the town away from the gothic nightmare of ogres, hooks and nets, they headed for the cliff-top. The three 'ogres', Don, Michele and Pierre, realised what was about to happen and stopped chasing the men and shouted a warning, but nothing was going to stop the headlong flight of the Japanese.

In the dark and concealed by the dead ground beyond the convex slope of the cliff-top, both Japanese men never saw the edge and plunged over it with a final fading scream of terror as they fell 200 feet onto the jagged rocks of St Martin's Point.

*

At 8.15 the next morning Gunn joined the queue outside the aesthetically ugly and fortress like Russian Embassy on the Boulevard Lannes. The consular section opened its doors promptly at 9.00 and after completing his application forms Gunn eventually emerged from the building two hours later with a visa in the name of Robert Bradfield, valid for 21 days.

The Boulevard Lannes was on the eastern perimeter of the City so Gunn caught the Metro back into the centre with the intention of finding a good restaurant and enjoying some lunch. He had time

79

to kill until eight that evening and had checked out of his hotel near the Gare du Nord after breakfast that morning. He found an unpretentious restaurant named Le Grand Pan on the Rue de Vaugirard near the Luxembourg Gardens and was just settling down with the menu, a glass of wine and the restaurant's home-baked bread rolls when his cellphone buzzed. Three people knew the number of his private cellphone, one of whom one had been murdered, which left Miles Thompson and Claudine's father, Jean.

'John, it's Jean, I need your advice.'

'Of course, fire away.'

'I'm using a friend's cellphone which is untraceable to me. I had a visit yesterday evening by two men exactly as warned by you.'

'Are you OK, Jean?'

'Yes, yes....I'm fine, but they aren't. I had the usual crowd with me at the cottage planning our night's fishing when Tom....the landlord of the Ship..... warned me that these two Japs were on their way. We armed ourselves with all sorts of improvised weapons from the sheds at the back. They tried to threaten me to find where you were, but the five of us managed to frighten them off and they ran from the house leaving behind two machetes.'

'Where have they gone?'

'Wait, the weirdest bit is they lost their sense of direction and both fell over the cliff top at that very narrow bit........'

'Yes I know it.....sorry, go on.'

'It was pitch dark, but we went down the cliff path to the bottom.....took us nearly ten minutes to find where they'd fallen. Both were dead with every bone in their bodies smashed. We took photos of them.....and before you ask....yes we pulled up their right sleeves and sure enough that tattoo, just as you described it, was there, so we photographed that as well. We also found a mobile phone on each of them so we took those.'

'So what did you tell the police?'

'We went back to the cottage and made sure we had our version sorted. We then phoned the police and told them that we were all on our way for a night's fishing when we passed these two. Moments later we heard a scream and both had vanished etc....etc.

The police were perfectly happy with that, but the paparazzi were all over the scene so it'll be in the mainland newspapers later today or tomorrow.'

'Well done! and congratulations to all of you......these cult thugs are vicious bastards....'

'Just one more thing, John...'

'Yes, sure.'

'We managed to record the conversation when they threatened Tony and me to find where you were.'

'Brilliant.....listen Jean, I'll speak with Miles and he'll arrange for someone to come over and collect all the evidence.....the knives, mobiles, photos and cassette. Thanks again.....and that bunch of pirates you call friends!'

'A pleasure and make sure you get the bastards behind all this, John.'

'I will....that's a promise,' and Gunn ended the call, glanced at his watch, ordered another glass of wine and dialled Miles' private mobile number. It rang several times.

'Hello.'

'It's me, can you speak?'

'Yes go ahead, your call has just given me an excuse to escape from a very tedious lunch in the Institute of Directors club in Pall Mall.'

'Two Japanese thugs from that *Seppuku-kai* cult tried to threaten Jean de Carteret last night.'

'Is he alright?'

'Yes, he's fine, but they're both dead.'

'Bloody hell! What happened?' So Gunn explained what had happened at St Martin's Point the previous evening ending by telling him that Jean had the knives, mobiles, photos and a recording of the threats made by the Japanese.

'Would it be possible to send someone over to collect that evidence?'

'Indeed it would........I finally persuaded the Director to let me allocate this as an assignment, but he insisted that it went to someone who could speak Japanese.'

'Makes sense, I suppose.'

'But I think that the evidence from Guernsey combined with some recent evidence in this building may have some far-reaching results over here.'

'OK....so who're you sending?'

'Tatanya Kazakova.'

'Right....heard the name, but not met. I leave this evening for Moscow and then on to Vladivostok via the Trans-Siberian railway.'

*

'What is it you want Ichiro–san?'

'An urgent matter, Kenji-sampai relating to the mission which you gave to your son, Davidson-san in London,' Ichiro Iwakami replied straightening from the deep bow he had made to the Director of not only the most powerful bank in Japan, but very close to being the most powerful bank in the World. That goal was in tantalising reach; if it was possible to devalue the assets of his rival banks, Yoshida Global Holdings and the Matsumoto Bank, then he could take over the latter and beat the former to a position of worldwide financial dominance.

In order to achieve that goal Kenji Tokukata – alias Peter Drummond and Peter Davidson – had set in train a conspiracy in two phases. The first phase was to destabilise the banking system of the G8 countries making the acquisition of other banks less expensive. The second phase, running concurrently with the first, was to ensure that nothing was known of his wartime service in Hong Kong, which required the elimination of the last surviving member of the Lequesne family and any papers concerning the Japanese POW camp in Hong Kong.

Phase one fell into his lap. Whilst the rest of the banks in the G8 Countries, including the Japanese ones, had greedily hamstrung themselves with staggering sums of unsecured loans and toxic debts in the futile hope of making even more money, the Toyohashi-Kimura Banking Group in its fortress-like, 72 storey building in Tokyo's Otemachi Square had amassed a multi-trillion dollar fortune; adequate funds to destabilise the economies of any of the G8 Countries. And that is exactly what had precipitated the worldwide credit-crunch. Without warning, the TKB Group had pulled the rug from under a selection of banks and building societies in the USA, UK and Europe, precipitating panic withdrawal of funds and savings in those financial institutions and, but for the injection of billions of dollars/pounds/euros and yen of taxpayers' money, the West's banking system would have collapsed.

Kenji Tokutaka was seated in his favourite chair looking out of the wall to wall plate glass windows of the penthouse at the top of the bank building. He never tired of the view to the east over Tokyo's bustling railway station to the Sumida River and the Kaschidoki Bridge. His banking group owned or had a controlling share in almost everything he could see from the Tokyo Tower to the south to the Tokyo Towers twin condominium skyscrapers on the east side of the river.

He swung round in his chair to face Ichiro Iwakami, the Chief Executive of his Bank and dedicated *kobun* of *Seppuku-kai*. At the age of 86, Kenji Tokutaka got up from his chair with the agility of a man half his age. He was over six feet tall with no stoop and towered over his Chief Executive. After his decision to betray his fellow officers in the POW camp in Hong Kong and flee to Japan in the *Lisburn Maru*, the Japanese Gestapo – the *Kempei-tai* - had even insisted on plastic surgery to stretch the facial skin at the outer edge of each eye to conceal his Caucasian ethnic origin. Every aspect of his western origins had been carefully concealed or destroyed making it impossible for both Ronnie Lequesne, and subsequently his son Rory, to find any trace of the traitor who had been directly responsible for the torture and deaths of so many POWs.

He had taken full advantage of Japan's miraculous post-war recovery to build his banking empire with the help of *Yakuza* and had surrounded himself with a small army of shamed – because of Japan's surrender - and dedicated followers of *bushido*, the code of the Samurai warriors. His goal was to destroy the country which he believed had robbed him of his degree at Cambridge to fight the Japanese – a nation he revered. It was he who, in 1995, initiated the Sarin attack on the Tokyo subway under the guise of the *Aum Shinrikyo* cult for no other reason than to satisfy his army of 'warriors' who were deeply dissatisfied with Japan's pacifism and wished to overthrow the Emperor and install their own man, Shoko Asahara – another of Peter Drummond's recruits - as Emperor.

The Sarin plot inevitably failed as Drummond knew it would, but it gave him the opportunity to strengthen *Seppuku-kai* as the dominant group of *Yakuza* – far more dangerous and focused than any other Japanese Mafia family. It was to his Chief Executive that he had given the task of destroying any evidence of his wartime service in Hong Kong.

'Take a seat, Ichiro-san, and tell me what this all about,' and Drummond indicated the low seats on either side of the circular table on which was laid the exquisite porcelain china for the ritual tea ceremony of the '*Way*'.

'Kenji-sampai, the British criminals whom we paid to kill Lequesne-san failed to kill Gunn-san although they did kill his woman. The failure was to be expected of the cheap criminal trash we were forced to hire in London from Semion Mogilevich, the Don of the Russian Mafia. You then directed that I should send our professional *Seppuku-kai* Samurai warriors to complete the task of stopping Gunn-san and his investigation to find you.'

'Yes, I'm aware of all this, Ichiro-san. So have they completed the task?'

'Shamefully no, Kenji-sampai. The warriors sent to kill Gunn-san in his house were both killed as were the two warriors sent to the island of Guernsey to find and kill him. They have disgraced us shamefully, but Keiko Tanaka has followed Gunn-san to Paris and assures me that she will kill him and retrieve the papers belonging to Lequesne-san.'

'She had followed him from London?'

'Yes, Kenji-sampai.'

'So, Ichiro-san; not a very encouraging report of your warriors who, you assured me, would complete the task quickly and efficiently with no publicity and no comebacks. You have failed.'

'I have failed indeed and will do the only thing left for me as a Samurai warrior, but first I must complete my report, Kenji-sampai.'

'You mean there is worse still to come?' Drummond exploded in fury, now pacing in front of the windows overlooking the Sumida River.

'Your son has failed in his task to bring disgrace to the Government of the United Kingdom and has compromised himself and his appointment as Director of British Intelligence. He is likely to be arrested by the British Police,' was gasped in a terrified whisper.

'Then do whatever is necessary to see that that does not happen. As we have been let down by the Russian Mafia, I suggest you contact Kushtrim Kraja, the Don of the Albanian Mafia in Paris, and assure him of a handsome payment in return for ensuring that this man Gunn is killed. Is that clear enough for you Ichiro-san?'

'That is clear, Kenji-sampai.'

✳

Miles returned to the table of his lunch appointment, made his apologies and left the gilded splendour of the IOD club. While waiting for a taxi, he phoned his office and asked his PA, Angela, to have Tatanya Kazakova waiting in his office by the time he returned, to have Mike Dimmock, the SE Asia AD, on stand-by to come to his office and to book Tatanya onto the first available flight to Guernsey. That done, Miles flagged down a taxi which dropped him off in Cale Street from where he walked to Kingsroad House.

By the time Miles reached his office, Tatanya's flight was booked and she was waiting in Angela's office. There was little resemblance to the auburn haired young woman whom he had interviewed some six months previously. Having been warned for an assignment in Japan, she had had her hair cut and dyed black and with the subtle use of make-up had even managed to make her eyes appear more almond-shaped.

'Come in Tatanya,' and Miles led the way into his office. 'I believe I'm right in saying that you prefer to be called Tanya?'

'Yes, that's right sir.'

'This will only take a moment as Malcolm Springfield is waiting to fly you to Gatwick. From Angela's note on my desk I see you're catching the 16.30 Flybe flight to Guernsey. You'll return on the 08.35 flight tomorrow. Now this is the purpose of the visit,' and Miles very briefly explained what she had to collect and then told her that her full assignment brief would be handled by both James Rayner and Mike Dimmock, the ADs for Russia and SE Asia, on her return.

'Any questions?'

'No sir.'

'Right, I'll see you back in this office tomorrow morning. Malcolm will meet your flight and fly you back here.'

Tanya left the office followed by Miles who asked his PA to get Mike Dimmock to come up to the office. Before the AD for South East Asia arrived, Miles walked down the corridor to Mike Carrington's office. His PA told Miles that he was just about to finish a briefing from the ADs of the Counter-Terrorist Teams, but said she would pass on Miles' request as soon as the briefing ended. Miles returned to his office followed in less than a couple of minutes by both Mike Dimmock and Mike Carrington.

'Many thanks both of you for joining me at such short notice. I will be as brief as possible at this stage. First of all, Mike D, would you translate the recorded telephone conversation on this tape,' and Miles handed Mike Dimmock the mini cassette. 'It's in Japanese with some English spoken in the middle. The conversation is between our Director and, if I'm right, a member of the Japanese *Seppuku-kai* cult. If I've got this wrong then I doubt if I shall be with BID for much longer. Please carry out my request as quickly as possible and only you, Mike, must handle this. Right, do you have a problem with this?'

'None at all, I'll be back with the translated tape in less than an hour,' and Mike Dimmock got up and left the office.

'Now Mike it's my duty to take you fully into my confidence so that you have all the information to make a decision on your next move.'

'Go ahead Miles....I'm aware of course of the background, but not the detail.'

'Right; in the last fortnight – coinciding almost exactly with the appointment of BID's new Director – there have been eight deaths....'

'Eight?'

'Yes, I'll cover that in a minute. Ever since Lequesne, the policeman and Claudine were murdered and we learned that these deaths were connected to something that occurred in Hong Kong in 1941, our Director has done everything possible to prevent an investigation. Even suggesting that John Gunn, who had survived two attempts on his life, was a loose cannon and should be sacked from BID.'

'I don't believe this.....'

'You'd better Mike, because there's a lot worse to come. Coffee?'

'Yes, I rather think I'm going to need a coffee.' Miles got up and poured two coffees from the jug on the hotplate.

'But to cut to the chase, the Director's PA overheard a conversation that he had yesterday with a Japanese person. She recorded it and recognised the words Gunn and Guernsey- even though the rest of it was in Japanese. Last night in Guernsey, an attempt was made by two Japanese men, both members of the *Seppuku-kai* cult, to intimidate Claudine's father into revealing where John Gunn was.'

'What happened, for Chrissakes?'

'Jean de Carteret was forewarned by Gunn and had a reception party waiting for the two Japs. They frightened them off and in their haste to escape they fell over the cliff. They're both very dead and it will be all over this evening's papers.'

'Jesus!'

'As a result of this we have a recording of the Director speaking to a Jap, two ceremonial Jap swords abandoned in flight, photos of the tattoos on the two men and their mobile phones which – with a bit of luck – will connect the conversation recorded here with the action on Guernsey.'

'Fucking hell!'

'Yes, I rather think that sums up the situation as I see it too. And we were about to parade our new Director at the JIC on Thursday where he would have learned of all the measures to cope with the *Seppuku-kai* threat.'

CHAPTER 9

Gunn had enjoyed a refreshing lunch of seafood with the restaurant's speciality mayonnaise, chilled white wine and freshly baked rolls. He was planning a walk along the Seine's Quay d'Orsay in the autumn sunshine to while away the time until he needed to check in at the Gare de l'Est for his Moscow-bound train. He had noticed the toilets at the back of the restaurant when he'd been shown to his table and thought it wise to visit them, after a couple of glasses of wine and before his walk by the river.

Right at the rear of the restaurant, which was barely a quarter full, was an Asian woman sitting on her own. Gunn glanced in her direction as he opened the door to the toilet and they made eye contact; Gunn smiled, but the gesture was not reciprocated and as he walked into the toilet Gunn realised that the eye contact had annoyed the woman. 'Why for God's sake?' Gunn murmured and then chided himself, 'for fuck's sake Gunn, wake up and stop wandering around as though you're a tourist....think....think. Have you seen that face before and if yes, where? London...at Victoria Station?...no, might have been there, but not seen. On the train to Southampton?...no.....stop!....yes...that was it....the plump blonde woman crossing her legs outside the toilet on the train....with black eyebrows clashing with the obvious blonde wig....could that be the same person? Bloody right it could,' Gunn berated himself. He'd been followed every step of the way. 'I bet they tracked me to Newhaven, either by boat or chopper. I'm certain now, I saw someone like that on the ferry........Oh shit!....my fucking backpack!' Gunn hurled himself out of the toilet cannoning into another customer and knocking him flying. As he reached the restaurant, the Asian woman had just bent down to pick up his backpack. She turned round as Gunn rushed out of the toilet narrowly missing a waiter carrying a loaded tray.

'Stop!' Gunn shouted at the top of his voice which succeeded in stopping everything and everyone else in the restaurant except for the Asian woman who grabbed the bag and made for the door. 'Stop or I'll shoot!' Gunn repeated, dropping to a crouch and drawing the Glock from his ankle holster. The woman spun round, pulling a small automatic from inside her padded jacket. A nano second check by Gunn to ensure that there was no one between him and the woman and then he fired twice as he rolled away to his right. She had fired, but the small .22 bullet had gone well wide to his left, fortunately causing no harm to anyone. Both Gunn's shots hit the woman in the head and she was stone dead before she crumpled to the restaurant floor. Gunn holstered the Glock 26, walked over to the woman and pulled back the right sleeve of her jacket. Sure enough, the *harakiri* lettering and the *wakizashi* sword of the *Seppuku-kai* cult were tattooed on her right forearm. He pried open the fingers of her left hand, removed the shoulder strap of his backpack and walked out of the restaurant seconds before the restaurant erupted in Gallic chaos, arm waving and shouting.

Gunn realised as he ran into a warren of streets taking him further and further away from 'Le Grand Pan' that he'd been functioning like an automaton since Claudine's death. Half a dozen times in the last ten days he'd only survived by the narrowest of margins which was totally unacceptable for anyone in his profession.

'How many people had got a good look at him in the restaurant? Plenty, probably,' Gunn reckoned; that meant all the rail stations would be swarming with police. It was now nearly four........three back in London. Gunn ducked into a small, dark bar largely patronised, it seemed, by Algerians and ordered a coffee. Once he'd received his coffee, he dialled Miles' number.

'Yes.'

'It's me......I've been followed here. Entirely my fault for not being sharp enough.......it was a woman who tried to take my backpack.

She was armed and fired at me but missed. I shot her.....she had that *Seppuku-kai* tattoo on her right forearm.'

'Where are you now?'

'I'm in a small bar about five hundred yards from the restaurant where I shot the woman.'

'Got all that. The package in Guernsey will be collected this evening. By this time tomorrow things may have come to a head, so you've got to survive and stay clear of the French police until then. Whatever happens in the next 24 hours, I'm assigning Tanya to cover your back and to help you with the language. Our in-country agent in Paris is Bruno Lauriant – he also works for the Deuxième Bureau; his phone number is 01-42-51-02-52 and you'll need Tanya's cellphone,' and Miles gave him the number.

Gunn smiled as he wrote the numbers on a stained menu card before entering them into his cellphone. The Deputy Director always referred to the French Secret Service by its wartime title rather than DGSE.

'I'll speak with Pierre Brouhard, the Director of the Bureau – he's just about to retire – to see if he can help to dilute the enthusiasm of the French Police – he owes me a couple of favours. As it's not your usual stamping ground you might need to know that the Bureau is at 141 Boulevard Mortier. The French sometimes refer to it as the 'Piscine' because it's right next door to the Piscine des Tourelles.'

'Thanks,' and Gunn was about to end the call, but Miles continued.

'Wait........you need more information as you weren't briefed for this assignment. Can I continue?'

'Sure, no one's paying any attention to me and I can see two other guys having conversations on their mobiles.'

'OK....as briefly as I can; criminal gangs in South-East Asia have difficulty when operating unnoticed in Europe and in countries where the majority of the population is Caucasian.......that's in spite of the ethnic immigrant population from that part of the World. In order to overcome this they contract out any assignments to the indigenous criminal fraternity. In Europe and the USA this means the Mafia.'

'Local or imported?' Gunn queried.

'Imported......in Paris it's the Russian and Albanian Mafias. After the collapse of the Soviet Union, a character called Semion Mogilevich – known as 'Don Semyon' was reputed to be the boss controlling the Russian Mafia gangs – particularly those operating in other countries. An ex-con by the name of Kushtrim Kraja is reputed to be the boss of the Albanian Mafia in Paris which operates out of St Denis.....that's a run-down suburb north of the Stade Francais on the east bank of the Seine. Both of these Mafias have strong connections with Chinese Triad gangs, the Sicilian Cosa Nostra and the Mafia in Japan.'

'That's the *Yakuza*.'

'It is, and if Shiro was unable to tell you before he was shot, there are five principal Yakuza families of which *Yamaguchi-gumi* is the most powerful – or was until the emergence of *Seppuku-kai*. Tanya will brief you in detail on all of that when you meet up in Moscow.

'Shiro Akagawa was briefing me about the Japanese Mafia when he was shot.'

'I know – that's what I asked him to do. I want to make sure that you realise that *Seppuku-kai's* task of eliminating you and preventing the investigation into Drummond's disappearance in 1941 might well have been contracted out to either the Russian or Albanian Mafias. The scope and ferocity of the Albanian gangs – who operate in Italy as well as France – dealing in arms sales, human body parts – usually removed while the unwilling donor is still alive - sex slavery, abductions, murder, forgery and drugs have prompted Interpol to rate them as a more severe threat to Western society than Al Qaeda. *Seppuku-kai* might well use the Russian or Albanian Mafias experienced and very effective assassins to kill you.'

'Got that,' and Gunn was about to end the call when Miles interrupted once more.

'Wait a moment..........Terry has just appeared with a message.' There was a pause and then Miles continued. 'We've just heard from Paris that the French have picked up a conversation on a DGSE-bugged telephone at a house in Rue Samson.....number 12...that's right in the centre of the Albanian Mafia's patch. The call came from Japan and no names were mentioned except yours. It would seem that after the Japanese failure to kill you in London and Paris the task has been handed over to the Albanian Mafia.'

*

'No sooner had Miles Thompson finished his call to Gunn and put his private cellphone away in his pocket than Angela told him that Mike Dimmock had returned.

'Come in Mike...........well what've you got?'

'Absolute dynamite! Here's the cassette that Melanie gave you and here's the version I recorded in English. Play it back and see what you think.' Miles took the tape and placed it in his hand-held tape recorder and pressed the 'play' button. When it finished, Miles sat in silence for a moment.

'He gave those *Seppuku-kai* thugs instructions to kill John Gunn.'

'I told you it was dynamite.'

*

Gunn was certain that he had not been followed after leaving the restaurant. Having tailed him to the restaurant, it was reasonable to guess that the woman was waiting for someone else to join her so that the two of them could deal with Gunn and get hold of the Lequesne papers. She had taken advantage of the opportunity offered by Gunn's stupidity at leaving his backpack at the table. Ten seconds later and she would have vanished with it. It was little wonder then that the eye-contact earlier had thrown her so badly. Going over the events of the last few days and the last hour in particular, Gunn shook his head in disbelief at his own lack of professionalism and how easy it had been for the Japanese Mafia to follow such a soft target.

Miles Thompson had hinted that there was enough evidence now to cause major changes at BID. That could only mean the removal or suspension of the new Director. So why was the Director so hyposensitive about the Lequesnes and the diaries kept by Ronnie and his son Rory? Had Ronnie managed to identify Peter Drummond's post-war activities in Japan and what was the connection to Ian Davidson? Certainly, the diaries revealed the direction of Ronnie's research but no proof of that connection was recorded. And how did the Lequesne papers link to the relatively new cult which had emerged from *Aum Shinrikyo*? Could Davidson, who had spent his entire childhood in Japan, be Peter Drummond's son? He was the right age to be Drummond's son and certainly, if it was ever revealed that it had been his father who was guilty of such a monstrous war crime as the murder of 1,200 British and Canadian soldiers, it would result in immediate dismissal of his son from any government appointment. But there was more to this than the stigma of his father's war crimes – if indeed that was the connection.

Gunn continued to weave together, mentally, all the incidents that had occurred since that fateful phone call from Miles Thompson that had set in train the events resulting in Claudine's death at his house and the murder of Professor Akagawa at SOAS. Either the *Seppuku-kai* Mafia had discovered the connection to Peter Drummond's war crimes – if such a connection existed – or it had dug up something else with which to blackmail Davidson into cooperating with their stated aim of destroying the G8's financial world domination. Japan was infamous for its use of Geisha girls to use as 'honey traps' for gullible diplomats and western visitors to the country – particularly during the post-war occupation by American GIs. What better blackmailed victim to have acquired than the British Ambassador to Tokyo?

Gunn had been weighing up the pros and cons of abandoning his reservation on the night train to Moscow in favour of finding some seedy 'pension' in the northern suburbs of the city until the situation at Kingsroad House and his assignment was clarified. There, in the run-down and decrepit housing estates, filled with immigrants from North Africa, the police were loathed and rarely patrolled the area, making it a haven for criminals and illegal immigrants......and, as he'd just been told.....the area controlled by the Albanian Mafia. Gunn wondered how much influence Miles would be able to exert on the Director of the DGSE. The police would have found the woman in the restaurant who had tailed him. They would also have found the small .22 automatic and the bullet fired from it which would have incriminated her.

The *Seppuku-kai* blog had announced that Richard Perrigot, the Director of France's largest energy consortium, was on its assassination list. If Miles told them that there was a BID agent in Paris assigned to the prevention of these assassinations would that take the heat off him? He knew he would soon find out. Gunn finished his second cup of coffee which had tasted like mud. Mind made up, he paid for the tasteless coffee and left the café. It was now 4.15pm; four more hours before the departure of the over-night train to Moscow.

*

By mid-day on Wednesday, Miles Thompson had received all the bits and pieces of evidence which confirmed the connection between BID's new Director and the *Seppuku-kai* cult. His desk was covered with the broadsheets and tabloids which had carried the story of the two Japanese tourists who had fallen to their deaths in Guernsey. On a slow news day in the Channel Isles – perhaps it was ever thus - the Guernsey paparazzi had had a field day with the story which had been syndicated to all the mainland dailies and evening editions. Banner headlines varied from the sublime – JAPANESE TOURISTS DIE IN FALL FROM CLIFF – to the ridiculous – JAP HARAKIRI GAY SUICIDE TRYST. There had been no comment from the Director.

Tanya had returned from Guernsey with the cassette of the recording threatening Jean de Carteret, the two *wakizashi* swords, photos of the two men's bodies and tattoos on their forearms and their mobile phones. From within BID Miles had the recording of the Director's phone conversation ordering the 'disposal' of John Gunn. Time was running out; the Joint Intelligence Committee was due to convene the following morning in Whitehall and before then Miles knew he had to convince, not only the Chairman of JIC of his Director's 'treasonable activity', but also the Prime Minister who had personally approved Sir Ian Davidson's appointment. The PM was still smarting from the discovery by BID that his security supremo had turned out to be a serial murderer. That had happened only two months previously on the eve of the PM's visit to the Beijing Olympics.

While a succession of people had come to Miles' office with various bits and pieces of evidence, Angela had contacted the JIC Chairman's secretary and arranged for a meeting at the Chairman's office for 13.30 that afternoon. Perhaps it was just as well that there had been no sign of the Director in Kingsroad House that morning. His PA had no idea where he was, having achieved no answer from her phone calls to his house or his cellphone.

While Miles sifted through the evidence making notes and cross referencing various incidents which included the removal of embargoed files from the ultra sensitive records vault, his PA placed a sandwich and coffee on his desk knowing that he would have no time for anything more substantial before his meeting with the JIC Chairman. At 13.25 Miles was delivered by BID car to 70 Whitehall for his meeting with Andrew Allen, the Chairman of the Joint Intelligence Committee.

'Miles, good to see you, come in,' and the Chairman indicated a comfortable chair and came round to join him. 'I've gathered that the purpose of this meeting is not only urgent, but highly sensitive.'

'That it is, Andrew, and if I've got this wrong or I fail to convince you, then it's highly unlikely that you'll see me in my present job much longer.'

'That sensitive....OK, fire away,' Allen said drawing a deep breath and taking a pen out of his pocket. Miles took him through the events that had started the day that Rory Lequesne was killed by a hit and run driver followed by the Director's reluctance to allow BID to investigate the Japan connection and lastly ended with the proof of the connection between Davidson and *Seppuku-kai*.

'Can you play those recordings once more?' Allen asked when Miles had finished. Allen was silent while he listened to the recordings. 'There can't be any mistake in the translation of that recording between Davidson and the man who was told to 'dispose' of Gunn?'

'No, none, Andrew; Mike Dimmock, my AD for South-East Asia, did the translation and is completely bi-lingual in Japanese,' Miles answered.

'I shall need copies of those tapes when I take this matter to the PM......' the Chairman looked at his watch..........'in half an hour.'

'These are for you. We have copies back at Kingsroad House.'

'He's not going to be happy with this.'

'That's of little concern to me, Andrew. My responsibility is the security of information and intelligence relating to the threat which *Seppuku-kai* poses to certain high profile figures and to this Country which the JIC will discuss tomorrow and the measures to be taken to deal with it.'

'Of course this really falls into Mike Carrington's Counter-Espionage Directorate,' Allen murmured while he digested the information he's just received.

'Both our Directorates, Andrew; 'E' was involved in putting John Gunn onto the case and now 'CE' are involved with the threat which *Seppuku-kai* poses to this Country. I am here in my capacity as the DD of BID. If there are any comebacks for placing this information before you and the PM then it's entirely correct that I take that responsibility.'

'And Mike is fully aware of all this, I'm sure.'

'He is.'

'Right, no point in wasting any more time. I'm convinced by the evidence........and I shall tell the PM that I cannot allow Davidson to attend the JIC..........' the office door opened and a worried secretary looked round it. 'I did say that I wasn't to be disturbed, Carol.'

'Sorry sir, but a most urgent phone call for Mr Thompson. May I put it through please?'

'Very well,' and the Chairman's secretary retreated and closed the door. The phone on the desk rang and Andrew Allen handed it to Miles.

'Miles.'

'Mike Carrington. Ian Davidson's hanged himself. His body was found by his wife half an hour ago in the attic of their house in Knightsbridge. She was away last night visiting her mother in Dundee and didn't return until mid-day. That's why Melanie was unable to raise anyone in the house when she phoned this morning. Looks like suicide, but SOCO and my CE4 team with Fiona Ransby are at the house now. Sarah Davidson's at the clinic under sedation. There are no children. That's all, Miles.........for the moment.'

'Thanks Mike,' he replaced the phone and turned to Andrew Allen. 'Davidson's dead.'

'That takes the pressure off both of us, Miles,' Andrew Allen said, 'but I'm still keeping that appointment with the PM in ten minutes to try and convince him of the risks of meddling with the proper selection process of a suitable Director of British Intelligence.'

*

Any wishful thinking that Gunn might have entertained about BID's ability to take the 'heat' off him was quickly dispelled as soon as he arrived at the Gare de l'Est. In order to kill time until he needed to board the night train to Moscow, he'd found another small café with a set tuned to the 'France TV' news channel and coffee which tasted marginally less like mud.

In between news updates on the developing banking crisis in the USA, Europe and SE Asia, a breaking news item showed the scene in Le Grand Pan and the body of the Japanese woman being removed on a stretcher. The camera zoomed in on the police Lieutenant in charge of the investigation who was holding a plastic bag containing the small .22 Beretta which the woman had fired at Gunn. The police officer then turned, and although Gunn couldn't hear what he was saying because the volume had been turned down, he pointed to an area where forensic officers in overalls were attempting to dig out the bullet from the wooden floor.

His cellphone vibrated.

'Yes.'

'A major development in the office; the boss has hanged himself,' was Miles' terse message. 'SOCO aren't convinced that it's suicide.

I've spoken with my opposite number in the DGSE after that call we had from our guy. He says he'll do what he can, but assume the police will be looking for you. Continue as planned, but in addition to the French Police you have the Albanian Mafia looking for you. Your back-up will join you in Moscow. Do you have any immediate questions for me?'

'None,' and Gunn ended the call. 'Thank fuck we're rid of that prat,' he added with conviction, finishing his coffee. 'Yuk, that still tastes like mud, but better mud than the last lot.'

As Gunn left the café on his way to the station, he was still bereft of any inspiration for some form of subterfuge to act as an effective disguise to divert police attention from a 'single, tall man'. Fifty yards from the café, workmen were gutting a building which looked, to Gunn, like an old school. In a skip by the pavement was a mass of detritus from inside the building including various lengths of white plastic electrical conduit pipe. Gunn pulled a four foot length of pipe from the skip and continued on his way to the station.

When he reached the imposing pillared facade of the Gare de l'Est, it seemed as though there were policemen everywhere. 'So much for any help from the DGSE,' Gunn muttered. Whether this was the usual police presence outside mainline stations, he had no idea. Gunn paused at the southern side of the square in front of the station entrance until he saw a middle-aged woman heading for the station pulling a wheeled suitcase along behind her.

'Excusez-moi, Madame,' Gunn approached her with a pronounced stoop and holding his white length of pipe out in front of him. The woman stopped and looked at him.

'Oui? Je ne donne pas de l'argent aux mendiants.'

'Je ne veux pas de l'argent, Madame,' Gunn hastily assured her that he was not begging.

'Et puis, qu'est-ce que vous voulez Monsieur?' she inquired, not unkindly.

'Je ne peux pas voir tres bien, madame. Pouvez-vous me guider à l'entrée de la gare si'il vous plait,' Gunn hoped that his accent and school French would pass muster and that he could convince her that he had very limited vision.

'Mais bien sûr, Monsieur. J'y vais moi meme,' and she reached out and took Gunn's arm and led him across the square to the station entrance. The police, if indeed they were on the lookout for him, paid him no attention at all as he entered the station.

'De quel quai départez-vous, Monsieur?' the 'Good Samaritan' asked as she led Gunn towards the platforms. He made a show of delving into his pocket and produced his purposely crumpled ticket and held it out to the lady.

'Pouvez vous me dire le numero du quai Madame?'

'Ah oui!' as she took the ticket and looked at the destination, 'ca c'est quai numero six,' and she led him to the barrier at platform six, showed his ticket and handed it back to him.

'Soyez prudent, Monsieur....adieu' and she waved goodbye.

'Vive La France,' Gunn murmured, when she was out of sight, as he disposed of his length of white plastic pipe in a litter bin and then headed for the blue and red coach at the front of the train indicated on his ticket and his self-indulgent first class two-berth sleeper.

CHAPTER 10

'Come in Andrew,' the PM welcomed the Chairman of JIC as he was shown into the PM's study. 'Presumably this is about tomorrow's JIC. Take a seat,' was offered to Allen although the PM had not risen from his seat behind the desk.

'Thank you Prime Minister; you will be concerned to hear that Sir Ian Davidson.......'

'Breath of fresh air and change of style for the Intelligence community, don't you agree?' the PM interrupted.

'Possibly, but now we will never know as he has hanged himself.'

'He's what?' Allen now had the PM's attention.

'He's hanged himself....or that's how it seems at the moment, but the police are not convinced that it's suicide.'

'For God's sake Andrew, what do you mean?'

'Quite simple Prime Minister, it means that it could well be murder. However, had this not occurred I would have had this meeting with you to let you know that as Chairman of JIC I could not have accepted Davidson's attendance at the JIC tomorrow.'

'What in God's name are you talking about? I personally approved Ian Davidson's appointment.'

'Indeed you did, Prime Minister, but in my briefcase I have overwhelming proof of Davidson's complicity with this Japanese *Seppuku-kai* terrorist group.'

'You're not serious.....'

'Prime Minister, I have never been more serious in my entire career. Davidson has already been complicit in three deaths........a member of the public, a police constable and a BID agent. Had he not died....by whatever means.....it is very likely that he would have been arrested tonight by the police.'

'What.....what happens now?' a somewhat chastened PM stuttered.

'Subject to your support, it's my intention to seek JIC's approval to appoint Davidson's Deputy, Miles Thompson, as BID's Director.'

'There's no doubt about Davidson's guilt?'

'None whatsoever.'

'Very well.'

'One thing in our favour.'

'What could that be?'

'His death has saved the Government the embarrassment of having to sack him only a fortnight after his appointment.'

∗

Fiona Ransby, the Assistant Director of CE4, showed her BID ID card to the police constable and was allowed through the police exclusion area around the entrance to Davidson's house in Knightsbridge's Hans Place. Up on the third floor, where an extending ladder led up to the attic, she met Chief Inspector Peter Nesbit.

'Oh, you've taken over from John Gunn,' was Nesbit's perfunctory greeting to Fiona after he'd studied her BID ID card.

'No Chief Inspector, John is involved on another assignment. I'm the Head of CE4 with a particular interest in all matters relating to Politicians, Diplomats, Embassies and Civil Servants.' Her response made it quite clear to the CI that she out-ranked him by some margin.

'Sorry Ma'am, I've 'ad so many big wigs wanting to know what's the score I've rather lost me normal cheerful disposition.' The gentle cynicism of the remark was not lost on Fiona.

'I'll get out of your way Chief Inspector just as quickly as possible. Are you able, at this stage, to tell me whether this was suicide?'

'The pathologist's up there now, Ma'am. 'e'll give you 'is opinion at this early stage. Davidson's 'anging from one of the roof joists – or 'e was until we cut 'im down. I've seen one or two suicide 'angings in my time, but in this case I'd say 'e was dead before 'e was strung up.'

'What makes you say that?'

'The colour of 'is face............' but Nesbit's explanation was cut short by the appearance, feet first, of the pathologist in his white overalls as he came down the ladder.

'OK Chief Inspector, I've finished, you can remove the body.'

'Thank you sir, this is Ms Ransby from BID.' The pathologist pulled off his overalls and then turned to Fiona.

'Davidson's only been with you for a couple of weeks hasn't he?' Fiona avoided answering that inquiry.

'We've met once before Doctor, back in that non-existent summer, when a woman at the Cameroon High Commission was electrocuted.'

'So we did.....you want to know cause of death. Not a hundred per cent able to tell you the exact cause of death but what I can tell you is that he was dead before he was strung up from the roof. Unless you fondly believe in life after death he certainly didn't do it himself. No, someone went to quite a bit of trouble to make it look like suicide. He was murdered. I'll get the exact cause of death to you and the police as soon as I've got the body back at the path' lab.' And with that definitive statement, the Doctor scurried off down the stairs.

*

The Joint Intelligence Committee had met half an hour earlier than usual on that Thursday because of its extended agenda. In addition to the Chairman and Miles Thompson, the meeting was attended by the Head of GCHQ, the Chief of Defence Intelligence, the Deputy Chief of Defence Intelligence Staff, the Chief of the Assessment Staff, representatives from the MOD and FCO and, on that occasion, the PM's adviser on Foreign Affairs.

The threat assessment of *Seppuku-kai* was still rated 'moderate' for the Country and 'severe' for targeted high profile individuals. There was an update on the risk of liquid IEDs on aircraft, further Al Qaeda and dissident IRA threats to mainland UK and a number of other up-dates. At the completion of all the items, the Chairman informed those present that there was one additional item which had not been included on the agenda.

'It's my sad task to let this meeting know that BID's recently appointed Director took his life yesterday.'

One or two of those at the meeting had picked up this bit of news before the meeting, but as for the remainder, it produced a stunned silence. The Chairman continued after a brief pause.

'We have no idea at the moment what set of circumstances led to this as his wife is still in a state of shock. What is most urgent, while this Country is faced with a sustained level of threat from Al Qaeda terrorists and this new threat from *Seppuku-kai*, is to have an experienced intelligence director ensuring the highest level of security possible that the Directorates of Espionage and Counter-Espionage can provide. Fortunately, we have just such a person and yesterday the Prime Minister approved the permanent appointment of Miles Thompson as Director of BID.

*

The atmosphere in Kingsroad House was as though Christmas had come early that year. The gloom of Davidson's two weeks as Director and the sadness of Claudine's death were replaced by delight at Miles Thompson's appointment as BID's Director. Even in the operations centre on the 14th floor where nothing louder than muted conversation was permitted, Terry Holt, the Controller, turned a blind eye to the animated exchanges of all the duty operational staff. Miles Thompson wasted no time in appointing James Rayner, the Assistant Director for Russia and Eastern Europe, as his successor as Director of the Espionage Department. James had been with BID as long as Miles and his appointment was well deserved and would be popular amongst the Western intelligence community world-wide.

No one showed more exuberance in Davidson's departure, however unpleasant for his sedated wife in BID's clinic, than Melanie, his PA. In the two weeks of his tenure as Director, Davidson had nearly succeeded in unravelling all the success achieved by Sir Jeremy Hammond's restructured Intelligence Directorate.

'Yes Melanie,' Miles responded to the flashing light on his telephone console.

'Terry Holt to see you, sir.'

'Yes, show him in...and Melanie.'

'Yes sir.'

'Miles will do just fine.'

'Right si.....Miles,' and the door opened to let Terry Holt into the Director's office.

'Yes Terry.......clearly hotfoot from the ops centre. What crisis have we now?'

'Just had a call from Boulevard Mortier, sir. Richard Perrigot has disappeared from his yacht en route from Nice to Marseille. It's also running on France TV.'

'Right, can I get that on my monitor over there?' and Miles nodded towards the large 42" flat screen LED and High Definition TV mounted on the wall opposite his desk.

'Sure,' and Terry picked up the remote from the Director's desk, pressed a couple of buttons and the France TV News appeared.

'Thanks Terry.' After watching the report on Perrigot's disappearance, Miles got up. 'I must speak to Mike,' and the two men left the office; Terry to the stairs leading to the 14th floor and Miles to Mike Carrington's office. The door to the Counter-Espionage Director's office was open and his PA, Jane Bristow, waved the BID Director through. Mike Carrington was just finishing a conversation on his mobile phone and pointed to the armchairs where he joined Miles.

'Sir David Istead,' Miles voiced the name of the British banker who had been identified by *Seppuku-kai* on its internet blog as a target for assassination.

'Not a nice character, Miles, but currently with 24 hour close protection by SO1 of the Met's Special Operations Command,' Mike volunteered. 'Why? I can see something's bothering you.'

'It is; the other seven people on that blog – three of whom it would seem have been killed – are, or were, very powerful movers and shakers, not only in their own country, but also on the international stage, which brings me to Istead. Until the Loughborough and Leicester Building Society went bust six months ago and had to be rescued by the Government with taxpayers' money, no one had ever heard of its Chief Executive. After watching the reaction of those people on the TV news who've lost their houses because of the profligate behaviour of the 'L and L', I reckon they would be delighted if Istead was bumped off.'

'In other words, well done *Seppuku-kai*.'

'Exactly; Istead's death won't even make a ripple on the surface of the City's efforts to re-establish its reputation. I can think of a slack handful of financial 'moguls' in this Country – starting with the Governor of the Bank of England and possibly ending with the Chancellor of the Exchequer – whose untimely death could really upset the return to financial stability.'

'Do you think that the Met should be keeping an eye on that 'slack handful'?' Mike Carrington queried.

'Sorry Mike, I'm really just thinking aloud, but if you don't think I'm being over cautious, why don't you have a quick heads-up with David Baines...........is he still the Head of Special Ops Command at the Met?'

'He is and a close pal. I'll let you know what he thinks.'

'Thanks Mike,' and Miles left his Counter-Espionage Director's office and returned to his own.

*

'Yes Tricia.'

'Tanya's here for her assignment briefing,' Tricia Wilson informed the recently promoted Assistant Director for Russia and Eastern Europe.

'Of course.....Jesus, is it that time already,' and David Simpson pulled the briefing folder out of his in-tray as Tanya was shown into the office by his PA. The knock-on effect of the Director's death had not only resulted in James Rayner's promotion from Assistant Director Russia and Eastern Europe to Director Espionage but also David Simpson's promotion from Controller to Assistant Director.

'Come in Tanya....grab a seat....Tricia!' was addressed to his PA as she made to leave the office, but stopped. 'Is Ben there and Marie from the EU?'

'They were both on their way a couple of minutes ago. I'll just check........ah! they're both here now,' and a young, stocky man with a short haircut and neatly clipped beard side-stepped past David's PA followed by Marie de Fonblanque, the Controller from the EU Department.

'Sorry I'm late, David, I.........'

'You're not. Ben and Marie meet Tatanya Kazakova who prefers us to call her Tanya. Tanya, this is Ben Warren who will be your Controller while you are in Russia on this assignment and Marie de Fonblanque who will cover you through France and Germany.....if that's needed. The mission for your assignment is to support John Gunn's investigation into the Japanese Mafia's threat to the financial stability of the G8 Countries. David Morris will be with us any minute from South-East Asia Department. He'll be taking over as your Controller as you move from Russia to Japan.'

Right on cue David Morris arrived in the office and all of them took their seats round the small conference table. David opened the briefing file and then addressed the small group.

'We know that the Japanese Mafia gang *Seppuku-kai* has close links with the most powerful of the Russian Mafia gangs.....the Izmaylovskaya bratva – or brotherhood. There have been many instances where each has helped the other by proxy – usually to remove an incorruptible policeman or politician. It's boss is Sergei Mogilevich – a Ukranian Jew who has achieved the title of 'capo de tutti capo' of the Russian Mafias. The work of this gang is almost solely confined to Moscow, but its influence is Russia-wide – a criminal version of the KGB would be an apt description. If the head of *Seppuku-kai* – he's an unknown......unknown to us, that is......asks Izmaylovskaya for help to prevent Gunn from reaching Japan then the Russian Mafia will carry out that task as far as its eastern seaboard.'

'Gunn will catch the Paris/Moscow train which leaves at 20.20 tonight. While he's in France and Germany we know that *Seppuku-kai* uses the Albanian Mafia to help out with any of its dirty work. I won't elaborate on the cruelty and bestiality of that Mafia. Gunn has just killed a *Seppuku-kai* woman in Paris and two others who broke into his house. A further two died in Guernsey.....you'll have seen that in today's papers.....which is very likely to trigger an immediate reaction. His train stops only once and that is at Berlin.... Marie....where it remains from 0900 hours tomorrow until 1315 hours Eastern European time. It then continues to Moscow where it arrives the following day at 2035 hours. That is where you, Tanya, will meet up with John Gunn.'

David Simpson then continued with the briefing for a further ten minutes before the meeting broke up and Tanya went off with the three Controllers to receive all the details of her assignment. That was followed by visits to comms' and ciphers on the 14th floor and Tony Taylor, the armourer, in the basement before she returned to her flat in Pimlico's Alderney Street at 5.30pm.

*

Ben Warren had booked Tanya on the BMI flight leaving Heathrow at 11.30 the next day arriving in Moscow's Domodedovo Airport at 18.30 hours local time. She had a reservation at the three-star Volga Hotel which was only 500 yards from the Belorusskaya Station where Gunn's express would arrive at 20.35 the day after her arrival.

Tanya was in two minds about acting as a 'language wet-nurse' for another agent. She had only completed one assignment for BID and that had been fairly low-key, keeping an eye on a UK Government cross-party fact-finding visit to Tibilisi. She had hoped that her next assignment might have been rather higher key than playing second fiddle to another agent. Slim and a keen athlete she had represented her college at Loughborough University in rowing, karate, distance running and hockey. She had dyed her dark red hair black and had it cut much shorter for this assignment so that she could blend in with the Japanese population.

Of John Gunn she knew very little except the BID grapevine gossip about his relationship with Claudine. Determined and fiercely independent, she dropped her shoulder bag on the bed in her first floor flat, which overlooked the trains entering and leaving Victoria Station, made herself a coffee and then sat down with her laptop.

She knew from her briefing that Gunn believed he'd been followed from the moment he had accepted the request by the Metropolitan Police to take on the investigation into the Lequesne papers. In order to avoid a repeat of that she had used the underground exit from Kingsroad House which brought her out in the King's Road and from there took a taxi to Alderney Street. Mind now made up, she switched on her laptop and used Google to find Easyjet's website. There was a flight leaving Luton Airport at 21.10 that evening which arrived at Berlin's Schoenefeld Airport at 00.20. The website indicated that there were plenty of seats available so she made a reservation and paid £30.99 on line for her single ticket. Two minutes later she had reserved a room at the Meininger Hotel Hauptbahnhof in Ella-Trebe Strasse which, as its name suggested, was less than 100 yards from Berlin's main line station. Her next task with the laptop was to find the website to reserve a couchette on the overnight express from Berlin to Moscow. That only took a further ten minutes and once she had paid with her credit card and downloaded her e-ticket she switched off the laptop.

It was now nearly six and smack in the middle of the evening rush hour. Tanya phoned for a private mini-cab and then threw some clothes and two passports with matching credit cards under different names into a small backpack. She pulled back the slide of her Smith and Wesson 9 mm automatic and ejected the chambered round which she inserted under the metal lips of the magazine. After replacing the magazine in the butt of the automatic, Tanya put it, the silencer and the spare magazine in her handbag and left the flat. The rush hour traffic was every bit as bad as she feared, but the cab made it to Luton Airport by 20.35 in time for her to check in for the 21.20 departure of her flight to Berlin. At the check-in desk she produced her BID ID and handed over a jiffy bag containing her automatic – with the chambered round removed as required by the airlines - silencer and spare magazine.

∗

At exactly 8.20 the Paris/Moscow express pulled out of the Gare de L'Est. The leaflet that Gunn had picked up from the ticket office had a diagram of the route to Moscow via Berlin. The route went via Brussels, crossed into Germany at Maastricht and then followed the Rhine via Cologne and Düsseldorf where it parted company with the river and turned north-east to Hannover and finally due east to Berlin. It was scheduled to arrive at the Berlin Hauptbahnhof at 09.03 the next morning where there was a six hour 'tourist stopover' before it departed at 15.15 for Moscow where it would arrive at 20.35 the next evening. Gunn smiled as he checked out his first class compartment. The punctuality of the French, German, Swiss and Russian trains was in direct contrast to the British rail network where the long-suffering traveller would consider it fortunate if the arrival or departure of the train was within ten minutes of the published time.

The express had twelve coaches sandwiched between two Czech 52 Series electric locomotives. Gunn's first class coach was the fourth one from the front locomotive and his compartment – number 22 - was the second one from the end of the coach closest to the lounge. Between the two first class coaches were a further two coaches; one was the restaurant car and the other the first class lounge with a bar, TV, reclining seats with video screens and a galley serving meals and snacks. The rest of the express was standard class which had a bar serving drinks and snacks. The first class compartments had two berths and the standard class had four berths. All the compartments were spotlessly clean and each berth had fresh linen, pillows and a duvet – or so the advertising blurb in the leaflet maintained. Certainly, his compartment was spotlessly clean, so having studied the leaflet, Gunn inspected his compartment with its en-suite toilet and washbasin. Best of all its assets was a very solid wooden sliding door with a key lock.

He removed the envelope from his backpack with the papers he had taken out of Lequesne's attaché case at Victoria Station and tucked it into the inside pocket of his anorak. He took the Glock 26 from his ankle holster, pulled back the slide and ejected the chambered round onto the berth. He then unzipped the small leather tool case and removed a slim black plastic oil bottle which had been part of the cleaning kit for his SA80 – L85A1 assault rifle when he was in the army. He stripped the Glock, oiled the slide and the dual safety/trigger mechanisms, reassembled the automatic, inserted the 9 mm round back into the magazine and inserted it into the grip. He then worked the slide and chambered the first round before replacing the Glock in his ankle holster and the spare magazine into one pocket of his anorak and the silencer into the other.

Gunn slid back the compartment door. The corridor was empty. To his right was compartment 21, the toilet and then the concertina-like coupling between the two coaches. The train swayed and the bogies rattled as it crossed a series of points in the north-eastern suburbs of Paris. He closed the door, locked it and pocketed the key before heading for the first class lounge.

The decor of the lounge was similar to that in his compartment. The seats were upholstered in a dull red fabric and the windows had bright red and white curtains. The bar was made of highly polished wood and already had two passengers seated on the fixed stools in front of it. Two of the lounge chairs facing the large flat screen TV were also occupied by passengers watching the France TV news channel. As Gunn reached the bar the news reader interrupted his interview with a scantily clad female 'celeb'- whom Gunn thought he ought to recognise but didn't – to switch to some breaking news. The picture changed from the TV studio to a large motor-yacht in Nice's marina. This was evidently archive footage about France's energy billionaire, who had been lost overboard earlier that day while the yacht was on passage between Nice and Marseille. Gunn was paying only scant attention to the TV as the volume was turned low until the news reader talking over the archive footage of the man on his yacht announced the name. Richard Perrigot – the fourth name on the *Seppuku-kai* assassination blog - had disappeared without trace.

CHAPTER 11

'Mesdames, Messieurs, vos billets s'il vous plaît,' the ticket inspector requested as he moved through the standard class section of the Paris/Moscow express. Rezar Niko had no ticket. He had received the phone call from Rue Samson while he was at Charles de Gaulle Airport waiting for a Cathay Pacific flight from Hong Kong. His contact at Hong Kong's Chek Lap Kok Airport had told him that there was a party of twenty unescorted Chinese school girls aged between 15 and 17 on the flight. The trip to Paris was a reward for successful exam results. The girls would be met at the airport by a junior attaché from the Chinese Embassy in Avenue Georges Cinq and the driver of the coach who would escort them to the Hotel Trianon Palace in the Rue de Vaugirard.

The coach driver was fast asleep when he and Jak Tosca forced open the locked door of the coach. The driver's death was instantaneous as Rezar stabbed him in the throat with a razor sharp double-edged lock-blade. The two men then bundled the dead driver into one of the luggage compartments underneath the coach and returned to the meeting point in the arrivals area of Terminal 1. Rezar had gone to the information desk and asked the girl behind the counter to make an announcement on the PA system requesting the representative from the Chinese Embassy to go to the meeting point.

When he returned to the meeting point, Jak Tosca had acquired a wheelchair from a stack of five by the trolley park. There had been only a handful of people at the meeting point; only one was of ethnic Asian origin and he readily confirmed that he was meeting the party of school girls. Amidst the noise and constant bustle of any airport, no one noticed as Rezar's needle sharp knife pierced the attaché's heart and he collapsed soundlessly into the wheelchair. The dead attaché was wheeled into the men's toilet and when no one was paying any attention they dumped the body and wheelchair in a stall, closed the door, left the toilet and returned to the meeting point. They were now in sole control of twenty young Chinese girls who would fetch a fortune in the sex-slave market once they had been 'conditioned' with a cocktail of mind-scrambling drugs in the cubicles at the warehouse in the Passage Meunier opposite Rue Samson.

It was at that moment that his cellphone had rung and he'd received instructions to go immediately to the Gare de L'Est to catch the 20.20 Paris/Moscow express. Even using the Metro, it had taken him nearly an hour to get get across Paris and the gate to platform six had been about to close as he squeezed through. He was told at the barrier that he could buy his ticket on the train from the inspector. He had been told in the call to his cellphone at the airport that he would receive instructions as soon as he confirmed that he was on the train. He had also been told to complete his task before the train arrived in Berlin so that he could leave it there and return to Paris.

Rezar used plastic to pay the €129 for a second class return fare to Berlin. As the Inspector handed him the ticket, his cellphone vibrated with the receipt of a text message. Once the Inspector had moved on down the carriage Rezar checked his cellphone message with its attached photo:

> *'yr tgt John Gunn. same train. poss use of other name. BID agent. ht 1.9m wt 90kgs. chk att photo taken 3 wks ago. armed. throw body off train. return asap. complete chinese task.'*

The thought of the enjoyment that he and Jak would have with the Chinese school girls, most of whom would be virgins, prompted a dribble of saliva to run down his chin which he wiped away with the back of his hand as testosterone fuelled blood pumped into his groin. Rezar left his seat, spurred into action by these thoughts of the drug-induced misery, abuse and degradation in which he was about to wallow which would destroy for ever the minds and lives of the young girls at the warehouse in the Passage Meunier.

Nick-named 'le rasoir' because of both his name and his preference for using a knife to mutilate his victims before and after killing them, Rezar had noticed that the ticket Inspector was carrying a passenger list to which his name had been added when he'd paid for his ticket. He needed that list. He caught up with the Inspector as he was about to leave standard class and move into the first class section at the front of the train. He told the man that he had hoped to meet up with a business colleague who had said he would be on the train.

'His name, Monsieur?'

'Monsieur Gunn....John Gunn.'

The inspector flicked through the pages of his passenger list.

'Non Monsieur, there is no one of that name on the train. Now I must go to the first class section if you will excuse me,' and the Inspector unsuspectingly turned his back on Rezar as he used his key to unlock the door into the first class section. Rezar removed the switch blade knife from inside the left sleeve of his jacket and stabbed the inspector in the neck, instantly severing the carotid artery.

He lowered the inspector onto the corridor floor, took the keys out of his hand and picked up the passenger list which had dropped to the floor. He then opened the door which led into the connection coupling between the standard and first class sections. Holding the door open, he dragged the body through the connection and then locked the door. The coaches had inwards-opening doors at each end. Rezar dragged the Inspector's body to the right hand door away from the track in the opposite direction and held it open with his body as he bundled the dead inspector out of the train. He shut the coach door, picked up the passenger list and walked along the corridor past the first class sleeper compartments as he wiped his hands on the seat of his stained jeans.

In the driving cab of the Czech 52 Class electric locomotive hauling the express through northern France a warning light and buzzer alarm sounded, indicating that a door had opened. The light went out and the alarm stopped. The driver turned to his co-driver and asked him to contact the inspector. The latter put down his sandwich and removed the radio clipped to his belt. He pressed the transmit button and called the inspector. There was no reply.

*

Day one as Director of Britain's Intelligence Directorate had been rather similar to the old adage of the 'curate's egg' – good in parts - for Miles Thompson. The 'good' had been the relief of the departure of Sir Ian Davidson – however traumatic - since it had become abundantly clear to him over the last fortnight that he could never work for such a man and would have to resign from the job to which he'd devoted himself for nearly twenty years. The 'bad' was the damage that Davidson had managed to do even in the short time since his appointment.

How had such a man – either a willing partner or blackmailed into cooperation with *Seppuku*-kai – managed to avoid, not only the vetting scrutiny of the Foreign and Commonwealth Office, but also the screening of all senior British Diplomats by both BID's Espionage and Counter-Espionage Directorates? That was certainly a black mark against both Government offices........unfortunate echoes of Burgess, Maclean and Philby.

What had Davidson really been doing amongst those files excluded from the 60 year Freedom of Information Act.......the ones which referred to the identity and activity of the SOE operatives in Japan during the Second World War and MI6 operations and activity after the war?

Gunn had killed two, so called *Seppuku-kai* 'Samurai warriors'; Jean and his fellow fishermen had dispatched another two and Gunn had killed a female member of the cult in Paris. How many more were in the Country and why was such an insignificant chief executive of a building society their stated UK target?

Before leaving the office just before seven that evening, he'd spoken again with Sir Marcus Lord, the Governor of the Bank of England, who had agreed that apart from the manpower drain on the Met's Special Ops Command to keep him alive, Sir David Istead's death would do nothing to upset the UK's treble 'A' financial rating with the World Bank. So why target him for assassination?

These and other questions to which he had no answers at the moment bothered Miles on the short journey to his house in Chelsea. Liz had said she was organising a small supper party for some close friends – there would be no more than ten of them round the table – and begged him to be home in time for the arrival of their guests at 7.45 that evening.

The Director's Jaguar XF pulled up outside his house in Durham Place. His BID bodyguard got out of the car and after a careful glance in either direction opened the door for Miles who said goodnight to both his driver and bodyguard and went into his house. Miles had yet to decide whether, for his daily commute, a driver and bodyguard were really either necessary or a sensible security precaution, but that was something that was too far down his list of matters requiring his attention to be resolved at the moment. Tonight he would enjoy his wife's supper party and the company of good friends.

∗

Tanya's Easyjet flight landed five minutes early at 15 minutes past midnight. Schoenefeld Airport resembled a huge building site as it was still being remodelled as Berlin's showpiece airport to take over from Tempelhof and Tegel. Although some ten miles from the centre of Berlin, the new airport had excellent bus and rail connections to the city centre. Tanya took the connecting travelator from Terminal B to the main Terminal and caught the train to Berlin's Hauptbahnhof. Having had no baggage to collect from the carousel, she was in her hotel by 1.30 am.

∗

Having had lunch at Le Grand Pan restaurant followed by some dreadful coffee in a couple of other cafés, Gunn had a light snack in the train's restaurant car washed down with a glass of mineral water. He walked back through the lounge where there were still only a dozen or so passengers of whom three were watching the France TV news channel. He decided that it was time to catch up on some sleep. The volume on the TV had been turned up and he paused as once again the news presenter interrupted his delivery with another breaking story about an incident at Charles de Gaulle Airport.

The commentary was rather too fast for Gunn's school French, but the camera work made up for that as it showed the airport's anti-terrorist police standing over a man whom they had shot. It appeared he had tried to abduct a group of Chinese school girls off a Cathy Pacific flight from Hong Kong. Gunn turned to continue on his way to his compartment and a few hours of sleep when even his lack of French linguistic skill couldn't mistake the news presenter's statement that the dead criminal was from the Albanian Mafia in Paris.

As he left the lounge and reached the coupling into the first class sleeping compartments, another passenger was coming in the opposite direction carrying a board with papers clipped to it and a bunch of keys. A steward? Gunn queried to himself; surely not, dressed in jeans, trainers, t-shirt and a leather jacket. He stood to one side to let the other man through. The latter walked past without any comment and opened the door into the lounge. Gunn continued on his way to compartment number 22. He closed and locked the sliding door, switched off the main light and switched on the light in the en-suite washroom leaving the door slightly ajar so that a thin strip of light illuminated the door to the compartment. He then lay down on the berth fully clothed with his Glock 26 beside him on the shelf by the window.

*

Rezar stopped inside the first class lounge still holding the door handle. "One metre ninety" the text had said. How many other men in this section were as tall as that? After a quick scan of the occupants of the lounge he was certain there was no one as tall as that. Rezar quickly went back through the coupling and just managed to catch a glimpse of the door to the second compartment along the corridor closing. He walked silently along the corridor, his trainers making no noise, and examined the door. It would need a sledgehammer to break through the lock. He returned to the lounge and sat down in one of the empty seats and studied the list of passengers' names in first class. There were only twenty-four. He got up and walked through into the restaurant car; he counted seven. Back to his seat in the lounge; another twelve passengers in the lounge. Nineteen passengers accounted for and if all had caught the train that meant five had retired to their sleeping compartments including one very tall male. He ran his finger down the names; there were only three names that did not appear to be French, German or Russian: a Mr and Mrs Maxwell, a Mr Robertson and a Mr Bradfield. Rezar took his cellphone out of his pocket and studied the photo of John Gunn – a photo that showed him with long hair and a beard. Imagine that same face, clean-shaven with short, dark hair..........he had just walked past Gunn and missed the perfect opportunity to complete his task before the train had even crossed from France to Belgium. 'Merde!' he swore under his breath. It would now have to wait until either breakfast, which was served from seven until the train arrived in Berlin at 09.03, or in the mêlée of passengers getting off the train at the Berlin Hauptbahnhof.

He had no intention of returning to his four berth couchette in standard class which had only one other male occupant whose snoring would ensure that no one else got any sleep. He reclined his seat in the first class lounge and decided to wait for his mark from that vantage point.

*

'Try Stepan again on the radio,' the train driver requested of his co-driver. It had been nearly ten minutes since the warning light had indicated an open door. The regulations stated that there must always be working communications between the cab of the hauling locomotive and the inspector.

'It may be that we were in a bad reception area when you last tried to get him. If you can't raise him then you had better go back and do an inspection to see if any of the doors are not properly secured. See if any of the sleeping car attendants can help. When you find Stepan, ask him if he's had a problem.'

'Very well,' and Petr stopped the process of making coffee, unclipped his radio and tried to contact Stepan, but with no success. 'Right, I'm on my way.' Petr removed a torch from its charging base and unlocked the door leading back past the powerful engine to the coupling. At the coupling he unlocked another door and entered the restaurant car of the Paris/Moscow express. It was now 21.45 and the stewards were clearing away the remains of the evening meal and laying the tables for breakfast.

Petr made his way back through all the coaches, checking each door with the powerful beam from his torch. None of the attendants he met could help him although they had seen Stepan earlier. He eventually reached the tail-end locomotive whose power was controlled by the front engine. The stand-by crew of driver and co-driver would take over from him and Igor at Berlin for the second leg of the route to Moscow, but were now both asleep in the bunks behind the driving cab.

Nothing; Petr quietly closed and locked the door behind him leading to the rear locomotive and retraced his steps meeting only a couple of the passengers and attendants as he made his way back to the front of the train. Once again he shone his torch at the 'slam-shut' closing mechanism of each door. As he approached the locked door leading from standard class into first he pulled the bunch of keys out of his pocket, stepped aside to avoid a passenger coming out of the toilet, fumbled and dropped his keys.

Petr bent down to retrieve his keys and saw that the passenger had trodden in some liquid which had been spilt on the floor leaving a clear imprint of his foot which had then left further footprints as he'd walked away. Petr was about to go back to the standard class lounge and get an attendant to come and clear up the spillage when he paused and shone the beam from his torch on the floor and then tentatively tested it with his forefinger. Blood; and a lot of it. What the hell had happened here to cause that? He shone the torch beam closer and saw that the trail of blood led through the door into the coupling.

Petr unlocked the door and followed the blood trail with his torch. There were smears of blood on the metal plates of the coupling, further smears on the door on the other side of the coupling and then the trail moved to the right, leading to the right-hand 'slam-shut' door which had blood smears on the inside panel and the door handle. It was hardly rocket science for Petr to conclude that someone bleeding copiously had been pushed out of the door – hence the warning signal and lack of response from Stepan's radio.

Petr reached into the side pocket of his driver's uniform and produced a handkerchief. With this he wiped the blood off the door and handle; there were no convenient finger prints......and replaced the handkerchief in his pocket. Perhaps that might be of use to the police? That meant that if Stepan had been pushed off the train, his killer was still on it. Anxious to get the information back to Igor, Petr hurried back to the front of the train. The first class lounge was almost empty; just one passenger in the seats and a couple at the bar. He broke the news as soon as he entered the driving cab.

'I think Stepan's been killed!'

'What d'you mean?'

Peter explained to Igor what he'd found at the junction of the first and standard class sections.

'Stepan always carries that list with him......'

'Of course, he needs it...........'

'No Igor, I know why he needs it.....it...it's just that there's an unlikely looking first class passenger in the lounge asleep in one of the seats with a clip-board just like Stepan's.'

'Right, that means we'll have to stop at Brussels and get the police on the train. Go back and see if he's still in that seat.'

Igor looked at the digital clock on the locomotive's control panel in front of him.

'We'll be there in eighteen minutes,' and he picked up the cellphone and dialled the emergency number for the SNCB control centre at the Gare de Bruxelles Central. He reported the incident and the fact that there was now no inspector on the train although there could well be a murderer. He was told that the train would be diverted from a through line at the Brussels-Midi Station onto one by a platform and that the police would enter the train through his driving cab. He was told to engage the emergency lock which would prevent any of the doors in the coaches from being opened when the train stopped at the station.

Petr reappeared in the cab. 'He's still there.'

CHAPTER 12

Gunn was dreaming; an eerie, echoing voice was trying to tell him something, but the words made no sense. With a jolt he came fully awake, his hand instinctively reaching for the Glock on the shelf by his head. The 'voice' was the train's PA system; he had just caught the tail end of an announcement in Russian. It was repeated in French followed by German and finally English informing passengers that the train would be stopping very briefly in a few minutes time at Brussels-Midi Station to pick up a technical component for the locomotive. Passengers were asked to remain in their compartments or the lounges. Arrival time in Berlin would be on schedule and breakfast would be served from seven in the morning until arrival at Berlin Hauptbahnhof at three minutes past nine.

Gunn glanced at his watch; just after ten. He'd slept soundly for an hour. He swung his legs off the berth, picked up the Glock and pushed it into the ankle holster. He sluiced cold water over his head and face from the tap on the small metal washbasin and then towelled his face and hair dry. The train was now slowing. Gunn pulled back the curtains which revealed that it was moving through the industrial suburbs of a large city which presumably had to be Brussels. The maze of rails and points, glinting under the cold, white halogen lighting gave way to the glass-vaulted dome of the station and the empty platform alongside which the train was about to halt.

Gunn put on his anorak, unlocked the door of his compartment and went out into the corridor locking the door behind him – chastened by a brief recollection of his stupidity in the restaurant.

The train stopped. Gunn went to the end of his 'wagon couchette' and tried the door onto the platform. It was locked. 'Thought so,' he muttered. Even as he turned to make use of the toilet as he was standing right beside it, the train started to move again.

Gunn closed the toilet door behind him and opened the door through the coupling into the first class lounge. As he entered the empty lounge it was as though someone had just pressed the fast-forward button on a digital recorder. A man sitting in one of the aircraft-type reclining seats in the lounge facing him - the same man he'd seen earlier at the coupling - looked up, saw him, checked that there was no one else in the lounge and launched himself at Gunn deftly drawing a knife from inside his left sleeve.

Gunn had no time to draw the Glock. He caught the man's right wrist with his left hand and warded off the man's left-handed karate chop with his right forearm. Then using his attacker's momentum he accelerated it further by dropping onto his back, slamming his right boot into the man's groin which acted as a pivot to catapult him over his head while keeping a vice-like grip on the right wrist. With an audible crack the wrist snapped, the man screamed as he crashed into the bar and the knife disappeared under the lounge seats. In spite of the broken wrist and a broken nose from the bar's brass foot-rail, the man reacted with snake-like speed to try and recover his knife. Gunn grabbed the man from behind with his right arm locked round his neck and with his left hand pulled the man's left arm behind his back and up into a 'full nelson' dislocating his left clavicle. Out of sight of the barman and steward peering out from the staff door behind the bar, Gunn switched his hold to bring his left hand up to the man's head and using both his hands, one on the chin and the other on the side of the man's head he broke his neck. He got to his feet, pushing away the lifeless body of his attacker. Gunn retrieved the knife from under the seat and placed it on the bar in front of the barman and two stewards who were peering out from the partially opened door behind the bar. At the same moment, the door at the far end of the lounge burst open and three armed police entered the lounge followed by one of the train's uniformed drivers.

*

'Hello Miles, Mike Carrington.'

'Yes Mike, what is it?' The phone in the study had rung just as the last of Miles' and Liz's guests were leaving. The secure phone in the study rarely brought good news and this night was to be no exception.

'I had a call from the Ops Centre a few minutes ago to tell me that Sir Marcus Lord is in trouble.'

'What sort of trouble Mike?'

'He left the Mansion House at 11.15 where he was a guest at the Lord Mayor's dinner for that group of financial experts from the G8 Countries. The Ops Centre heard from one of Fiona's guys who was following him and then a brief message that he was also being tailed.'

Miles looked at his watch: 11.45. 'Is his wife at the apartment?'

'Yes.'

'PM know about this?'

'No, not yet, I wanted to speak to you first.'

'There's no confirmation that he's been killed or kidnapped yet?' Miles queried.

'None.'

'Anything from your side of the house, Mike?'

'After our last conversation about this I got Fiona to keep an eye on three people, Sir Marcus Lord, Hamish McGregor, the Chancellor, and Peter Black, the Head of the Stock Exchange.......'

'......and?'

'Tony Baines, one of Fiona's CE4 team, was at the dinner tonight with instructions to ensure that the Governor arrived home safely. We've lost communications with him, but I'm hoping that we'll have some news shortly. I really don't believe that anything more can be done that isn't being done at the moment.'

'I agree; thanks for putting those safeguards in place Mike; please let me know when you get any news.......good or bad,' and Miles ended the call.

'Bad news, Miles?' Liz asked from the doorway.

'Possibly love; I'll sleep down here tonight so I don't disturb you.'

*

Tony Baines had kept a close watch on Sir Marcus Lord throughout the evening at the Mansion House. Having had a lucrative job with Goldman Sachs in the City for three years before he decided that he needed a more active career, he had little difficulty in contributing to the financial aspect of the dinner conversation around him.

When the after-dinner speeches were over and he saw that Sir Marcus was preparing to leave, he left the banqueting hall, went down the stairs to the cloakroom, handed in his ticket and collected his motorcycle leathers and helmet. It took him a couple of minutes to get dressed and transfer his 9 mm Beretta from the shoulder holster inside his DJ to the left thigh pocket of his leathers. He checked the automatic's de-cocker before he went out of the Mansion House, unlocked his 865cc Triumph America, started it and pulled up in the deep shadow some 20 yards from the main entrance to the Mansion House from where he identified the number plate of the Governor's Bentley Arnage official car.

Sir Marcus Lord came out of the Mansion House accompanied by the Lord Mayor. They shook hands and Sir Marcus got into the back seat of the Bentley. Baines pushed back his sleeve, checked his watch – 11.16 – and then pressed the transmit button on the right handgrip and spoke into the integral mike in his helmet. 'Charlie Echo four this is Tango Bravo, time now twenty-three sixteen hours; leaving dinner venue behind official car, over.' The duty operator in the Counter-Espionage section of the Operations Room in Kingsroad House acknowledged the transmission.

Another 50 yards behind Baines' Triumph the 1,000cc engine of a Ducati Superbike rumbled into life. The rider pulled the visor down on his helmet while his accomplice on the rear seat checked the MAC 10, .45 calibre machine pistol before the bike pulled out into the road behind the Bentley and its motorbike escort. The machine pistol was fitted with a Sionic suppressor and slotted into a canvas holster in front of the accomplice's left knee.

Baines made his tail after only 100 yards. Geraint Owen, the driver of the Governor's Bentley, was from CE4 and in direct communication with both Baines and the BID ops centre. Tony Baines pressed the transmit button: 'we've got company......bike behind me......possible drive-by......plan B.....go like the clappers as you enter the underpass...over.'

'Roger out,' was acknowledged calmly by Owen as he removed the Glock 17 from his shoulder holster, placed it in his lap and asked Sir Marcus Lord to tighten his seat belt. Earlier that afternoon Baines and Owen had recced three routes to and from the Governor's apartment in Smith Square. Plan A had been the Strand, Plan B the Embankment and plan C south of the Thames via Blackfriars Bridge. Some 200 yards from the underpass exit onto the embankment, at the junction with Temple Lane, there was a right lane restriction for road works with heavy plant parked alongside the central reservation.

The Bentley took the left fork off Queen Victoria Street round White Lion Hill and down to the underpass at a sedate pace. As soon as the Bentley reached the underpass, blue smoke erupted from the rear tyres as it took off like a rocket, propelled by its 4.4 litre, Cosworth-engineered, supercharged BMW V8 engine. Baines was ready for this move and the Triumph leapt forward, front wheel clear of the road. The Ducati was out of sight on White Lion Hill when the move was made, but was quick to respond. The two or three seconds delay gave Baines the gap he wanted to skid to a halt on the blind side of a large yellow JCB opposite the Temple Lane junction and a gap in the central reservation.

The Ducati howled past Baines chasing the Bentley which was now a clear 400 yards away under Waterloo Bridge. Baines accelerated the Triumph at maximum revs up through the gears in pursuit of the Ducati. Masked by the screaming whine of the high-revving Ducati, its rider never heard the Triumph closing the distance between the two machines. The Ducati was now only 100 yards behind the Bentley, both car and bike weaving in and out of the fairly sparse traffic.

The Ducati's passenger reached down with his left hand and lifted the MAC 10 out of its canvas holster. Baines saw the pistol appear with its elongated suppressor barrel. Time had run out. Any second now a stream of bullets would enter the back of the Bentley, killing or fatally injuring the Governor of the Bank of England. Baines took his left hand off the handgrip, pulled the Beretta out of his thigh pocket and pushed down the de-cocker with his thumb. The Ducati was nearly level with the Bentley.

Tony Baines was some 30 yards behind the Ducati rider when he fired. The shot missed, but must have been close because for the first time the Ducati rider realised that he was being tailed. His accomplice reached behind him with the MAC 10 and sprayed a handful of rounds which hit neither Baines nor any other car or person.

'Enough of this shit!' Baines muttered through gritted teeth and emptied the remaining 14 rounds from the Beretta's magazine at the men on the Ducati. The Bentley and both bikes were fast approaching Westminster Bridge. Baines groaned as he thought that all his shots had missed. He saw the brake lights of the Bentley and he also started to brake for the red traffic lights against them, but allowing traffic from Parliament Square cross onto Westminster Bridge. The Ducati shot straight over the red lights, across the bridge, somehow missing all the traffic, took off as it hit the pavement on the far side of the bridge and disappeared with both men over the bridge parapet into the Thames opposite Big Ben.

*

There was a classic performance of Gallic pandemonium as the Belgian Police and the Russian and French train employees all tried to make themselves heard at the same time. The police wanted to arrest Gunn, while the train driver, the stewards and barmen all tried to volunteer their witness accounts and statements at the same time. Gunn got his breath back while he waited for a moment of calm to evolve out of the chaos. Eventually the Police Inspector approached Gunn.

'Vous parlez Français, Monsieur?'

'Pardon, mais non,' Gunn replied; 'only very bad school French.'

'That is no matter as I and my colleagues all speak your language,' was said with Gallic superiority. 'The train staff say that you suffered an unprovoked assault by this man whose neck was broken when he fell against the bar rail,' and the Inspector indicated with his foot the body of Gunn's attacker.

'That is correct Inspector; the knife he used is on the bar over there. I.........' but Gunn was interrupted by the police Sergeant who spoke rapidly to the Inspector, from snippets of which Gunn gathered that the identity of Gunn's attacker was known. The Inspector turned back to Gunn.

'Your name please?'

'Robert Bradfield.'

'Your passport.' Gunn handed over his passport.

'Why would someone in the Albanian Mafia who is wanted for a number of serious crimes in both France and Belgium - including the murder of the Inspector on this train - attack you?'

'I have no idea. There was no one else here and I suppose he wanted to rob me.'

'Very well.....one of my men will take a statement from you.' The statement was written and signed, the body was removed and the Inspector told him that he could continue his journey to Berlin, but should expect to hear from the British Police on his return to the UK.

It was nearly 11.45 by the time statements had been taken and signed. The train made another unscheduled stop at Liège where the police departed with Rezar Niko's body. As the train moved away from the platform, Gunn got up from his seat in the lounge and walked over to the bar.

'Scotch please, no ice.' Service was instantaneous and he was told there would be no charge.

*

Miles was just making himself comfortable on the sofa in his study when the phone rang.

'Yes Mike.'

'Some good news; Sir Marcus is OK and now back at his apartment. It was an attempted 'drive-by' killing which failed. Our man dealt with the killers at Westminster Bridge.....they and the bike went into the river. The Met Marine Support Unit has recovered the bodies of the men using one of their fast response boats which, fortuitously, was dealing with an incident at the south side of the bridge. Their divers will have the motorbike out of the river soon.'

'The men are dead I presume?'

'Very.....no less than eight bullets in one and four in the other. We have names too; Viktor Bout and Yugo Volkov. The Met know that they work for the Russian Mafia........the Izmaylovskay bratva which has cells in most major European capital cities. The gang has a hand in every type of criminal activity, but its speciality is contract killing. After two failures, it would seem that *Seppuku-kai* has decided to contract out the killing of its victims.'

'So it would seem,' and Miles left the sofa and went upstairs to bed.

*

'Monsieur Kraja?'

'Oui, c'est moi, qui parle?'

'Alain Coblin; Sergeant Coblin at the Headquarters of the Belgian Railway Police in Brussels.'

'I believe that Monet was the greatest of the Impressionists.'

'I would have to disagree; I prefer Van Gogh,' Coblin replied with the correct response for that day. Both the Albanian and Russian Mafias were run with military precision; some gangs had a rank structure, others had adopted the military signals procedure and the use of passwords and codes was universal throughout the gangs and brotherhoods in all the European capitals. What was equally universal was the use of 'moles' throughout the majority of government departments – the police in particular, the financial sector and major business corporations. Neither the Belgian nor the French Police were in receipt of generous salaries, so a regular income from another source was much appreciated.

'And what news do you have for me today?' Kushtrim Kraja, the Don of the Albanian Mafia in Paris asked.

'You have a man known as 'Le Rasoir'?'

'There are many men with that nickname.'

'A man named Rezar Niko was killed on the Paris/Moscow express. The body was removed at Liège and is now in the mortuary below this headquarters.'

'That is an interesting bit of news,' and Kraja ended the call. 'Merde!' was muttered as he dialled a number.

'Bushati.'

'Valmir, I have a job for you. Be in my office in twenty minutes. You will be catching a flight to Berlin.'

'Bien sûr, patron,' and the call was ended.

*

The budget airline 'German Wings' flight 2D 341 from Paris' Orly Airport to Berlin landed at Schoenefeld Airport at 07.58. Valmir Bushati had no hold baggage to collect from the carousel. Kraja had told him that he would be met at the airport by Eduart Kamani who would act as back-up. He would be driving a red Mercedes taxi with the registration B 536 DW. As he arrived at the taxi rank, he identified the taxi which had been parked to one side of the rank with its bonnet raised. He walked across to the taxi.

'Bonjour Monsieur!'

'Guten morgen, besser auf Deutsch.'

The code was correct, the bonnet was closed and ignoring the rude comments shouted across from the taxi drivers who were parked in the rank, Bushati got into the back of the Mercedes. On the back seat was a cardboard box which he opened as the Mercedes moved off. He removed the 9mm Sig-Sauer automatic, pressed the magazine release and ejected all 14 hollow-point rounds into the cardboard box. He then worked the top slide and ejected the round from the chamber. After a careful examination of each of the rounds, he replaced them and inserted the magazine into the grip, chambered the first round and flicked on the safety with his thumb. The automatic went into the right-hand pocket of his anorak and the silencer into the left. Up to that moment not a word had passed between driver and passenger other than the coded greeting. The Mercedes was now making good progress through the Berlin rush hour traffic.

'We will be at the Hauptbahnhof in three minutes. The time is now 08.51 and the train is scheduled to arrive at 09.03. You will have nine minutes to get to platform two. As soon as you have completed your task call me at the number on that card;' a card was handed back over the driver's right shoulder, 'and I will collect you from the taxi rank. The taxi crossed over the River Spree and pulled into the drop-off point in front of the twin glass tower blocks supporting the curved glass dome covering the platforms and track of the Hauptbanhhof. Bushati got out, slammed the door and walked away into the station.

*

In spite of the two unscheduled stops at Brussels and Liège, the Paris/Moscow express pulled into Berlin Hauptbahnhof at 09.02 – one minute earlier than scheduled.

Gunn had slept soundly from shortly after midnight until 7.30 when he had been woken by his sleeping car steward announcing that breakfast was served. Unsure of how quickly the news of the man's death would have reached the Mafia in Paris and what sort of reception might be in store for him at both Berlin and Moscow, he put the Glock 26 into his anorak pocket where it was ready for instant use. He went to breakfast and spent the last hour of the journey in the first class restaurant car. Even after 17 years since the reunification of East and West Germany there was still a marked contrast as soon as the train crossed the now non-existent border from West to East. Gunn checked his watch as the train rattled over the myriad of points at the major rail junction leading into the Hauptbahnhof; 9.01. Smack on time. He drank the last of his coffee, slung his backpack over his shoulder and went into the lounge car to await the arrival at the platform. As he walked into the lounge his cellphone rang.

'Yes.' Only Miles Thompson knew his cellphone number.

'Robert, it's Sandra; we were going to meet in Moscow, but I had to change my plans. I'm at the station waiting for your train. See you shortly, bye,' and the call ended.

So Tanya had decided to change her travel arrangements from catching up with him in Moscow to a meeting during the six hour stop-over in Berlin. Gunn returned the cellphone to his pocket as the train pulled into the station.

CHAPTER 13

Valmir Bushati entered the impressive concourse of Berlin's new mainline station which had only been completed two years previously. Seven minutes before the train arrived. The open-plan concourse resembled a mega-enclosed-mall shopping centre rather than a station. Escalators headed upwards to shopping arcades, multi-screen cinemas, restaurants, a hotel and offices and downwards to the Berlin U-bahn – the underground rail system. Six minutes and he could see no sign indicating the location of Platform 2. He saw the sign 'AUSKUNFT' above a circular counter with four uniformed women providing information to bewildered passengers.

'Bahnsteig zwei bitte Fräulein?' Bushati asked pushing in front of a couple laden with suitcases and backpacks. In reply the girl turned to her right and pointed to a sign which he'd failed to spot. Without thanking her he turned and ran. Three minutes to the arrival of the train.

*

Tanya returned her cellphone to her jeans pocket and then took up position where she could see everybody exiting from the barrier at Platform 2 and anyone going to the meeting point some 20 yards away. Three times a week until the twice-weekly winter schedule started, the Paris/Moscow express stopped at 09.03 at Platform 2. It would leave at 15.15 for the second leg of the journey to Moscow. This provided the passengers with a six hour 'window' in which to do a guided tour of the city or whatever else they wished to do.

This opportunity to tout for trade was not missed by either tour operators or taxis and the exit from Platform 2 was surrounded by agents carrying small placards advertising tours, hotels, restaurants and even a massage parlour which made Tanya chuckle.

As the train pulled into the station, Tanya spotted a new arrival at the barrier. Out of breath and checking his watch, the new arrival pushed his way through the throng of tour, hotel and taxi touts to reach the barrier just in front of her as the train came to a halt alongside the platform. He took a card from his pocket – or perhaps it was a photo, Tanya thought as she moved closer. Yes, it was a photo. She had never met John Gunn and, like the man studying the photo, she had been given a photo of Gunn at her assignment briefing.

The doors on the train opened and the platform soon filled with passengers heading towards the barrier. Tanya was now standing only a yard or so behind the man who had pushed his way through to the barrier at the last minute. He put the photo into the back pocket of his jeans and then put his hand into the left pocket of his anorak and brought out a short black tube which he held under his anorak. Tanya moved so that she could see his right hand which emerged, unseen by the press of people around him, from the right anorak pocket with a black automatic which was quickly concealed under his anorak to be connected to the silencer in his left hand.

*

Gunn had spotted Tanya amongst the crowd waiting beyond the barrier. If there was going to be another attempt to kill him, getting through the hustle and jostle of the greeters and tour touts would offer as good an opportunity as any other. He had just made way for a tractor pulling three loaded trolleys and was toying with the option of hanging back until all the passengers had gone through. A commotion within the crowd of greeters caught his attention. The crowd had separated and pulled back from something which Gunn couldn't see. He tightened his grip on the Glock in his anorak pocket.

*

Tanya glanced up at the approaching crowd of passengers and spotted Gunn, because of his height, at the back of the crowd. She swung her handbag round on its shoulder strap so that it was in front of her, put both hands inside it, connected the silencer to her Smith and Wesson automatic and pushed the safety off. She then purposely stumbled against the man.

'Es tut mir leid, Mein Herr!'

He glanced over his shoulder at the pretty, dark-haired girl behind him.

'Pas du tout, M'meselle,' and turned back towards the approaching passengers, but now Tanya had the photo from his back pocket. It was a photo of Gunn with much longer hair and a beard. The barrier gates opened and the passengers jostled their way out into the station concourse. Gunn was at the back of the crowd with his backpack slung over his shoulder. His eyes were studying the faces of the people surrounding the gates and for just an instant he looked straight at Tanya but gave no hint of recognition. The station staff pushed the crowd of greeters and touts back to let a small tractor come through pulling three trolleys of cardboard boxes. Gunn was now only ten yards from the gate.

The man in front of Tanya was pushed back by the people in front of him as they made way for the tractor. She held her handbag against his spine and pulled the trigger of the automatic twice with her right hand still in the bag. The 9mm ballooning hollow point bullets at point blank range severed his spinal cord killing him instantly. He fell forward onto the people in front of him amid gasps initially and then screams as the Sig-Sauer silenced automatic fell from his hand and clattered onto the concourse paving.

Tanya joined in the general confusion as the touts and passengers nearest to the body pushed back while those who couldn't see what had happened pushed forward to gawp at the man lying face down on the paving. With all eyes focused on the man, Tanya was able to melt away out of the throng of people towards the meeting point. One of the station staff at the barrier knelt down beside the man and felt for a pulse. He shook his head and then unclipped a small radio from his belt and spoke into it.

*

Eduart Kamani left his vantage point on the galleried shop level from where he had had a dress circle view of Bushati's death and the departure of the woman who had shot him. He took the down escalator two steps at a time and followed the woman to the Meininger Hotel. He then returned to the Mercedes in the Hauptbahnhof car park, removed the taxi sign from its roof, changed the number plates and drove to the Meininger Hotel.

*

Green-uniformed German Police seemed to appear from nowhere and cleared away the onlookers from the body lying on the paving. There were still more than fifty or sixty passengers in front of Gunn waiting to leave the platform. Gunn dialled Tanya's cellphone.

'Hello.'

'Thanks, I'm guessing I owe you one. Leave now and then text me with an RV.'

'OK,' and Tanya ended the call.

The police corralled all the people on the concourse side of the barrier for questioning, leaving a channel for the passengers to exit the platform. The police were checking all passports as the passengers went through the barrier. Gunn handed over his passport.

'You are on holiday or business Mr Bradfield?' was asked in perfect English.

'Holiday with my girlfriend.' The policeman looked around.

'And where is she?'

'I hope she's at her hotel where we're planning to meet.'

'I hope so too, Mr Bradfield. Enjoy your holiday in Berlin. I'm sorry that you should have been inconvenienced by this incident,' and his passport was returned to him. As he walked away from the barrier his cellphone buzzed with a text message tone.

'Meininger hotel 9 ella-trebe strasse 100 yds from station left outside stn and left again into ella-trebe str hotel on left. coffee shop.'

There were now five policemen at the scene armed with automatics and machine pistols who were none too gentle in the way they dealt with those awaiting questioning. The wailing sound of approaching police sirens indicated that more were on the way. As Gunn walked away from the scene he felt a chill sweat of apprehension tingling down his spine. Would there be that shout of "halt!" followed by a back-shattering burst of fire from a machine pistol? Perhaps he was letting his imagination conjure up too many ghosts from the past. His assignment was to resolve a war crime and find its perpetrator – if he was still alive. That man was responsible for an act of treachery in a POW camp so heinous that its ramifications now threatened people's lives and the financial stability of the G8 countries. Ghosts or not, Gunn couldn't help recalling a similar scene from The Great Escape. The much-repeated cult film of the mass escape of air force POWs from Stalag Luft III had starred Richard Attenborough in a similar scene at a rail station before being caught by the Gestapo and executed with the other escapees.

Gunn followed the text directions from Tanya and after walking out of the station's main entrance and turning left he immediately saw a square white building with 'MEININGER' in large red letters. He walked through the lobby into the coffee shop and spotted Tanya in a corner booth with no one near her. He sat down opposite her and immediately sensed in her body language how tense she was.

'Thanks again for dealing with that guy. How.....' Gunn paused as a waitress appeared at their table.

'You wish to order sir?'

'Yes please, a coffee for me,' and then he turned to Tanya.

'Yes please, another coffee for me.'

The waitress took Tanya's empty cup and returned to the servery. After a short pause both of them started to speak at once. Gun smiled.

'You go first.'

'I think you were going to ask how I knew that man was planning to kill you.'

'I was, and also why you decided to fly to Berlin rather than Moscow?'

'Second part's easy; surveillance by *Seppuku-kai* agents has been so effective that anything I could do to disrupt that would be good......I reckoned. After the briefing I went back to my flat and then spent twenty minutes on my laptop changing my itinerary.'

'Thank Christ for that!'

'First part's beginner's luck I expect. This man arrived at the barrier out of breath and only as your train stopped at the platform. I had been watching all the other greeters and sales reps and all seemed genuine. He was the first person who looked nothing like a greeter or rep. So I stood close to him and saw him look at a photo which he put in his back pocket. That photo was of you.......you with long hair and a beard. He then took a silencer out of his pocket and fitted it to an automatic which he hid under his anorak. The rest I think you know.' Gunn had let her talk without interrupting. Talking about it had visibly relaxed her and eased some of the stress.

'It sounds too tame to say 'thanks' when you've probably just saved my life, but thanks again anyway. That's the third attempt to stop me since I left London. The second attempt was on the train last night and the first attempt in Paris before I caught the train. Someone really doesn't want me to get to Japan.'

'Who was the man I shot?' Tanya asked.

'No name, but if he's from the same stable as the man I killed last night then it's the Albanian Mafia. The Belgian Police identified the guy on the train immediately...... a guy called Rezar Niko.'

'Does this mean that *Seppuku-kai* is now using other Mafias for its contract killing, having failed no less than three times – I was told at my briefing - to get you in London?'

'Looks like it. Miles warned me about the Albanian and Russian Mafias, both of which have close links with the Japanese *Yakuza*.' Gunn's cellphone vibrated with an incoming call. 'Hello.'

'James...... can you speak?'

'Just a second,' and Gunn covered the cellphone and looked at Tanya; 'James?' he mouthed quietly.

'James Rayner's now the Director of Espionage,' she said quietly and Tanya pointed at herself and shook her head. Gunn nodded.

'Ah!' and Gunn uncovered the cellphone. 'Yes, go ahead, sorry about that, my coffee was being delivered.'

'Are you able to give me a quick up-date?' James Rayner asked.

'I'm in Berlin and will leave at 15.15 this afternoon for Moscow where I should arrive at 20.35 tomorrow. There have been two attempts to stop me; one on the train last night and one this morning on arrival at Berlin. As the Germans have suffered a casualty on that hit list you may decide it's worth speaking to your opposite number in either the BND or the BfV to explain my presence in their country.'

'Got all that. Your back up should meet your train on arrival at Belorusskaya Station.'

'OK...incidentally, the same might apply to the Russians as they have also lost a person on the hit list. Worth speaking to the FSB?' Gunn asked.

'I'll get back to you on both of those within the hour.'

'Thanks,' and Gunn ended the call and turned to Tanya. 'What's your German like?'

'I can get by........you?'

'Ditto........were you planning to come on the train or are you flying to Moscow?'

'Train......I've bought my ticket; Standard Class.'

'Does the ticket have a name on it?'

'No......just the coach and couchette numbers.'

'OK....you won't have missed the CCTV cameras all over the station. The German Police and the BfV......'

'BfV?'

'Bundesamt für Verfassungsschutz.....as usual, a right mouthful in German. That's their equivalent of BID's CE Directorate. They will be studying the tapes of the cameras pointing at the crowd waiting at the barrier to Platform 2. Because they are super efficient they will then compare that with the people they've interviewed to see who's missing. Make sense?'

'Oh shit! Yes, makes a lot of sense; suggestions?'

'Do you have an identity with blonde hair?'

'Yes; Tracy Mason.'

'I told the policeman who checked my passport and ticket that I was meeting my girlfriend. We have to assume that he won't have forgotten that and that he will be there to check passengers returning to the train for the Berlin/Moscow leg. Does that make sense?'

'Again, yes; if I turn up as a single person to board the train with my hair as it is now and the police have been as thorough as you say, I'm going to make their job a lot easier for them,' Tanya agreed chewing her lip.

'Right, go and buy..........'

'It's in my back pack.'

'Terrific...then I suggest that you go up to your room.... what number and what time must you check out?'

'215 and by twelve.'

'Dye your hair and then we'll find a hairdresser to give you a really short hairstyle. Then when we return to the station to board the train we'll act the part of recently united lovers.......I'll even buy you a large bunch of flowers to make it more convincing. OK?'

'OK, meet you back here in an hour,' and Tanya picked up her backpack and left the coffee shop.

✳

'Yes.'

'Bonjour Monsieur.'

'Guten morgen, besser auf Deutsch.' The current day's recognition code was correct.

'Eduart; Bushati's dead. Gunn had a woman as back-up waiting at the Hauptbahnhof. I've followed her to the Meininger Hotel. Gunn has also come to the hotel. She has just gone to her hotel room. Your instructions Patron?'

'Kill both of them!' was almost shouted at Kamani, but Kraja then changed his mind. 'No! Wait! Do you have any one to help you there?'

'Yes, I can get Mergin Daka to meet up with me in a matter of minutes.'

'Good; listen carefully. My aircraft – the twin-engine Cessna Titan, registration Foxtrot five, six, six, eight, is parked up at Schöenefeld Airport waiting to embark the Turkish girls we're bringing to Paris. Jeton Pervishi is flying it with Luka Madhi. We are giving him instructions while I'm talking to you. As soon as you have the woman, take her to Tempelhof Airport.....'

'That's closed now.'

'Yes I know it's closed to the public but it's still used for cargo and some sort of flying club and the runway is in good condition. Jeton will take off from Schöenefeld and then contact air traffic control telling them he has a technical fault and will land at Tempelhof. ATC will object, but he will fake radio problems and land anyway. You will load this woman from BID onto the Cessna and then make yourself scarce with........who was it?'

'Daka.'

'Yes, Daka.'

'And Gunn?'

'Kill him. Have you got all that?'

'Yes Patron,' and the call ended.

*

Gunn glanced at his watch: 11.15. Tanya had been gone for 35 minutes. His cellphone rang with an incoming call.

'Hello.'

'Terry, from the Ops centre. This is urgent. DGSE has intercepted another call at 12 Rue Samson. You are under surveillance at the Hotel Meininger and the intention is to kill you. A team of two – Kamani and Daka - either have kidnapped, or are about to kidnap Tanya and take her to the disused Tempelhof Airport from where she'll be flown to Paris to suffer the same fate as the other trafficked women.........'

'Is that it Terry.....'

'No....wait. The aircraft is a small twin-pin Cessna, registration Foxtrot five, six, six, eight........its also got some Turkish girls being trafficked for the sex trade.'

'Got all that, thanks Terry,' and Gunn ended the call and left the coffee shop. His hand was on the Glock in his anorak pocket, but there was no one in the lobby who took any notice of him. He stopped by the tourist counter. 'The route to Tempelhof Airport, please.'

'It's no longer in use.....'

'Thank you, but I need to go there.'

'Easy sir; road number 96.....right outside this hotel goes south all the way to Tempelhof.........'

'How far?'

'About ten kilometres.'

'Thanks.'

Gunn hurried to the bank of three lifts and entered as soon as the first set of doors opened.

With the exception of the housekeeping lady and her trolley the corridor was empty. He knocked on the door to Tanya's room. There was no reply. Gunn turned to the cleaning woman.

'Please open the door. I have left my key card with my wife.'

'Bitte?' the startled cleaner queried. She was holding the plastic pass key in her hand.

'Oh shit!' and Gunn snatched the plastic card from her hand, pushed it into the slot on the door and opened it. The cleaner shrieked something unintelligible and Gunn entered the room with Glock drawn.

There was no one in the bedroom, and Tanya's backpack was on one of the twin beds. Gunn dumped his back pack beside it on the bed and pushed open the bathroom door.........no one. The basin was full of black hair cuttings and the shelf above with empty plastic bottles of hair dye and toiletries. Back in the bedroom Gunn spotted Tanya's handbag under the bedside table. Gunn opened it. Her purse was still there as was her automatic. Gunn crammed the bag into her backpack ignoring the non-stop tirade from the cleaner.

He turned to leave just as the hotel day manager appeared and added his stream of Teutonic remonstrations to the cleaner's, but his were interspersed with frequent references to 'die polizei'.

'Sorry mate, no time for introductions,' as the man made a half-hearted attempt to restrain him. Gunn struck him clinically with the Glock which ended any further interest in events by the day manager. He picked up both packs and dashed out into the corridor where the cleaner was still shrieking hysterically. Two or three doors had now opened, but quickly closed as Gunn left Room 215 and headed for the stairs. 'Must have only just missed them by minutes,' Gunn muttered as he took the stairs two at a time carrying both his and Tanya's backpacks and hurried out of the back of the hotel into the car park. Even as he did so a red Mercedes erupted out of a slot in the park, rear wheels burning rubber as it smashed through the car park barrier and swung into the road causing a clarion of squealing brakes and blaring horns.

They'd got Tanya.

CHAPTER 14

Two parking slots to the right of the place from which the red Mercedes had shot out of the car park was a bulky Volkswagen Touareg 4x4. Gunn was sure that its male driver would have seen Tanya being man-handled into the Mercedes before its dramatic exodus from the car park. The driver was standing beside the open door dialling a number on his cellphone.

'Just the car I need,' Gunn muttered as he ran across the car park to the 4x4. He pulled his BID ID card out of his pocket and holding it with difficulty in his right hand with the Glock, shouted at the driver of the 4x4. 'Achtung polizei!' It was unlikely that his German or the BID card had much of an effect, but the Glock certainly did and the man stepped away from his car. The key was still in the ignition. Gunn threw the two backpacks across to the right seat, started the diesel engine, shouted 'danke shön!' over his shoulder as he engaged first gear and floored the accelerator, closing the car door as the 4x4 raced across the car park to the road. The exit barrier had already been smashed by the Mercedes and was lying in two pieces which Gunn drove over before turning to his left onto 'road number 96' heading south through the Tiergarten Park.

The traffic was relatively light for lunchtime on a weekday and although Gunn was tempted to floor the accelerator and to hell with the police attention that decision would attract, common sense indicated a different course of action. The last thing that Tanya's kidnappers in the Mercedes wanted to do was to attract the attention of the police. Gunn reasoned that they would drive as fast as possible within the speed limit of 50kph. The man at the tourist desk had said

144

ten kilometres. Gunn glanced down at the SUV's odometer: 51,346. 'OK,' Gunn said aloud, 'so at about 51,355 I should be close.'

He constantly glanced in the rear-view mirror for any green and white police cars, but so far it was almost an empty road behind him in the wooded park. The SUV was doing a shade under 60 kph. As he came out of the park, the road curved to the right at the entrance to a four-lane tunnel which presumably took the bulk of the north/south traffic under the park. The road signs indicated a major T-junction ahead.

'Oh shit, now where the hell does the 96 go?' But even as Gunn cursed, a very clear sign showed that the 96 was a left turn along the City's Landwehr Canal. Lights were in his favour. Over the intersection and take a left. The canal was on his left now as he headed south-east on a dual carriageway. The north-east traffic was on the other side of the canal. His carriageway went under a rail bridge, presumably carrying an over-ground section of the City's U-Bahn onto the left hand side of, and above the canal.

Gunn's eyes were riveted on the road signs, but like the French who marked their roads regularly with identifying road numbers, the Germans did likewise with black numbers on a yellow background. He was still maintaining a speed of just under 60kph, hoping that would not attract any police interest.

Another major intersection lay just ahead. Odometer reading was now 51,350; half way, if the tourist guy at the hotel was accurate. Another road sign appeared. A right turn for '96' heading due south with a right lane filter avoiding the lights onto the new road. There was still very little traffic. Gunn edged his speed up to 70kph. He was on a tree-lined dual carriageway. Red lights at the intersection! Fierce braking as he begged the lights to change. Lights turned to amber; up through the gears again. Odometer reading was now 51,353. Should be nearly there.....large sign........TEMPELHOF – PRIVAT FLUGHAFEN......even he, with his rudimentary German, could understand that.

There in front of him was the red Mercedes! Or was it? A red car had pulled over to the outside lane for a left turn where another sign pointed to the private and commercial airfield. Yes, it was a

Mercedes! It turned across the other lane and into the entrance to the airfield. Gunn had to wait for three cars before he could follow. He saw the Mercedes take a sharp right turn between office buildings and warehousing. Mustn't get too close and spook them.... Gunn forced himself to hold back. The Mercedes turned left round the end of the office block and Gunn followed in the Touareg. In front of him was the wide open expanse of the airfield.

On his left was a half-moon shaped concrete park-up area for aircraft. There were aircraft of all sizes from four-engine Boeing cargo jets to single-engine Pipers and Cessnas. Ahead and to the right were a number of cars and vehicles parked up. The Mercedes had slowed right down and was heading in the direction of those vehicles. As yet there appeared to be no sign of a twin-engine Cessna.

The Mercedes stopped on the edge of the parking area; presumably waiting for the arrival of the Cessna. It was time for action. Gunn drove the Touareg into the car park and parked out of sight of the Mercedes. He reached into Tanya's handbag in the backpack and removed her automatic and silencer which he pushed into the left pocket of his anorak. He opened the door, got out of the SUV and, in a crouch, worked his way along the line of parked cars until he was beside the Mercedes. Now on all fours, he crawled to the back of the car and went round to the passenger's side. The passenger wouldn't have the benefit of vision through the rear-view and side mirrors.

Any second the car could leap forward in a dash to RV with the Cessna. Gunn inched forward until he was beside the right rear back door and eased up off all fours until he could just see into the back of the car. It was empty. She must have been pushed into the boot; makes sense, Gunn thought, in case they'd been stopped by the police. The passenger's window was down and smoke drifted out. He fitted the silencers to both automatics and got to his feet holding the Glock in his right hand and the Smith &Wesson in his left. He stepped forward level with the front window. The bullet from the Glock went through the driver's right ear and blasted the left side of his skull and brain out of the open car window. The passenger nearer to Gunn turned towards him and was rewarded with a bullet from the Smith & Wesson in the centre of his forehead.

Gunn walked round to the driver's side of the Mercedes and removed the key from the ignition and opened the boot. Tanya was bound with tape and cable ties and with masking tape across her mouth. Gunn lifted her out of the boot and sat her on the ground with her back against the car while he eased off the tape around her mouth.

'Thanks, John.'

'I told you I owed you one,' Gunn smiled as he removed the tape from her legs. 'Bugger, I need something sharp to cut these ties.' He looked in the boot, lifted the carpeted floor panel, exposing the spare tyre and tool kit, and removed the pliers which made short work of the cable ties. 'Can you stand up?'

'Think so.....circulation's returning to my legs with lots of pins and needles....ooh!.....OK....that's it.'

'Right, just stand there as you get your circulation back.' Gunn went round to the driver's side, dragged the man out of the car and over to the parked cars where he dumped him between two cars. He then did the same with the passenger. Tanya was massaging her legs and looking better by the second. Gunn gave her the Smith & Wesson automatic.

'I fired it once.' She took the automatic, removed the silencer and put it in her anorak pocket.

'What now, John?' she asked as he closed the car boot.

'Get into the front passenger seat and I'll tell you what's going to happen. Fit for action?'

'Damn right I'm fit and fucking mad at myself for being caught like that. Thanks again,' and Tanya got into the Mercedes and shut the door. Gunn got into the driver's seat and closed his door.

'Now we wait and I'll tell you what happens next.'

*

Miles Thompson walked into James Rayner's outer office. Tricia, his PA, indicated that he should go through into the Espionage Director's office.

'Hello James. Would it be an inconvenient moment for me to drop by for an up-date on Gunn's progress across Europe?'

'No, you've just saved me from the long walk along the corridor to your office.' James Rayner glanced at his watch; 12.45. 'Tricia, could we have some........' but even as he spoke, she appeared with two coffees. Both men took their coffees and sat on either side of the low coffee table. 'Tanya changed her travel arrangements and decided to meet up with Gunn in Berlin.....at the station on his arrival. I'm not sure why she did this, but she probably saved his life as the Paris-based Albanian Mafia had sent an assassin to kill him.'

'Has this come from Gunn?' Miles asked.

'No, the DGSE has a tap on the phone at 12 Rue Samson in Paris and has been feeding information to our Ops Centre as soon as they get it. Gunn dealt with another of their contract killers on the train. Tanya spotted the man waiting for Gunn at the barrier in Berlin and dealt with him, but was identified by the assassin's back-up. She was kidnapped from her hotel next to the station by the Mafia and the last we know of that is that Gunn was going to follow the Mafia's car to the old Tempelhof Airfield – famous for the Berlin Airlift – but now used for commercial cargo flights and an aero club.'

'Let it run, send more back-up or get them back to start again?'

'I'm inclined to let it run, Miles. This really is Tanya's baptism of fire. We need answers on this Japanese *Yakuza* threat to the G8 countries and while *Seppuku-kai* is focusing its attention on preventing Gunn from getting to Japan it may make our task of protecting their published targets easier.'

'A cynical but realistic assessment; I'll go with that, but please keep me in the loop if we need to send in the cavalry. Thanks for the coffee,' and Miles got up and returned to his office.

*

'You told me that you would be able to confirm the death of this man Gunn twelve hours ago. I have heard nothing and I wish to know what has happened,' Ichiro Iwakami demanded in his call to the Don of the Albanian Mafia in Paris.

'The contract you gave us is proving not only more costly financially, but also in the lives of my men. I don't believe that you were totally honest when you asked me to accept this contract. Two of my experienced men have now been killed by this man Gunn. If you want me to continue with the contract and provide you with three young Caucasian virgins as part of it then the price has just doubled. I will retain the 500,000 Euros you have already deposited in my Cayman Islands account, but the contract is now two million Euros; a million now and a million when Gunn is dead. You will transfer another 500,000 Euros to my account to make up the one million deposit. When Gunn is dead you can send over your company aircraft and we will provide you with the virgins in exchange for the balance of another million Euros. Is that clear?'

'This is disgraceful extortion.......we....we....had a contract,' Iwakami stuttered.

'Yes, you're right Ichiro, it is extortion and that's what I'm bloody good at. Take it or leave it.'

'Very well then, I will transfer the 500,000 Euros now and you will tell me when Gunn is dead. Yes?'

'Of course, I shall be heading south so divert your company Learjet to an airport on the south coast,' and Kushtrim Kraja ended the call on his landline and then dialled another number on his cellphone.

'Fatos.'

'How many have we got in the warehouse at the moment?'

'Eleven, Patron.'

'And the youngest?'

'There are three aged between twelve and fifteen.'

'Virgins?'

'The fifteen year old is a virgin but the other two have been used by the men, Patron.'

'Make sure the fifteen year old remains a virgin.'

'Very well, Patron.'

'Are those three we are preparing ready for the auction?'

'Very shortly, Patron.'

'Good,' and the Don ended the call.

*

'Before we do anything else we need to get the two backpacks into this car,' and so saying Gunn got out of the Mercedes, removed the two packs from the SUV and threw them onto the back seat of the Mercedes.

'OK....time for explanations; any minute now a twin-engine Cessna should make an emergency landing here. It's taken off from the main international airport at Schönefeld with some girls. These girls are being taken to Paris to be sold to the highest bidder as part of the Mafia's human trafficking for the very lucrative sex trade. You were destined to become a part of that once you had been 'prepared'..........'

'What sort of preparation?' Tanya asked.

'Your brain scrambled with drugs and then your body sold to the highest bidder.......the Arabs, Chinese, Koreans, Japanese and Africans are particularly partial to young Caucasian girls. Life expectancy.....say a couple of months........until abused, raped, battered and beaten to indulge the warped sexual fantasies of these creatures, the girls are thrown onto the scrap heap as drug-addicted wrecks, commit suicide or are murdered.'

'Yuk.......that was too close for comfort.'

'Not only young girls and women, but young boys as well......... highly prized in the Middle East.'

'Can't something be done to stop it?'

'Very difficult...........' Gunn scanned the skies for any sign of the Cessna........'you see it's much easier than drug dealing and more profitable than identity theft. What's more, the girls are available everywhere.'

'What do mean John.....available?'

'Any idea how many girls go missing or run away of their own volition each year in London alone?'

'Hundreds I expect.'

'Ten thousand.......in London alone....now tell me what happened in the hotel while we wait.'

'I'd just finished dyeing and cutting my hair when there was a knock on the door. I stupidly thought it was you. God! What a cretin! I won't make that mistake again. I opened the door and the rest you know. What happens when this plane arrives?'

'The pilot will be expecting a red Mercedes to drive up to the aircraft so we will oblige him. He will be keen to take off as quickly as possible before the police, customs or air traffic control can inspect the contents of the Cessna.'

'Do you have to climb onto a wing to get into this plane?'

'Fairly certain 'no'; if it's carrying four girls it must have at least that number of seats for passengers. I think that model has about eight seats and a door in the fuselage........probably on the port side.'

'And then?'

'I'm pissed off with being used as some sort of coconut in a fairground shy with these Japs and Mafia hoods taking pot shots at me. It's time to turn the other cheek. I'm no Sir Galahad, but I would like to throw a spanner in the Mafia's sex trafficking. You don't have to go along with this Tanya....in fact, if you want to bail out now, please do; very understandable. My investigation of a war crime is a personal matter which our new boss has sanctioned. It's waited 65 years so it won't harm to wait a little longer.'

'You're planning to go to Paris aren't you?' Tanya stated it.

'I am.....you?'

'You try and stop me! My flesh is still creeping from the mauling I got from those two hoods........look! is that the plane?' and Tanya pointed.

'Could well be....registration will be Foxtrot, five, six, six, eight.... usually on the tail-plane.' Gunn started the Mercedes. 'I'll approach the plane from the rear port side so that the crew don't see you. I'm expecting the co-pilot to come back from the cockpit to open the door and help with loading you into the plane. Do you have that silencer?'

'Yes, I put it back in my bag.'

'Right, fit it and let me have it.' Tanya reached into the back, removed her bag from the backpack, fitted the silencer to the Smith & Wesson and then gave it to Gunn. 'When we stop, I'll get out of the car and come round to your side. You'll pretend to be drugged. I'll heave you out of the car and walk you up to the boarding steps.........they fold out automatically when the aircraft door is opened. I'll take out the co-pilot and then go forward and deal with the pilot. I'll leave you with the girls.....I've no idea what state they'll be in. Questions?'

'None......oh yes, one: are you going to fly the plane to Paris?'

'I am......is that a problem?'

'No.....I was half way through my PPL when I applied to join BID. I've been solo on a Cessna 152 if that's any help.'

'Damn right it helps........he's on his down-wind run now. I'll move a bit closer so that the pilot can see the Merc.' Tanya was shielding her eyes from the low Autumn sun.

'The registration definitely has an 'F' at the beginning.'

The small plane banked steeply to starboard at the down wind end of the runway and started its run in. Gunn drove the Mercedes further towards the runway. The Cessna landed, quickly came to a halt and then turned through 180° and taxied back so that it was ready to take off as soon as its new passenger was embarked.

Gunn drove onto the runway, staying to the right rear of the Cessna. The registration was correct. The small aircraft reached the runway threshold and turned to port through 180° into the wind. As it turned Gunn was able to confirm that the passenger door was on the port side immediately behind the trailing edge of the wing.

'When I drag you out of the car, put your hands behind your back as though they're tied.' Gunn reached into the driver's side door pocket and removed a duster. He leant over and tied it around Tanya's head as a gag. 'Right here we go, don't forget to throw the backpacks into the plane.'

Gunn got out and went round to Tanya's side. He opened the door and, none to gently, dragged Tanya out. Then, supporting her as though she was drugged, he approached the aircraft door.

'Open the sodding door!' Gunn muttered as they got closer. The inset handle on the door turned and it opened releasing the boarding steps. The man in the aircraft had to stoop because of the lack of headroom. Gunn and Tanya were now at the foot of the boarding steps. As the man reached out to drag Tanya into the Cessna, Gunn pulled the silenced Smith and Wesson out of his pocket and shot him twice through the heart. The co-pilot was thrown back into the fuselage followed by Gunn who walked over him to be confronted by the frightened faces of four young girls. Speed was now vital.

He smiled at the girls and walked quickly to the curtain screening off the cockpit. The pilot shouted something to his co-pilot which Gunn failed to understand so he made what he hoped was a suitable Gallic non-committal noise, pulled back the curtain and shot the pilot in the back of the neck. He then reached over, removed his earphones, undid his seat harness and dragged him out of the cockpit. Amazingly, having been ignored by whoever owned and controlled the airfield since their arrival, Gunn now saw a vehicle approaching as he dragged the pilot out of the cockpit. Tanya had closed the door.

'Time to go. You OK back there?'

'No problem.'

'Ready for take off?'

'All ready.'

Gunn clambered into the left hand seat, grabbed the check list from the door pocket and glanced at those serials that he knew were vital to check. Although not familiar with the Cessna, he had enough experience to get it safely into the air. The warning panel showed no red lights and the engine gauges all indicated in the green sector. He checked that the flaps were extended, released the brakes and pushed the throttles forward. The vehicle driving towards the Cessna swerved to one side of the runway as the aircraft raced towards it. Gunn held the aircraft down for some 400 yards and then eased back on the control column. The Cessna Titan left Tempelhof Airfield below as it climbed away to the west.

CHAPTER 15

'You aren't going to believe this,' Tanya said as she climbed into the co-pilot's seat.

'What's that?' Gunn asked as he spread out the flight chart on his lap after engaging the autopilot.

'That lot in the back thought that they were being flown to Paris to train as fashion models. They said that there was a competition and they were the winners.'

'It's so bloody easy, isn't it.......this craving for the so-called fifteen minutes of fame......these dumbed- down TV talent shows and the wretched 'celeb' culture; are they German?'

'No. They're all Turkish, but speak German fluently and a bit of English, so we managed. Their parents came to work in Germany from Turkey in the seventies and eighties as 'Gastarbeiters' – doing all the hard manual labour to rebuild the great German fatherland ....or whatever.'

'Are they alright?.....and what did you do with the bodies?' Gunn asked as he alternated his questions to Tanya with responses to the German Air Traffic Control. He had been asked about the diversion from his declared flight path from Schönefeld to Paris Orly via the beacons at Frankfurt, Luxemburg and Reims. He explained that there had been a problem with the warning light for the fuselage door, which was a false alarm, but requested reactivation of his flight plan and an altitude ceiling of 5,000 feet. The request had been granted reluctantly and he'd been given the frequency to speak to Frankfurt ATC.

'I told them you were a policeman.....sorry I couldn't think of anything more heroic than that......poor mites. One of them can't be more than twelve or thirteen.....barely out of puberty and the eldest is no more than sixteen. The real tragedy is that this was done with the full support of their parents who thought their daughters were going to earn lots of money as fashion models. Oh yes, the bodies, I dragged them to the tail and pushed them into two seats and moved the girls forward behind us. What do we do when we get to Orly?'

'Been thinking about that. How does this sound? For starters we're not going to Orly.....there'll be police and Christ knows what other bureaucracy waiting for us there. No, I intend to put this plane down in the countryside south of Paris and then dial 112 on my cellphone and let the French Police get involved in sorting out the young girls and the bodies. I'll back that up by contacting Miles so that he can inform the DGSE what has happened. I don't intend to tell Miles at this stage what my plans are for the Albanian Mafia in Paris.'

'What time will we get to wherever you find a place to land this Cessna?'

'It's about 500 miles....' Gunn paused as he glanced at the fuel gauge. 'We have a full load of fuel.....we're flying at 230mph......so let's say no longer than three hours. I have no weather report so have no idea of head or tail winds, but with a lot of luck we should be there by five giving me plenty of daylight to put this machine down safely.'

'Would it be worth speaking to Miles before the French Police?' Tanya suggested.

'Probably....I'll do that,' and then Gunn was called by Frankfurt ATC.

"Foxtrot six eight, switch to one three five decimal eight for Reims ATC."

'One three five decimal eight, Foxtrot six eight, thanks and goodbye,' Gunn changed frequencies and turned to Tanya. 'Here, take this cellphone. Miles' number is the only one in the contacts.

See if you can get him and then I'll speak.' Tanya scrolled to the contacts and then dialled.

'Hello.' Tanya handed the cellphone across to Gunn.

'Thanks for the warning from DGSE. I have my backup with me and we're on our way back to Paris. I'm flying the Albanian's plane. I have four girls who were destined for the warehouse in Paris. My flight plan is for Orly, but I don't intend to land there and will look for a suitable site south of Paris. I've decided to pay a visit to the Albanians unless you order me not to do so. I will then continue with my previous mission. It was my intention to abandon the plane and then phone the police to come and take care of the girls and the bodies of the pilot and co-pilot. Are you able to get any help from our Gallic friends.'

'Got all that. How long 'til you land?'

'Hour and a half.'

'I'll call you back,' and Miles ended the call.

'I thought you said you weren't going to tell the boss about the visit to the Albanian Mafia.'

'Changed my mind........probably because I detected a certain lack of enthusiasm for my macho bravado,' Gunn replied with a smile.

'Possibly.........I'll go back and see how the girls are,' and Tanya undid her belt and clambered back into the back of the Cessna.

*

Miles Thompson ended the call from Gunn and buzzed his PA.

'Yes Miles.'

'Angela, please get me Pierre Brouhard, Director of the French DGSE on 'secure'.'

'One moment,' and she dialled the direct line and then spoke in French to Brouhard's PA at 141, Boulevard Mortier in Paris. 'The Director's on the line now, Miles.'

'Bonjour Pierre, comment ça va?'

'Ca va bien, Merci, Miles. And what can I do for BID today?'

'Pierre, you have already been most helpful with the timely information you've sent us from Rue Samson. With the information you gave us that situation has developed and I have an agent flying a twin-engine Cessna from Berlin to Paris registration - F5668. The Cessna is either already in French airspace or will be very shortly. The plane is the property of the Albanian Mafia. My agent has killed the pilot and co-pilot. The plane was due to deliver four girls for the Mafia's sex trafficking who were abducted in Berlin. On the plane is another of my agents – a woman – who had been abducted by the Mafia. It is my agent's intention to land the plane to the south of Paris and then contact the police to deal with the girls and the bodies of the pilot and co-pilot. This operation has all been a part of BID's involvement with Interpol's coordinated plans to find the killers of your Richard Perrigot, Russia's Lazarenko and Germany's Mayerling and to prevent any further killing. Incidentally, an attempt was made on the life of the Governor of the Bank of England last night by a member of the Russian Mafia who we believe was under contract to *Seppuku-kai*. Any advice you can give me on a landing site for the plane and any other help would be gratefully received. The plane is an hour and a half away from Paris.'

'Thank you Miles; then we have no time to waste. I will call you back in no more than five minutes. Au revoir,' and Pierre Brouhard ended the call.

*

The ring tone on Gunn's cellphone made them both start. Tanya picked it up and answered, recognising Terry Holt's voice from the Operations Centre. She held the co-pilot's marker crayon over the plastic millboard.

'You are cleared to land on the airfield at Bretigny-sur-Orge. Location is 48° 35' North, 02° 20' East. The frequency of the outer beacon is 438.5. It's a military airfield. You will be met by a BID friend. Officials will take care of your passengers. You are cleared for follow up action as there is currently insufficient evidence to secure a conviction. Questions?'

'Wait.........' Tanya turned the millboard towards Gunn who read it and shook his head. 'No questions,' and she ended the call.

'Here,' and Gunn passed the chart across to Tanya. 'See if you can find that airfield, but it looks as though

Miles has done a good job with his opposite number at the DGSE which means we might well get some help from French ATC.' Even as he spoke, Gunn was interrupted by a call on the radio.

'Foxtrot 5668 this is France ATC.'

'Foxtrot 68 - go ahead.'

'Squawk on 340.5.'

Gunn switched the transponder to that frequency and provided France ATC with the signal it needed to identify the Cessna.

'We have you Foxtrot 68. Remain at flight level five. Once you clear the Reims beacon turn left on 236°. That flight path will take you to the east of Paris and clear of traffic at Orly. You will cross the Seine at Corbeil-Essonnes. Turn right on 266° and you are then ten kilometres from Bretigny-sur-Orge. Contact Bretigny tower on 39.5. I say again, the airfield beacon is 438.5.'

'Foxtrot 68,' Gunn acknowledged the instructions.

'Got it,' Tanya announced. 'And that Corbeil-Essonnes place on the Seine. 'What are your plans when we get to Paris?'

'Much simpler now that we've been given the green light from both BID and DGSE. A lot will depend on what we hear from Bruno Lauriant – BID's in-country agent in Paris - and I expect that he's the 'friend' who'll meet us at this airfield. Whatever we do needs to be done quickly. The Mafia is bound to have people meeting the Cessna at Orly to maintain the image of a fashion competition. I've no idea if the pilot would have contacted Rue Samson by cellphone during the flight, but we have to assume that he would have and that the Mafia will know that something has gone wrong. The longer it takes us to get to Paris the more time the Mafia has to cover its tracks.'

'What'll they do with all the girls in the warehouse?'

'Again, we have to assume that they have contingency plans to evacuate both the warehouse and the building in Rue Samson at short notice. They probably have another building, or buildings, not too far away where they can shift everything.'

'Doesn't sound very promising.' Tanya was unable to keep the disappointment out of her comment. Gunn glanced across at her. She now had a bleached blonde 'gamin' hairstyle which suited her features. But it failed to hide the grim determination to exact revenge to make up for her perceived failure in her hotel room.

The Cessna passed over the Reims beacon and Gunn changed course to 236°. 'Should be about 80 miles now to Bretigny and 25 minutes to go. Would you like to do your stewardess bit and let the girls know that we'll be landing shortly?'

'Sure,' and Tanya climbed out of her seat and went back to the four girls.

*

'Damn! Damn! Damn! What the fuck has gone wrong now?'

Kristi Fatos knew from bitter experience that to volunteer an explanation when the Don was in one of his explosive rages would only invite retribution on himself. Kushtrim Kraja was pacing back and forth in his office, furious that he had heard nothing from his pilots or from Kamani.

'How many men have we lost in less than 24 hours?' Kraja rounded on his deputy. 'How many?' he shouted.

'We don't know yet about the pilots or Eduart and Mergim,' was offered hoping to appease the Don's rage, but if anything it made him even more furious.

'For Christ's sake who is this fucking man 'Gunn'?' The shouted question was rhetorical and it would have been an unwise deputy to offer an answer. 'I've now lost eight men because not one of them was capable of putting a fucking bullet in the head of a British agent.' Kraja stopped pacing and glared at Fatos who was now too terrified to offer anything in case he suffered the same fate as had happened at least once before to a colleague. The man had misjudged the Don's rage and had replied with a flippant suggestion. Kraja had whipped out an automatic from the drawer in his desk and shot the man.

'I await your orders Patron,' Fatos replied meekly.

As quickly as rage had engulfed Kraja, it now vanished. He sat down at his desk and looked at Kristi Fatos as though he hadn't noticed him before.

'How quickly can you be ready to move?'

'An hour and half..........'

'Have the girls ready to move in 45 minutes. I will get Marku and Bekim to clear this building. You take Leutrim and Agron to help you. Now get out of here!'

*

Gunn switched the radio frequency to 39.5 and contacted the control tower at Bretigny-sur-Orge Airfield. He was told to descend to 3,000 feet. Gunn eased back on the throttles and pulled out the flip-chart of pre-landing checks from a pocket in the instrument panel as Tanya reappeared.

'They're all strapped in back there,' she told Gunn as she secured her own harness. He handed her the flip chart.

'About eight minutes to our final turn onto 266° as we cross the Seine.'

'Foxtrot 68 this is Bretigny tower, descend to 1,000 feet, runway 25.' Gunn acknowledged and Tanya began the check list with "carburettor heat to on" followed by "flaps to 17°" and ending with "landing gear down". The Cessna crossed the Seine, turned onto 266° and then lined up to land in a south-west to north-east direction on runway 25. Even as the Cessna's landing gear touched the threshold of the runway at Bretigny-sur-Orge, Gunn saw five or six vehicles move out from the airfield buildings to meet them on the taxiway.

'Let's hope this is a friendly greeting party as I don't fancy a night in a French jail,' Gunn commented as he applied reverse thrust to the props and eased forward on the throttles. A yellow guide buggy separated from the other vehicles as the Cessna turned off the runway onto the taxiway and took up station in front of the Cessna leading it in the direction of two large hangars. The other vehicles followed in convoy behind. As they approached the hangars the doors on the nearer one opened. It was empty except for a police

Alouette helicopter parked up on the right side of the hangar. The buggy led the Cessna into the hangar and then with the signal of crossed batons Gunn was told to shut down the engines.

Tanya was already in the aft portion of the Cessna and as it came to a halt inside the hangar she released the catches on the door and swung it open. First up the steps as soon as they touched the concrete floor of the hangar was a man of medium height and build with crew-cut dark hair who introduced himself to Tanya as Bruno Lauriant before heading towards the cockpit. The French Gendarmerie and Air Force Police officers waited at the foot of the steps as Tanya guided the four young girls out of the Cessna to a woman police officer who led them to a minibus. Two ground handling Air Force personnel had already opened the baggage hatch of the Cessna and removed the pathetically sparse girls' personal possessions which were loaded onto a trolley and followed the girls to the minibus.

Gunn climbed out of the cockpit and greeted BID's in-country agent who, not unsurprisingly, spoke perfect English. Before leaving the Cessna and dealing with 'French officialdom' waiting at the foot of the steps Gunn impressed on Bruno Lauriant the urgency of moving quickly if there was to be any hope of retaining the element of surprise.

'That is not a problem, John. France's equivalent of our Joint Intelligence Committee has been urging the Government to take more positive action to curtail the activities of both the Albanian and Russian Mafias in France. Sadly, the DGSE has had to operate with their hands tied.'

'By what?' Gunn asked picking up his and Tanya's backpacks.

'Police corruption; the police force is riddled with moles.......the pay is not good and the bribes that are offered by the Mafia make an enormous difference to the quality of life of a policeman's family. It is now so bad that the Mafia hierarchy is aware of police strategy even before the Inspector General and his senior police officers.'

'How long will it take to get through that bunch out there,' and Gunn nodded in the direction of the group of officials gathered outside the Cessna.

'Just as long as it takes to get you and Miss Kazakova to that helicopter,' and Bruno pointed to the dark blue Alouette........that will get you to your target in the St Denis District in less than ten minutes. Problems?'

'None.......many thanks.'

'My pleasure,' and Bruno went down the steps ahead of Gunn, collected Tanya and led them to the Alouette where the pilot had already commenced the engine start-up process. Gunn gave Tanya her backpack and the two of them climbed into the back of the helicopter. The Observer in the front left seat turned round as soon as they'd fastened the seat belts and handed each of them a headset on an extension lead.

'We will be landing on a football pitch just 100 metres to the north of the Stade de France and just south of the Canal St Denis.... many helicopters land there so it will not cause any interest in that area of St Denis. You will be less than a kilometre from the Rue Samson. Here is a map of the area,' and the Observer handed back to Gunn a section of a Paris street map. 'You will see that I have marked the house in the Rue Samson and the warehouse in the Passage Meunier. It would only take you three or four minutes to walk there, but our Chief thought you might need a car. At the west end of the football pitch you will find a black Peugeot 308 – sorry, no Aston Martins were available!' was said with a chuckle.

Gunn couldn't quite detect whether the French Police thought that the whole episode was a grand joke or whether it was just good humoured camaraderie. He could just remember enough of his French to remark 'quel domage!' with the appropriate expression which produced chortles of laughter over the headset.

'This is the number plate for the car and the keys will be in the ignition.' Gunn was handed a slip of paper with a Paris registration plate written on it. 'Bonne chance mes amis!' and with that cheerful greeting the pilot clutched in the rotor and taxied the helicopter out of the hangar and onto the airfield apron.

CHAPTER 16

There was chaos inside the warehouse in the Passage Meunier. The place had once been a brothel and had been divided into the maximum number of cubicles that could fit into the building without making it too claustrophobic for the fee-paying clients brought in off the street by the girls. Even so, the thin fibre-board walls between each cubicle ensured that everyone could enjoy the grunts, groans and squeals of real or pretence orgasms from both sides. That occupancy seemed harmless compared to the misery and degradation of the present one.

There were 11 young girls in the building – their ages ranging from just 12 to 19. They covered the spectrum of ethnic backgrounds – Black, Caucasian, Asian, Chinese, Arabic and Indian. Those from India and China had been willingly sold by the parents; had they not been sold they would probably have been killed and their bodies thrown on the vast rubbish tips in both countries or put to work in the filthy brothels of Kolkata, Mumbai, Beijing and Shanghai. The others had been abducted or tricked into thinking that they were going to a fashion shoot or party. They were all drugged with various addictive amphetamines and Class A drugs. Of the 11, three had already taken their own lives with heroin overdoses and their pathetically thin and wasted little bodies lay in their own sweat, blood, body fluid and excrement on filthy soiled beds. Others lay naked on their beds where the Mafia, of both sexes, would make use of them whenever they wished. Then there were the select few; these were really very pretty young girls with good figures who were being prepared for discreet auctions at secret addresses where they would become the property of the highest bidders. Among the latter, potential bidders included politicians, financiers, corrupt African and South American dictators and Arab sheiks. They were drugged, but not nearly as heavily as the others and any member of the Mafia caught messing around with any of this select group risked instant death.

Parked outside the warehouse was a large panel truck with the commercial logo of PNEUS GUILBERT stencilled on both sides. The truck was backed right up to the warehouse to conceal what was being loaded into the back from prying eyes. In the parallel street of Rue Samson everything possible in the way of incriminating evidence was either being burned or stuffed into plastic sacks and then loaded into the back of a Nissan Patrol 4x4.

For the third time Kraja phoned Fatos; 'for Christ's sake how much longer will it take to get those fucking women into the lorry?'

'What do we do with the bodies?'

'Leave them you cretin! There're a hundred of those a day in Paris overdosing in squats and derelict buildings. How much longer?'

'Ten minutes max, Patron.'

'Phone as soon as you're ready to leave.'

'OK Patron........' but Fatos was speaking to a dead phone.

Kraja's landline phone rang. He was in two minds whether to pick it up or rip the lead out of the wall socket and smash the phone. He picked up: 'yes.'

'Phoenix from the Prefecture of Police on the Île de la Cité; I'm on my cellphone at the Quai d'Orsay.'

'Monet.'

'No, Van Gogh.' The authentication was correct.

'What is it?'

'I have no details, but I believe that your place in St Denis is about to be raided.'

'You have just confirmed what I already suspected,' and Kraja slammed down the phone splitting it in two and then threw it across the room as he ripped the line out of the socket. 'Merde! merde!

merde! Come on all of you. Time has run out. Down to the car. Fatos!'

'Yes Patron.'

'Phone Marku and tell him we're leaving. Tell him if he doesn't come with us now he'll be spending the rest of his life in la Santé Prison.' The phone call was made, the last two plastic sacks were shoved into the back of the Nissan and the SUV pulled out of its parking slot into the Rue Samson driven by Fatos with Kraja and Bekim as passengers. The panel truck slotted in behind the SUV in the Rue Lorget driven by Marku with Leutrim and Agron as passengers and in convoy the two vehicles headed for the St Denis Porte de Paris and the autoroute south.

*

The pilot of the police Alouette had taken a flight path that went in a curve out to the west of Paris over the northern bend of the Seine so that his Observer could point out the Rue Samson and the parallel Passage Meunier before they landed on the football pitch next to the Stade de France. The helicopter had just done a right turn over the Canal St Denis onto a southerly bearing for the run-in over Rue Samson to the football pitch when the Observer interrupted his monologue guide of St Denis.

'They are leaving the warehouse!.....and the house in Rue Samson,' was added as the helicopter dipped and increased speed. 'We are getting this from the tap on the land line. Une taupe...... how do say in English please?'

'A mole,' Tanya offered.

'Yes that's it...a mole at the Préfecture has warned them of your visit. Look! That is the warehouse with that lorry outside at the back and that is the house in Rue Samson......the one with the red roof.' The pilot spoke rapidly in French on the intercom to his Observer who then turned back to Gunn and Tanya. 'We will drop you now at the football pitch and then we will follow where these people go. That is OK?'

'That's fine. Thanks.' Gunn identified the lorry outside the warehouse and as the helicopter passed over it and gave an angled view of the side of the vehicle he saw the logo of PNEUS GUILBERT.

The helicopter made a fast descent onto the football pitch and the moment the tricycle undercarriage touched the ground, Gunn and Tanya baled out with their backpacks, ran clear of the rotor, waved and ran for the car park to collect their car.

Exactly as briefed by the Observer, the Peugeot 308 was there and the keys were in the ignition. The backpacks were thrown into the back of the car. Gunn got into the driving seat, handed the little street map across to Tanya and drove out of the car park. Tanya guided him under the autoroute onto the dual carriageway north to the Porte de Paris where they turned left into the Rue Lorget.

'That's it,' and Tanya pointed at the street sign of Passage Meunier, 'and there's the warehouse.'

'Right, we do this by the book. No heroics, especially by me. We have no idea if they've left anyone behind or if the place is booby-trapped. Full magazine?' Tanya nodded. 'Let's do it!' and the two jumped out of the car and burst through the unlocked Judas gate in the roll-down metal warehouse door. Gunn went through first covered by Tanya. Room by room and cubicle by cubicle the two of them first cleared the building. There was no one. They paused at the point where they started, both visibly shaken by the tragic sight of the three dead girls in the cubicles.

'We'll come back to this,' Gunn said through gritted teeth, 'but we'd better clear the other building first. Ready?' Tanya nodded. Gunn led the way out of the warehouse on the other side, across a deserted passageway between the rows of houses and into the back of 12, Rue Samson. Again the door was unlocked confirming the hurried exit they'd seen from the helicopter. The interior of the Mafia headquarters told the story of the hurried departure.......papers scattered on the floors, even an abandoned Tec 9 sub-machine pistol under a desk and drawers full of 9mm ammunition.

'Right, back to the warehouse after I've made this call,' Gunn said, dialling the number.

The call was to Bruno Lauriant. Gunn briefed him on what they'd found in St Denis and told him that the police helicopter was following the lorry which had left just before their arrival. He finished by telling him of the grim scene inside the warehouse and stating the urgent need for a forensic scenes-of-crime team. He ended the call and turned to Tanya.

'C'mon....let's get it over with. There's just an outside chance that one of the girls might have been able to leave behind some clue or message if they had overheard that the place was to be raided by the police.'

The two of them began the unpleasant task of searching for anything that might give a clue as to the destination of the pathetic human cargo which had been bundled out of the warehouse into the lorry. This was a delicate task as it needed to be done without contaminating the evidence for any follow-up forensic investigation. All the cubicles were in much the same state – an iron bedstead with a soiled mattress and filthy sheets, a chair and bare floorboards on which were scattered any number of needles and other drug abuse paraphernalia. After searching the cubicles which contained the bodies of the three young girls, Tanya emerged red-eyed and part-traumatised by the tragic and squalid end to three young lives. Gunn was much the same – both of them lost for words at the bestiality and brutality of what they had just seen.

The last three rooms they searched were completely different.... these were rooms rather than fibre-board cubicles. They were carpeted and had a wash basin in one corner, a wardrobe, bedside table and a chair and a decent, reasonably clean bed. None of the three rooms appeared to have any evidence of drugs.

'Who do you suppose occupied these?' Tanya asked Gunn as they finished their search of the first two rooms.

'God knows, but I suspect that these girls may have been due to appear at an auction and so would need to look in perfect unblemished condition. They were possibly on milder drugs and sedatives. The other girls were destined for brothels I would imagine. It's wishful thinking on my part, but it's just possible that one of these three girls might have overheard something and have been able to leave some indication of where they were being taken.'

'In their state? Do you really think so,' and with that disparaging comment on Gunn's wishful thinking, Tanya went into the next room. But it was Tanya who let out a 'whoop' of excitement only seconds after entering the room. 'John! quickly! Look at this!'

Gunn left the room he'd just entered and went across the corridor to the room which Tanya was searching. She had stripped back the counterpane and duvet of the bed. On the sheet covering the mattress a message had been written in felt pen or biro.

'Guilbert R Rabelais Marseille puis Japon'

He immediately returned to the other room, stripped back the duvet and revealed the same message. They both went into the third room. All three had the same message.

'Where do you think they got the felt pen to do this?'

'No idea, but that shows they aren't zombies. They must have overheard one of the Mafioso mention the destination.'

'Who are you phoning?'

'Bruno.'

'You won't tell him about the message?'

'Damn right I won't.........ah! Bruno, any news from the chopper.'

'No, sorry. They lost the lorry and SUV in the Paris traffic. I suspect that the Mafia had spotted the helicopter and waited under a bridge or in a car park somewhere. Any clues where you are?'

'Not as yet. I think we'd better leave it to the forensic guys to go over this hell hole.'

'Scenes of crime officers should be there in five minutes.'

'Good, we'll have gone. Thanks again and be in touch no doubt,' and Gunn ended the call. 'Quick Tanya, get the sheets off the beds. I'm not going to risk some fucking French police mole in their Headquarters passing this on to the Mafia.' Within seconds they had all three sheets off the beds and put the duvets back in place. 'Better just check the other cubicles quickly to make sure there are no messages there.' And the two of them returned to the filthy cubicles, but were unable to find anything. 'OK, we're out of here!' and Gunn led the way out to the Peugeot where they stuffed the sheets into the boot of the car and drove out onto the autoroute via the Porte de Paris.

*

It was five minutes to six in the evening and already starting to get dark in the fortnight before the clocks went back an hour. It had been a long day for everyone, but Miles Thompson was left with no option but to have a meeting at that hour as those now sitting at the conference table in his office had been away all day. The subject being discussed was the *Seppuku-kai* threat to key people in the UK and the current state of play of BID's two agents, John Gunn and Tanya Kasakova.

The newly appointed Director of Espionage and Deputy Director of BID, James Rayner was on Miles' right. On his left was David Simpson, the new Assistant Director for Russia and Eastern Europe who had replaced James Rayner. On the right of the latter was Mike Dimmock, the AD for South-East Asia and opposite him was Charles Gardner the AD for the European Community. At the far end of the table was Mike Carrington, the recently appointed Director of Counter-Espionage.

Mike Carrington had briefed the meeting on the assassination attempt on the Governor of the Bank of England and the subsequent increase in threat level assessment from 'substantial' to 'critical' this had triggered for other key personalities in the UK. The raised threat level had put a huge strain on the manpower of both the police and BID's CE teams. Mike Dimmock was at the meeting because of his fluent knowledge of Japanese and his department's shared control of John Gunn and Tanya Kasakova with David Simpson's and Charles Gardner's Department.

'Much has happened over the last 48 hours apart from BID's management merry-go-round. I left my appointment with some unfinished business and I'm aware that the same situation exists with some, if not all, of you here. So, for the first and, I hope, the last time

I am going to interfere. I have authorised freedom of action for both our agents, currently in France,' and here Miles glanced at Charles Gardner. 'However this is subject to your recommendation, Charles, as the operation progresses and may well have to be reassessed if the operation moves to either or both Russia and Japan. We have had considerable co-operation from the Deuxième Bureau and there is just a chance that we may be able to do them a favour if Gunn and Kasakova are successful. May I know now if there are any objections to this course of action or any alternative suggestions,' Miles asked.

'When they have finished in France, do you expect them to return to the Trans-Siberian route to Vladivostok and then ferry to Japan or to fly direct?' was asked by David Simpson.

'My guess is that they will fly. The only reason that Gunn was travelling overland was because at the time he set out he was on leave and had no authority from BID for his assignment, so was unable to take firearms on a flight.'

The meeting broke up very shortly after this question, but any hopes of a quiet night would very soon be dashed.

*

Sir Peter Istead, the CEO of the Loughborough and Leicester Building Society, was pleased with life. Had it not been for the infusion of £70 billion of taxpayers' money, the Building Society which he had signally failed to manage responsibly would have gone into administration. This would have resulted in thousands of families losing their homes or their savings, or both. He had been removed from his appointment – that had been inevitable – but he had a handsome pension pot of £2 million and could now find himself another CEO appointment when all the ridiculous fuss had died down.

It was a balmy October evening as he walked back to his house with his two Rottweilers along the Croxton road, some five miles to the north-east of Leicester. The police had offered to accompany him, but he told them to go into the house and have a cup of tea. All the leaves were just beginning to turn and the following day he would be leaving on a fortnight's business trip to Spain. Life had been good to him. He metaphorically patted himself on the back. A fortnight spent with his mistress in Santander while Janet, his wife, coped with the half-term exeat of his two boys from their boarding school.

'This is the life!' he said out loud to the hedgerows on either side of the empty road........at least it had been empty, but now a very noisy motorbike was approaching. The bike slowed as it rounded the corner behind Peter.

'Gracious, that's unusually courteous,' he muttered as the bike with its rider and pillion passenger approached him. All too late the profligate banker realised that his nemesis had arrived in the form of two men in black leathers and black opaque visored helmets.

When the police found him some two hours later in the ditch at the side of the road, the body was riddled with bullets. The alarm had been raised when the two Rottweilers returned to the £1.8 million farmhouse without their master.

*

The section of Paris street map which the observer in the helicopter had given them only covered the area in St Denis from the Stade de France to just north of the Rue Samson. Tanya directed Gunn onto the dual carriageway which ran due south from the the Porte de Paris in St Denis to the Porte de la Chapelle where it intersected with the Boulevard Péripherique – the ring road around Paris. She checked the glove pocket of the Peugeot; no road map.

'Pull in to the first garage you see and I'll buy a Michelin road map of France. It's ages since I was last in Paris. I know this ring road connects with all the main autoroutes going north, south, east and west out of Paris, but there is no way that I can remember the road numbers.'

'OK, got that.........ah! here we are,' and Gunn moved into the right-hand lane and then into the forecourt of a large 'ELF' service station with pump facilities for at least 50 vehicles filling simultaneously. While he filled the car's tank to the brim, Tanya went into the shop and reappeared with a road atlas. When Gunn had paid for the petrol and returned to the car, he suggested that they park up and buy something to eat and drink as neither had eaten since breakfast that morning in Berlin. 'In order to get to Marseille ahead of the lorry and check out the Rue Rabelais, we're going to have to take it in turns to drive. Let's stock up with things to eat and drink here and then there should be no need to stop, other than for petrol.'

'I'll go and do the shopping,' Tanya offered, 'if you'd like to check the route. I had a quick glance and it looks like the A6 south to Dijon and Lyon and then the A7 to Marseille,' and Tanya disappeared into the mini-supermarket to buy supplies for the 400 mile drive.

She returned with a plastic bag full of supplies to the table where Gunn was studying the road atlas. It would be at least a 9 or 10 hour drive south to Marseille. Gunn swapped the Michelin atlas for the plastic bag and they returned to the car.

Five miles further round the anti-clockwise carriageway of the ring road at the Porte de Clichy, the Nissan Patrol and Iveco panel lorry joined the Boulevard Péripherique and headed south.

CHAPTER 17

It was at the third ring-tone that Mike Carrington reached out and picked up the phone beside the bed. He dropped it, found it on the carpet and pressed the connect button.

'Yes.'

'Mr Carrington?'

'Yes.'

'Richard Preston....Ops Centre duty officer.'

'Yes Richard....what is it? Do I need to switch to secure?'

'No sir.....Sir Peter Istead has been murdered.'

'Got that......I'll be in the Ops Centre in about twenty minutes.' Carrington replaced the phone in its charging base and swung his legs out from under the warm duvet.

'Problems?' Christine, his wife, mumbled from under the duvet on the other side of the bed.

'That banker whose building society was rescued by the taxpayer has been murdered.'

'Poetic justice,' was mumbled from even further under the duvet. It was just before midnight when Carrington entered the Operations Centre on the 14th floor of Kingsroad House. Richard Preston, the Assistant Director for the Indian Sub-Continent, who was the duty officer for that night, met him as he entered the Centre.

'Coffee sir?'

'Yes please....black no sugar. What went wrong with the close protection team from the Met.'

'It seems that Istead was out on his own with his dogs.........it was the dogs which alerted the SO14 guys in the farmhouse to the murder.'

'What?.........run that by me again,' Carrington said, stifling a yawn as he sipped at the scalding coffee.

'The dogs.....two Rottweilers......returned to the farmhouse on their own.'

'Where the hell were the two constables from SO14?'

'In the house watching TV........it was the ManU/ Arsenal match.'

'Bugger! They've made us look like a bunch of bloody amateurs. I'm sure that performance with the Governor of the Bank of England was a feint.......and succeeded in making us, or certainly the police on duty at Istead's house, drop their guard. Who gave you the information?'

'Chief Superintendent Lochart,' Preston replied having checked the log. Carrington went over to the desk on the controller's raised rostrum and sat in the comfortable high-backed leather seat. He pulled out his cellphone and scrolled through his list of contacts and pressed the call button.

'Lochart, SO14.'

'Hello Bruce, it's Mike Carrington, see you've got the graveyard shift again. What went wrong in Leicester?' It was less than a month since Mike Carrington had resigned from his appointment as Assistant Commissioner and Head of SO15 in the Metropolitan Police having applied and been selected for the appointment of Director of Counter Espionage in BID.

'Just about everything, sir. It's clear in hindsight that the assassins had had the farmhouse under surveillance for some time and as soon as Istead went out on his own a phone or radio was used to alert the guys on the bike. There were no less than 28 bullets in his back. They used a machine-pistol, the firearms guys reckon....something like a 9 mil Scarab Scorpion. Lot of red faces here, sir. I expect the Commissioner will be on to your Director in the morn.........oh, it's morning already....a bit later.'

'Thanks Bruce,' and Carrington ended the call.

'Contact the Director?' the duty officer queried.

'No, let him have a decent night's sleep. Richard, I want you to contact the intelligence services of the other targets....the ones that are still alive of course....and find out if there have been any attempts to assassinate them.'

'Very well sir.'

'I'll be down in my office.' and Mike Carrington left the Operations centre and returned to the 12th floor.

*

Other than providing clear and precise navigation instructions to Gunn as he drove the Peugeot 308 anti-clockwise round Paris' Périphérique in the fading light, Tanya was silent. The silence suited Gunn's mood; the sordid degradation of the drug-littered premises in the Passage Meunier had left its mark on both of them. Apart from his own thoughts about the depravity of the Albanian Mafia, Gunn needed all his concentration to avoid the indigenous Paris drivers who gave a convincing impression of treating the circular route round the French capital as a practice lap for a Formula 1 race. If Gunn showed the slightest hesitation or indecision, he was reprimanded by a cacophony of blaring horns.

As they passed a sign for the Porte d'Orléans at the '6.30' position on the circular route, Tanya warned him that the next exit would be the Porte d'Italie and the start of the A6 Autoroute du Soleil to the South of France. Gunn moved over to the right lane, slowed to the 'rappel' indicated speed limit of 90kph and left the Périphérique for the A6.

'It must've been ghastly to lose Claudine.........I mean........' There was a silence. 'Sorry John, I didn't mean to.........' Tanya's attempt to create a more genial atmosphere into the tangible and thunderous silence petered out as she saw the expression of fury on Gunn's face. That expression faded almost as quickly as it had hardened his features. He turned to Tanya and smiled.

'I owe you an apology..........no, first of all, my thanks for your professional navigation through this nightmare Paris traffic and secondly, an apology for my boorish behaviour...........'

'No, I mean......'

'No please......hear me out. I haven't spoken about Claudine since the paramedics took her away from me in my house......'

'The autoroute divides in about a mile,' Tanya interrupted quickly. 'Take the right fork marked A6/E15/E60.'

'Thanks........ours was a fatal relationship. In this job it's madness for us to have imagined that there was any prospect of permanency. In fairness, we didn't.....we just let things.........ah! that'll be the right fork,' and Gunn joined the majority of traffic heading south on the A6. Tanya said nothing, hoping that she had given him a chance to talk about Claudine's death. 'She had some very strong views about most things, but about BID in particular. We had a number of clashes during my last assignment........that was when I got myself shot in St Vincent and our agent there was killed.' Gunn reached down for the main beam switch as dusk turned to night.

'I had just completed my induction training and was being shown round the Operations Centre by BID's Training Director from Maidenhead,' Tanya explained. 'I was with two other new guys when that information about you came through from the St Vincent Police. I think it brought home more clearly than anything we'd been told in the lectures how dangerous the job could be.'

'Claudine believed that I was far too 'cavalier'.......I think that's how she might have described it. She said that I expected everyone to share my enthusiasm for danger and risk-taking........something like that. She was right. I never thought to ask the Vincentian police sergeant who was married with two young children if he had any reservations about the dangers which might face him and his family.'

'Did anything happen to them?' Tanya asked before taking a drink from a bottle of water. She unscrewed the cap from another bottle and passed it across to Gunn. He drank and passed it back.

'No.'

'So where does that leave the argument?'

'Her point was that I had no right to ask him because, of course, he couldn't and wouldn't refuse. She believed that I had retained too much of my military training where a soldier has no option to decide whether it's a good idea, plan or whatever.......he, or she, just has to get on with it. She was right. Ever since I was a boy, I always assumed that my friends wanted to do the same hair-brained things that I wanted to do. I've learnt a little restraint since I joined BID,' Gunn turned and smiled at Tanya who had unwrapped a sandwich.

'Here,' and she passed the sandwich across to Gunn.

∗

The Nissan SUV driven by Fatos with Kraja in the passenger seat and Beckim in the back was closely followed by the Iveco panel truck driven by Marku with Leutrim and Agron in the other two front seats. The two vehicles were 15 miles ahead of Gunn and Tanya. The leading two vehicles had covered 185 miles and were now 20 miles away from the junction of the A31 south out of Dijon and the A6 where the latter turned due south. What had started as intermittent drizzle on the southern outskirts of Paris had now, at 10.45pm, turned into steady rain. It was a weekday evening and the late hour and the rain had cleared the southbound carriageway of the autoroute of the majority of cars, leaving just the occasional articulated heavy goods vehicle to take advantage of the empty road to make up time on the journey south.

In the back of the truck it was pitch dark. Half-a-dozen mattresses had been thrown into the back of the panel truck together with a large plastic bottle of water and bucket before the girls were either carried or led out of the warehouse in Rue Samson. The five heroin-addicted young girls had been dumped on the mattresses from where they hadn't stirred since leaving the warehouse. The water and toilet bucket were concessions for the three high-priced girls awaiting auction to the highest bidder. The old mattresses reeked of stale sweat, urine and faeces. The three mildly sedated trio did what they could to make the five pathetic little girls as comfortable as possible, but once the daylight turned to night the thin pencil beams of light through the cracks in the truck's bodywork disappeared, leaving all of them in stygian darkness.

It was during one of these efforts to help the drugged girls, groping around in the dark that the trio discovered the two youngest girls, barely more than ten years old, had died. One of the three girls banged furiously on the back of the driving cab.

Marku was still driving. Leutrim was asleep.

'What the hell's that noise?' Marku asked as he wiped the windscreen which the demister had failed to clear.

'One of the girls wants to take a toilet break,' Leutrim replied in a feigned prim accent and then laughed at his own twisted sense of humour.

'Laugh you may you cretin; if anything happens to those three girls then you can answer to Kraja.'

'No wait,' Leutrim answered hastily, I'll phone Kraja.'

'You do that,' and Marku passed across the cellphone. Leutrim dialled the number.

'Yes.'

'The girls are banging on the back of the cab. Do we ignore it or investigate, patron?'

'Wait.'

'Wake up Agron. It's time he took a turn at the driving,' Marku suggested as they waited for directions from Kraja.

'Two miles ahead of us is the service station of Bligny-sur-Ouche. Follow me and we will park well clear of any other vehicles. Got that?' Kraja demanded.

'Yes patron.'

The SUV and truck had just entered the eastern edge of the Forêt Domaniale de Detain Gergueil. The dense forest crowded in on both sides of the autoroute only relieved by the bright lights ahead of the 24/7 service station. As they drove into the service station, Kraja noted that there were no cars at the pumps and only two trucks parked up for the night in the lorry park. He drove right to the far end of the parking area for cars and lorries and then pulled in beside a gravel track which led off into the woods – "probably to the waste water and sewage treatment plant which serves these remotely located service areas" were Kraja's thoughts as he got out of the SUV and inspected the red and white padlocked bar preventing access to the track. The panel truck pulled in beside the SUV.

After checking to ensure that there was no one around, Kraja gave instructions for the rear doors of the truck to be opened. His men were positioned to prevent any of the girls from escaping – if capable of such an action in their sedated and disoriented state. The rear door was unlocked and opened. All of them involuntarily turned their heads away from the opening as the nauseating odour of urine and excreta drifted out into the rain-filled air. The three valuable girls fell out of the back of the truck where they had been lying on a mattress by the door to try and get even a minute draft of fresh air.

Kraja called Marku over who appeared from the front of the truck with a syringe and small rubber-capped bottle of Butophanol. He was the only employee allowed to administer drugs. His previous employment had been as a nurse in the Centre Médical Europe in Paris's rue d'Amsterdam until he was caught removing drugs and selling them. After 8 months in La Santé Prison where he met his fellow countryman Agron they both moved to the north of Paris and a life of petty crime which led eventually to the Passage Meunier and the Albanian Mafia.

With a jerk of his head, Kraja indicated the three girls and while they were held by the other men, Marku injected the sedative. Because it took a few minutes to become effective the girls were led over to the SUV, placed in the back seat and the car was locked. Once the girls had been removed, Kraja climbed into the back of the truck and walked forward to the pile of mattresses and its pitiful heap of what had once been healthy children.

*

In January 1998 the Borsa Italiano was acquired by a consortium of banks which controlled it until October 2007 when the London Stock Exchange Group acquired it for $2.15 billion, making it the largest exchange market in Europe. The Borsa wass based in Milan and in 2005 the companies listed on the Borsa – ranging from Indesit to Fiat and Pirelli – were valued at $890 billion. When acquired by the LSEG, the Head of the Borsa became the Deputy Head of the LSEG. The latter was now due to retire and all sorts of rumours were circulating in the smart financial district of Milan as to his successor.

Signore Biaggio Campano – a flamboyant and stylish banker - was determined that the appointment would go to him. He was just emerging from Boeucc, which was rumoured to be not only the smartest and most expensive restaurant in Milan, but also the oldest in the World with a history dating back to 1696. Behind him, emerged a collection of some of the wealthiest and most influential bankers and industrialists in Italy. Those who had chosen to leave their wives at home were accompanied by stunning young female escorts whose scanty clothing was barely coping with the chill October evening breeze that blew across the Piazza Belgioioso. The cost of the meal he had just paid for would have kept the starving children of Ethiopia alive for a year. Waiting on the pavement as the 'Glitterati' appeared from the famous restaurant was a throng of photographers, TV cameras and papparazzi – all carefully forewarned by Campano's Head of Corporate Communications.

One person in the media throng had received his instructions from a different source, far away from Milan and Italy. His TV camera had some unique modifications which had nothing to do with film quality.

*

'Come in!' Mike Carrington called from his desk in response to the knock on his office door. Richard Preston, the Assistant Director for the Indian Sub-continent and the duty officer from the Operations Room came into the office. 'Yes Richard, please take a seat.'

'You asked for information on the four remaining men who had been threatened by *Seppuku-kai*.'

'I did and I can tell by your expression that the news is not good. I've no intention of being facetious, but this gets more and more like Agatha Christies' mystery novel 'Ten Little Niggers', but of course now for PC reasons that title has been renamed to 'And Then There Were None'.

'I would have to agree, sir. The eight men published by *Seppuku-kai* on their blog could hardly be described as paragons of virtue – just like the characters in Christie's mystery 'whodunnit'. The Russian was closely linked to the death of Polonium-poisoned Alexander Litvinenko, the German was involved in that Formula 1 scandal, my young 8 year old son could manage a bank better than Istead and the Frenchman, Perrigot, was being investigated by the DEA.'

'So what's happened to the four remaining men?' the Director of Counter Espionage asked.

'Three still alive but the Italian was shot half-an-hour ago in Milan – no protection and carrying on in his usual flamboyant lifestyle. He leaves behind a long-suffering wife and five children.'

'Method of assassination?'

'Bullet through the head; initially, the Italian Carabinieri were rushing around searching for snipers on top of buildings in the piazza.'

'So what changed their minds?'

'A sharp-eyed Scenes of Crime Officer who pointed out that there were minute traces of powder burn around the entry wound which meant that the assassin was no more than five metres away from the victim.'

'*Seppuku-kai* has picked its victims well. Their deaths appear to be designed to cause as much hiatus in the financial world as possible with little public concern or regret at their demise,' Mike Carrington muttered as he twisted a pencil round in his fingers. 'I'm straying into your side of BID now Richard, but *Seppuku-kai's* threat list affects both E and CE. What is known about the other intended victims – the Canadian Martinez, the American Nebelberg and the Japanese guy.....'

'Kurobashi.'

'That's him; what do we know about them? I know that Nebelberg was one of a number of executives of Enron responsible for hiding billions of dollars of corporate debt from the company's auditors which led to bankruptcy and any number of indictments and law suits, some of which have ended in custodial sentences.'

'Correct sir; Martinez was alleged to have had dealings with an international media holding company whose chairman was convicted of fraud and sent to prison, but nothing was ever proved and he is still Chairman of the Quebec Imperial Bank which has its headquarters in Toronto and has recently, in financial assets and number of employees, joined Canada's big five, headed up by the Royal Bank of Canada.'

'So could be that there is something adrift there?'

'A possibility.'

'And Karabashi?'

'Jiro Kurobashi.'

'Sorry, never could get my tongue round some of those Japanese names,' Carrington apologised.

'He, of course, is the Chairman of the most powerful bank in the World which has achieved that status with its recent merger with the Matsumoto Bank to create Yoshida Global Holdings Inc which employs over 80,000 people and has over a thousand branches worldwide.'

'So what scandal is he hiding behind?'

'None.'

'You said 'a possibility', so what?'

'The possibility was in connection with Martinez sir, but in the case of Kurobashi, competition between banks is notorious and there was another bank involved which attempted to take over the Matsumoto Bank. That would have made it the largest and most powerful bank in the World. It was defeated by Kurobashi's bank.'

'And which bank was that?'

'The Toyohoshi-Kimura Bank.'

'And who is the top guy of that outfit?'

'Quite an old man – Kenji Tokutaka.'

'Here's a thought from an ex-policeman who is neither an expert on oriental or world financial matters.'

'What would that be sir?' Richard Preston asked.

'Could all these assassinations be a smoke screen for the real target........this man Kurobashi who defeated the other man.....'

'Tokutaka.'

'That's him.'

CHAPTER 18

Gunn's hand on her shoulder was enough to wake Tanya who had been fast asleep for the last hour as he drove through the rain. She put her seat upright, wiped her hands and face from a packet of wet-wipes which she had bought at the service station and asked Gunn where they were.

'We're just coming up to a service station in the forest to the north-west of Beaune. We've done about two hundred miles,' Gunn added, glancing down at the odometer. 'I could do with making use of the facilities and was hoping that you might take a spell at the wheel.'

'Sure and yes, me too....for the facilities as you put it so politely. I'm busting for a pee so the sooner we stop the better!'

'Here we are,' and Gunn pulled over to the exit lane and entered the brightly lit filling station. 'You dash for the loos while I top up the car again. I'll park just over there,' and he nodded towards some parking slots in front of the service station's cafeteria and shop. No sooner had the Peugeot stopped by the pumps than Tanya hurried away through the glass doors of the cafeteria. Gunn checked his watch as he pulled the unleaded pump out of its socket and started filling the tank. 11.05. There was no point in trying to race down to Marseille. They just had to rely on the message the girls had left for them. Provided that they kept going they couldn't be far behind the Iveco truck and SUV that had left Rue Samson just before they got there. These were Gunn's thoughts as he finished filling the tank, closed the cap and returned the pump into its slot. He dug out his credit card and went into the shop where a very weary receptionist who was flicking through the French edition of Vanity Fair looked up as he entered.

'Numero Monsieur?'

Gunn glanced back at the Peugeot.

'Neuf, s'il vous plait.'

She pressed various keys and then pushed over the credit card touch pad. Tanya reappeared looking refreshed.

'Your turn, John. May I have the keys and I'll adjust the driving seat and get myself comfortable.'

Gunn handed over the keys and headed for the toilets at the back of the cafeteria. He took advantage of the remarkably clean toilets, ample hot water and fresh roller towels to freshen up.

Once Tanya had backed out of the parking slot, various white arrows painted on the tarmac directed them round the back of the service station and then out through the parking areas for trucks and cars. The rain had eased slightly, but still kept the wipers busy on the constant rather than the intermittent setting.

'Pretty deserted....only a couple of cars and a petrol tanker........ hey! What's up over there?' Tanya asked.

'Where?' Gunn had been studying the Michelin road atlas.

'There, do you think they're drunk or what?'

'Not drunk, there's blood all over the man and he's almost carrying the woman. Pull over Tanya and stop but keep the headlights on the couple,' Gunn said removing the Glock from his ankle holster. He got out of the car and shoved the Glock into the right pocket of his anorak. The man seemed to be middle-aged but looked older because of his dishevelled state, the rain and the head wound which had bled over his clothes. As soon as they saw Gunn walking towards them, he could read in the man's eyes that he was terrified that Gunn might be another thug about to mug them. Gunn turned and beckoned to Tanya. The presence of a woman might reassure the couple. She caught up with him as he reached the couple. Her presence did have a calming effect.

'Nom de Dieu! Aidez-nous gentils gens, Je vous supplie.............' but the man was almost in a state of collapse and the woman no better and she also had terrible bruising to her head which Gunn had just noticed.

'Tanya, can you bring the car over and then we'll get them to the cafeteria and call the police and ambulance.' She was away before Gunn had finished and brought the Peugeot alongside the couple pointing back to the service station. With care and some difficulty they got the couple into the back of the car and drove them back to the service station. The weary receptionist came to life and phoned for the police and ambulance while the couple were made as comfortable as possible. Tanya came over to Gunn. Her French being far more fluent than Gunn's she had picked up what the injured couple were saying to the half dozen or so people who had gathered around them while they waited for the police.

'They were sitting in their Volvo SUV having coffee when two men came up to them asking if they might borrow a jack to change a flat tyre on their car. As soon as the man opened the door he was hit on the head and his wife was dragged out of the other side and knocked unconscious. They had only just regained consciousness when we found them. All the stuff they had in the car was thrown out and the car was taken.'

'That has to be the crowd from Rue Samson.....but why did they need to take the car? Something's gone wrong with that truck of theirs. Come on Tanya before we get held up explaining everything to the police. Can you tell the receptionist that we've gone to collect the couple's luggage.' Tanya told the receptionist who nodded briefly and then busied herself caring for the casualties and bossing around the inevitable crowd of gaupers.

Gunn and Tanya jumped in the car and drove back to where they had found the injured couple. They quickly found the spot where the Volvo had been parked. Bags, clothes, picnic basket, boots and hats were scattered exactly where they had been pulled out of the four doors and rear hatch of the Volvo. It was very dark and there was no lighting in this part of the parking area of the service station.

'Have you got a torch?' Gunn turned to Tanya who went to the Peugeot and returned with a neat Maglite torch. The two of them set off along the forest side of the parking area looking for a broken-down truck or anything which might explain the need to hi-jack the Volvo. The rain had made any tyre tracks that might have been left behind fairly indistinct. After they had gone about 200 yards and just before the exit road led back out to the autoroute, the torch picked out the red and white barrier pole. From where they were they could see that the barrier was padlocked and were about to turn round when the loom of the torch showed faint tyre tracks leading off the parking area onto the gravel.

'Let's take a closer look at that padlock,' Gunn muttered. The hasp of the lock had been cut-through with bolt cutters and put back together to ward off a casual inspection.........as theirs had very nearly been. They both ducked under the barrier and walked up the track. Gunn had removed the Glock from his anorak pocket and the small 9mm Smith & Wesson automatic had appeared in Tanya's hand.

'What the hell's this track for?' Tanya asked in a whisper.

'God knows, but its been properly laid with a hardcore, tarmac and gravel........mains electricity transformer or something like that would be my guess.......that's the truck!' Twenty yards ahead of them was the back of the truck.

'Must be something wrong with the truck so that's why they hi-jacked the Volvo.'

'What's that smell?' Tanya asked wrinkling her nose.

'Sewage.........possibly a treatment plant for the service station.' Gunn went up to the back of the truck, pulled down the locking bar and turned it releasing the clips. He pulled the doors open. The foul odour from inside the truck made them both recoil.

'Oh shit!' Tanya gasped clasping her hand over her mouth and nose.

'Correct assessment........in a word,' Gunn agreed putting his Glock back in his pocket as he climbed into the back of the truck. He reached down for the torch. 'Just let me take a quick look and then I'll give you a hand up.'

As he went forward he took in the upturned bucket which had spilt its contents over the floor and the empty plastic water bottle. At the far end was a pile of four or five mattresses on which were the bodies of five very young girls. Gunn bent and quickly checked for a pulse in any of the necks, but the skin was cold to the touch and not a flicker of a pulse. The girls were in much the same state as the three which they had found in the warehouse in Rue Samson. Two of them had been shot. Gunn returned to the back of the truck. He shook his head.

'Dead?'

'All dead.'

*

After all the failed attempts to kill Gunn and the loss of seven men by the Albanian Mafia, at last something had gone right for Ichiro Iwakami, the Chief Executive of the Toyohoshi-Kimura Bank and *kobun* of the *Seppuku-kai* Mafia. Istead and Campano were both dead, but the rest of the world still thought that the hit list was a terrorist threat. His Chairman swept into the room.

'Your report please.'

After completing his bow, Ichiro gathered his papers and faced Drummond.

'Istead-san and Campano-san are both dead, Kenji-sempei. Is it time yet to deal with Kurobashi-san?

'Not yet, Ichiro-san. Martinez-san next; we already have 43% of the stock of the Quebec International Bank. Arrange for his death to take place in the most sordid of circumstances; in other words entirely within keeping with the way in which he has led the rest of his life.'

'It shall be done, Kenji-sempei.'

*

Henri Martinez had led a gifted career in the Canadian financial world. Always immaculately groomed, clothed and shod, he had flitted from one lucrative appointment to another. He always seemed to arrive just in time to take advantage of a share deal or bonus scheme. This was not just luck. Henri was as sharp as a needle and never allowed himself to become involved in any relationship that might slow down his meteoric rise to the board of the Quebec International Bank, the sixth largest bank in Canada, at its headquarter offices in Toronto's Bay Street, a stone's throw from Canada's largest bank, the Royal Bank of Canada.

He had just moved into a new condo at the junction of Yorkville and Bay Street which was purported to be not only the most expensive in Canada, but the most expensive in North America. From arrival in the bank's boardroom to taking over as Chairman of the bank had only taken just over two years and would have been even faster had it not been for his first ever mistake when he very nearly went to prison with another Canadian banker over fraudulent share deals. Now secure as the Chairman of the Quebec International Bank, he was all set to guide his billion dollar financial group through the credit crunch. Henri was single and the gutter press constantly hinted at his sexuality, but was unable to produce any mud which would stick.

As he walked out of his condo building on a crisp and chilly October evening his chauffeur-driven Cadillac was parked in its usual place. He walked over to it, waved to his driver and got into the back. He shut the car door and opened his brief case to have one more read of the notes he had made for the speech he was required to give at the dinner at which he was the guest of honour. The man driving the car reached down, removed the Taser from under his legs, turned to his right and released the compressed-air propelled probes at point-blank range into Martinez's chest. The banker slumped forward over the papers which had been removed from his brief case. The Cadillac pulled over by the kerb and two men got into the back.

*

Miles Thompson arrived at Kingsroad House shortly after 8.30am having walked from his house in Chelsea's Durham Place. His first port of call was the Operations Centre on the 14th floor. From there he went to his Deputy's office on the 12th floor.

'Morning Mike, the Ops' Centre told me that you were called in during the night. Can it wait or would it help to talk now?'

'Now's fine Miles if you have a few minutes.'

'I've lots of minutes, so shoot,' Miles said as he took a seat in one of the armchairs in his Deputy's office. Mike Carrington grabbed some notes he had made and came round his desk and joined his Director in another chair.

'I didn't really need to come in as Richard had everything tied up neatly by the time I arrived. He phoned to let me know about Campano's murder.'

'So the assassinations continue?'

'Very much so.'

'Just a moment.......why did Richard phone you and not James.......?'

'He did. Both of us. But there was precious little if anything to be done. James decided not to come, but as this whole business affects both E and CE I thought some solo time in the office making some notes might be useful.'

'And was it?'

'Yes.....at least I think so. Do you still have lots of minutes so that I can bounce my theories off you?'

'I do,' Miles confirmed removing a small notebook and pencil from an inside pocket.

'As can be expected from a copper.....or more accurately, an ex-copper, what I say may sound a bit cheeky, but say it I will.'

'That sounds a bit daunting, Mike, but refreshing so let's see what your experience in detecting has teased out of this *Seppuku-kai* business.'

'Right, here goes. It seems to me that the whole business was obscured by the extraordinary behaviour of Davidson. This made most of us focus on what his next ridiculous action or pronouncement might be. Had it not been for Gunn's determination to follow up the Lequesne papers, with your tacit support, I feel we would still be chasing our tails and worse still, Davidson would still be the Director.'

'Some generalisations there, Mike, but I go along with that,' Miles commented jotting down a few notes. Mike Carrington shuffled the pieces of paper in has hand and then continued.

'I'm going back to my first day as a Detective Constable when my DI gave me a piece of advice which I've never forgotten. "Find the motive and you'll find the guilty person". So what seems to be the motive in this case? Every effort was made to destroy the Lequesne papers and kill anyone who had seen the contents of the papers. That is undoubtedly -undoubtedly to my mind, that is - what Davidson was doing with those embargoed papers in our vault. He was looking for - and with the obvious intention of destroying - any documents that might reciprocate, enhance or support the research notes in the Lequesne papers. Although Gunn is the only person who has seen the papers, from him we know that they concern the betrayal of British and Canadian officers in a Japanese POW camp in Hong Kong during the Second World War. Gunn has told you that the papers are a diary of both father and son Lequesne's search for a British officer called Peter Drummond; the traitor responsible for the deaths of more than a thousand officers.'

'We know that Davidson was connected to Lequesne's, Claudine's and Professor Akagawa's killers and that those killers belonged to or were hired by *Seppuku-kai* which claimed responsibility for the internet blog threatening those international financiers. Richard and I discussed this last ni.....I mean in the early hours of this morning.'

'Any conclusions?' Miles asked.

'Yes, I think so. All eight of them, except for one – Jiro Kurobashi – are considerably less than squeaky clean. The Litvinenko assassination, drugs, banking incompetence, scandal........you name it they were into it. All except one man..........' There was a knock on the door and Terry Holt, the Controller of the Operations Centre put his head round the door.

'Sorry to interrupt sirs, but thought you ought to know that we've just heard from the RCMP that Henri Martinez – number five on the hit list – was found dead shortly after midnight in a casino mostly frequented by gays in the St James District of Toronto. He appeared to have lost more than $200,000 US on the Blackjack tables. That leaves just two sir: the American, Nebelberg and the

Japanese, Kurobashi. Our financial experts in Admin reckon that this will knock at least 10% off the Quebec Bank's share value.'

'Thanks Terry,' from the Director and the Operations Centre Controller closed the door behind him. 'Go on. Mike.'

'This morning when I was discussing all this with Richard after the death of Campano, I compared it somewhat facetiously to Agatha Christie's non-pc titled mystery 'Ten Little Niggers'. Now I'm tempted to draw another comparison with one of her Inspector Poirot mysteries, the 'ABC Murders'. In order to disguise the motive for killing the intended victim, the murderer kills two or three others, apparently working his way through the alphabet. All of those banking guys who've been murdered have a pretty unpleasant background except one, and he's as clean as a whistle and is now the Chairman of the World's Largest Bank.'

'OK, Mike but......'

'No bear with me a little longer. There was fierce competition in Japan to acquire the Matsumoto Bank. That competition was between Kurobashi's Yoshida Bank and the Toyohoshi-Kimura Bank. Kurobashi defeated the Toyohoshi takeover bid, acquired the Matsumoto Bank and now Yoshida Global Holdings is the largest bank and fund manager in the World.'

'So who was the Chairman of the defeated bank?'

'A man named Tokutaka; Kenji Tokutaka.'

'And what do we know about him?'

'Not much except that he's very old.'

'But what about the Japanese Mafia.....*Seppuku-kai*, is there a connection?'

'If we could find a connection between the Mafia and Tokutaka it would establish the motive. In order to prepare himself for the position as head of the World's most powerful bank he would have to ensure that there was nothing in his past which could be used for blackmail. Davidson spent many years in Tokyo and during that time must have done something which made him vulnerable to blackmail by the *Yakuza* – probably a honey trap using Geisha girls. It seems that he was given the task of removing Lequesne and any evidence linking the POW camp betrayal with the Toyohoshi

Bank. I'm well out of my depth now, Miles, and this falls into James' Department. But I would like to think that I might have identified a possible suspect with a motive for the killings – the oldest motive of all - revenge.'

'So you think that this man Tokutaka could be the traitor Peter Drummond that Lequesne was trying to find?'

'Why not?'

CHAPTER 19

It was nearly 01.30 before Gunn and Tanya were able to continue with their drive to Marseille. They would not have been able to continue at all had it not been for Tanya's excellent French, their BID ID cards and a phone call from Gunn to BID's Operations Centre which resulted in a call to the French Police at the service station from the Préfecture on the Îsle de la Cité in Paris. Once the police at the service station had been reassured that Gunn and Tanya were not the villains, the clear-up of the incident proceeded quickly.

The middle-aged owners of the Volvo were taken to hospital together with all their belongings and the scenes of crime officers sealed off the area around the abandoned Iveco truck with its grizzly cargo. A call was put out for the Nissan and the Volvo with a warning that the men were armed and there were three female hostages.

Tanya took over the driving and told Gunn to get some sleep. It was just over 100 miles to Lyon - A6 all the way and then A7 from Lyon to Marseille. He gratefully dozed off after insisting that she wake him before they reached Lyon so that he could help with the navigation around the tortuous interchange of autoroutes around the city. Gunn woke up as the Peugeot came to a halt beside the petrol pump at the Morières Service Station. He glanced at his watch. 05.10. Tanya got back into the car, drove over to a parking slot and suggested that a freshen-up and coffee was called for.

'Where are we?' Gunn asked undoing his safety belt and getting out of the car.

'Just to the south of Avignon.........about another 70 miles to Marseille. Sleep well?'

'Like a log, see you in a minute,' and they separated into their respective washrooms. When Gunn reappeared Tanya was already at a table, having bought the coffees and croissants and a street map of Marseille.

'There,' and Tanya pointed to a spot on the opened street map and finished her mouthful of croissant. 'Rue Rabelais; it's in an area behind the commercial port.'

'Difficult to find?' Gunn asked, noting the maze of streets stretching like a web across the old port.

'Don't think so......the A7 turns into the A55 which we stay on right to the end then take a right and two roundabouts later another right and we're in Rue Rabelais.'

They finished their breakfast and returned to the Peugeot. Gunn took over the driving and they left the service station at 05.45.

'The mafia must know that the police would put out a call to have them stopped. Would they have stayed on the autoroute?' Tanya mused aloud.

'The service stations are reasonably numerous, but even so it was by complete chance that we chose the same one as the Mafia. If the Mafia had been less brutal when hijacking the Volvo or had stolen a parked car then the truck would never have been found. They may believe that no one has found that truck, in which case they could still be on the autoroute, but I think it's highly unlikely. The Volvo's number plate would be spotted at the toll booths. The N6 and N7 follow the autoroute nearly all the way so I think they'll use those or even minor roads to get to Marseille. That'll slow them down quite a bit.....even at this hour,' Gunn added as an afterthought as the very first streaks of dawn appeared in the eastern sky.

The remainder of the drive to Marseille was uneventful. The A7 did as indicated in the Michelin atlas and turned itself into the A55 which descended quite steeply from the foothills of the Luberon and Provence Alps through a tunnel into the north-east suburbs of the port just after 06.30.

'Second roundabout take a right.......that should be Rue Rabelais,' Tanya instructed as Gunn left the autoroute at its terminus cloverleaf and joined the Avenue André Roussin heading south towards the port.

'Keep a lookout for 'Pneus Guilbert'....I'll concentrate on the right and you take the buildings on the left,' Gunn suggested.

The Rue Rabelais climbed up the side of a knoll with houses, shops, warehouses and streets leading off mainly on the right. On the left there was but one row of buildings and then the ground fell away steeply to the coast road and the commercial harbour.

'There!......about fifty yards ahead of us.'

'Got it........I'll drive past, turn round further along the road and come back and park. Any signs of activity?'

'Not a thing,' and Tanya was unable to keep the disappointment out of her voice. 'It looks like a fairly old warehouse with a house attached. Presumably it was originally a storage depot for Guilbert's tyres.'

'If that is the Mafia's Marseille address........the message from the girls could not have been clearer....we could hardly expect to find the cars parked outside. It's quite possible of course that we've got here before them.'

'No, you're right,' Tanya acknowledged. 'There's a roundabout about another 100 yards further on. You can turn there and there's a bit of waste ground just before the Guilbert place, but not overlooked by it, where you can park the car.'

'OK...now these guys have never seen either of us. So here's how we tackle it. We get out of the car and then walk past the front of the building as though we're on the way to work. As we do this we check to see if there are any windows from which we might be seen. Once we've done the walk-past, let's stop out of sight and decide how to enter the place. Last thing, as we walk past look closely at the ground for tyre tracks leading up to that large wooden door at the front of the warehouse part of the building. OK, what have I missed?'

'Nothing, but what about our backpacks?'

'Take them with us, I reckon.'

'OK.......there's a boulangerie right beside that bit of waste ground so I'll go in and buy a couple of baguettes which will help to make us appear part of the local scene.'

'The thought of a freshly baked baguette is making me hungry,' Gunn smiled as he drove round the roundabout and headed back down the Rue Rabelais to the waste ground spotted by Tanya. He pulled off the road and parked the Peugeot beside two rain-soaked cars. Tanya removed the automatic from her handbag flicked off the safety catch and replaced it in the bag. Gunn pushed the Glock 26 into his anorak pocket. First stop was the boulangerie where Tanya bought two long baguettes. They left the shop and walked along the road towards the warehouse.

After the last building before the warehouse, there was a cobbled courtyard. At the back of this was the house connected to the warehouse forming the shorter part of an 'L' with the warehouse forming the long part of the 'L' stretching out to the road with the large wooden doors fronting onto Rue Rabelais with the 'PNEUS GUILBERT' logo in faded black paint above the doors. There was a metal bar with a hinged piece at the end which swung over and slotted into two metal brackets and then folded over a ring. Through this ring was the recessed hasp of a large secure padlock which would have defeated any bolt-cutters.

'We'd need a bulldozer to get through those doors,' Gunn commented as they came level with the doors.

'Look at the cutaway part of the pavement in front of the doors,' Tanya whispered.

After the overnight rain and because they were probably the first pedestrians to walk along the pavement, nothing had obscured the two clear sets of dissimilar tread patterns leading off the road up to the warehouse door. The tyre marks could only have been made by vehicles which had driven through the overnight rain.

'Keep walking and stop at that scruffy café up ahead of us with those tables and chairs on the pavement.'

*

During the 'good' years at Enron, Charles Nebelberg had been able to put aside hundreds of thousands of dollars into an account in the Cayman Islands. The account was so intricately concealed by a multitude of transfers through numbered accounts all over the world that it would have taken an army of fraud experts in the FBI to trace it back to him. But the purpose of the Senate inquiry to which he had been summoned was to give him the opportunity of disclosing his knowledge of the large sums of money, still unaccounted for, which had disappeared in the two or three days before the 'bubble' burst and Enron collapsed.

The appearance of his name on the *Seppuku-kai* blog worried him not at all. He believed that this was just another ploy by either the FBI or some other federal agency to get him to reveal what had been done with the money in return for his personal protection; either that or some freak who wanted to abduct him for a ransom. This bravado was in spite of him reading in the Herald Tribune of the deaths of the other men threatened on the blog. His solicitor had begged him to be more contrite and cooperative with the investigation and to consider some form of plea bargain to reduce the length of sentence he could be facing.

One of the assets his embezzled funds from Enron had acquired was a luxury, 53 metre Bagliotto steel-hulled super-yacht which he kept berthed in Antigua's Falmouth Harbour Marina. No one knew of the existence of this yacht which he owned under a false identity, passport and ship's papers. He was currently on bail for $500,000 to appear before the Senate sub-committee on the Monday.

Charles glanced at his watch; 08. 45. His solicitor, David Abrahams, was due to come to his luxury condominium in the Galleria District of Houston at 9.15 that morning to discuss his defence. He had chosen his solicitor with considerable care from a selection of the top five law firms in Houston. This had been before the Enron bubble burst, but when the burst had become inevitable and he was making plans to disappear. He had found what he wanted in the law firm of Samuel and Solomans. David was exactly the same height, had the same hair colour and same unremarkable facial features, but best of all David sported a designer beard.

Charles knew that every form of communication was being monitored by the FBI. Although he hadn't had to serve his bail in the State Penitentiary at Huntsville, for all intents and purposes he might just as well have been there. His condominium was watched 24/7, his mobile and landline were tapped and any electronic emissions from his personal computer would be picked up. The bell rang at his front door. Charles glanced at the CCTV monitor which showed his solicitor standing at the door. He opened the door and welcomed him.

'Come in David; go on through into the lounge and you'll find a percolator and cups on the table. Help yourself to coffee and I'll be with you shortly. I'm just finishing off a draft I've been working on which I hope will be of help to you.'

'That's good news, Charles, thanks,' and his solicitor went into the lounge with its panoramic views over the up-market residential district of Houston. As he poured the dark Colombian coffee into the cup he wondered what would happen to the condo' when Nebelberg was inevitably sent to the State Penitentiary for a very long time. Perhaps he would buy it? He smiled at the prospect as he sipped the strong and bitter coffee. Four minutes later Charles came through to the lounge from his study. The transformation was astonishing had there been anyone there to see it. Nebelberg was now Abrahams, complete with designer beard.

The solicitor was comatose on the floor and would be in that state for at least eight hours. Charles lifted him onto the sofa, removed his tie which he put on, took the car keys from his trouser pocket and picked up the briefcase. He removed the papers from the brief case and replaced them with a considerable amount of money and his false passport in the name of Christopher Mount. He paused at the front door to do a final check and then walked out, closing it behind him.

The FBI agents saw the solicitor leaving the condo' and made a note of the time. Charles drove away in the Solicitor's BMW and headed for David Wayne Hooks Airport – a private airfield hosting a number of flying clubs and private aircraft. He had left his cellphone in the condo' – switched on – where it's GPS gadgetry would tell the FBI that he was in residence. In his pocket was a new cellphone which had never been used. At the airfield he was greeted by the mechanic who had serviced his Piper Saratoga, signed for the maintenance work that had been done and for a full fuel load.

'Where's Jackson?' Nebelberg asked of the mechanic as he was signing the acceptance sheet.

'He's away Mr Mount,' the mechanic replied.

'Oh OK. Everything OK?'

'Yes sir, no problems.' The last word was pronounced as 'ploblems', but Nebelberg was in too much of a hurry to notice his stand-in mechanic's ethnicicity as he completed his checks of the outside of the Piper and climbed in.

The Piper had a range of 1,100 miles so his flight plan to Antigua was via Punta Gorda in Florida, Montego Bay in Jamaica and San Juan in Puerto Rica before the last 350 mile leg to St John's in Antigua. All legs of the flight crossed the Caribbean where in places the depth was over 5,000 metres.

Charles Nebelberg, alias Christopher Mount, took off from the Houston airfield in his Piper Saratoga at 11.20 am on the first leg of his flight plan to Antigua.

*

'Right, let's see if a brief mind-clearing session can throw any fresh light on the banking assassinations and Mafia contract killing here and in Europe,' Miles Thompson addressed the meeting in his office.

Seated round the conference table in the BID Director's office was James Rayner, the recently promoted Director of Espionage, Mike Carrington, recently appointed Director of Counter-Espionage and three Assistant Directors covering SE Asia, Europe and Russia and lastly, Barry Windsor, the Assistant Director of CE1 – Counter Terrorism.

'Let me kick this 'think-tank' session off by bringing you all up to date, including the events of last night.' It was a few minutes after 9 am and those who had not been involved in the night-time events would not have had time to catch up with the daily sitrep covering the last 24 hours circulated by the Operations Centre. The Director continued: '*Seppuku-kai* or contract killers hired by that cult of the *Yakuza*, killed the sixth victim last night........Henri Martinez, the Canadian Chairman of the Quebec International Bank.'

'And in the same night, in Milan, Signore Campano, Head of the Borsa Italiano and until last night, Deputy Head of the the London Stock Exchange Group, was shot dead. Of the eight names published on the *Seppuku-kai* blog, only two remain alive: the American Nebelberg and the Japanese Kurobashi. Just over an hour ago I was discussing this with Mike when the news of Martinez's death was sent to the Ops Centre by the RCMP. Mike had a theory about the killings as, I hope, all of you have. I am going to give you Mike's theory and then the floor is yours for either constructive criticism or alternative theories.'

'Of the eight intended victims, seven have anything from criminal pasts to thoroughly unpleasant lifestyles. The eighth, Kurobashi, has nothing criminal or unpleasant, as far as we know, about his past or present lifestyle. He has recently become the Chairman of the World's largest bank after defeating the Toyohoshi-Kimura Bank in the takeover of the Matsumoto Bank. Mike's theory is this; there are two separate objectives of *Seppuku-kai*: one is to silence anyone who has had access to the Lequesne papers and the other is to seek revenge for losing the takeover battle for the Matsumoto Bank. Implicit with this theory is that there is a connection between *Seppuku-kai* and the Toyohoshi-Kimura Bank.....a link that Miss Yoshiwa, our agent in Tokyo, has yet to confirm. Mike suggests that the seven other murders of international financiers with unsavoury backgrounds is merely a smoke screen for the real target which is Kurobashi.'

'Now I find nothing unrealistic or lacking in objectivity in this theory so let me hear your assessment gentlemen,' and the Director stirred his coffee and awaited any comment.

'May I just ask for an up-date on the whereabouts of John Gunn and Tanya Kazakova?' Barry Windsor asked.

The Director turned to James Rayner; 'James?'

'They are in Marseille. I approved Gunn's request to deal with Kushtrim Kraja, the Don of the Albanian Mafia in France in order to secure the release of abducted young girls due to be auctioned to the highest bidders in the next 48 hours. Gunn says he has evidence that these girls are to be auctioned in Japan. The Albanian Mafia has also been complicit in the assassination of international financiers as contract killers for *Seppuku-kai*. Succeed or fail in that mission, Gunn and Kazakova then re-route to Japan to meet up with our agent there to identify the link, if it exists, between *Seppuku-kai* and the Japanese banks.'

'Thank you sir; one more question. Why wasn't it left to the French Police to deal with the Albanian Mafia, thus releasing Gunn to deal with the Japanese Mafia?' Barry Windsor directed his query back to the Espionage Director.

'Good comment; unfortunately, there is a very effective 'mole' or 'moles' in the French Police HQ in Paris who is/are known as 'Phoenix'. They are able to provide the Albanian Mafia with adequate warning of any police raid or intervention in the Mafia's activities. Phoenix, in conjunction with the Mafia's highly-rewarded solicitors, ensure that no criminal charges stick. Pierre Brouhard, the Director of the DGSE, has indicated his tacit agreement to Gunn's mission, particularly if it halts, or helps to halt the revolting trade of young people – of both sexes – for the sexual gratification of the highest bidders.'

'Has anyone else in BID seen the papers passed to Gunn by Rory Lequesne?' David Simpson asked.

'No. Gunn discussed the contents with me on his return from visiting his father,' Miles Thompson answered. 'However at the time he was operating under some considerable duress – as indeed others were while Davidson was here – and had placed the papers in a left-luggage box at one of the mainline stations. The papers were a diary of Rory Lequesne's efforts to trace Peter Drummond, the man who had betrayed his fellow officers in a POW camp in Hong Kong. That betrayal led to the death of hundreds of men in the *Lisburn Maru* as they were being shipped to Japan as slave labour. Rory Lequesne was unable to trace Drummond despite several fruitless visits to Japan.'

'This meeting might wish to know that just a few hours ago a truck owned by the Mafia was found at a service station on the A6 south of Paris containing the bodies of five young girls.' This was volunteered by Charles Gardner, the EU AD, whose Controller, Marie de Fontblanque, was currently supervising Gunn's mission. 'Two of them had been shot and the other three had died in the filth of their own urine and faeces. The oldest was just 15 and the youngest 10. It's just possible that one of the girls abducted by the Mafia and who is still alive, might be destined for Japan which connects Gunn's current mission with the future one of closing down *Seppuku-kai*.'

'Thank you for that update Charlie,' the Director acknowledged, 'I............' but there was a discreet tap on the door and his PA came in.

'The FBI has just told the Ops Centre that Charles Nebelberg has failed to appear before a senate sub-committee inquiry on the Enron affair. No one has seen him since before the weekend, sir.'

*

What are you grinning at?' Gunn smiled, 'that bloody chair was about to do considerable damage to my manhood.'

'I thought that's what was bothering you,' Tanya laughed as two large cups of coffee were placed in front of them. Scruffy and gloomy the café might have been, but the coffee was some of the best Gunn and Tanya had tasted since their arrival in France.

'That's just what was needed! Right, now how are we going to tackle this warehouse?'

'Would it be time to call in reinforcements?'

'You mean the police?'

'Whatever.'

'I agree it would be very useful to go in there with a little more firepower,' Gunn conceded, 'but police forces by their very nature have to act within the law and so take an age to get going – they would need a warrant and that would require the French equivalent of a magistrate. Do you think there'd be a magistrate out of bed at this hour?.....very unlikely. I don't think we have the luxury of that sort of time lag if we hope to have the faintest chance of saving those girls and following the trail to Japan.'

'How many are there do you think?'

'At least four, including Kraja and at the most....say eight. That'd be four or five in the lead vehicle and two or three in the second plus the three girls....quite a squash. The warehouse looks pretty secure so it looks as though we've got to get into the house.' Gunn got up and left a five Euro note on the table. 'Ready?'

'As I'll ever be.'

'OK, I'll take the right-hand route and you the left. We'll meet up at the far right end of the house.' They parted at the corner of the warehouse, Tanya covering the left side of it along a very narrow alleyway. She threw away the baguettes as soon as she was out of sight of the street. Gunn crossed in front of the warehouse doors again and then followed the buildings' 'L' shape round the cobbled yard. Tanya could find no access until she turned the corner to walk along the back of the building. Just off-centre was a door in the house part and a flight of steps leading from it down the steep slope to the coast road about 50 or 60 feet below and the commercial port on the other side of it. All the windows in the house had the shutters closed so there was little likelihood of her being seen as she walked along the narrow strip of level ground at the rear of the building. She met up with Gunn at the far end of the house.

'Any joy?' she asked quietly.

'Not really; all windows shuttered and just the one door in full view of the road. You?'

'Door at the back and windows shuttered, but the shutters on the immediate left of the door can be forced, I think.'

'Well, at least it's out of sight of the road. Let's give it a go,' and Gunn led the way along the back of the house to the door. 'Just let me try the door first before we force any of the shutters. I'll leave my backpack here.' The door was inwards opening – hinges on the right door handle on the left. Holding the Glock in his left hand, Gunn depressed the door handle. The door opened noiselessly without any squeaking of hinges or creaking of the wooden door jamb. Gunn turned to Tanya and raised his eyebrows; she shrugged, now holding the Smith and Wesson in both hands.

The door opened into a large kitchen – stone flagged floor, heavy beams across the ceiling and large central wooden table with six chairs around it. There were two ceramic sinks on the left with wooden draining boards, plate racks and a view out of the window if the shutters had been open. On Gunn's right was a cooking range with work surfaces and directly in front of him a piece of furniture very similar to a Welsh dresser. Tanya slid past Gunn and moved over to the left covering him. There wasn't a sound. Gunn pointed at the door on the other side of the room. Tanya nodded and moved across the room to cover him. The door led into a hallway - lounge on the left, stairs on the right and a door which had to lead into the warehouse. Gunn pointed at the lounge and covered Tanya as she pushed the door open with her foot. Empty. There was a small washroom at the foot of the stairs. Empty. Gunn put one foot tentatively on the first step of the stairs. Solid – no creaks. Tanya covered him as he went up the stairs to the landing and then silently followed him. Upstairs possessed a bathroom and three bedrooms; all clean and in good condition and....empty. They both went downstairs to the hall and over to the door leading into the warehouse. The door opened towards Gunn. The inside of the warehouse was similar to that in Rue Samson; the part nearer Gunn was divided into cubicles and the part nearer the road was used as a garage. The Volvo SUV and another 4WD vehicle were both parked in this space; absolute silence. Gunn and Tanya went from one cubicle to another, but all were empty and tidy. They stood looking at the two vehicles; there were footprints everywhere on the concrete floor. Gunn touched the bonnets of both vehicles........still warm.

'They could only have got here an hour ahead of us......at the most,' Gunn whispered. 'We seem to be just too late again,' and then Gunn stopped whispering and spoke in a normal tone. 'There weren't any other doors which we missed were there?'

'Pretty sure there weren't, but let's have another look,' Tanya suggested, leading the way back into the house. Their search revealed no doors in the house or in any of the cubicles. They ended up back in the garage. Gunn put the Glock back in his pocket. He walked over to the 4WD Nissan Patrol and opened the driver's door. The keys were still in the ignition. He removed the keys and idly spun them round his finger on the key ring. 'Where the hell would they have gone in such a rush, particularly if they had the girls with them?' Gunn queried aloud, having silently dreaded during the search of the house a repeat of the macabre scene in the back of the lorry. The keys spun off his finger and fell onto the concrete floor. He bent down to pick them up. 'Oh ho! what have we here?'

'What's that?' Tanya asked coming round to his side of the Nissan.

'Take a look under the car.' Tanya got down on her hands and knees.

'Oh, it's only a drain inspection cover,' she said, unable to keep the disappointment out of her voice.

'I think it's too large for a drain cover. Let's have a look,' and having retrieved the keys he got into the Nissan, started it and reversed away from the cover. He examined the metal cover closely. Instead of being manufactured from cast iron it appeared to be made of steel or a lighter alloy. Gunn stood up, put his finger to his lips and whispered to Tanya. 'Have your automatic ready.' He got his hands into the handholds at either end and lifted. The metal cover came away easily and made a loud clatter as he placed it to one side of the rectangular aperture. 'Shhhhhit!' he muttered.

It was no drain cover. At one end of the hole was a brick wall disappearing down into darkness with a metal-runged ladder let into the brickwork. Not a sound came from the darkness below. Gunn got up and walked away from the opening, beckoning Tanya to follow him.

'If those bastards are down there, I can't for the life of me think of any way not to be sitting duck as I climb down. Any ideas?'

'If they are down there, wouldn't they have had to leave someone behind to drive the car over the hole?'

'Don't think so. If you look at the high ground clearance of the Nissan, I, and certainly you, could slide underneath into the hole and then position that metal plate over your head.'

'Oh.....OK...so do we assume that they are all down there?'

'No alternative.....you still got that torch?'

'It's in my backpack by the kitchen door.' Tanya was away for only a couple of minutes and returned with both backpacks. She handed the Maglite torch to Gunn. He lay down on his stomach beside the opening and shone the torch into the aperture. But all the torch beam did was to illuminate a small area of concrete at the foot of the ladder.

'Right, there's only one thing for it if this all goes wrong. You've got my backpack with the Lequesne papers. Contact Marie de Fontblanque and tell her what's happened and then respond to whatever instructions she gives you. Problems?'

'Yes, just one. Is it really necessary to go down....I mean would this be the time to ask for police support?'

'Possibly, but the longer I think about it the less I feel inclined to go down,' and without another word Gunn swung his legs down into the opening and with the torch switched off, he lowered himself down the metal rungs and disappeared into the darkness.

*

Peter Drummond sat at his ornate antique Japanese Taisho desk in the cavernous lounge-cum-study of the penthouse at the top of the Toyohoshi-Kimura building. The bank had been built on the most valuable piece of real estate in Tokyo in the Otemachi District to the east of the Imperial Palace. That piece of real estate was the former site of the ancient 17th century village of Shibazakai – the oldest part of Tokyo. The room was filled with exquisite pieces of antique Japanese porcelain, furniture, Samurai suits of armour, *katana*, *wakizashi* and *tanco* swords, a priceless collection of miniature *bonsai* trees and delicate displays of *Ikebana* flower arrangements which were changed or refreshed every day.

His first wife, Haruko, was the eldest daughter of Colonel Ishikawa, the Commandant of the Argyle Road POW camp in Hong Kong. She had died on 6th August 1945 while visiting her family in Hiroshima. The entire family, the house and all their possessions had been close to ground zero of 'Little Boy' – the first of the two atomic bombs to be dropped on Japan - and had been vaporised in the fireball temperature of 4,000°C. His second wife,

Beryl Adams, had been a typist in the British Embassy whom he had met at a reception at the Embassy in 1961 and married six months later.

There had been one child, Ian, who was born in 1963 and who took his father's adopted English surname of Davidson. Beryl had died in childbirth and the son had been brought up by a succession of *'ubas'* or nannies, until he reached the age of seven when he was dispatched into private education in England. After university, his fluency in Japanese assured him employment in the Diplomatic Service followed by a number of tours in Japan alternating with desk jobs in King Charles Street. Ian Davidson had absolutely no idea of his father's wartime service in Hong Kong until his second diplomatic appointment to Tokyo as Head of Chancery and Deputy Head of Mission.

Davidson had married Sarah Pelham-Downes, a Third Secretary in the Embassy in Tokyo on his first tour as a Diplomat in the Commercial Section. Sarah was the first woman to succumb to his charmless advances, as indeed she had succumbed to the advances of just about every other male in the Embassy. Not without reason had Sarah earned the nickname of 'Sarah Pull 'em Down'. That union produced no children and during that tour he developed a taste for the charms of Geisha girls. That brought him to the notice of *Seppuku-kai* as a suitable target for blackmail.

It also coincided with Rory Lequesne's efforts to trace Peter Drummond. The latter summoned his son who was confronted with photographs and videos of his Geisha dalliances and given explicit instructions on what he was to do if he hoped to achieve his ambition of a Knighthood and appointment as British Ambassador to Tokyo. The consequences of his failure to prevent Rory Lequesne or his sister from making the connection between the Head of the Toyohoshi-Kimura Bank and the POW camp traitor were made abundantly clear to Davidson by both his father and the Mafia *kobun*.

With the help of *Seppuku-kai*, Rory Lequesne's sister had died in a contrived car accident in Australia and Rory himself had been killed in a hit and run accident in London. Davidson's failure to destroy the Lequesne papers and bungled efforts to silence John

Gunn had required swift excision by Drummond of his own son in order to preserve his goal of becoming the Chairman of the World's most powerful bank. Just two tasks were left for Peter Drummond as he sat at his desk looking out across the Sumida River and the financial empire which he controlled; the removal of Jiro Kurobashi and John Gunn. He summoned Ichiro Iwakami, the *kobun* of *Seppuku-kai*.

*

'Yes Melanie,' BID's Director acknowledged the pulsing LED light on his desk.

'Martin King would like to know if you have a few minutes for him to brief you on the enhanced security of the files in the restricted access vault.'

'Of course; is he with you now?'

'No, he's on the other line.'

'Now would be a good time Melanie.'

'He'll be with you shortly.'

Since his reprimand from Miles Thompson for allowing the previous Director to bully him into releasing embargoed files, Martin King had initiated much stricter rules for access to highly sensitive files. These were files which had no 'Freedom of Information Act' access date. BID's Head of Finance and Administration was shown into the Director's office by Melanie.

'Come in, Martin,' and Miles came round from behind his desk and sat down in one of the armchairs, indicating the one opposite him to Martin.

'I'm sure you'll remember sir,' Martin began, 'that when you came down to check on those missing folios, it appeared that they were all in the correct position in the files.'

'Yes I do,' Miles said wondering if another security breach had occurred.

'I went through all the files that Davidson removed........' Miles noted the slightly derogatory use of his predecessor's surname.......'and discovered that those folios which you had listed and which appeared to have returned to the files, were all forgeries.......very professionally forged....but forgeries nonetheless.'

'Here I have to say that I only glanced at them,' Miles admitted, but they looked original.'

'As I said sir, very professional forgeries; all the documents related to the Japanese defeat of the Allied Forces defending Hong Kong in the Second World War......the British, Canadian and Indian Regiments. The alterations to those folios focused on the names of officers in the British 5th Regiment Royal Horse Artillery, activities in the POW camps and the loss of the ship *Lisburn Maru* while transporting prisoners from Hong Kong to Japan for slave labour in the mines..........'

'But everything in those files is backed up on CDs,' Miles interrupted.

'And before the advent of CDs, on Microfiche, but Davidson either didn't know this or thought that just by removing the information from the folio it would be enough to prevent attention focusing on one particular person.'

'And that was......?'

'Second Lieutenant Peter Drummond.'

After Martin had left his office, Miles sat for some time wondering what connected Davidson and Drummond. 'Japan was obviously one connection, but was *Seppuku-kai* the main link?' he pondered, 'or could Davidson be related to Drummond. Davidson was about 51 so his father could be still alive.......just.' He pressed the touch-sensitive button on the intercom for BID's Armourer, Tony Taylor.

'Armourer.'

'Tony, Miles; are you busy at the moment and if not, could you come to my office please.'

'No I'm not sir and will be there in a couple of minutes.'

Tony's expertise in almost every form of weapon was largely due to his Army service in the Small Arms School Corps, but his personal file showed that he had transferred from the Royal Artillery as a young sergeant to the SASC. He had retired from the Army as a Lt Colonel in 1995 and joined BID in the same year. His personal file also showed that Tony was a Military Historian and organised small groups of tourists on battlefield tours in France, Gallipoli, Hong Kong and North Africa.

'Tony, I have a small task for you which has nothing to do with your Armourer duties, but requires your knowledge of the Army and Military History,' Miles said when Tony was seated in a chair opposite his Director.

'Right, fire away sir,' and Tony had a notebook and pencil at the ready.

'After all these Defence Reviews and cutbacks since the end of World War Two, does the Royal Artillery still have a 5th Regiment Royal Horse Artillery?'

'Yes sir, but it's now 5th Regiment Royal Artillery; it lost the 'Horse' title back in the fifties.'

'Where is it,' Miles asked.

'In Catterick sir.'

'Good. When the Japs defeated the Allies defending Hong Kong, 5th Regiment was part of the British Forces.'

'It was sir, and equipped with 5.5" medium guns.'

'I'm looking for a photograph of a young officer, 2Lt Peter Drummond, who joined the Regiment in 1941 from Cambridge and was taken prisoner by the Japs in December of the same year. A group photo which we can enlarge and enhance will suffice, but ideally an individual photo if one exists. Can do?'

'Of course sir. I'll get back to you later today with an update,' and with that Tony left the office.

CHAPTER 20

Not a sound came from the black hole into which Gunn had disappeared. Tanya lay on her stomach beside the rectangular aperture peering down in the hope of catching a glimpse of anything below. There was nothing.

'Damn you John Gunn!' she swore under her breath, 'say or do something to let me know if you're OK.'

'Hi there!' Gunn's head suddenly appeared out of the blackness below Tanya frightening her out of her wits.

'You bastard! John, I nearly had a heart attack. You alright?'

'Yes, I'm OK, but there are three guys down there who aren't.'

'Kraja's men?'

'I'll show you in a minute,' Gunn answered as he climbed out of the manhole in the middle of the garage.

'What's down there?'

'Not totally sure myself,' Gunn answered brushing off some of the dirt and dust. 'The battery in this was rapidly losing power,' and he showed her the little Maglite which was reduced to a dull orange glow, before switching it off. 'What's down there is a cross between Madame Tussaud's Chamber of Horrors and a medieval dungeon. There are three dead men......'

'Any of the girls?'

'No girls, just three men; all shot. Presumably Kraja's men. Look, we need to get new batteries for this torch and another torch. I think I remember passing a bicycle shop on the other side of the road.'

'If it's just Kraja's men down there do we need to go down again? Surely we now need to find Kraja and the girls....how, I'm not sure, but that must be the priority.'

'Quite right, and that's exactly what we're going to do and as quickly as possible. Come on,' Gunn said as he led the way back into the house talking as he went. 'That underground chamber is ancient, as I suspect is this house – the garage would've been a much later addition – perhaps a renovated coach house or stable. I was unable to examine it properly, but at the side furthest away from the front of the garage there was the entrance to what could well be a passage.'

'D'you think that's the way he's gone with the girls?' Tanya asked as they retrieved the backpacks from the kitchen on their way out of the back of the house.

'I'm fairly certain that no one came back out of that chamber once they'd gone down. To me it looks as though Kraja's making a run for it – with the girls who will fetch a huge price – and has no intention of sharing the proceeds with any more people than he has to. I would've thought he'd need at least two others to help him with the girls,' Gunn added as he led the way across the road which was now much busier. 'Ah there! Look! About fifty yards further along....that looks like it might sell torches and batteries. What's a 'torch' in French?'

'Same word.....spare batteries as well?'

'Yes. You go on, I'm just going to send a text to Marie de Fonblanque to let her know where we are. Gunn paused in a shop doorway while he sent his text to their current controller before catching up with Tanya.

Five minutes later, equipped with two large torches and spare batteries and new AA batteries for the Maglite, the two of them returned to the Pneus Guilbert house. Gunn climbed into the manhole first and Tanya handed him the backpacks before following him down the metal rungs into the pitch black void below.

Chamber of Horrors was an accurate description of the underground chamber. It was square and about twenty feet long on each side. The stone work of the walls was old but dry and the worn flag-stones on the floor gave a rough indication that it had been there for hundreds of years. At various intervals around the walls were rusty ringbolts, some with even rustier chains hanging from the bolts. Turning her torch up to the ceiling of the chamber, Tanya noticed with a shudder that two huge hooks with needle-sharp points hung down in the centre of the room. Under the hooks were the bodies of three men.

These had to be Kraja's men as the bodies were barely cold and the blood from the multiple bullet wounds was still sticky. Tanya swung the beam of her torch slowly round the chamber pausing at the door on the far side and then moving on until it stopped again at the rungs of the ladder leading up to the garage above. Beside the rungs and about five feet from the floor was a switch; the wiring to the switch came down from the corner of the garage nearest the house and then went horizontally along the stone wall through a wall-mounted light covered by a metal grill until it disappeared through the stonework by the door on the far side of the chamber. She walked towards the light switch.

'Tempting, but I think we'd better do without that,' came Gunn's warning as her hand reached out to the switch. Tanya withdrew her hand. 'The wiring looks in good condition and disappears through the stone wall and down the steps on the other side of that door. I'm pretty certain that's the way Kraja's gone and if we switch on the lighting it could warn him that he's being followed.'

'Shit! That was stupid.'

'Then we're both guilty of stupidity as I nearly did that when the batteries died on your small Maglite – natural reaction. Your knowledge of history couldn't possibly be worse than mine so what do you reckon this is.........? apart from something from your worst nightmare' Gunn asked.

'Not at all sure,' Tanya replied, returning to where Gunn was standing in the centre of the room looking down at the three bodies. 'When I was at the back of the house – by the back door – I noticed a ship leaving the commercial port and directly above the ship.....say about a mile offshore.......was this castle.........'

'Chateau d'If!' they both said in unison.

'Of course.......as infamous in its day,' Tanya continued, 'as Alcatraz was in the twentieth century for hardened criminals, so the dreaded dungeons of Chateau d'If were for the Huguenots who were fleeing from the 'sans-culotte' of the French Revolution. Hundreds, if not thousands were locked away and, like Alcatraz, if the myth can be believed, no one ever escaped. Would this have been a secret way of transporting the prisoners to the dungeons of Chateau d'If?'

'Only one way of finding out,' and Gunn led the way to the door on the other side of the chamber.

*

'Adjutant.'

'Captain Carr-Smith?'

'Speaking.'

'Tony Taylor, may I speak to your Commanding Officer please. He may remember me when I was a Sergeant and he was a Second Lieutenant in 50 Missile Regiment.'

'Just hold the line please,' and Robert Carr-Smith pressed the mute button to kill any conversation being overheard on the phone while he buzzed his Commanding Officer.

'Yes Robert.'

'I have a Tony Taylor on the phone, Colonel, who says he knew you when you were a Second Lieutenant and he was a Sergeant.'

'Christ! That's a name from the past. Yes, put him through Robert.' A click told Tony that he was being connected. 'Tony! Mike here, what can I do for you? Last I heard you had disappeared into the world of spooks.'

'It's connected with that line of work, Mike. I would very much like to come and visit you in Marne Barracks at Catterick.'

'Yes....yes of course...when would this visit be?'

'Tomorrow, as early as possible please.'

'That urgent?'

'Yes Mike; would 8.30 be OK?'

'That is early; you coming by train or car?'

'Chopper; could I ask your Adjutant to gather together every photo album, picture or group photo of officers who were in the

Regiment when it was in Hong Kong in 1941 at the time of the Japanese invasion?'

'May I know who it is you're looking for?'

'Yes, of course, Mike – when I see you tomorrow, oh yes, one more request, your regimental history records for the years 1939 through 1941,' and Tony ended the call with a cheery goodbye and before he was asked any other questions over an open phone line. He replaced the phone in its charging base and shook his head. 'Not the sharpest pin in the cushion, but solid and reliable – I bet that was written on every one of his confidential reports,' Tony smiled as he picked up the phone again and dialled Malcolm Springfield's number in the heliport on the 15th floor.

The 250 mile flight from the heliport on the top of Kingsroad House to Marne Barracks at Catterick took the Gazelle one hour and forty minutes; it landed in front of the headquarter building of 5th Regiment Royal Artillery at 08.26 allowing Tony Taylor to walk through the front entrance of the Headquarters at exactly 08.30. All he had with him in a slim manuscript briefcase were various photos of Sir Ian Davidson – for a brief period, the Director of the British Intelligence Directorate. Tony was met by the Adjutant and taken into the CO's office.

In the office, laid out on a six foot table with folding legs, was a collection of albums, framed photos and brown envelopes containing more photos – so the writing on the outside stated. On a separate table were the box files of the Regimental History covering 1939, 40 and 41. Coffee was produced and then the CO, who was dressed in full desert combat uniform, excused himself saying that he was off to take part in a preparatory training exercise for Operation Herrick, the British military commitment in Afghanistan.

Tony Taylor started with the regimental history. In each file was every detail of what the regiment had done in that year and included the names of every officer and other rank. It covered every detail from operational commitments to the wining battery of the regimental rugby seven-a-side competition. From these files he discovered that 2/Lt Peter Drummond had joined the regiment in Tidworth in January 1940, a fortnight before it deployed to Hong

Kong to augment the artillery support for the increased number of infantry battalions which had been sent to defend the territory against the perceived threat of a Japanese invasion from the sea.

He then seated himself at the six foot table and started with the framed photos, followed by the loose photos and finally turned to the albums. At the outset of the Second World War, an efficient quartermaster had packed up all the regimental silver and historical memorabilia and sent it back to the Royal Artillery's home at Woolwich in London. Had it not been for this sensible precaution all the memorabilia would have been burnt and the silver stolen by the Japanese invading army which sacked all the barracks of the Hong Kong based garrison.

Because of his fluency in both Mandarin Chinese and Japanese, Peter Drummond had been posted to the Headquarter Battery of the Regiment as the Assistant Intelligence Officer. Gradually Tony Taylor amassed a small pile of photos and opened albums where he had identified Peter Drummond. He walked next door to the Adjutant.

'Robert, do you have a facility for enhancing and enlarging a particular character in a photo?'

'With the target identification equipment we have in this Regiment, sir, we could enhance a pinhead to the size of a football. What is it you need?' Tony showed Robert the person in each photo he needed enhanced, restraining a wry smile that he was now addressed as 'sir'.

'No problem.' The Adjutant made a phone call and within five minutes a young sergeant appeared, had the task explained to him and departed with the albums, photos and framed group photos. While he was waiting for the result, Tony received a call on his cellphone from Malcolm Springfield to tell him that the Gazelle had been refuelled. The sergeant returned after twenty minutes with A4 size photos of Peter Drummond. The quality and clarity of the photos was unbelievable. He took them into the CO's office and removed the photos from his briefcase of Ian Davidson.

Tony had been prepared to be disappointed at the result. He was well aware that sons did not necessarily take after their fathers in looks, but the photos laid out in front of him proved, almost conclusively, that Ian Davidson was Peter Drummond's son.

*

The door in the chamber opened soundlessly on well-oiled hinges. Gunn shone his torch into the short passageway on the other side revealing the 21st Century cabling and lighting which he dared not use however tempting. The underground passage ran for about ten yards before it disappeared steeply down a flight of steps. The stonework was dry and in an excellent state of repair.

The steps continued down in flight after flight with a level stretch of passage between each flight that varied in length from five to ten yards. Tanya tapped Gunn on the shoulder on one of the level stretches. He stopped.

'Do you think this tunnel goes all the way to the castle?'

'No idea, but the more I think about it the less I believe that this was a covert way of transporting prisoners to the castle dungeons. I think that this old house – somewhere above us – was the equivalent of some sort of 'safe-house'. A bit like the 'priest holes' in old houses where they hid Roman Catholic priests in Elizabethan England. In this case a place where those fleeing from persecution, or whatever, could be hidden until they were moved on by ship. I seem to remember that the majority of the Huguenots fled to England via the Channel ports of France, but Robespierre's reign of terror against France's aristocracy must have been just as blood thirsty down here in the south.'

'The air in this tunnel is really quite fresh. Would it be this fresh if the tunnel ran all the way out to the Chateau d'If? I dunno,' and Gunn shrugged his shoulders. 'Come on, only one way of finding out,' and he set off again down the next flight with Tanya close behind him. After several more flights of steps, the stonework showed increasing signs of damp and then the steps ceased and the passage levelled out. Gunn paused. 'We must be at sea level....or perhaps even below it.' Tanya shuddered.

'I hope you're right about this not going all the way to the Chateau.....'

'Shhhh......steps ahead of us going up,' Gunn interrupted. They climbed one flight of steps and then came a short passage and a heavy, wooden steel-bound door. Gunn tried the door. It was very firmly locked. 'Bugger!' he mouthed quietly. 'I suppose I half expected that.'

'Those of any use?' Tanya whispered behind him, shining her torch on a row of steel hooks on which hung three keys.

'Well spotted....let's hope so,' and Gunn took down two of the keys and examined them closely under the light of the torch. 'These two are identical.' He took down the third key, 'and so is this. There must be a system of unlocking the door, taking the key, relocking from the outside and then returning the key when the tunnel is used next.' He returned two of the keys and quietly slotted the third one into the lock. He then removed the Glock from his pocket, turned to see that Tanya was holding her automatic and turned the key.

The door fitted snugly into the jamb, but opened inwards without too much effort. Daylight flooded into the tunnel. In front of them was a small stone jetty in a secluded arm of the commercial port. Three small fishing boats were moored stern-on to the jetty with their bows out in deeper water tied up to buoys. There wasn't a person in sight. The small jetty was completely hidden from the commercial port. They both walked out of the tunnel onto the jetty.

'I think you were right; this is how the Huguenots escaped the guillotine. From here they would have been taken by boat with muffled oars at dead of night and mist hanging low over the water out to a clipper, anchored out of sight round the headland and then to England and safety.......how delightfully Daphne du Maurier!' Tanya added with a chuckle.

Gunn smiled, 'I thought it was Baroness someone or other who invented the Scarlet Pimpernel.......'

'........Orczy,' Tanya prompted.

'........so it was; with a bit of luck we can forget about oars as all three of those boats will have diesel engines.'

CHAPTER 21

'*Kon'nichiwa*, Iwakami.'

'Hello Mr Iwakami this is Kraja.'

'Oh, hello Kraja-san, do you have any news for me?'

'Some; but I need to know where your Learjet is?'

'The Learjet is at Toulon-Hyères Airport; I gave instructions to move it there when you told me that you were heading south with the packages.'

'That is excellent Mr Iwakami. Contact your pilots and tell them to be ready for an immediate take-off on full tanks with a flight plan to Tokyo.'

'That will be done Kraja-san, now where is this man Gunn?'

'Don't worry about him Iwakami. We will deal with him. You just make sure that plane of yours is ready for an immediate departure, goodbye,' and Kraja ended the call on his cellphone.

'How are you planning to deal with Gunn, patron, when we don't know where he is?' Marku asked.

'Gunn can wait, Marku, he is of no immediate threat to us. Has Bekim gone down to the jetty to get rid of all the tourists?'

'Yes patron, he's just phoned to tell me that the last boat has left. When the tour guides objected to being removed from the island, he told them that the castle was about to be used by the army to test a new biological agent. They couldn't get off the island fast enough after that!'

'And the helicopter?'

'It's already taken off from the airport at Toulon and should be here in ten minutes.'

'And Duka's in the helicopter with the pilot?'

'He is and the pilot has been told that he is picking up three candidates for the Miss France event in Cannes next week. Duka told him that they had been on a pre-event shoot using the Chateau d'If as background. He will deal with the pilot when the helicopter gets here and then he'll fly it back to Toulon. It's just as well we haven't got the other three here, patron, as the helicopter only has a capacity for six passengers.'

'All three had become a liability. I could no longer trust them. There'll be nothing left but bones by the time anyone discovers them. Now let's get the girls ready for the helicopter flight.'

*

'Morning Marie, you're bright and early. How's John's and Tanya's assignment going?' Charles Gardner asked his controller as he passed her office door. Each area Assistant Director in BID had a small suite of offices which consisted of the AD's office, another for the PA, a controller's office, an empty office for an agent's use and lastly a washroom and small kitchenette. Charles Gardner was the AD for the European Community and was known as 'Charlie' by everyone in BID.

As the European Union grew in size it was finally decided to provide Charlie with an assistant. Helen Szyra, whose family had emigrated from Poland to the UK just days before Hitler's forces invaded in September 1939, now occupied the 'agent's office' and shared the services of Simone – Charlie's PA. Charlie looked after the 'old EU' and was the Head of the Department while Helen dealt with the 'new EU' countries. Peter Bancroft was her controller who shared an office with Marie.

'Ah! Charlie, good morning,' Marie replied, getting up from behind her desk. She had been at BID since seven the previous evening in case Gunn needed any support as he drove south with Tanya in pursuit of the Albanian Mafia and the lorry-load of young girls for auction.

'Any news?' Charlie asked as Marie followed him into his office.

'Yes, I had a text not long ago. Kraja has left a trail of bodies behind him. In addition to those at the warehouse in Rue Samson and the ones in the lorry abandoned on the A6 south of Paris, Gunn and Tanya have found three more........'

'Not girls?' Charlie interrupted.

'.........no, not girls, men; possibly his own Mafia. For some reason which is not clear, Kraja has used an old underground tunnel from the house in Marseille to remove himself, the girls and however many of his Mafia, to the Chateau d'If......... yes, that's the castle just off the coast,' she added as Charlie made to interrupt. 'John reckons he's about to leave Marseille. The only reason he can think of for the move to the isle of If is because it offers both the space and security for a helicopter to land and take off. I get the feeling that this assignment is coming to a conclusion – certainly France and the Albanian connection. BID's in-country agent, Bruno Lauriant, is keeping an eye on events in Paris and minimising the damage potential of the Mafia's mole 'Phoenix' in the Police Headquarters. I believe that I would be of more use to John and Tanya if I was in Marseille.'

'Makes sense. When are you off?'

Marie looked at her watch. 'In about ten minutes. Malcolm will fly me there in the Lynx - direct to Toulon Airport.'

'Let me have an up-date as soon as you are able so that I can brief the Boss.'

'Will do Charlie,' and Marie left his office, picked up a small backpack from her office and headed for the lift to the 15th floor and BID's heliport.

*

Gunn dropped his backpack on the jetty and climbed down into one boat after the other to check the fuel tanks. All three of the boats had the same model of two cylinder diesel engine.

'This one has a tank that's half full,' he announced. Tanya handed him the backpacks and jumped down into the boat. The engine was positioned in the centre of the fishing boat inside a wooden box. Gunn lifted the lid of the box and decompressed the cylinders.

'When I say 'now' flick that lever that I've just moved back to the compressed position. OK?'

'OK.' Tanya moved to a position where she could get at the small lever while Gunn turned the engine over.

'Now!'

Tanya flicked the lever over; the engine fired and then stopped.

'OK, let's try again.' The next time the engine fired and then settled to a steady thump, thump, thump.

'I'll let go the stern line if you could untie the bow line from that ring on the buoy.

'Clear now.'

'Thanks,' and Gunn pushed the gear lever forward and then increased the rev's with the hand throttle. The small boat came out from its secluded jetty into the main part of the commercial port. Tanya moved back from the bow to where Gunn was sitting at the tiller.

'I suppose that metal-lined box in the bow is for storing the catch. Any thoughts on a plan of action?'

'Lots, and most of them pointless until we get a bit closer to that island. Have you got a spare mag' for your Smith and Wesson?'

'Two.'

'And a silencer?'

'Check.'

'Good, and my two mag's and a silencer for the Glock. We've been just too late at each stage of our pursuit to get even the slightest advantage, but that may be in our favour.......oops!' and Gunn swung the tiller over as a powerful pilot pinnace suddenly appeared at full speed from behind the stern of a large cargo ship and gave him a series of imperious blasts on its klaxon as it headed out to escort another vessel into the port. Gunn pointed the little boat into the steep bow wave. 'That's our one advantage; Kraja doesn't know that we are this close to him. The last he heard of us would have been from his mole in the police headquarters. He knows that we will have raided his place in Rue Samson, but believes that no one knows where he's gone. He managed to shake off the police chopper easily enough. If we believe the message left behind by the girls, their final destination is Japan. Kraja couldn't possibly take the girls on a scheduled flight whatever excuse he conjured up. Agreed?'

'Unless he transported them as patients.....drugged of course, on an air-ambulance flight,' Tanya suggested.

'Yeees,' Gunn acknowledged, 'but I don't think he's had time to arrange all that even if he does have members of his Mafia all over France.'

'Why go to the house in the Rue Rabelais and not directly to an airfield?'

'I believe he's trying to cut himself some time to make a clean getaway. He knows that the police would have the registration numbers and description of both the cars in the garage at Rue Rabelais. That would have been circulated to every police region in France and certainly to every airport and port. So by leaving the cars under cover in a garage, unknown – he thinks – by anyone pursuing him, he has achieved that. Of course he knew that the police would eventually find the Rabelais house and also the underground chamber, bodies and tunnel, but by then Kraja would be long gone on his way to Japan. So somewhere on the south coast there has to be a private aircraft capable of making that sort of long-haul flight......that could be at a private airfield or an airport like Nice or Toulon. In my text to BID I said that I thought that the reason for his move to the castle was to secure a landing site for a chopper to get him, the girls and however men he has left to the RV with an aircraft.'

Their fishing boat was now clear of the main port breakwater and rose and fell in the slight chop of the open sea. Gunn checked his watch; it was just before ten. The low autumn sun spotlighted If Island and its sheer-sided rock cliffs topped by battlements and gun embrasures providing a formidable barrier to anyone wanting to get onto the island anywhere other than by the only landing jetty. From the jetty, the zig-zag flights of steps cut into the rock-face led up to the plateau on which the square, three-turreted castle stood on the western end of the island with a lighthouse at the eastern end.

Gunn judged the lozenge-shaped island, lying east/west, to be no more than four or five acres in area.

They were now less than half a mile from the island and both of them could see a couple of boats tied up alongside the jetty.

'The tourists around here get going early.....it's not even ten and some of them seem to be leaving the island,' Tanya remarked, shading her eyes from the bright sunlight. One of the tourist boats was already moving away from the island and heading towards them.

'They're all leaving the island. Look at all those people coming down the steps. I'm going to head towards that boat. With your mastery of the lingo, see if you can find out what's happening.' Gunn adjusted the heading of their boat so that it would meet up with the tourist boat. Tanya stood up and waved. A couple of the tourists waved back, but the boat slowed. Tanya waited until less than twenty metres separated the two boats.

'Qu'est-ce qui se passe?' she shouted cupping her hands around her mouth to make her voice carry. Some of the tourists shouted various unintelligible responses until the tour guide appeared with a megaphone.

'L'accès à l'île est interdit pour des raisons militaires.'

'Pourquoi?' Tanya shouted back.

'Parce qu'il est toxique de gaz.'

'Merci beaucoup, merci,' and Tanya turned to Gunn, 'you get that?'

'Yes, cheers, so that's the excuse that Kraja's using to clear everyone off the island.'

After more waving, the two boats separated and Gunn headed the small fishing boat obliquely at the island to try and make it look as though they were going to pass by it.

'One man could prevent anyone from using those steps up to the castle,' he commented.

They were now only a couple of hundred yards from the jetty and only one tourist boat remained taking on board the last of its passengers. There was a man standing at the foot of the first flight of steps cut into the rock face.

'And that's the man,' Gunn said nodding his head in the direction of the jetty. 'He's the first item on our plan of action. He'll be armed and will either have a radio or a cellphone. We have to get rid of him before he warns the others or we will have to find some other way up that rock face.'

'Agreed, but whatever we do must be done quickly because if you're right about the chopper it could be on its way here already. How's about this; when we're out of sight of that guy, you strip off and go over the side of the boat. I'll run the boat up to the steps in the jetty and with a bit of luck that will make him come over to warn me off. He'll be no more than ten yards away from you. Shit! I think I can hear that chopper now.'

'Can't think of a better plan,' and so saying Gunn stripped off and shoved his clothes and the two backpacks into the fish storage box in the bow. Tanya took over the tiller and swung the boat round heading back towards the jetty steps. Gunn used the end of the stern warp to tie a bight round a midships thwart, leaving a two foot loop hanging over the side to use as a handhold. He slipped over the side of the boat, hanging on with his left hand and holding the silenced Glock in his right. The sound of the approaching helicopter was now much louder.

'Another fifty yards to the steps..........he's seen me and is waving me off,' Tanya gave Gunn a running commentary as she stood up and waved back to the man. 'He's coming towards the steps now........he's about thirty or forty yards away.......his right hand is behind his back.......could have a weapon in that hand.'

'Bonjour M'sieur! Qu'est-ce qui se passe?' she raised her voice as she addressed the man.

'Va-t'en, Mme'selle!' was the immediate rough response and then in a more conciliatory tone, 'Il est interdit de rester ici aujourdhui. C'est peut-être possible demain.'

'He's coming towards the steps........about five yards to go.' Her commentary was almost drowned by the deafening clatter and beat of the helicopter's rotors as it banked above them into a hover before landing.

'Bonjour M'sieur,' Gunn greeted the man guarding access to the castle as he hooked his elbows over the boat's gun'le. The man's reaction was instantaneous. His right hand appeared in a split second holding an Uzi-type machine pistol. The Glock's two 9 mm bullets from Gunn's 'double tap' aimed at the man's chest knocked him off his feet and the machine pistol out of his hand, but not before his dying muscular finger contraction squeezed off a burst of five rounds into the air; fortunately, the sound was swamped by the heavy thwack, thwack, thwack of the helicopter's rotors biting into the thin warm air to hold it in the hover as it descended onto the open ground beyond the castle.

'What's all this "bonjour M'sieur" bit then?' Tanya queried as she tied the boat's bow warp to a bollard on the jetty. Gunn heaved himself over the gun'le and quickly pulled on his T-shirt and jeans.

'It's a bit like shooting a game bird that's not flying,' Gunn answered with a chuckle, putting his wet feet into his trainers. 'We didn't know whether he had a weapon or not. In spite of them all deserving to go to the guillotine, I still have a faint hint of a qualm about executing an unarmed person. C'mon, I'll get rid of the body and then let's see what's happening up at the castle,' and Gunn dragged the man's body over to the edge of the jetty, kicked it into the sea and picked up the machine pistol.

'Just as well that chopper was there to cover the sound of his gun discharging,' and Tanya followed Gunn to the steps.

'And that's the first thing we need to do,' Gunn said over his shoulder as he took the steps two at a time.

'What's that?'

'Disable that chopper.'

CHAPTER 22

'Where are the girls?' Kraja shouted at Marku, trying to make himself heard above the deafening racket of the Augusta helicopter's twin turbo-shaft engines. They were both standing in the arched entrance to the castle, shielding their eyes from the dust storm raised by the rotors.

The entrance opened onto the centre courtyard of the castle which was constructed in the form of a hollow square. Within this hollow square steps to the four above ground floors had been constructed on the outside of the walls providing access to the cells on each floor. Steps from the ground floor of the castle led down to the deepest dungeons which had been hewn out of the island's sandstone rock. These dungeons had no windows and in the 16th Century the occupants were incarcerated without any form of sanitation in permanent darkness. For the benefit of tourism there was now lighting on all floors so that tourists could 'ooh, aah and shudder' at the horrific cruelty of Europe's medieval era.

'They're in cell 3 on the ground floor of the courtyard – it's the only cell which had a key to lock the door,' Marku answered, removing his hands from shielding his eyes as the helicopter's engines were shut down.

'What's happened to Bekim?'

'Still getting rid of the tourists I expect.'

'If he doesn't appear soon we'll go without him.'

'I'll go and get him,' and Marku set off at a jog trot in the direction of the steps leading down to the jetty.

Duka stepped down from the observer's seat of the helicopter and walked over to Kraja.

'Any problems?' Kraja asked.

'None, the flight plan is approved and the pilot believes that he's about to fly three potential 'Miss Cannes' back to Toulon Airport. The Lear Jet chartered by the Toyohoshi-Kimura Bank to fly all of us to Tokyo is ready to depart on a logged flight plan via Dubai, Delhi and Hong Kong. Where are the girls?'

'Marku has locked them in cell number 3 on the ground floor. He's gone to collect Bekim from the jetty where he's been keeping the tourists away from this place. I want you to go and collect the girls; here's the key. I'll deal with the pilot,' Kraja added as he checked his automatic, flicked off the safety and returned the 9mm Ruger to his jacket pocket.

'Will do,' and Duka went into the courtyard and headed for the cells on the ground floor.

*

Gunn went up the last eight steps on all fours stopping when his head was below the top step. Once over that step any part of him would be in full view of the castle and the open area around it. The racket from the helicopter's turbines was dying down. He cautiously peered over the top step. Two men were standing at the entrance to the castle and, as he watched, a third man climbed down from the front port-hand door of the helicopter.

'That makes three of them plus the pilot.......watch out Tanya!........ one of them is running over here. Quick, go back down to the bottom of this flight.' The two of them hurried down the steps to the place where the next flight down of the 'zig-zag' staircase was out of sight from anyone coming down the top flight. Gunn heard the man pause on the top step, no doubt Gunn thought, to see if he could signal to the man on the jetty and save himself the effort of going down to find him. He would have already discovered that he wasn't answering his cellphone. The man took the steps two at a time in his anxiety to get to the bottom as quickly as possible. As he reached the turning point where Gunn and Tanya were concealed he was taking the stairs at a reckless pace and certainly off balance.

Gunn stepped out at the last second, tripped the man and at the same time brought down a crushing blow with the side of his clenched fist at the base of the man's neck. He disappeared over the metal hand rail with no more than a gasp to fall seventy feet to the concrete jetty below.

'That leaves two plus the pilot. C'm'on,' and Gunn led the way back up the steps, again going down on all fours before reaching the top. Both of them peered over the top step. The pilot was walking round the helicopter doing his various pre-flight checks. The man who Gunn had seen standing at the castle entrance was walking slowly towards the helicopter which was about 50 yards from the top of the steps. When the man was about halfway between the helicopter and the castle, another man came out of the castle entrance and hurried across to him. The pilot paused in his checks and looked in the direction of the two men. The one who had run out of the castle was talking in an animated fashion, pointing back at the castle.

*

'What the hell's the matter?' Kraja asked as Duka ran out from the castle courtyard.

'You're sure it was number 3?'

'Yes, of course I am. They couldn't possibly have got out from the cell unless Marku forgot to lock it.'

'No, it's not that. I can't get the key into the lock to open the door.'

'Oh for Christ's sake do I have to do everything. Go on,' and Kraja followed Duka back into the castle and across the courtyard to the cells. The door was clearly marked with the number 3. Five foot off the ground was a small barred aperture in the door. Kraja peered in, but there was no sign of the girls. The door opened outwards. He snatched the key off Duka and tried it in the lock. It wouldn't go in. He bent down and looked into the keyhole. It was completely blocked. 'The bitches! They've jammed something into the keyhole from the other side. Go and find something like a nail which can be hammered into the keyhole to force out whatever it is that's jamming the lock.'

'Where in hell am I supposed to find a nail for Christ's sake?'

'For fuck's sake do I have to do everything myself. You saw that building to the right of the castle entrance?'

'Yes.'

'That's where the castle and island maintenance staff live and store all their equipment. There's bound to be a toolbox there.'

'What about the maintenance staff?'

'There were two of them. One of them left without any trouble with the tourists. The other refused to go so Bekim shot him. Now for fuck's sake get a move on while I get rid of the pilot.'

*

'Something's gone wrong. What do you reckon it is?' Gunn whispered.

'It must be to do with the girls. Look, I reckon the pilot's one of the good guys. Let me go over there and talk to him. It'll only take me a couple of seconds to run there. I know all pilots have to speak English, but I'm the one who speaks French and may be able to explain to him quicker than you. OK?'

Gunn paused for only a second; 'go on, off you go,' and Tanya leapt to her feet and ran across the open 50 yards between the steps and the helicopter. Gunn had his Glock ready to cover her if anyone appeared from the castle or if the pilot suddenly turned hostile. Neither happened and Tanya arrived at a rather bewildered looking pilot and led him out of sight behind the fuselage. They had only just moved behind the Augusta when a man appeared at the castle entrance, glanced in the direction of the helicopter and then ran across to the single storey building to one side of the castle. As soon as the man disappeared into the building, Tanya reappeared from behind the helicopter and waved urgently to Gunn, beckoning him towards her. Gunn got to his feet and sprinted across the short distance.

'John, this is Captain Chevalier who is employed by Charte de L'Air et cie based at Toulon-Hyères Airport. He was told that today's charter was to take one passenger to Chateau d'If and return with three girls who'd been on a photo shoot and four cameramen and fly them to Toulon airport.'

'Hello Captain, how quickly can you take off in this helicopter?' Gunn asked the pilot.

'No more than one minute........but I was....,'the reply ended in mid sentence as the pilot looked with increasing apprehension at the silenced automatics being held by both Gunn and Tanya.

'No time to explain Captain. Get back into your helicopter and take off as soon as possible if you want to stay alive. Once you're clear of the island, please contact the police.....we could do with some help here.'

'Who are you?' the pilot asked as he climbed back into the Augusta.

'British Intelligence working with your Sécurité Extérieure. Here.......' and Gunn put his hand in his back pocket. 'Oh shit! it's in my anorak in the boat.'

'It's OK....here's mine.' and Tanya produced her BID ID.

The pilot barely glanced at it as he started both engines. Gunn and Tanya backed away from the Augusta and hid behind the battlements overlooking the precipitous edge of the plateau. Gunn glanced at his watch.

'Come on, come on man; go for an emergency take off,' Gunn urged looking from the helicopter to the castle. As if he had heard Gunn's exhortations, the pilot clutched in the rotors which rapidly built up speed. The man who had gone into the maintenance building reappeared, holding what looked like a toolbox. It was only at that moment that another man appeared at the castle entrance. He waved his arms at the helicopter making a cutting signal across his throat. When there was no response from the helicopter except the roar of the turbines going to full power the man pulled an automatic out of his pocket.

With both his forearms resting on the wall of the old gun embrasure, Gunn took careful aim and fired as the man raised his automatic. It was a long range shot and the bullet missed the man, but must have been close, Gunn reckoned, because he dropped to the prone position making himself a much smaller target.

With a lurch the Augusta helicopter heaved itself off the ground, swung round so that it's tail rotor faced the castle offering the least vulnerable aspect to the gunman and clawed its way east into the sky from the Chateau d'If.

*

After emptying his magazine at the departing helicopter, the man leapt to his feet and ducked and weaved his way back through the castle entrance, hoping to make himself as difficult a target as possible. Gunn wasn't prepared to attempt a shot at a range of nearly a hundred yards.

'Right, that's two of them plus the girls and the only way off for the two men is in our boat or a body-bag. What d'you reckon's gone wrong inside the castle?'

'No idea, but it seems that whatever it is it needs a toolbox to sort it out.'

The man with toolbox ran back to the castle. It was obvious that he had neither heard nor noticed the shot fired by Gunn's silenced Glock or had even seen the two of them behind the gun embrasure. He disappeared through the castle entrance.

'We need to be very quick while they're sorting out whatever's gone wrong. Cover me while I run to the castle. I'll then cover you. OK?'

'Ready!'

Gunn sprinted the hundred yards across to the castle. No sooner had he reached the entrance than Tanya followed. No one made any effort to fire at them.

'I'm going to find out what's gone wrong....if I can,' and Gunn edged round the carved stonework of the archway. At first there appeared to be no one.....until the sound of hammering on the far side of the courtyard revealed the two men trying to do something to one of the cell doors. Gunn turned back to Tanya. 'I don't think these guys even know we're here. The one who fired at the chopper must've thought that it was the pilot who shot at him. I'll work my way round to the left and you go to the right. All the doors to the cells appear to be open so there's plenty of cover.'

Tanya moved across to the other side of the arch and as Gunn moved into the courtyard on the left side going from one cell door to the next, Tanya did the same on the right. Until they had both worked their way round the courtyard and were on the same side as the two men still engrossed in the task of trying to open the cell door. Tanya waved at Gunn and then held her fist out in a 'thumbs up' sign.

'Kraja!' Gunn shouted, 'stop what you're doing and both of you........'but he got no further as both men spun round drawing their automatics as they turned towards Gunn. One man dropped to the ground in a crouch and emptied an entire magazine at the area from where they had heard Gunn's shouted order. While Gunn ducked back into a cell door as bullets ricocheted off the stone walls around the cell door, the other man made a dash for the archway on the opposite side of the courtyard to the entrance.

The volley of shots fired at Gunn was followed by the sound of one shot from Tanya's Smith and Wesson. The man outside cell number 3 was taken completely by surprise. His automatic dropped from his grasp as he collapsed on the stone paving of the courtyard. Gunn ran across to him. There was no need to check for a pulse. Tanya's 9 mm bullet had gone into the back of his head as he faced in the opposite direction towards Gunn. There was very little left of the front of the skull or the man's face.

Gunn crouched by the man's body covering the archway where the other man had gone. Tanya joined Gunn.

'Good shooting; can you stay here and talk to the girls. This looks like the key to the door,' Gunn said handing a large key to Tanya which had been lying on the ground by the dead man.

'Sure,' she replied taking the key and turning to the door where a frightened young face had appeared at the grilled window. Gunn removed the silencer from his Glock and pushed it into his pocket. He edged along the wall past two open cell doors to the archway. As he reached the archway he dropped to a crouch and swung round

233

holding the Glock in both hands as he covered the area beyond the arch. There was no one........nothing, except an empty stone hallway and a large notice "Pour les Donjons" at the top of a circular stairway descending into the darkness.

*

As soon as BID's Lynx landed at Toulon Airport, a black Citröen pulled up beside it. Marie de Fonblanque stepped down from the rear door of the Lynx and was handed her backpack by the co-pilot.

'Marie de Fonblanque?' queried the be-suited man who had got out of the back of the Citröen.

'Oui, c'est moi........aah! Jean-Paul Lefevre,' and the man from the DGSE and Marie embraced. 'That's really kind of you to meet me, Jean-Paul.'

'Not at all, my boss insisted on it. Your John Gunn and the young woman with him have helped us greatly by taking action against the Albanian Mafia when we found that our hands were tied.' They both got into the car. 'First of all we will go to the control tower as I know from your phone call that you want to check on a particular aircraft.'

'Yes please, that'd be fine.'

'There has been a call from the pilot of a helicopter from Charte de l'Air who flew out to the Château d'If this morning to collect three girls. The pilot told the police that they should go out to the Château and help two agents from British Intelligence.'

'And are the police going to the Château?'

'Yes they are, but you will know how it is with these things..... the bureaucracy and procedures....I hope they will be on their way shortly. The pilot has offered to fly them there if it will speed up things,' Jean-Paul added with a Gallic lift of the shoulders.

They had now reached the entrance to the control tower and Lefevre led the way into the lift and pressed the button for the floor below the control room. They were met by the Director of the flight control centre and taken into the busy office where all the flight plans were received, checked, approved or modified and then approved.

'Yes Madame, what can we do for you and the British Intelligence Directorate?' Marie was asked after the introductions. After the formality of introductions, Monsieur Girard, the flight control director turned to Marie.

'Do you have either at this airport or at Nice any private aircraft for which a flight plan to Tokyo has been filed?' Marie asked him.

'Not to my............'

'Mais oui patron.' This came from a woman behind a desk that had no less than three computer screens facing her. 'I can answer that immediately. There is a Lear jet from Yokohama Eachata, registration JARC 4154, parked out at Stand 14, fully fuelled and waiting for the arrival of its passengers, who, we are told, will arrive by helicopter.'

'Thank you Madame, that is most helpful. Will you excuse me Monsieur Girard while I call my office?'

'Of course.'

As Marie left the office she saw the Director pull his shirt sleeve down which had been rolled up. It still didn't quite cover what was either a birth mark or a tattoo. She dialled the Operations Centre at BID.

'Ops.'

'Marie de Fonblanque; there is a Lear jet currently parked up at Toulon Airport belonging to Yokohama Eachata, registration number JARC 4154 with a logged flight plan to Tokyo. I want to know who has chartered this aircraft – not the front organisation or any cut-out companies – but the main player behind the charter and I need this information within one hour or sooner if possible.'

'Got that; on the number you're using?

'Affirmative.'

'Got all that,' and the call was ended.

CHAPTER 23

On the wall by the archway leading to the underground dungeons was a metal plate with four switches on it. Gunn went over to it and tried each switch in turn. The first one turned on a light in the hallway, the second appeared to do nothing and the third and fourth switches operated lights in the courtyard. Gunn tried the second switch again looking at the lights on the wall of the spiral staircase leading down to the dungeons, before he realised that the light had been smashed and there were glass fragments on the stone steps. The man who had disappeared down to the dungeons must have had enough time to smash each light on his way down.

The steps were in their original 16th Century state with no balustrade and worn into a depression in the middle of each step by the countless feet of wretched prisoners, heartless wardens and modern day tourists. The spiral staircase wound down clockwise around a central open shaft of unknown depth to Gunn. Daylight from the hallway above would make anyone descending the staircase as easy a target as a china duck at a funfair........particularly if he went down the stairs upright. He lay down on the stone floor holding the Glock in his right hand and leopard-crawled across the floor to the head of the staircase. Taking care to avoid the broken glass from the stair lighting, he eased his way over the top step and began his headfirst descent down the spiral stone steps, tucked close in to the wall on his left.

The worst part would be the first couple of spirals where the daylight from the hall would always be to the advantage of his adversary. The further down into the darkness that Gunn went so the odds stacked against him would even out. By the second spiral he had avoided the broken glass from three smashed lights, but there was no sign or sound of the man below him. At the foot of the third spiral, in almost complete darkness, he reached the first underground cell level. As his eyesight became more and more accustomed to the dark, he could just make out that he was now in a circular chamber, extending out from the open central shaft with cells leading off all the way round to the point where the stairs went down to the next level.

Halfway round the chamber there appeared to be a corridor heading away from Gunn and presumably leading to many more cells. He rose first to a crouch and then slowly stood up. No reaction from anywhere or anyone. Starting with the first cell on his left, Gunn went from cell to cell. Each was the same; nothing but a stone bench for a bed. 'How did anyone survive imprisonment in such fucking awful conditions,' Gunn thought as he checked all the cells before once again going down on hands and knees and starting to crawl down the next flight of the spiral staircase.

Even though his night vision had managed to cope with the conditions on the first underground level, it now became a matter of feeling his way in total darkness. A further three spirals and he reached the next level down. Again he rose first to a crouch and then stood up. Not a sound.......anywhere. He edged slowly over to his right to a point where the next flight of stairs down would start; nothing. He was on the lowest level of the dungeons. This was a much larger chamber and by feeling his way round the walls he bumped into all sorts of strange objects.

'Aaah,' Gunn thought to himself, 'this is where the poor bloody prisoners would be treated to the delights of all the macabre medieval torture machines..........'CRASH!.......hardly had the thought come to mind than Gunn tripped and fell against something metal and as tall as himself. He spun round when he'd regained his balance, dropping to a crouch to make himself as small a target as possible because the noise must have given away his exact position to his quarry.

No response at all; Gunn's heart was pounding so hard he thought it must be audible. Slowly, slowly he stood up and felt for the metal casing he had crashed into. It was taller than him.......so about seven foot high and in the shape of a large bomb standing on its base. His knees felt damp from where he had crouched after bumping into the 'metal bomb'. He put his hand down.......the moisture on his knees was sticky. 'Oh shit! that's blood,' he thought as he rubbed the sticky fluid between his finger and thumb. He wiped his hands on his jeans.

Still holding the Glock in his right hand he ran his left hand over the metal casing until he found a catch on the right side. The catch eventually moved after he had tried pushing and pulling it and with no warning the curved metal front piece swung open towards Gunn, knocking him over......again.

'John?' his name shouted by Tanya echoed down the labyrinth of floors, corridors and cells from the hall two floors above. Gunn got to his feet, now realising how the man he had been following had met his fate. A fate thoroughly fitting for the appalling cruelty inflicted on the young girls in Rue Samson and the abandoned lorry on the A6.

'OK Tanya,' Gunn shouted back, 'have you got your torch?'

There was a pause and then: 'yes.'

'Watch out for the broken glass on the steps. I'm at the bottom of the second flight of stairs.' Moments later, he saw the loom of her torch as she descended the spiral staircase.

'Where's Kraja?' she asked as she reached the foot of the stairs.

'Is that who it is?'

'So the girls said after they'd seen the......oh my God!' The exclamation came as the beam from Tanya's torch illuminated what remained of the man Gunn had followed down to the dungeons.

'Not a pretty sight.........I think this particular piece of horrific medieval gadgetry was known as the 'Iron Maiden'.' Tanya's small torch illuminated the full horror of the lethal punishment inflicted on the man's body in the iron sarcophagus. Long needle-sharp daggers protruding from the open sarcophagus lid had pierced both his eyes, his mouth his chest, abdomen and groin. Blood had pooled at the base of the base of the casket and then seeped out onto the stone floor and was now smeared over Gunn's jeans.

'Did you.......?'

'No, but I would like to have done. No, this was a DIY job. If you look at the bottom of the 'Maiden' where his feet are you'll see there's a hinged metal plate. He probably thought that it would make an excellent bullet proof place to wait and shoot me as I reached the foot of the stairs. He must have then broken the last of the lights........over there......and then stepped into the casket not realising that by opening the Iron Maiden's lid he had cocked the closing mechanism.'

'Yuk!....come on, the girls are at the top of the stairs,' and Tanya turned away from the ghoulish sight of Kraja's eyeless and eviscerated corpse.

'Coming, just a sec,' and Gunn felt in the man's pockets until he found his cellphone. 'This might help the police to identify the 'mole' in their Paris Headquarters,' and Gunn followed Tanya up the stone steps. They were greeted by three anxious faces as they reached the hallway.

'John, this is Michelle from Ontario, Noelene from Adelaide and Zoe from Liverpool. All three of them were on their GAP year before university. They met up at the Anne-Marie Verder YWCA in the Rue Blomet in Paris. The girls were having a drink in a local bar when they were joined by what seemed to be three very nice guys. The next thing that any of them remembers was waking up in the warehouse at Rue Samson.'

'Do they need to phone families?' Gunn offered holding out his cellphone.

'Done.....while you were down there,' Tanya said, nodding in the direction of the dungeons.

'How did you manage to stop Kraja and co opening that cell door?' Gunn asked the girls.

'We found a rusty nail which we pushed into the key hole. They tried hammering a nail in from the other side, so we removed our nail, but as soon as they pulled their nail out we stuck ours back in again,' was explained by Noelene.

'Simple, but incredibly effective; all your families know you're safe?' Gunn queried as the now familiar sound of the Augusta helicopter could be heard approaching the island.

'Yes thanks,' they answered in unison.

*

'Hello.'

'Ops here, we have that information you requested. I won't bore you with names of the circuitous routing for the payment of that charter. Suffice to say that funding for the private charter of that Lear jet was channelled through three different banks – as far apart as Zurich and Nova Scotia – two holding companies and three private accounts in the Cayman Islands. Breaking the privacy coding of the latter took most of our time. You need to know that the real source of the funding came from an account at the Toyohoshi-Kimura Bank in Tokyo's prestigious Otemachi District. That's the bank that lost the takeover battle with the Matsumoto Bank. It's owned by Mr Kenji Tokutaka and his Chief Executive is a Mr Ichiro Iwakami. You will recall that the Head of the Matsumoto Bank which defeated the Toyohoshi Bank is Mr Jiro Kurobashi – one of the names on *Seppuku-kai's* death list. That's it.'

'Got all that, many thanks,' and Marie ended the phone call.

'Got the information you needed?' Jean-Paul asked as Marie pushed the cellphone and a small notepad into her large shoulder bag.

'Yes thanks.'

'Can I offer you a lift in the Augusta helicopter? It's ready to return to the island together with a police helicopter.'

'Thanks,' and Marie followed Jean-Paul out of the Control Tower across to the helipad where Captain Chevalier was waiting by the Augusta helicopter.

*

The Augusta helicopter landed as Gunn, Tanya and the three girls walked out of the Chateau d'If. The first person out of the

Augusta, which had landed a few minutes ahead of the French Police Eurocopter, was Marie de Fonblanque who hurried over to them.

'You alright John?' she asked, looking at Gunn's blood-smeared jeans.

'Yes, I'm fine. The blood belongs to Kraja, the Don of the Albanian Mafia. Whoever looks after this place will need to do quite a clean-up in the lowest dungeon down there,' Gunn said nodding in the direction of the castle entrance. 'The girls have all spoken with their families, so if I may I'll leave it to you and the police to get statements and look after them.' Gunn paused as the second helicopter landed and then continued when its engines shut down. 'There's another dead guy in the courtyard and two down on the jetty. Can I leave you to handle the police? Tanya and I will return to the mainland in the boat we used to get here.'

'Yes, go now. We'll take care of the girls and all the questions.'

'Don't forget the house in Rue Rabelais where you'll find another three bodies. Nothing to do with us; they were Kraja's handiwork,' Gunn said as he turned to go.

'I'll deal with all of that,' Lefevre volunteered.

'Jean-Paul Lefevre,' Marie introduced her colleague from the DGSE.

'Hi Jean-Paul, sorry to have made such a mess of your castle. We'll leave these with you,' and Gunn and Tanya gave Marie their automatics, silencers and magazines which she pushed into her shoulder bag.

'Yokiko will provide you with anything you need when you get to Japan. You might find this information useful,' and Marie took her notebook out of her shoulder bag and tore out a page which she gave to Gunn. 'I'll be handing over to David Morris who'll be your controller from now on. Quickly, go now before the French Police get here and hold up your departure.'

Bye girls,' and as Gunn and Tanya turned to go the three girls came over and hugged them. Farewells over, Gunn and Tanya jogged across to the steps leading down to the jetty and disappeared from view.

*

'Yes, Ichiro-san, what is it at this time of night?' Peter Drummond asked who had been woken by the call from his Chief Executive.

'I have received a call from Marseille,' this statement was followed by silence while Ichiro Iwakami agonised over the best way of telling the *Oyabun* of *Seppuku-kai* that something had gone seriously wrong.

'And.........' Drummond prompted.

'Our charter aircraft at Toulon to bring Kraja-san and the girls to Tokyo has been impounded and both pilots and crew have had their passports confiscated by the French Police.'

'And how has this come about?'

'Our informant believes that Kraja is dead and that Gunn-san is now on his way to Tokyo.'

'How helpful of Mr Gunn. As it seems that we have been incapable of finding and killing him he has now helped us by coming to Tokyo. He will, of course come by air, so you are to have your men at every airport......and, of course, our main line station here in Tokyo........however many that takes. Understood?'

'Yes *Oyabun*.'

'He will be easy to identify as he is over six feet tall and you will issue photos to all your men. He is to be killed and the body disposed of without any further mistakes. Is that clear?

'Yes *Oyabun*.'

*

After three days and two nights at sea, the twice-weekly ferry from Vladivostok to Japan berthed at the ferry port of Fushiki in Toyama Bay on the west coast of Japan's Honshu Island. In a zealous effort to avoid both the wrath of the Oyabun of *Seppuku-kai* and any further mistakes in the hunt for John Gunn, Ichiro Iwakami had not only covered all the airports and the main line stations on the train services into Tokyo, but also the west coast ports of Hokiado, Honshu and Kyushu Islands.

Jinzo Nomoto had been unimpressed when given the task of checking all the arrivals at Fushiki on the Tuesday and Friday ferries arriving from Russia. He spent much of his time watching sub-titled DVDs of American Westerns, 1930s gangster movies and playing mindless sadistic computer games. Jinzo's heroes were Billy the Kid, Butch Cassidy and Al Capone. It was for these very immature character attributes that he had been selected by Ichiro Iwakami for this unlikely mode of arrival in Japan by John Gunn.

As soon as the ferry had berthed, the cars and lorries were released first. Jinzo positioned himself close to the immigration booths where passports were being checked. There were very few cars and none of them had a 'long nosed' Caucasian at the wheel. The same applied to the lorry drivers. Once the last of the lorries had driven down the ferry's ramp, the walking passengers disembarked. The majority of those would be heading for the station to catch the train to either the local area or to the mainline station in Toyama City with a 'Bullet Train' high speed link to Tokyo. There was no man over six feet in height amongst the passengers nearly all of whom were Japanese men involved in the motor trade between Japan and Russia. As soon as the last of the passengers had walked out of the port towards the station, Jinzo jumped on his Suzuki motorbike and went home.....back to his DVDs and X-Box computer games.

CHAPTER 24

It was only a twenty minute train journey to Toyama where Yokiko Yoshiwa, BID's in-country agent in Japan, was waiting for Gunn. Like Jinzo Nomoto, Yokiko had been expecting a tall Caucasian until she received the text message from Tanya before the Aeroflot flight left Chek Lap Kok airport in Hong Kong for Vladivostok.

'Hello Yokiko.'

She spun round, but the only person near her was an old man in a wheelchair and his nurse, or perhaps it was his daughter. It was the old man who spoke.

'If you could help Tanya push me in the direction of the train, we'll do all the introductions when we're seated in our carriage.'

Tanya greeted Yokiko in Japanese and, like long separated family, they embraced for the benefit of anyone watching them. Once the three of them were seated in an almost empty carriage and the train was on its way for the three hour journey to Tokyo, Yokiko explained what she had managed to find out after receiving the text message from Tanya.

'I'm sure you've been told that the Toyohoshi-Kimura Bank is one of the largest in Japan and occupies the most prestigious building in the Otemachi District, next to the Imperial Palace – that would be the equivalent of it being close to your Queen's Palace in London.' This was added for Gunn's benefit. 'The head of this bank is Kenji Tokutaka; he is old – estimates vary, but it seems he must be in his eighties so if he was eighteen in 1941 that would make him eighty-five. So yes, he could be Peter Drummond. That is the only photo I could find of him,' and Yokiko dug in her shoulder bag and produced a photo which had been copied from a very grainy newspaper photo. 'That was taken during the time of the Sarin gas attack on the Tokyo subway in 1995. He has never been seen in public since that date and is supposed to live in a sumptuous penthouse apartment at the top of the bank in Otemachi.'

'Thanks for all your work, Yokiko. I suppose that it's impossible to get anywhere in the bank building other than the banking hall on the ground floor?'

'Absolutely impossible, but your idea is a possibility. We will pay a visit to the bank to familiarise you with the area. When we get to my flat I will tell you what I have arranged so far.'

*

After bowing deeply, Ichiro Iwakami spoke; 'you sent for me Tokutaka-sempai?'

'Yes Ichiro-san; do we have any news yet of Gunn's arrival in Japan?'

'None at all, *Oyabun*; we have access to all passenger lists for flight arrivals in Japan. He has not arrived by air. The men I posted at the ferry ports have confirmed that no Caucasian matching his description has come into the country by that method in the last 48 hours.'

'And Kurobashi-san; when will he be removed?'

'He is very well guarded, *Oyabun*.'

'Of course he is. I expect......' but whatever Peter Drummond expected was cut short by the phone ringing.

'Shall I.........?

'Yes, you answer it.'

'It's a woman wishing to speak to you, *Oyabun*.'

Peter Drummond took the phone from his Chief Executive.

'*Kon'nichiwa*.'

'Hello Peter Drummond, this is John Gunn. I shall be paying you a visit shortly.'

The phone dropped out of Drummond's hand as though it was red hot. In contrast, he was deathly pale as he turned to his Chief Executive.

'Where has that call come from?'

Ichiro Iwakami picked up the phone and spoke to the exchange.

'It came from a payphone in the banking hall of this building, *Oyabun.*'

*

The three of them returned to Yokiko's apartment which overlooked the Tama River in the Setagaya-ku district of Tokyo. Gunn disappeared into the bathroom to rid himself of the talcum powder in his hair and other makeup Tanya had used to age him for his wheelchair role. While both Gunn and Tanya took the opportunity to shower and change clothes from the meagre selection each had packed in their backpacks, Yokiko prepared the living room for the arrival of two men she had recruited after receiving Tanya's text from Hong Kong.

When Gunn appeared from his bedroom, Tanya was already chatting with the two young Japanese men. The conversation switched to English.

'John, I want you to meet Saburo Kagawa who used to work for Kawasaki Robotics and Goro Kochi who is a pilot and owns his own aircraft.' Gunn bowed and shook hands with the two men. 'Both Saburo and Goro have worked with BID before and it is they who believe your idea to get to Peter Drummond to be perfectly feasible.'

Spread out on the carpet was a large scale map of Tokyo, a floor plan of the penthouse and an aerial view, courtesy of Google Earth, of the Otemachi District of the city.

'Right John, this is what the boys have come up with. The only way for you to get at the Drummond penthouse on the top of the bank building is by air. The plan is simple, its execution is not,' and Yokiko smiled at Gunn. 'In summary, you will free-fall from 5,000 feet at night onto the top of the building. It has a marked helipad, but at night that will be very hard, if not impossible, for you to identify. So we must mark it for you. Close by the bank building is the Palace Hotel, which, at 75 storeys, is higher than the 72 storey bank building.' Yokito had armed herself with a bamboo cane and was pointing out the various buildings.

'At the top of the Palace Hotel is a roof-top Japanese garden to which anyone can have access. Saburo has a contact at the hotel who will see that he has a secluded part of the garden to himself where he can set up a floodlight directed at the helipad. Saburo will switch on the floodlight when you are within 1,000 feet of the helipad. OK so far?'

'OK,' Gunn couldn't fail to be impressed by the speed with which Yokiko had acted after receipt of the text message.

'Goro has made up two Semtex shaped charges for you which have suction cups. These will stick to the armoured plate glass of the penthouse windows. Each charge has an eight second delay once you have armed it. He has already experimented with the charges and they will shatter the glass, but do little damage to anyone or anything in the penthouse unless, of course, anyone has their nose pressed against the glass.' Yokiko paused, 'have another beer John.'

'Thanks, I will; you guys?' Both accepted a can of beer. 'Right, I'm on the helipad with two explosive charges.' Yokiko moved the tip of her bamboo cane to another chart which was the ground plan of the penthouse.

'These are the two windows we suggest that you blow – they are south-facing from his study and overlook the Sumida River. Now you will be in the study. What you do then is your business, not ours. Our business is to get you into and away from that penthouse. You will be equipped with two chutes – one for the freefall from Giro's aircraft and a second one to do a base jump from the edge of the helipad on the east side of the roof down into Otemachi Square. We will be waiting for you in the square and will dispose of the chute and get you away as quickly as possible. All of us will be in contact by radio throughout this operation. We have all the weapons you might need. Now we must wait for a weather forecast and hope for a night with no rain or wind. That's it. Now lots of questions I expect,' and Yokiko concluded her efficient briefing.

*

For 48 hours the weather was just about as unsuitable as it possibly could be. Tropical storm 'Rita' had moved north-west towards North Korea leaving in its wake an unsettled weather pattern of pockets of low pressure. The associated wind caused by these anti-cyclones prevented any thought of a free-fall drop onto the bank building. Gunn had made two visits to Tokyo's Haneda Airport to the south of the city, which handled mostly domestic air traffic. Yokiko had understated Goro's support for BID. He had his own company based at Haneda which operated six small aircraft. The one he had selected for Gunn's free-fall was a high-winged Beaver with an up-rated turboprop which had replaced the original Pratt and Whitney radial engine.

Gunn had been offered a wide selection of weapons, but had settled for a silenced Glock 17. The wait for the weather to improve was particularly frustrating for Gunn as he was confined to Yokiko's apartment except for the airport visits when he was collected by Goro from the building's basement car park. He did make one other visit in his wheelchair to the roof garden of the Palace Hotel at night. Saburo took him to the site he had selected to mount the floodlight from where Gunn had a clear view of the penthouse and the helipad. It was just unfortunate or bad timing that neither of them saw the security guards who had been deployed to guard against any access to the roof.

On the third day high pressure moved in from the west, the temperature dropped and the forecast for the following day indicated a maximum easterly wind of 7mph. Yokiko and Tanya had made two visits during this waiting time to the Toyohoshi-Kimura Bank and returned reporting a significantly increased presence of armed security guards. Tanya questioned the wisdom of the phone call Gunn had made to Peter Drummond, but accepted his justification that he wanted the traitor who had been responsible for so many deaths to experience just a fraction of the terror of awaiting his own nemesis.

On that fourth day time seemed to drag by as they all waited for nightfall. Shortly after ten that night, Gunn was taken to the airport. There was only one other person in the small hangar where the Beaver was parked up. Goro needed a co-pilot to assist Gunn out of the aircraft and then close the door after his jump. Like Goro, his co-pilot had been used on other BID assignments. Gunn changed into a black jumpsuit, boots, black ski-mask, helmet and goggles. His main Delta II parawing chute went onto has back and his low speed BASE rig chute – totally different from the high speed opening freefall chute – went on his midriff below his altimeter. The two shaped charges were strapped to his legs and his Glock, radio, spare magazines and hook knife for cutting away a fouled chute went into the padded pockets of his jumpsuit. Once he had landed, he would discard the parawing and the BASE rig. The latter would be hidden and then he would strap it on – preferably, as Gunn had commented during his briefing – before he jumped off the side of the building.

Just before 11pm, Goro got his clearance from the tower to taxi for a flight plan filed to Niigata, 150 miles to the north on the west coast of Japan's main island of Honshu. He turned onto the runway and went straight into a rolling takeoff. Gunn sat in the front beside Goro. The co-pilot was in the first row of seats behind Gunn. His task was to pull back the sliding front door for Gunn's exit, then close it and take the front seat beside Goro. The Beaver headed out into Sagami Bay to the south of Tokyo to gain altitude before turning onto a course of 350° for Niigata and the over-flight of the Toyohoshi-Kimura Bank.

Yokiko's voice came through clearly on the frequency selected for their communications. 'Hello all stations this is zero radio check, radio check, over.' Gunn, Saburo at the Palace Hotel and Goro all replied.

'Three minutes, John,' Goro warned Gunn and his co-pilot. Gunn gave the pilot a thumbs-up and turned in his seat towards the door and did one last check to make sure his hook knife was on its safety line in his breast pocket.

'Barely any wind at all, but what there is, is coming from the west,' came from Saburo on the hotel roof.

'One minute,' from Goro, then, 'thirty seconds....open the door!' A great rush of noise and buffeting cold air followed by Goro's countdown on the radio which Gunn received on the earphones inside his helmet......'five, four, three, two, one, go!' and Gunn dived out of the door into the cloudless night above the myriad lights of Tokyo below him. The Beaver's door was closed, the co-pilot moved into the front seat and the small aircraft continued on its approved flight plan to Niigata.

*

Yokiko had hired a small panel van which she considered would make the task of disposing of Gunn's Base-rig chute and his parawing - if he still had it – much easier. She and Tanya dropped Saburo and his floodlight equipment at the hotel and then drove into Otemachi Square where they had little difficulty finding an empty parking slot at that time of night. Yokiko had just parked the van when she and Tanya heard Goro's countdown on the radio.

*

For Gunn, the trickiest part of any parachute jump, whether static line or freefall was getting out of the aircraft. Once clear of the aircraft, the adrenalin rush and sensation of flying never failed to exhilarate him. Below him was a carpet of lights with the moon-lit Sumida River estuary marking the southern edge of the city. Before taking off from Haneda Airport, Gunn had zeroed his altimeter with that on the Beaver and it now unwound rapidly from 5,000 feet as his body accelerated to a terminal velocity of 120 mph. The lights below him became clearer as the altimeter unwound past 4,000 and then 3,000 feet – Gunn could even identify the area of the Imperial Palace to the west of the bank because it had considerably less lighting than the commercial part of the city. The needle passed 2,000 feet – Gunn brought in his right arm from the spread skydive posture, grasped the handle on the end of the rip cord and pulled..... the pilot chute deployed instantly dragging out the parawing. Gunn felt the tension come onto the risers at his back followed by the dramatic deceleration as the chute deployed and the air rushed in to fill the pockets on the rectangular chute.

'900 feet and now about 200 yards to the west of the target,' Gunn pressed the transmit switch on the side of his helmet and spoke into the minute boom mike attached to it. He grasped the steering lines attached to the risers on his back and concentrated on the task of landing on his target. Even as he spoke, over to his right, he saw the powerful beam of Saburo's floodlight lance across from the hotel roof and light up the white 'H' on a blue-painted circle. Now just seconds to go......and then Gunn saw the security guard appear from behind the penthouse building.

The guard walked onto the helipad and stared directly into the beam of the floodlight. Gunn steered his chute round in an arc and then brought it back into the wind and behind the guard who was just raising a radio to his mouth. He stalled the chute at the same moment as both his boots hit the back of the guard's head, snapping his neck instantly. The floodlight was switched off as Gunn landed at a jog trot on the helipad. He immediately threw away his gloves and removed the Glock from his jumpsuit thigh pocket, discarded the harness and started to gather in the zero-p fabric of his ram-air chute as he knelt on the helipad.

This was the exact moment that the next guard appeared from the other side of the penthouse. There was very little wind, but what there was, was blowing towards the guard. Gunn released the light-weight fabric which billowed across the helipad and enveloped the guard. Cocooned in the chute fabric, the guard made a perfect target and two silenced shots from Gunn's Glock finished the business. He removed his helmet, took the hand-held radio from another pocket, pressed the transmit switch and whispered; 'down safely and two guards killed.'

CHAPTER 25

Gunn dragged the bodies of both guards into an alcove between the helipad and the penthouse wall and used the weight of their bodies to hold down the rolled up chute fabric. There was still no sign of any other guards. He unclipped the harness of his BASE-rig chute and placed that with the other chute and bodies. Helmet, goggles, gloves and altimeter joined the pile. As Gunn turned away from the pile of bodies and equipment, the guards' radios burst into life.

'Time to move,' Gunn muttered, pushing the Glock back into his thigh pocket. The penthouse was surrounded by a wide gravelled area filled with potted plants, *bonsai* trees, a swimming pool and jacuzzi. He made his way to the south side of the penthouse where the two large plate glass windows overlooked the view across the city to the Sumida River. The sound of voices came from the other side of the penthouse where Yokiko's diagram had shown the penthouse kitchens and a maintenance exit onto the rooftop.

Thick curtains were drawn behind the plate glass windows. Gunn removed the first of the shaped charges from his leg, moistened the suction cups, placed the charge on the glass and then pushed over the small lever which depressed the cups clamping the charge to the glass. He moved on to the second window and repeated the procedure with the second charge. The male voices were getting louder. At least two men were approaching from the west side of the penthouse. As soon as he had clamped the charge to the window he pulled out the pin from the detonator, quickly moved back to the first charge, removed the pin and then threw himself on the ground behind an ornamental bridge. Goro had said an eight second delay on the charges. Two men came round the corner of the building about thirty yards from where Gunn was lying prone on the gravel.

One of the men spotted the charge on the window, walked over to it and tried to pull it off. A shattering explosion was followed split seconds later by another. Both windows imploded, shredding the curtains. One man had vanished and the other staggered back round the far end of the penthouse. Gunn got up from behind his ornamental bridge and walked into Peter Drummond's living quarters to be greeted with a bizarre and macabre spectacle.

There was a man kneeling on the floor in front of a much older man who Gunn recognised as Peter Drummond. The man on the floor had self-impaled himself on a *wakizashi* sword; his right hand on the hilt and his left on the blade – protected by a cloth bound round the blade – which he had used to drag the razor sharp sword diagonally from low left to high right, eviscerating himself. There seemed to be blood everywhere, mostly coming from the *seppuku* victim, but some came from Drummond who had been hit by shards of glass from the shattered windows. Drummond turned to Gunn.

'I suppose you have to be John Gunn.' Gunn said nothing. 'That's Ichiro, my Chief of Staff, who should have killed you, but failed. *Seppuku* was the only honourable course of action left for him.'

'And what about you and the hundreds of British officers you murdered in the Argyle Street POW Camp and in the sinking *Lisburn Maru*. What is the only honourable course of action for you?'

'Oh, that was a lifetime ago. We've all moved on since then and anyway why should you care?' As Drummond spoke he was gradually edging towards a table that had a long ceremonial *katana* sword and scabbard on a display stand - the traditional sword carried by the Samurai.

'Your treachery led to the death of an officer known only as 'Horse' to everyone in the camp. He was the escape officer. The Japanese guards beheaded him.'

'He was stupid and made life worse for all of us. The Japanese are a civilised race. They were civilised, when we Angle-Saxons were still grubbing around in mud huts and painting ourselves in woad. Had we all signed that agreement not to escape, we would all have lived through the privations of the camp in some degree of comfort. Anyway why should you be interested in that man?' Drummond had moved a little closer to the sword.

'He was Captain Graham Gunn – my grandfather. His nickname came from his initials 'GG'.' Drummond paused and for the first time seemed to focus clearly on Gunn.

'Oh, I see....yes I suppose that does make it personal.....' and at that he dived for the sword which he swept off the display stand. The bullet from the Gunn's Glock hit Drummond in the shoulder and the sword fell to the carpet. Drummond staggered back against the edge of his desk. Gunn stooped and retrieved the sword and with a sweeping backhanded slash, the gleaming razor edge removed Drummond's left hand which he had raised to defend himself before it beheaded him.

OTHER BOOKS FEATURING
JOHN GUNN

BY BRIAN NICHOLSON

GWEILO

The theft of a birthright has been the motive for murder since Jacob usurped it from his elder brother Esau. The loss of the birthright to the immense riches of Hong Kong leads to a plot by two men, one Chinese and the other a 'gweilo' – a descendant of the first settlers to arrive in Hong Kong. The catastrophic meltdown of the Chernobyl nuclear power station provides the solution – the destruction of Hong Kong rather than hand it back to the China. Fluent in both Cantonese and Mandarin Chinese, John Gunn is recruited for this assignment by the British Intelligence Directorate. But the countdown to this nuclear holocaust has already begun.

AL SAMAK

This is a rocket-paced thriller about a conspiracy by die-hard communists to sell nuclear warheads to Saddam Hussein. The conspirators are led by an ex-KGB psychopath whose bloodthirsty brutality even sickened the KGB and the Soviet leadership. Their choice of arms dealer is Hassan Hussein whose Kurdish village has been destroyed by Saddam's chemical gas attack. Horribly disfigured by the gas attack, Hassan has his own plans for the nuclear warheads.

This is John Gunn's second assignment with the British Intelligence Directorate. It's a story of intrigue, treachery, revenge and unbelievable violence during the summer of 2002 when the USA, UK and IAEA were searching for the 'smoking gun' to justify the invasion of Iraq.

ASHANTI GOLD

The priceless ingots of Ashanti Gold are secured in the vaults of the Bank of Ghana. Gold will buy weapons and weapons are needed by the West African exiles, ruthless arms dealers, corrupt diplomats and politicians on both sides of the Atlantic conspiring to overthrow the governments of all West African countries. This is John Gunn's third assignment with the British Intelligence Directorate which has sent him to Ghana to investigate the disappearance of an SIS agent from the British High Commission.

FIRE DRAGON

Colliding tectonic plates, erupting volcanoes, earthquakes and tsunamis make Indonesia the most volatile geological archipelago in the World. This explosively unstable geology is matched by the volatile conspiracy of Romano Rusman who is determined to return Indonesia to a communist dictatorship. He has stumbled on the vast treasure hidden by Admiral Yamamoto at the end of World War 2 and uses this limitless source of funding to conspire with North Korea to place its nuclear weapons in space orbit out of the reach of the IAEA inspections and US spy satellites. A fatal error occurs while the nuclear warheads are being shipped from North Korea to Indonesia, which results in John Gunn's fourth assignment with the British Intelligence Directorate and his confrontation with man-eating komodo dragons in the 'ring of fire'.

CALYPSO

How can five yachts disappear without trace on a Caribbean cruise? What has happened to the British Warship sent to investigate? Where are Iraq's chemical weapons? Why is London lobbying for the release of a Camp Delta prisoner and why has a WW2 Dakota been shipped to the UK from the Mojave Desert? John Gunn is pitched into a desperate race against time on this assignment for the British Intelligence Directorate, as the answers to these questions reveal a conspiracy for a catastrophic terrorist atrocity in London.

SHARK

What is the secret that lies buried in the sand of the Iraqi Desert and why has this led to the murder of a British Intelligence agent? What was the name the gunman tried to utter before he died? Who is blackmailing senior members of the Cabinet Office and Intelligence Services? Who was the eighth man and who is the mole crippling the British Intelligence Directorate? Desperate urgency is needed to answer these questions because the next agent to be murdered is John Gunn.

TRAITOR

The spectre of a traitor who betrayed fellow soldiers in a Japanese POW camp in Hong Kong has risen from the grave to haunt the British Intelligence Directorate. A deliberate hit-and-run murder in London of the son of an ex-POW is followed by the murder of an agent during a break-in at Gunn's London house to search for war crime papers and diaries relating to the betrayal in 1941. Twice Gunn escapes the 21st Century Samurai warriors from a proscribed Japanese Mafia cult thought to have been responsible for the Sarin gas attack on the Tokyo subway.

Every effort is made by both the Director of the British Intelligence Directorate and the Japanese Mafia to prevent him taking over the investigation. This turns Gunn into a fugitive from the British police and the Counter-Espionage Department of BID as his search inevitably leads him back to Japan.

BRIAN NICHOLSON

Excitement started at an early age for the author; returning from India with his parents and sister in June 1945, aged 3, the ship in which the family was embarked was chased by a Japanese submarine which fortunately had run out of torpedoes. Brian Nicholson had an equally exciting career in the army for 35 years of which the last 10 were spent working with the officers of the Secret Intelligence Service in various overseas appointments in Hong Kong, Ghana and Indonesia.

He was made an OBE in 1985 and received a Commendation from the Commander British Forces Hong Kong in 1987 for his success in the negotiations with the Chinese Government on the handover of Hong Kong. At the request of the Royal Navy Funeral Department, while he was Defence Attaché in Jakarta, he solved the mystery of what happened to Sub-Lieutenant Gregor Riggs. He was the last of the 23 Commandoes on the ill-fated Australian Commando raid, Operation Rimau, on Japanese shipping in Singapore Harbour in World War 2. The author discovered the remains of the young officer on a remote island in the Indonesian Archipelago and returned them to the family for burial with full military honours at the Changi Military Cemetery in Singapore. In 1990, as Military Advisor to Jerry Rawlings, Ghana's President, he was directed to plan the successful West African military intervention in Liberia after the horrific videoed torture and assassination of the country's despotic dictator, Master Sergeant Samuel Doe. These are but a few of the exciting experiences in a colourful career which formed the backdrop to the seven books which he has written. He is currently researching his eighth book. Brian Nicholson is married with two adult daughters and lives in Richmond where his time is taken up with writing, golf, shooting, sailing, travel and caring for his classic British sports car.

THE AUTHOR